Reprise

by the same author
Sisters

Reprise

CLAIRE RAYNER

Hutchinson
London Sydney Melbourne Auckland Johannesburg

For Terence Blacker,
with thanks for fighting back

Hutchinson & Co. (Publishers) Ltd

An imprint of the Hutchinson Publishing Group
3 Fitzroy Square, London W1P 6JD

Hutchinson Group (Australia) Pty Ltd
30–32 Cremorne Street, Richmond South, Victoria 3121
PO Box 151, Broadway, New South Wales 2007

Hutchinson Group (NZ) Ltd
32–34 View Road, PO Box 40–086, Glenfield, Auckland 10

Hutchinson Group (SA) (Pty) Ltd
PO Box 337, Bergvlei 2012, South Africa

First published 1980

Set in Times by
Input Typesetting Ltd

Printed in Great Britain by The Anchor Press Ltd
and bound by Wm Brendon & Son Ltd,
both of Tiptree, Essex

British Library Cataloguing in Publication Data
Rayner, Claire
  Reprise.
  I. Title
  823'.9'1F   PR6068.A949R/

ISBN 0 09 140840 7

1

When Theo had come and told her that Dolly was dying she didn't believe him. Not at first. She had stood there in the middle of all the crazy hubbub backstage at the Roundhouse and stared at him, at his tight expression of concern mixed with urgency, and thought, 'He looks nice. That black shirt was the nicest one I ever bought him. He looks nice.'

'Darling, do your hear me? She's dying. I'm sorry to be so brutal about it, but Oliver said there's no doubt, and she's asking for you. It's really very urgent – '

'Dying?' Maggy said.

'I know it's difficult to take in – Christ, but this is one hell of a place to – look, I've got the car outside. I can have you there in under half an hour. I'll give you all the details while we go. Come on, love.'

'I'm not going anywhere, Theo,' she had said, trying to sound reasonable and pleased with herself because she did. 'I've heard these panics before. And I've got a gig here, in case you'd forgotten. Have you forgotten?'

'A gig – for Christ's sake, Maggy, a *charity* thing? So they'll manage without you. There just isn't the time now to – '

'Now, what sort of attitude is that? Only a charity thing? I'm ashamed of you.'

She had smiled at him, bantering and still reasonable; very, very reasonable. 'That from you, Theo? And here's me thinking you're a show-must-go-on-man!'

One of the other bands pushed past them on their way to the stage as a roar went up from the audience, six sweating men wearing old tail coats and celluloid collars over shirtless chests, humping brass instruments. A hell of a group to follow a punk band; she'd told them that when they planned the bloody evening in the first place, but whoever listened to sense in this lousy business? By the time her own group were on, top of the bill though they were, the poor bastards out there wouldn't know their arses from their elbows, let alone her sort of music from the crap they'd had thrown at them before. She'd been half minded to walk out anyway once she'd realized what a stinking show it was. To hell with the Musicians' Benevolent –

But not now. Not now that her mother was dying.

So, she hadn't gone. Theo had argued for five minutes or so, trying to convince her it was real this time, a real emergency, and then had gone to phone Oliver. And she'd taken her people on the stage and salvaged the evening, making the sort of hit she always did. Maggy Dundas. Who could touch her? No one. Not even her mother, dying.

She'd gone to the funeral though. Golder's Green Cremato-rium, a stinking hot afternoon, one of the only hot afternoons in this whole miserable summer. She'd gone so that she could wear casual ordinary clothes and look blank and unconcerned while the others sat around looking ostentatiously lugubrious. Oliver, his face pouched and sodden, had obviously been crying for hours, sour-faced Ida, looking even more sour than she usually did, if that were possible, and the chamber maids and kitchen staff and that supercilious bitch from reception, all looking embarrassed when they caught her eye. Oh, that had been good. And she had done it exactly as she had meant to, sitting still and silent until that whey-faced creature in his black cassock began intoning words over the coffin, waiting there to be slid into the furnace behind, and then when he'd started on about how good and compassionate Dolly had been, how careful of her staff's happiness, how beloved by her friends, getting up and quietly walking out. Past Theo's straight-ahead stare, and Oliver's mournful cow eyes and Ida's glare. Oh, that had been a good moment. That had paid back some of the anger of the years.

Some of it. She stood now on the hot pavement of the Hay-market staring towards Leicester Square, feeling the heat bite through her thin shoes and her throat thick with the stink of diesel fumes and fried onions from the hot-dog stalls and sweating tour-ists, and thought about it. All that misery and humiliation and shear frustration that Dolly had inflicted on her. Whether she had meant it or not, that was how it had been. Maggy thought of Gerald and Oliver and her father and let anger seep back into her. Dolly had been stupid and mindlessly unkind and the fact that she had meant so little of it somehow made it worse, not

6

better. If she'd been deliberately cruel, it would have been easier. Then I'd have a right to hate her, she whispered deep in her mind. As it is, I don't, I don't hate her. No I don't. Yes I do. Oh, hell, why can't I just stop *caring*? Damn Dolly. Damn her to hell and back. If only I could forget it all. I'm thirty-seven years old. Thirty-seven years old and I'm still feeling the miseries of sixteen. Bloody Dolly.

Someone stopped in front of her, clutching a map in one brown hand, jabbering and gesticulating first at the map and then towards Leicester Square, looking at her hopefully, and she stared down at him, a small brown man, probably Malaysian, and said wearily, 'Oh, get out of my way. Bloody tourists – ' and turned and walked into the big building waiting there for her. She wanted to shout aloud to the people she passed, wanted them to know that she wasn't coming here out of greed. She didn't want any of Dolly's possessions; rejecting them, whatever there was, would be the final insult, the final shutting of the door on all the miseries of those years that had pleated themselves into such a burden of memories. But that would be silly. For a moment she managed to stand back from her self-pity and her rage and grin, a little. The sooner all this was settled the better. Then she'd be able to push it all into the past, and get on with living now. Wouldn't she?

'Where is she, then?' Ida said, and poured another cup of tea. It was tea the way he liked it, strong and dark, not the weak scented stuff Maggy went in for, and he felt comforted by it and smiled up at Ida. She nodded briefly back, because Ida never smiled. But he knew she liked him, and it didn't matter to him that she never smiled, though it had always infuriated Maggy.

'She's meeting Mr Friese', he said and sipped his tea, not looking at Ida now. 'In the Haymarket.'

She put the pot down on the table, thumping it hard on its cork mat and staring at him. 'The Haymarket? D'you mean she's going to the safe deposit?'

'That's what Friese said.' Theo drank some more tea, and felt discomfort rising in him. Friese had had no right to tell him as much as he had. The man was supposed to be acting in Maggy's interest, dammit. He's been Dolly's man, originally, of course, but now Dolly was dead and Maggy was her only relation so it was Maggy he should be loyal to. Yet he'd chattered on to Theo about all sorts of things, even though Theo had tried to stop him.

Thinking of it now, he was embarrassed. And somewhere deep underneath excited and something else; frightened? He shook his head sharply, with that tic he sometimes suffered and drank some more tea.

'She kept that box as the most private thing she had,' Ida said heavily. 'Not even I ever got to see it. I mean, I knew the thing was there, and that was as close as anyone ever got. She never told *her*.' Ida still could not bring herself to use Maggy's name. 'Dolly said to me once that all her life that had been worth living was in that box. Never wanted no one to see it but herself. And now that Friese is taking her to it.'

'It seems Dolly told him to,' Theo said. 'Look, Ida, I'm sorry, but I really couldn't help it. Dammit, I didn't want to pry into anyone else's affairs! I told him that Maggy and I – he knows we only live together. Why he should try to treat me as her husband I don't know. But there it was – he just went on and on, even though I told him it was none of my affair.'

'You're the nearest to a husband she's ever had. Or likely to, more fool you.' Ida sat down and began to drink her own tea with a controlled ferocity that made it seem she would finish by biting the cup itself and chewing it up. 'And that's more than she deserves.'

'Look, Ida,' Theo said and stopped, and then tried again. But first he got to his feet and walked across the little room to peer out at the reception desk and the big foyer beyond that. Not that anyone could hear anything outside this room; Ida was much too canny not to provide herself with anything but the safest and most private of offices, but you never knew. And it embarrassed him to be talking about Maggy in this way.

'Look, Maggy isn't the easiest of persons in the world. I know that. You've got your own ideas about her and they're yours – no – ' he said quickly as she opened her mouth to say something. 'No, I just don't want to know. I – Maggy and I have been together a while now, and we suit each other. We've no claims on each other, no boring ties we don't choose to have, but you might as well get used to the fact that I'm not prepared to listen to you slanging her. I won't listen to her slanging you, either – frankly, it's too damned boring. But I like you, and I'd like to see you happy. You've been part of this place a long time, one way and another, and from what Friese told me, I think you will be for a lot longer. No, he'll tell you himself. Or Maggy will. Right now, let's get it clear – I'm not taking sides, all right? Willing to be – oh, I don't know precisely – not referee, that's for sure, but well, an arbitrator if you like, if you ever need one. But don't ask me to listen to you going on about Maggy. Because I won't.'

'I thought you'd left her?' Ida said, her voice flat and conversational. 'What's all this about when you've left her?'

'I've moved out of the flat for a while, that's all,' Theo said after a moment, and sat down again. 'That doesn't mean I've left for good, though, does it? Like I said, Maggy and I have been together a long time. One way and another. You don't end that in a hurry, especially at a time when – well, it's stressful, for Maggy. In her own way she's suffering – '

'I'll bet,' Ida said harshly. 'I'll bloody bet. And you're looking at this place and thinking it's worth more than tuppence ha'penny? Could that be part of it?'

His jaw tensed, but he didn't rise. A very Ida crack, that. Always on the look out for a way to make a man feel cheap and bad, however altruistic his motives, even if she liked him. But he wasn't going to let her get through to him, not this time. So he just looked at her and shook his head with exaggerated patience and said nothing.

She drank more tea and then said abruptly. 'What else did he tell you? That Friese? About the box?'

'Nothing. Just that Dolly had it and had left instructions that Maggy was to be given access to it as soon as possible after her death. That's all.'

Uncomfortable again Theo said, 'I gather it's one of the conditions of the will. She can't inherit anything else until she's been through the box. Something like that – '

Ida looked triumphant suddenly, her heavy face lifting, though still with no trace of any smile on it. 'Christ, you're a right pair, aren't you? You hanging around to see what she gets, and her doing all she can to get her hands on Dolly's bits and pieces! A right pair.'

Theo stood up, and picked up his hat. He was wearing a wide-brimmed straw, very fetching, very trendy this summer. 'If you're going to follow that line, Ida, I'm going. I came because I thought you might like a little company. I've always liked you, in spite of yourself, and I was sorry for you, with Dolly dead. I thought you might be in need of a little company. But I can see – '

'You can see bloody clear that you were wrong. The last thing

I need is anyone crying into their beer over Dolly for my comfort. I'll sort myself out well enough. No call for you to come patronizing me, any more than there ever has been. So sling it.'

'I'll see you in a few days.' Theo was being imperturbable now. He was quite good at that when he put his mind to it. 'When you're feeling better. Don't bother to see me out – '

She didn't move, sitting there staring at him over the rim of her cup, which she was holding in both hands, and he smiled and bobbed his head and went, pushing out past the reception desk into the foyer.

The receptionist, a thin narrow-faced girl with her hair pulled back into a sleek knot, very unfashionable but curiously attractive all the same, was fiddling with the flowers in the big *jardinière* in the far corner, and as he came out she bobbed her head at him and went away towards the cloakrooms to fetch water, leaving him alone there.

He stood and looked round, almost as though he were seeing it for the first time. Not a big place, but big enough, the Westpark, and it compared reasonably well with the rest of the myriad of small hotels clustered around this part of Bayswater. The foyer where he was standing was warmly carpeted, leather furnished, welcoming, and certainly clean, which was more than you could say for many of the other places around. He grinned then; as if any place that Ida was involved with would be other than clean! He could see the dining room on the far side, tables set ready for dinner, every knife in place, even though it was still only four in the afternoon, and the lounge on the other side with its big sofas and velvet curtains equally perfect and empty of people, and thought briefly of Dolly, dead Dolly. How much part had she actually had in running the place? Would it all slip now, become sleazy and tatty the way other small hotels were, now she was dead? Not if Ida had anything to do with it, he told himself. Ida would carry on as she always had, being Dolly's prop and stay even though Dolly wasn't there.

And how would she react to the information that Friese had so indiscreetly let drop in his ear, but not yet told Ida herself? He thought of Ida going on working for Maggy as she had for Dolly and shook his head, and looked round again. The place must be worth – what? It was made up of three big old houses, so there must be around thirty bedrooms, maybe half of them with bathrooms of a sort, and there were the public rooms, and the kitchens

– it could hardly fetch much under two or three hundred thousand, depending on the length of the lease of course. And there was the goodwill –

He tightened his jaw and pushed the thought away. It wasn't a safe one, not at the moment, now that he'd moved out of Maggy's flat. Not that he intended things to stay that way. Give it a week or two until all the tension had loosened a bit, and he'd go back. She'd have him back, of course she would, and then they could think about the future. Maybe a quarter of a million. Not to be thought about.

The receptionist came back and he nodded at her and walked towards the double doors that led to the hot street outside, but as he came level with the archway that led to the lounge there was a soft sound and Oliver came out. He stood there staring at him lugubriously and then said, in that odd breathy voice he used sometimes, 'Theo. Old Theo. How're you, friend? Theo.'

'Good afternoon,' Theo said repressively, and tugged at the brim of his hat, to make it as clear as he could that he was leaving, had no time to stand and talk, but Oliver didn't get the message.

'Where're you going, Theo? Don't go – come and have a drink, hey? Just a little drink.'

'No thanks, Norwood. I must be on my way. Things to do, you know – '

Not that he couldn't do with a drink. It had been a rough day, one way and another, and there would be no point in going back to the office now, not at two in the afternoon. But the pubs wouldn't be open yet so he'd have to do without. But Oliver seemed to pick up his moment of uncertainty and came and put his hand on his arm, and urged him towards the small bar at the far side of the foyer, next to the dining room.

'Come on, ol' man. We can have a quick one here. Resident, you see. I'm resident, so I can – '

His hand was hot through Theo's sleeve, and he felt a shiver of distaste. There was something about Oliver that he found repellent at the best of times, but now, with his aura of misery and his sagging face with its hangdog eyes he was even more unpleasant.

'Really, Norwood,' he said sharply. 'I don't – '

'Oh, God, don't call me Norwood like that. I need my friends, Theo, got to have my friends. Don't call me Norwood as though I wasn't a friend. *Oliver.* Call me Oliver. Let old Oliver give you a drink. Whisky's yours, isn't it? Yes, whisky – '

He went behind the bar, busying himself with bottles, and sourly Theo watched him.

'I can't stay long,'he said as curtly as he could and Oliver nodded. 'I know, Theo. Busy man. Got all these pop stars to look after. But spare me a minute or two, eh? All on my own, now, you know. All on my own – ' And he sniffed, a small shuddering sound, as his hands did expert things with whisky and ice and ginger ale. He mixed Theo's drink exactly the way he liked it, and pushed it at him over the little bar counter with a winning smile, or what tried to be one, but which made his pouched cheeks look more disagreeable than ever.

He poured tonic water and bitters for himself, with some ostentation, but Theo ignored that. He had had enough boring talk in the past about Oliver and his problems with alcohol and the rest of it.

'Where's Maggy?' Oliver said and now his voice seemed sharper, and he looked up at Theo with a new brightness in his eyes. 'Not with you?'

'No. She's gone to the Haymarket,' Theo said, unthinkingly and then was furious with himself. What the hell business was it of Oliver where she'd gone?

Oliver sighed softly, an oddly satisfied little sound, and bent his head to his drink.

'To the safe deposit?' he said softly. 'I thought as much.'

'What do you know about the safe deposit?' Theo said sharply. 'It's none of your affair.'

'Of course it isn't, Theo ol' man. Of course it isn't. But I'm Dolly's friend – I mean, I *was* Dolly's friend – ' Abruptly his eyes filmed over and his sodden grief-stricken look came back, and Theo felt disgust again. Bloody man! Posing lump of –

'So I know what's what, don't I?' The grief disappeared as fast as it had come, and again Oliver was looking at him with those sharp eyes gleaming between the pouches of his lids. 'She used to go there once a year, Dolly did, when she was well, poor darling. I used to take her and sit and have coffee over the road, and there she'd be for a couple of hours, sometimes, to come back all – ah well, that was a long time ago. Hadn't managed it this past two years, the poor lamb. It was her legs, you see. They got so swollen she couldn't put her feet to the floor, and there she'd sit up there in her room, and wouldn't let anyone but me and Ida do a thing for her. Commode, the lot – '

'Shut up,' Theo said savagely, and finished his drink in one gulp. 'I'm not interested in your reminiscences. Have a bit of decency, man, for Christ's sake – '

'Decency? And you in the record business?' Oliver tittered, a thin sound that seemed to ring among the bottles on the shelves behind him. 'I should cocoa! And what about the way you're hanging round here? What's decent in that? Thought you'd left Maggy? There's nothing here for you any more, is there? Or is there? Making up your lovers' tiffs then? Going to marry the heiress, then?'

'I'm going,' Theo said. 'You make me sick, you – you – '

'Poof's the word you're looking for, darling,' Oliver said, and grinned. 'But sick or not, I dare say you'll be back, eh? You're not the sort to make strange, not now that Dolly's dead and there's this place to sort out.'

But Theo had gone, pushing past the receptionist with a muttered apology for making her spill some of her flower water, and Oliver stood there behind the bar for another moment or two, and then meticulously washed Theo's glass and his own, and wiped the bar surface, whistling softly between his teeth.

Ida was still sitting at the table in the inner office when he came in, and he stood leaning against the door jamb, staring at her.

'She's gone to the safe deposit,' he said abruptly after a moment.

'I know.'

'So now what?'

'How should I know? I'm not psychic, for God's sake. There's a lot I don't know. Any more than you do.'

'More than I do, for all that. But I'll find out, don't you fret. I'll find out. What will *she* find out?'

'I told you. I'm not psychic.'

'Yes, you bloody are,' Oliver said, and his voice was vicious suddenly. 'But you don't fancy me as a mate, do you? You're a fool, you know that? Because you'd do better with me than against me. You may know a lot, but we were very close these past few years, Dolly and me, and you're a fool if you forget it.'

'I won't forget it,' Ida said, and got to her feet. 'And don't you forget I've been around a lot longer than you have. A lot longer. Now get out of my way. I've got work to do.'

'Yes,' Oliver said, and now he sounded abstracted. 'Yes, I know you have. Me, though, I got time on my hands. I think maybe I'll take a train ride. Eh? Down to the Haymarket.'

'And what good will that do you?'

'Oh, I don't know. Might bump into an old friend – have a drink. You know?'

'Oh, go to hell,' Ida said contemptuously, and picked up the tea tray. 'You bore me, you with all your posing – '

' – and tricks. Yes. I know. See you, Ida. Don't work too hard, will you?' And he went away towards the street doors, whistling again. He looked younger suddenly.

The man across the street watched him go, and sourly sucked his back tooth; he'd have to get the damned thing filled some time, the hell it was giving him, but when? These bloody people leaping in and out of the place but never any sign of the girl herself; how the hell was he supposed to get the information they wanted if the bloody girl never came? He contemplated the injustice of his situation gloomily and shifted the weight on his feet.

Oliver reached the end of the street, and looked back with a curiously furtive movement before disappearing round the corner, and on a sudden impulse, the man moved after him. There was no point in staying here, really. The Cordery bloke had gone, the Guthrie woman never budged out at this time of the day – you could set your watch by that one – and maybe Norwood was going to the girl? They'd been close enough once, he'd found that out, and now the mother was dead maybe they were getting together again. He picked and teased at his thoughts as he turned the corner, and saw Oliver disappear into the underground station. This was going to be an easy tail, and he had nothing to lose by it, and maybe he'd get something to tell them tonight –

He looked at his watch. Two o'clock. If he phoned them at six tonight that'd be one o'clock their time, wouldn't it? British summer time. He calculated, trying to count the hours backwards as he bought a 15p ticket from the machine and followed Oliver down to the east-bound platform. Maybe he'd better leave it till around nine tonight. That way he'd be sure to get 'em. And there'd be trouble if he didn't. They'd been very nasty the last time he'd called and hadn't had enough information for them.

This time, somehow, he'd have to get *something*.

2

The lift whispered its way down to the basement and the air was cool, and she relaxed. It had been disagreeably hot up in the street, humid and heavy, but the air conditioning in here was good, even if it smelled a bit phony, pretending to be scented with spring flowers. But it was better than diesel fumes.

Fool, she thought, discussing the weather with yourself! Why not think honestly about what you're here for? Why not face up to it? You've still got time to turn round and walk out, and tell them they can do what they like. Plenty of time. No one's exactly forcing you to open the bloody box, are they?

The lift stopped and the doors sighed open and he was there leaning against the opposite wall and as he saw her he straightened up, became every inch the Family Solicitor, his face taking on an expression of polite and controlled commiseration. Poor Lady, having to deal with a Bereavement; it was as though he had said it aloud, and the moment of goodwill she'd felt at first sight of him shrivelled and died.

'Don't stand there looking at me like a sick cow, man, for God's sake,' she said. 'I'm not exactly heartbroken, you know, and you might as well get used to the fact. I'm not about to pretend anything – '

At once Ian Friese's expression changed, and he became every inch the Business-like Solicitor. 'Of course. I've got everything ready. Shall we go in?'

'Just a minute.' She leaned against the wall beside him, staring at him. There was still time. Time to press the lift button, go back up to the hot street and forget all about it, about Dolly, her box, her will. 'Just a minute. I want to be sure I've got the facts clear. Okay?'

'Of course. But we have been through it all. I did explain – '

'I know you did. But me, I'm thick – put it down to me being thick. Tell me again. Simply. No fancy legal language. Can't be doing with that. Just simply.'

He folded his hands over his brief-case and looked solemnly at her, and she wanted to giggle. This man had seen too many movies when he was a kid. He changed poses so often it was ridiculous. Now he was being avuncular and protective towards a Poor Little Rich Girl –

'Your mother's will was quite clear, Miss Dundas. The hotel, the Westpark, is to be yours entirely, under certain conditions. First, that you pay off the mortgages with which it is at present heavily encumbered, and that you do so with means that will be made available to you via the contents of your mother's safe deposit box. And secondly that you employ Ida Guthrie for as long as she chooses to be employed as manager and housekeeper, at her present salary plus a bonus on turnover.'

'And if I refuse to employ Miss Guthrie – '

'Then the estate reverts to her entirely,' Friese said smoothly, and then smiled. 'It's an interesting will, isn't it? I told your mother at the time she made it that I thought so. It is a very – *kind* way to ensure the well-being of an old employee. Very kind.'

'You reckon?' Maggy said. 'What about my feelings in the matter?'

'Well, I can understand that you'd probably rather employ your own staff, of course, but after all, Miss Guthrie was part of the business for a very long time as I understand it. Long before your mother – ah – consulted me. Right from the beginning.'

'Yes. Right from the beginning. She's always been there – '

All my life, Maggy thought, staring bleakly at the self-satisfied face in front of her. She was always there, in the way, interfering. Getting between her and me, spoiling things –

She blinked, and then frowned. So what if Ida had come between Dolly and herself? What did that matter? She hated Dolly, didn't she? So why should she care about Ida and Dolly?

But she cared. She cared too much, and now she said abruptly, 'There's no way out of that? Either I take Ida on, or she takes the lot?'

'That's the size of it,' Friese said, and smiled again. 'Shall we go along, then? Time's getting on, you know, and I have a great deal to do back at my office.'

He turned and went to a little door along the heavily carpeted corridor, and for a moment Maggy hesitated, still leaning against the wall. Still time to press the lift button, still time to cut and run.

And let Ida get it all. I don't want it, I really don't want it, but I want Ida to have it even less. She took enough from me, being Dolly's friend, being always there. She took enough – I shan't let her have this as well, I shan't. And anyway, who do you think you're fooling? The Westpark – it's got to be worth a lot. Quite a lot. And though I don't need much more than I'm making, there are things I could do, work I could try –

'What's the market value of the place?' she said abruptly, staring at Friese and he let his lips curve into a smile, knowing and a little sneering.

'How much?' she said sharply, refusing to let his opinion of her matter. 'You should know.'

'At present? Well, there's a bit of a slump in hotel property at the moment – the developers, you know how it is – but unencumbered, well – say two hundred and fifty thousand. Give or take a hundred or two.'

'Two hundred – 'A quarter of a million. Ye Gods. A quarter of a million. *Pounds.*

Someone came out of the little door, hurried along the corridor and pressed the lift button, and at once the doors opened and he stepped in and the doors closed again, and the lift went whispering away upwards and she straightened. It was as though her last chance to back out had been lost, the lift taking away with it her final opportunity of choice. She would do it. She'd take on the hotel and Ida with it and the safe deposit box. There was nothing else she could do. She'd be mad to do anything else.

Beyond the little door there was a narrow cubby hole of an office, with a counter and another door beside it. Friese was talking to the woman behind the counter, papers in front of them, and the woman looked up at her sharply as she came in and then at Friese.

'I see. And this is the death certificate? Yes. And the proof of Miss Duncas's identity – yes, I see. And this was arranged, you say, with – ah, yes, here's the release. Well, yes, that seems to be in order – Miss Dundas, I'll need your signature.'

Now she had decided there was to be no more hesitation, Maggy moved forwards briskly and signed the form that was put in front of her, calm and relaxed. She felt Friese hovering at her shoulder as the woman behind the counter pushed a bell and the other door opened from inside.

'This way, please, madam.' A man in black clothes, not precisely a uniform but giving him an air of police-like authority, stood just inside the door, which she could see was a very thick and heavy one, and she stepped forwards.

'Ah, Miss Dundas – ' Friese put a hand on her arm, and she looked at it and then up at his face. No posing now; he looked eager and curious and she felt her own curiosity sharpen.

'Er – shall I wait for you? No doubt there'll be matters you will want to discuss, items to be – um – elucidated – '

'I thought you were in a hurry to get back to your office?'

'Well, yes of course, I'm busy, very busy. Always am, you know. But of course I'm at your disposal, at any time. Glad to wait if you need me – '

She smiled slowly, staring at him. 'Mr Friese, do you know what's in this box?'

He dropped his hand, took a step backwards. 'Know? Of course not! A safe deposit box, you know, is a very – a very *private* matter! Of course I don't know! Your mother put all her business affairs in my hands, naturally, but I didn't *pry*. Wouldn't dream of asking her – but she said that the means to settle the heavy debts on the hotel were here, you see, so I thought – '

'You thought there's some sort of treasure in there, and you're dying to know what it is! Is that it?' She spoke loudly and clearly, very aware of the fascinated stare of the woman behind the counter and the man in the doorway, even more aware of Friese's discomfiture.

'Not at all, not at all!' He was stiff now, very proper, and folded his hands over the handle of his brief-case again and nodded frostily at her. 'Merely offering my professional services, as it is my duty to do. However, I am sure you will come to my office when you are ready. Good afternoon, Miss Dundas.'

'Good afternoon, Mr Friese,' she said and smiled sweetly. 'Thank you so much for your – *interest*.' And she stood and waited until he had gone, bustling out into the corridor, leaving the door to swing closed behind him. And then, and only then, she followed the uniformed man through the other, heavier door.

It was odd, inside. Heavy carpets, still, an air of opulence still, and the spring-flower-scented air-conditioning still, but there was a heaviness, a brooding suffocating sense of weight pressing down on her, and she felt uneasiness creep into her. There was another door on the far side of the one she had come through, a great heavy safe door that looked two to three feet thick, and she

18

glanced up at the ceiling, almost expecting to see bars there. It stared back down at her, white and plain, but she felt she could almost see the huge building above it, pressing down, felt that the walls on each side of her were as thick as that safe door, and it was a horrible feeling. Like being in an underground train when it stopped between the Embankment and Waterloo; knowing the river was above, feeling all the weight of water pressing down –

She shivered and pulled her jacket a little closer about her, and the uniformed man nodded at her and said 'Tis cold, ain't it? I tells 'em, all the time I tells 'em they keeps it too cold dahn 'ere, but there, they don't listen. Says it's get to be cool for the good o' the combination on the safe and the boxes and that, but I reckon they just don't know what it's like to be down 'ere all the time. What's your number, please, miss?'

'Number?'

He pointed to her hand, and she looked down at the key she was holding. The woman had put it there after she had signed – she remembered now, and stared at it. A small ordinary key with a number engraved on it.

'Ah – B.11 – is that it? B.11?'

'That's it, miss. This way, miss.'

The room inside the heavy safe door was lined with square-fronted boxes, each with a letter and number engraved on it, and the sense of oppression increased. She had seen a morgue once, a long time ago, when George had died. A long time ago. That had been lined with drawers like this, big heavy drawers each big enough for a body. These were small drawers, though, and she had a brief vision of each one holding a tiny gnome of a corpse, and wanted to giggle.

'Ere y'are, miss. B.11. This way, miss.'

Portentously carrying the box under his arm, the man led the way to yet another door and opened it, switching on a light, and led her in. No bigger than a lavatory, a blank-walled place with a shelf along one side and nothing else. He put the box down on the shelf, and nodded affably at her. 'There y'are, miss. Just you ring the bell as soon as you're ready – ' He pointed to the bell push beside the door and then he was gone, closing it behind him, and for a horrible moment she panicked, almost banged on the door to be let out; but took a deep breath and closed her eyes and waited for the feeling to ebb away. And it did.

She turned then and looked at the box. A long narrow rectangle of dull grey metal, deep sided, with a flat lid over it. She put her bag down on the floor, and stood in front of the shelf for a long moment, still staring at the box. What was in it? Money? Bank-notes in wads? Or handfuls of jewels, like the ones in children's stories about pirates? Twinkling gold and silver and diamonds, heaped high?

'Stupid.' She whispered it aloud, and the sound came back at her dully from the heavy in-pressing walls. 'Stupid.' The box was too small to hold a pirate's hoard. It was no iron-bound fairy-tale chest. But there had to be something in there of value; Friese had been quite clear on that. The wherewithal to settle the mortgages that encumbered the Westpark hotel, that was what was in there. Somewhere in the region of two hundred thousand was owed, Friese had said, in mortgages and debts to private set-ups as well as to banks. A lot of money. Unless it was paid off, and paid off soon, the whole place'd be lost. She wouldn't get it, and neither would Ida.

Maybe that's what I ought to do, she thought suddenly. I hadn't thought of that before. If I refuse to open this box, refuse to take the legacy, then Ida gets the hotel, *and* the debts and that'll be that. She'll lose it anyway, just as much as I will. Unless – she lifted her head and stared at the ceiling. Unless her mother had also arranged that if she refused, *Ida* should have access to what-ever was in this dull grey oblong? She would know as well as anyone else what would happen if Ida was left the Westpark with nothing to help her pay her way. So she was back where she started. Facing the box and having to open it.

She had put her hand out and lifted the lid. Beneath it was a pile of paper. Envelopes tied up with white tape; squares of pasteboard, grubby and dog-eared, with rubber bands round them; folded sheets, held with little bulldog paperclips.

She put out one finger and touched the pile of pasteboard, thinking 'Photographs – ' and suddenly a scent arose from the box; faded and far away, like the sound of a piano played in a distant room in a big house and she closed her eyes as memory overwhelmed her, almost physically, for her throat tightened and her chest felt as though someone had taken hold of it in a tight grip.

The smell of chypre, that flowery yet heavy scent Dolly had always used. Her face climbed up out of the depths of memory and hovered in front of Maggy's closed eyes; the faded red hair

20

dyed to a ridiculous flame with streaks of brassy yellow in it, the round chipmunk cheeks and the soft drooping mouth, the brown eyes so big and dark in that pale face. And then another vision; a smooth plumpness, the way Dolly had looked when Maggy first remembered her, Dolly young and soft and –

Maggy snapped her eyes open and stared furiously at the blank wall in front of her. Oh, Christ, but this was going to be awful. For years now, she had hated Dolly. She'd made up her mind to that, tried hard to keep to it. Why should she suddenly remember her as she used to be, and feel like crying?

With a business-like movement she picked up the first sheaf of paper that came to hand. They were the folded sheets, and she took the bulldog clip off and spread them out on the shelf in front of her.

They were bills, mostly, and letters to do with leases and rentals and whether or not rates were due, and she picked them over with fastiduous fingers. The address all these related to was the one in Brixton; Effra Road, and she stood and stared at the shape the words of the address made on the paper and could see the house. Peeling stucco and a weedy front path that had once been handsome with black and white square tiles, but which the years had battered and made pitted and dangerous; the stained-glass window set into the front door, with a green slant-eyed girl with rippling hair in among blue and yellow and violet fishes under a turquoise sea; the smell of cooking that pervaded the narrow hallway, the broken sign over the front door reading 'Hanover House, Rooms Available at All Times.' It was extraordinary how vidid the picture was, for she had been very young when they had left there – barely eight or nine. If that.

She shook her head again, and riffled through the rest of the papers. They seemed to be a record of the whole of the Brixton time, starting in 1945, at the end of the war, when they had come there from – where? Maggy didn't know. She had been barely – she did the sum in her head – four years old at the time; and they had stayed there until 1949. It was as though Dolly had taken those four years of their shared life and wrapped them up in a few legal documents; as though having a receipted rates bill made those years solid and real, not just lost time.

She went through them again, wonderingly. Could these carry some information about the 'means that would be made available' to disentangle the finances of the Westpark hotel? Surely not.

Thirty-year-old scraps of yellowing paper to do with a building long since derelict, signed by council officials and bank managers long since retired, probably dead, like Dolly herself; how could there be anything here?

She clipped them together again, and set them on one side, beginning to relax a little. There was clearly no treasure of any kind in the box, nothing that would make that Friese character's eyes brighten. He could have these bits of paper and welcome for all the good they would do him. The whole thing was a nonsense, one of Dolly's foolishnesses.

She picked up the next pile. It was the same again. This time the papers related to the place in Acton. Creffield Road, Acton. Dolly had called that one the Windsor Hotel, her grandiloquent ideas enlarging from a mere Hanover House; that had been bigger, made of two semi-detached houses knocked into one, with a scrubby privet hedge in front and the remains of the front gardens covered in white-flecked black pseudo-tarmac which went sticky in hot summers and smelled of pitch. Maggy had hated that house too, sitting there in the middle of the would-be genteel but run-down suburban road, with battered dustbins huddled against the front hedges and rubbish thrown over by passers-by; there had been that time when she had found what she thought was a discarded toy balloon there and taken it to Dolly, and Dolly had gone white and hit her and told her she was a filthy little bitch to touch such a thing. Her nine-year-old fury and bewilderment rose in her again now, remembering. How was she to know what the bloody thing was? How could poor little Margaret Rose possibly know? For she had still been Margaret Rose then, Margaret Rose in white socks and black patent ankle strap shoes.

She began to flick the pieces of paper over more rapidly; bills and receipts, letters to do with an argument with the council about rubbish collection and another series all about noise complaints from the neighbours. It seemed, reading them, that Dolly had won that battle, for it had all happened in 1951, and they had still been there five years later. It wasn't until – when was it? Maggy lifted her head and stared again at the blank wall. When did I leave at last? When did the end come? I was fifteen. I remember that, fifteen, 1956. So long ago. Only yesterday to think about, but so long ago.

These too she clipped together again, for there was nothing there that was of the least interest. Nothing that pointed in any way to those mysterious means to pay off mortgages. Unless correspondence about old mortgages was a clue of some kind? She looked again, but there was nothing. Nothing that made any sense of today at all.

And so it went on. She rifled through pile after pile of paper, finding nothing but receipted bills and dull letters, and in one pile, menus. Lists of meals long since eaten and forgotten, and she was diverted for a while, reading the prices. Two shillings and sixpence for a three-course lunch, with soup and a main course and a pudding, coffee thrown in as well. Twelve and a half pence today – she felt old, then, for a moment. To remember such differences in prices was a very old thing to do.

The last two packets were different. One was apparently all newspaper cuttings, and she unfolded them carefully, because they were old and the paper was fragile and tore easily. There were a lot of them and she looked only at the first few and then folded them again, quickly. Reports of her own doings, reviews of concerts, scraps from the gossip columns – she had seen these before and had no wish to see them again. But she felt uneasy as she slipped them back into the envelope in which they had been. It was somehow an uncharacteristic thing for Dolly to have done, to have kept her daughter's cuttings. That was something sweet loving mothers did, not the Dollys of this world. Why should she have done such a thing?

Because she didn't feel towards you as you've always thought she did. As you've always tried to persuade yourself she did, a secret voice whispered deep in the recesses of her mind. Because she was a sweet and loving mother, after all, and –

'No.' Maggy said it aloud and pushed the cuttings back into the bottom of the box. She was here to look for – well, she wasn't quite sure precisely what. But it was certainly not digging over of the old coals that had once burned between Dolly and her daughter. No way was she interested in that. Not to be thought about, now or ever. So she picked up the last package, uneasily, and turned it over.

And found herself staring down at Dolly's face. A black and white photograph, crumpled a little at the edges, but clear enough. Dolly, sitting on a stool and looking coquettishly over her shoulder into the camera, her hair in tight marcel waves, yet still contriving to look bushy and hard to control; her eyebrows plucked and arched but with the faint shadows of her own natural ones showing underneath, even in this old photograph; her mouth set in a silly cupid's bow pout. Dolly, about eighteen years old in a sleeveless dress with fringe over the skirt and white stockings with pointed one-bar satin shoes. Dolly, young and hopeful and looking for all that absurd 1930s tat so like Maggy herself that she couldn't bear to look at it.

And she pushed the photographs back into the box, slammed the lid on it, and thrust her finger hard at the bell beside the door. She'd had enough, more than enough. If she didn't get out of this place right away she'd lose control, or be sick, or something. She'd had more than enough.

3

The Haymarket was as hot and stinking and crowded as ever, but she stood there on the pavement taking deep breaths and willing the glittering lights in front of her eyes to fade away, to leave her in peace again. The stumbling journey out of the cool sub-basement had been dreadful, with nausea threatening to overtake her at every step, but she had managed it, somehow, willing herself to be controlled. The woman had made her sign another form on the way out, and told her that from now on she was to keep the key and could return at any time she chose; the uniformed man had nodded at her brightly and tried to get her to stand and listen to him complain about the air conditioning, and she had managed not to shriek at either of them, or to throw up on the carpet at their feet. Now, standing on the pavement as the afternoon crowds thickened into a rush hour mob, she began to feel better. This was now, today, and she could cope with that. Down below was yesterday and a lot of pain she didn't want to remember, and that was what made her feel so sick.

'Well, well, if it isn't my dear old Maggy, then.' The voice almost made her jump, coming as it did from behind her, and seeming incredibly loud, even in the roar of Haymarket traffic, and she whirled to stare at him.

'Oh,' she said after a moment. 'Oliver. What are you doing here?'

'Just a little stroll, lovey, that's all. Felt a bit bogged down, you know? Thought I'd take a walk, and look what happened – finished up here! Must have been walking for ages, didn't realize how far I'd come – '

'Really?' she said, uninterested; becoming aware of the heat, she took off her jacket so that she could sling it more coolly over her shoulders. At once he helped her, and as he touched her she felt the old feeling creep into her again, that mixture of revulsion and fascination.

'I can manage fine, thanks,' she said sharply. 'And I must go.'

'No – not yet, lovey! Can't just go like that! Come and have a quiet drink with me, eh? For old times' sake? I'm awfully lonely now, Maggy, and it'd be good to talk to you for a while – We would pop over to the Cabin and have a quick one – '

'No, Oliver, really, I don't think – I want to get home – '

He looked at her sharply then. 'You're looking a bit green, love! What is it that got to you? Come on – I insist on a drink. You look as though you need it.' And he took her arm and with a masterful air led her across the road towards the pub they had gone to so often when they used to record for the BBC at the Paris Theatre, long ago.

This time she felt no reaction to his touch. She was drooping now, as suddenly tired as she had been suddenly sick, and it was easier to go with him than argue. And she was thirsty too; there was a metallic taste in her mouth she would be glad to wash away.

He found a corner of the already crowded pub where there were two stools and then brought her a vodka and tonic and a tomato juice for himself, and she sat there, her shoulders sagging and her hands floppy on her lap and waited, her mind empty. She felt lousy, too lousy even to wonder why.

But the drink cooled and refreshed her and after a while of sitting staring moodily into space she stirred herself and sat up a little straighter.

'That's better,' Oliver said. 'What happened, then? You really were feeling it in there for a bit, weren't you?'

'Yes,' she said absently, and then looked at him. He looked very comforting, suddenly. He'd made her very unhappy, once, but that was a long time ago now, and it really didn't matter; at least, at the moment it didn't, though heaven knew whether she'd think the same way this time tomorrow. So she smiled at him.

'Thanks, Oliver. I needed that drink.'

'So tell me what happened.' He leaned forwards cosily.

'I don't know. Mad, really. I just felt ill suddenly. Not a bit like me.'

'Oh, I don't know love. You aren't quite as tough as you make yourself out to be, you know. You always used to go on about how strong you were, never ill, never tired, but I knew better. Remember? This is Oliver, sweetie, not one of your Johnny-come-latelies. This is old Oliver. And you've every right to feel a bit off. What with the heat, and the upset of Dolly and then having to go through the box – '

26

At once she was all edge, sitting up very straight and staring at him. He looked back at her with his eyes wide and limpid, his face blank of any expression, just the usual soft look, the sagging muscles that made him seem like a wax doll that had been left out in the sun too long.

'What box?' she said sharply.

'Dolly's safe deposit box, darling. You'd just come up from there, hadn't you? When I bumped into you? What else would you be doing standing on the pavement just there?'

'What do you know about that box? What business is it of yours?'

'Sweetheart, do be reasonable! I lived with your Mum for fifteen years, remember? There wasn't much about her I didn't know! 'Course I knew she had it!'

'Well, so what if she had? What has it got to do with me?'

'She left it to you, didn't she?' Oliver opened his eyes even more widely. 'Who else would she leave it to? Not me, darling, nor Ida either. You, of course – so don't go getting all agitated at me. It was natural I should ask – '

'Maybe. But it's not natural for me to answer. So I shan't.'

'Bless you, darling, you sound like a naughty little girl – shan't, shan't, shan't! All right, then, ducks, don't. No one's forcing you. I was just interested in why you felt ill so suddenly. I thought, there must have been something there that upset her, poor kid, I thought. That's all.' He turned his head to look round the pub, ostentatiously relaxed and she stared at his profile and thought – he used to look so marvellous. The first time I saw him I – have I changed so much, as well?

Aloud, she said abruptly, 'What if there was? What difference can it make to you?'

'Would you believe I love you? In my own stupid way, I love you?'

'Really?' There's a turn-up for the book, then,' she said harshly, and couldn't look at him. 'And there was me, all those years ago – oh, go and get me another drink. And shut up.'

While he was at the bar, she tried to sort out her confused thoughts. Why be so upset by the stuff in that damned box? What possible reason could there be for getting in such a state? Mad, really mad. She didn't *care* about Dolly. Dolly was dead, and just didn't matter. The only reason for going to the box in the first place was to stop Ida getting her hot little hands on it, to stop her

27

from robbing her even more than –

'Oh, damn, damn, damn,' she said aloud, and then wanted to laugh; it sounded so stupid. And Oliver, coming back, grinned comfortably and said, 'That's better. Even the smell of a drink and you look like you're enjoying yourself. Drink it up and we'll really have a ball.'

She drank, and he leaned forward after a while and said earnestly, 'Look, Maggy, I'm sorry if I upset you, prying. I wouldn't upset you for anything, you know that. I mean, I hurt you enough in the past, didn't I? But that's all over, and I want us to be friends. Truly, sweetie, I need you, and you know something? You need me. No, don't look like that. You do. Who else is there you can be really comfortable with? No need to put on any sort of sexy act for me, the way you have to for other men. Theo and – well, no need with me. And I really know you well, you know that, Maggy? I'm one of the few people who do, if not the only one, now poor old Dolly's gone. You put on that great show of being all tough and hard-boiled and you're as soft as marshmallow underneath. Purest, softest marshmallow. You're so vulnerable it hurts to look at you sometimes, and the more you try to be hard the more vulnerable you are. I'm right, aren't I? And who else is there who knows about you? Only Oliver, silly old Oliver. So who else can you trust the way you can trust me?'

She looked at him through the faint haze the vodka had set before her eyes and thought – he's right. He is the only one I can be comfortable with, if I let myself. He's certainly the only one I never have to be on guard with. Never have to pretend with. If I want to hate him I can, and then I can come back and he's forgotten or never cared –

'There was a pile of photographs there. I only looked at the top one,' she said, and then, absurdly, giggled. 'I only looked at the top one.'

'Well?' His voice was comfortable, encouraging rather than probing.

'It was Dolly – around, oh, I don't know how many years ago. She looked about – eighteen, maybe. You'd have liked the clothes she was wearing. All cross-cut satin and fringes – camp as a troop of boy scouts. And her hair and her make-up – honestly, it was straight out of Gold Diggers of 1932. You'd have loved it.'

'May I see it?' He sounded casual now. Her bag was on the table between them, and he pushed it towards her, with an almost absent-minded gesture.

'I left it there. Couldn't look at anything else. Shoved it back in the box and left it there. It upset me so much – '

There was a little pause and someone put a coin in the juke box, making the noise triple as people standing around shouted louder to be heard above it. 'Why?' he said, and then repeated it, louder. 'Why?'

'Because she looked like me,' Maggy said, and tipped up her glass to swallow the last of her drink, and got up. 'I've got to get out of here. Too much noise – I'm going home. I've got a recording tomorrow – there's things to do – ' She picked up her bag, and thrust it under her arm, threw her jacket over her shoulders. 'Lots of things to do.'

'What else was in the box?' He followed her out, threading a way through the now jam-packed bar, trying to keep up with her, trying to sound as relaxed as he could. 'Anything else apart from photographs?'

'Papers,' Maggy said vaguely. They were out in the street now, and she began to walk quickly up the narrow pavement back towards the Haymarket, watching for a taxi. 'Bits of paper. Is that taxi's light on? Damn – someone's got it – '

'I'll find you one when we get to Trafalgar Square – it'll be easier there.' He took her elbow, tried to slow her down. 'What sort of bits of paper?'

'Oh, a lot of rubbish. Nothing important. Old receipts, bills – menus – things like that.'

'Nothing else?' He pulled on her arm now, slowed her down even more.

She looked at him then over her shoulder and there was a new look on his face, a familiar one and she frowned, still a little hazed, what with reaction from feeling ill and the vodka, and tried to place it, and then did; it was the look that had been on the solicitor Friese's face. Eager, almost avid, solid with curiosity.

'What should there be?' she said lightly. 'Damn – there's another taxi gone. I'll try in the middle of the road, I think – ' and she plunged into the traffic, forcing him to let go of her arm. But he followed her, and together they stood on the island in the middle as her eyes raked the oncoming traffic for a taxi.

'Oh, I don't know – but safe deposit boxes – you expect them to have something really worth hiding in them, don't you? I mean – ' He moved closer, trying to make her look at him instead of

29

looking so assiduously for a taxi. 'When that safe deposit place in Baker Street was turned over a few years ago – d'you remember? They dug a tunnel from the place next door and got away with God knows what – and people said then a lot of the boxes had money in them. Black money.'

'Black money?' She couldn't avoid looking at him; his head was thrust directly in front of her now.

'Oh, tax fiddles, you know? And jewellery of course – hedges against inflation, all that sort of thing. And why not? Why else have a safe deposit box? If you've got legitimate money you invest it, or put it in a normal bank account. The only reason to have a safe deposit is for secrets – '

She moved away enough to see over his shoulder, and then, gratefully, waved furiously, 'Taxi! Taxi, damn you – Glory be, I've got him. Goodbye, Oliver. See you around – '

The taxi slid to a halt beside them, the driver put his arm out to open the door for her, but still Oliver held on to her.

'There must have been something else in there,' he said, very loudly. 'I mean, just photographs, bits of paper? Or were some of the papers stock certificates or something of that sort? There must have been more than – '

'Goodbye, Oliver!' She slammed the door shut, and said urgently to the driver, 'Royal Crescent – just off Holland Park Road – fast as you like – ' and then leaned back as the taxi moved away into the traffic, leaving Oliver staring after it in the middle of the road.

All the way home she sat huddled in the corner of the taxi as it crept through the nose-to-tail rush hour traffic, taking almost three-quarters of an hour for the six-mile journey, staring out sightlessly at Oxford Street and then the Bayswater Road, trying to sort out her feelings, and put her thoughts into some sort of order. Why had Oliver been so interested in the safe deposit box? Why had he probed so hard? Why had he been there at all, come to that? She had accepted his presence there in the street as one of the coincidences that happen so often in London, but now she wasn't so sure. Dammit, the Haymarket was one of the busiest streets in the whole town, and it had been half past five, the start of the rush hour. He *must* have been hanging around waiting for her to have met her quite so pat; and, taking that and his behaviour in the pub into account, his probing afterwards began to seem much more sinister. She had been warmed and comforted by the things he's said to her there, staring at her over his tomato juice. There had been warmth and, she had thought, real affection, and even though the feelings she had for him all those years ago were dead now, there were enough of their ghosts left for her to have welcomed that. Had she been beguiled, softened up, deliberately? Usually when they met he was barbed, made bitchy little jokes and digs that smarted badly; why had he been so gentle tonight?

Christ, she thought, I'm getting paranoid. This really has to stop – it really must stop, right now! Deliberately, she made herself think about tomorrow. She was working only with the basic band, Dan on the percussion, Komo on the double bass, and Chalky with the clarinet. A wierd line-up for her sort of music, they'd told her once, until she'd shown them just what sort of sound she could make with it. As long as there was Maggy Dundas on the piano to tie them together, you could take anything from a tin whistle to a jew's harp and make it work. But only as long as Maggy Dundas was on the piano. Tomorrow they were working on the Elgar variations and the Stravinsky Symphony in C. And anyone who laughed at the idea of making jazz out of those two would laugh again on the other side of their faces when they heard what she could do with them.

I'm trying too hard, she thought bleakly. If I have to build myself this high before I even begin, I'll get nowhere. Come on, woman, admit it. You're rattled as hell, and you've got a big job on tomorrow and you're scared. That's what it is. That's why you're in such a state. You need a bath and something to eat and an early night, maybe a couple of Mogadon. It's been a rough day, one way and other.

She leaned forwards to speak to the driver. 'Can't we do any better than this? Try the back doubles, maybe?'

'It's like barley soup all the way from here to Shepherds Bush and beyond,' the man said, leaning back wearily. 'Been like it all day. You'll do better on the tube, tell you the truth. This time of night they're mobbed, but the trains at least run. More than this bloody traffic does. Take you pick, ducks, no skin off my nose.'

'Oh, all right, all right – ' She leaned back. The underground – she should have picked up a train at Piccadilly; she'd have been home by now. But the throught of getting out of the taxi now and joining the mobs at Lancaster Gate station – she shook her head. She'd stick it out. Here at least she was sitting down.

31

By the time she reached home, she was feeling a bit less tense, had even managed to close her eyes and relax in the cab, going over the Stravinsky score in her head, and she paid the taxi driver cheerfully enough and then started the long climb to her flat.

She had been dubious when she'd first seen it. A super flat in lots of ways, of course, a magnificent living room with windows at each end, because the house was on the corner, with views high across the chimney tops for miles, a good bedroom, a really well-fitted kitchen and a bathroom with a shower, a rare pleasure in a conversion like this one. Hundred-year-old houses don't take easily to modern plumbing. But it was on the top floor and every time she was faced with six flights of steep stairs she told herself she'd have to move. Get somewhere modern, with a lift, garbage chutes. And then she'd get to the top and into her big cool white room, with its Collard and Collard piano dominating it, and think – what modern flat could take a grand? And would have walls and floors thick enough to keep the sound out?

Now, plodding heavily upwards, her bag held under one arm as she held on to the curving banister with her other hand, she counted the steps as she went, as she often did, a childhood trick that had never left her. Thirty-*three*, thirty-*four*, thirty-*five* – fifty-*one*, fifty-*two*, fifty-*three* –

She muttered irritably as the reached the top flight. The blasted light had gone again. She'd complained to the landlady often enough about it, but every time she put in a new bulb, it went again. Maggy sometimes suspected the man in the flat below of coming up to steal the bulbs; he was a pernicketty penny-pinching old miser, and the light fitting could be reached easily from the landing outside her own front door. One of these days she'd set some sort of trap for him, and then there'd be arguments –

The thoughts, silly, childish, mumbled through her head as she climbed on into the dimness, while the step counting went on behind them, as a sort of counterpoint; seventy-*eight*, seventy-*nine*, eight –

The attack when it came was so ridiculous that it was surprise that knocked her over more than the impact. One moment there she was counting steps and thinking sour thoughts about her downstairs neighbour and the next there was a hand tugging at her bag, and another pushing against her chest for all the world as though she was a child, and someone was trying to take a bag of sweets from her. She was being pushed against the banisters so that her ribs seemed to crack against them, and she gasped and let go of her bag and heard the attacker, whoever it was, fall back against the wall and grunt with pain as he hit it, for clearly he was as startled with the ease with which he got possession of the bag as she was; and then he was half falling, half scrambling down the staircase, making a great clattering noise and leaving her in a heap on the top flight with one arm curled round the banisters and her head aching abominably where she had hit it on the banister rail.

The man with toothache stood on the kerb and watched the taxi go, and could have shouted aloud with the frustration of it. The bitch, the stupid bitch, to go by taxi at this time of night. He hadn't got a dog's chance of getting another one in this hubbub and even if he did it wouldn't get him anywhere. He'd tried the 'follow-that-cab' routine before and both times the drivers had told him to piss off out of it, they weren't getting involved in nothing like *that*, thanks very much. So he had to watch her go, helplessly, had to stand there on the kerb and watch the taxi bury itself in the clotted traffic and could do nothing about it.

What the hell would he tell them tonight when he called? There'd be all murder let loose if he didn't do something, didn't find out a little bit more. They'd been very pressing, very pressing indeed about it the last time he'd called. And the really maddening thing had been the way he'd been so pleased with himself, getting the first bit of info for them. He'd called the man himself, direct on his private line, something he hardly ever dared do before and told him, flat out, 'She's dead. Dolly Dundas, handed in her dinner pail. Heard about it from someone up at the studios.'

And he'd been pleased as Punch with the reaction he'd got. 'Is she indeed?' the smooth voice had murmured, as silky as hot custard, even over three thousand miles of phone links. 'Is she *indeed*. Well, well. That takes a little thinking about. I'll call you back.' And he had not half an hour later, with very precise instructions. 'Find out who gets the hotel. Find out who gets access to her property. It's probably the daughter – in fact I'll be amazed if it isn't. But make sure. And then watch her, and tell me everything she does, everywhere she goes, you understand me? Everything.'

It had sounded so easy. Just follow some dim female. But she was so dim she never did the right things; only the dimmest of idiots would take a taxi in the middle of the rush hour, he told

33

himself bitterly, and he turned and went along the street, pushing irritably through the crowds. He'd have to make it the record office building again, even though that hadn't got him anywhere so far, hanging around outside there. Damn it all to hell and back, he hadn't even managed to find out where the bloody woman lived, yet –

'It's getting complicated,' the man at the desk said, and twirled his chair so that he was staring out of the window at the East River. 'I hadn't expected this.'

The other man said nothing, sitting and watching, his arms folded neatly across his chest.

'You're sure he said the girl had gone to a safe deposit?'

Yes, sir, Mr Lancaster.'

'Nothing more than that?'

'No, sir. Not a word.'

'I should have foreseen it. She was that sort of woman. I should have guessed it.'

'Sir?' the young man said, polite and a little remote, and uncrossed and recrossed his legs.

'We've got to get this right, Greening.' The man at the desk twirled his chair again so that he was looking across it at him, and his voice was softer, deeper, less abstracted. 'It's difficult for you, I know. You don't understand what it's all about, do you?'

'That isn't important sir. As long as you do.'

The man at the desk smiled, and leaned back. His face was more shadowed now that the window was behind him. 'Yes, I do. The ways of providence – I have to understand. To help you.'

'That's so, sir.' For the first time the young man showed some animation, his mouth lifting in a smile. 'To help us.'

'Well, let me tell you a little. Just a little. Like you, I was different. I lead you now, but I *was* different. And before I was as I am now things happened – bad things. You understand?'

'Bad things happened to me too, sir,' the young man said, and leaned forwards. 'I – '

'Not now, Greening. Now now. *I'm* explaining to *you*. Listen.'

'Sir.'

'The bad things don't matter to me any more. But they could matter to the lost ones. The ones we must help. You understand me? It's important that you should.'

'Sir.'

34

The man at the desk sighed, a sharp almost irritated little sound and then smiled, wide and soft. 'No, I suppose you don't. Let me put it on the line. There are facts about my past that could be bad for us. For you as well as me. It could discredit all our work. That would never do, would it?'

'No *sir*. Never.'

'So. I'm telling you we have to ensure, don't we, that the – these facts stay where they are. Not talked about. Forgotten.'

'We do indeed, sir.'

'And that girl – '

'That girl knows the facts? Whatever they are?' The young man was as quiet and polite as ever, but there was a smoothness about him that made the other look at him sharply. But he had imagined it. There was no guile there, none at all. Just obedience and interest. That was all.

'This old woman knew. The one who died. I thought it would die with her, I suppose, but now I'm not so sure. A safe deposit box – so I'm not so sure. That's the problem.'

'Not the man that Gibbs looks after? I thought he was the problem, sir.'

The man at the desk laughed easily, and leaned back in his chair. 'Well, of course, he could have been. And you're right. He was part of it too. But I'm dealing with him. Stupid creature – ' and there was a note of venom in his voice, just for a moment. 'Believe me, he's in the same boat as I am, in his picayune fashion. But he hadn't the wit to see it, so he's more worried about what I might say, instead of trying to worry *me*. He's a fool. Forget him. I want you to concentrate on the girl. Because if she finds out, then – she's not a fool. And she's not soft, the way her mother was. The old woman never worried me, because of the sort of woman she was, but this one's different. So watch her, you hear me? Because one way and another, there's a lot to worry about here. Quite apart from the money.'

'Money, sir?'

The other man lifted his brows at him, smiling again. 'Didn't I tell you? There's a lot of money involved, I rather think. A lot. Enough to do a good deal of the work we have to do, hmm? The sort of money that'll make money. So you see, there's a lot to think about. And a lot of reasons to keep an eye on her. I'm relying on you, now.'

'Sir,' the young man said, and smiled.

4

'I think I'd better move back in, darling, don't you?'

'If you like.' She was staring at the wall, her eyes fixed on one of Saul's fancy etchings, but not really seeing it. Her head still ached a little, and the coffee she had had as soon as she got here had been a mistake; it had made her headache even worse.

'Only if *you* like, Maggy. No way am I going to force anything on you. But you need looking after, for God's sake. I mean, if I'd been there as usual last night, it wouldn't have happened.'

She looked at him now and managed to smile, a twisted little grimace.

'That's one hell of a way to talk to a woman these days! Christ, man, you'll get yourself dragged in front of the Equal Opportunities Commission or something – '

'Oh, let's not get on to that tack!' he said and made a face at her. 'I wasn't doing the male chauvinist bit – just making the point that you wouldn't have been so likely to be mugged on your own doorstep if someone else had been on the other side of the door. Man or woman. If you know a woman you'd rather share your flat with, great. Go call her. I'm just making the point that you shouldn't be living on your own, and I'm here and ready – '

'I know, I know.' She was bored with the talk, now, irritated by his solicitude. 'I take your point. Come back if you like. We both know you were going to anyway. Might as well be now as later.'

And I am frightened. And I would be happier to know there was someone else around. And I do miss you. She would never have said any of it, but thoughts couldn't be controlled as easily as speech.

There was a slam of the door at the far side of the big studio and Saul came bustling towards her out of the shadows. 'Sweetie! What's this I hear? Mugged, my darling, in your own flat? I tell you, we're getting as bad as New York here!' He said it with melancholy pride. 'Such a thing to happen – I'm shattered! So tell

36

me all about it, darling, every bit – what did they get? Did the bastard hurt you any? Did he – ' His voice dropped. 'Did he try anything?'

'Oh, Saul, for Christ's sake, leave the poor girl alone! Bad enough it happened, and she had the police to talk to and the rest of it – don't you go putting her through a catechism – '

'No, Solly, he didn't try anything,' Maggy, perverse suddenly, smiled cheerfully at the fat little man, ignoring Theo, bringing Saul into a cosy chattiness with her, wanting to make Theo feel shut out. 'Must have been an Irish mugger, because the silly idiot took my bag, bashed my head on the banisters, and then dumped the bag in the front area, without taking anything from it – daft, isn't it?'

Saul's eyes opened wide. 'Took nothing? Didn't try anything on you? You're putting me on!'

'Honestly! He turned my bag upside down on the front step, the police reckoned, went through it looking for something, and didn't find whatever it was, and then just dropped it over the railings into the area – and I had a fair bit of cash in my purse too. I knew I wouldn't have time to get to the bank today, being Friday and all, and no banks tomorrow, so I'd taken out a lot of cash. I'm going down to Dorset in the morning for a couple of days – or I was – so there was a lot of cash there, over a couple of hundred quid, and he just left it. Really weird.'

'You didn't tell me that!' Theo said sharply.

'Didn't I? Maybe you didn't ask the right questions.' She smiled at Saul again.

'Anyway, that's what happened. A real non-starter when it comes to a robbery.'

'Terrible, terrible,' Saul said, but now his concern sounded a little abstracted. No money gone and no sexual assault meant nothing to get really excited about. He looked over this shoulder as the distant door slammed again. 'Ah – the fellers – so where you been, you lot? We've been here ready and waiting for hours!' He bustled away, all bonhomie and cheerfulness as Komo came out of the shadows, lugging his double bass.

'Hi, Maggs – hi, Theo, Fuckin' parkin' round here – if you don't get those bleedin' wardens organized, Solly, I ain't goin' to come here to work no more, you hear me? I got better things to do in the mornin' than have fights with bleedin' traffic wardens – '

'So give me your keys, and I'll send one of the boys to park

37

you. What do you want of my life? Don't I lay on the best of everything here, don't I give you the best damned studios in the whole of London, including the Beeb, and you expect we should let you drive your van right inside? Maybe you'd rather park in my office, hey? I'll move my desk out for you, hey? – '

Arguing pointlessly they went away, and Chalky and Danny, who had followed Komo in, grinned at Maggy and made expressive faces at Komo's departing back.

'He's in a bad way, Maggy, I warn you. Really tied one on last night,' Danny said, and began to set up his drums, pushing the big instruments about as though they were made of butter. 'He's been moaning all the way from Balham. Here, Chalky, give me a hand with this – '

'Did he, then?' Maggy said grimly, and got to her feet. 'I'll soon deal with *him* – I've not had the best of nights myself, and I'm in no mood for one of his temperaments, that's for sure. Go talk to him, Theo. Make yourself useful – '

She felt better now. The day had started properly and as the studio lights began to snap on and the engineers got themselves organized in the booth behind the plate-glass walls at the far end of the big room she felt her headache recede. There was work to be done, and she was going to do it, and do it well.

Theo picked up her crisp mood and nodded and went away after Komo, and after a moment appeared on the far side of the glass wall, and began to talk to the engineers, their mouths moving dumbly, and Saul and Komo followed him in there. Maggy stood for a moment watching them, as Komo waved his arms about and shouted soundlessly and Theo made soothing gestures at him.

More coffee appeared, brought by one of the blue-jeaned boys who were always hanging around the place, waiting to be discovered by one of the Greats while they worked for Saul as dogsbodies for tuppence a week, and this time she took it gratefully. She had had no breakfast, waking late from her Mogadon-induced sleep, and she needed a lift.

Chalky did too. 'Here, pretty boy – you with the face – go get me a bacon sandwich. And a hot Danish to follow. I don't blow good on an empty belly.'

He arranged himself on a tall stool, his heavy buttocks flopping over the edge and his belly resting cosily on his thighs. 'C'mon, Maggy, let me buy you a nosh. You look like you haven't eaten for a week.'

'You'll make us all as fat as you are, Chalky. But I could do with some breakfast. Make it a fried-egg sandwich, on brown, though. And no Danish – Chalky, how'd you get on with the new top page I gave you? Better, eh?'

'Like always, me darlin', like always!' Chalky picked up his clarinet and blew a few notes, cascading them into a ripple of sound that was soothing and yet exciting at the same time, and she grinned at him, and Danny, catching the lift in her mood, rattled a short cadenza, flourishing his sticks like a drum majorette. They all laughed then, and Komo came and joined them, grinning and cheerful, his black face as amiable now as it had been scowling a few minutes ago.

They slipped into the comfortable pattern of a morning's work, going over the score, working through a few bars at a time where the tricky sections came, Danny extemporizing a little, Maggy leading him at the piano. Their food came, and they ate, still talking, stopping sometimes to play another few bars to sort out a difficulty and then eating again, and Theo came and joined them now, leaning on Maggy's piano, watching her as she worked.

There was a little smear of egg yolk on her chin, and that warmed him; it made her look younger and softer, exposing the vulnerability he knew was in her. She was looking good this morning, her red hair, tightly curled, standing up in an aureole and her usual pallor seeming thicker and whiter. It was not an unhealthy pallor precisely, but it did show how tired she was, as did the shadows under her chin and at her temples. But for all that, she seemed alert and tense in a creative sort of way, as though she were like an overstrung violin. Even her clothes added to the tense look; tight black leather pants, a baggy black sweater and streaming yellow silk scarf; all very now, very trendy in its fifties nostalgia. Clever Maggy, he thought, as the group slid at last into a full run-through. Clever Maggy, using the best of yesterday to make today her own. She did it with her music as well as her clothes, coming on as strong as any of the twenty-year-old kids who littered this business. But Maggy wasn't twenty, hadn't been for a long time. Maggy was a very grown-up lady, a very complex grown-up lady, with a lot to offer a man, in lots of ways. She looked up at him and frowned suddenly; she hated being watched when she worked, so he nodded and grinned and went back to the booth. There'd be time, eventually, to say what he wanted to say.

He waited until they had taped the ninth run, going over and over the score in Maggy's usual meticulous way, and everyone was beginning to look frayed; it had been a long morning and a hard one, but the work was beginning to sound good. He came down from the booth and went over to her where she was sitting on her piano stool, the headphones over her ears, listening to the playback. She sat there with her eyes tight shut, her fingers moving over the invisible piano keys on her lap as she concentrated on the tape and then grunted as it came to an end and she pulled off the headphones.

'These cans are bloody awful,' she said dispassionately. 'They'd make Paganini sound like a honky-tonk player. Solly!' She turned and waved to the plate-glass wall. 'I need new cans – or there's something sour up there. Come and listen to this! You too, Hal!'

Solly, in the booth, threw his eyes up in exasperation and came scuttling out with Hal Isaacs, the producer, behind him, and there was a bustle with the earphones as Danny stretched and lit a cigarette and Chalky began to choose the runners for the afternoon's races at Sandown Park.

'Maggy, where are you going tomorrow?'

'Mmm? How d'you mean?' She had her head down over her score, marking it yet again in her meticulous handwriting, going over and over again the pauses, the emphases, the shape of the piece they were recording. Usually he admired her painstaking professionalism, but now it irritated him. But he knew better than to let her know that.

'You said you were going down to Dorset.'

'Oh – yes. I'd thought about it – ' She looked up at him then, her lower lip caught between her teeth, suddenly doubtful. 'I don't know now, though – '

'Why not?'

She sat silent for a moment, as Hal and Solly began to argue about the technical quality of the tape, shouting at each other with great energy but no real acrimony.

'I'm silly, I suppose, but it was this daft business last night. I mean, it was really mad, wasn't it? Someone sits hiding on the top flight of my stairs, goes to the trouble of picking the lock on the street door to get in – so the police said, anyway – takes the bulb out of the light, hangs around for God knows how long till I get there, shoves me over to pinch my bag, and then doesn't take anything. It's mad, it did me no harm apart from a minor bash on the head, and it's left me shit-scared. You know that? I was shaking like a baby by the time the police had gone and I went to bed. Terrified – which is crazy, when you think about it. So, I thought – ' She shrugged. 'So I thought I'd better stay home for the weekend after all. You know, climbing back on the horse you just fell off? Or something – ' Her voice trailed away.

'Maybe if you can work out why the chap mugged you, whoever he was, you'll feel better,' Theo said, carefully.

'Why? But why does anyone ever do such a thing? That's a daft – '

'You said it was daft because he didn't do what you'd expect. He left your money behind. So – working out why would be a very relevant thing to do.'

She stared at him, her forehead a little creased. 'But how can I work out why? I mean, damn it, where do I even begin?'

'Begin with what he did with your bag when he took it.'

'Nothing! I told you that!'

'Not at all! He definitely did something. Went through it, and then chucked it into the area. Looking for something that wasn't there. You said that youself.'

She shook her head. 'I suppose so – I've really been rather thick, haven't I? All shook up, I suppose, too shook up to think straight. Yes, that's what he did. Looked for something that wasn't there – ' She bent her head and looked at her score again, avoiding his eyes.

'Well, what might that have been?' Theo said, still tentative, still not wanting to alarm her.

'You tell me.' She looked at him with her eyes so blank of expression they seemed almost opaque. 'You tell me.'

'Where had you been yesterday? The bank, of course – you said that. But it couldn't have been cash the guy wanted or he'd have taken it. So it wasn't someone who saw you at the bank and then followed you – '

'I wasn't followed. I was laid in wait for. Really, you'll have to do better than that.' All her suspicion was aroused now. She remembered fleetingly how she had felt about Oliver's behaviour the previous afternoon and thought – am I mad? Getting paranoid delusions? Thinking everyone is after me?

Theo went on as carefully as ever. 'Well, what do *you* think? Where did you go that might have encouraged someone to think that you had something valuable? Valuable enough to – er – go ahead of you, wait for you – '

She laughed now, as the engineers joined the group of men in the middle of the studio arguing over the equipment. There was something wrong with one of the leads, and an engineer began testing it, and she laughed again, looking at them.

'Honestly, Theo, you're as bad as that lot there, digging around to find a gremlin in the works. Why don't you just come out with it? You know where I went yesterday afternoon, don't you? Just as Oliver did.'

'Oliver?'

'Yes, Oliver. He was waiting for me when I came out of the place. Said he just happened to be taking a walk, but I reckon that was one hell of a just-happened. Don't you? And now here's you digging around to find out where I went yesterday. Could it just happen that you know perfectly well where I was? You spent enough time talking to Friese after Dolly died. And Friese is a great talker, isn't he? So, come on, Theo. Tell me all. You know where I was yesterday afternoon, don't you?'

He was silent for a moment. 'Yes,' he said at length, and looked across at the engineers now arguing furiously with Solly while Hal tried to calm them all down. 'Look, this is going to take ages to sort out. Come out for lunch, what d'you say? We can go to that Chinese place up the road. I'll tell Hal and Solly – '

She let him do as he chose, let him send the others off for their usual liquid lunch at the pub and let him bring her jacket and put it over her shoulders. Not until they were sitting at the oilcloth covered table at Kuo Yuang and had ordered their seaweed and Peking duck did she speak again. And then only said, 'Well?'

'Well, what?'

'What was the catechism about? You complained when Solly wanted to ask questions, but your own – about as subtle as a bulldozer, and about as efficient, too – '

He sighed and leaned back in his chair, holding his teacup between his fingers with great delicacy. He looked a little foolish suddenly, the small cup seeming incongruous in his big hand, and some of her suspicion melted away. Damn it all, this was Theo. She'd lived with him, one way and another, for three years. Why suddenly look sideways at him now, just because he was asking questions?

'Look,' she said. 'I went to the safe deposit yesterday, as you obviously know. Friese said that I'd find enough there to pay off

42

the debts the Westpark's lumbered with. Okay. So I expected to find – I don't know. Money? Share certificates? Something. I imagine you expected the same – '

'Yes, I did. Friese said there was a box, so – well, what else could there be in there? There'd be no use in the thing otherwise. What *was* there?' He looked at her solemnly, no hint of the eagerness that had so filled Friese's expression, and later, Oliver's. Just an owlish stare, and she laughed at him.

'Go on. Guess. Tell me what you imagine was there – '

He shook his head, angry suddenly. 'Stop playing silly buggers, Maggy. I'm not playing games, believe me. You were pushed over last night by some hoodlum or other and would you believe, I'm upset about it. Yes, I was curious about that box – I'd be a bloody liar or a fool if I said I wasn't – but I really am far more concerned about who got to you last night. I thought it might be linked with the damned box in some way – that's why I asked. Okay? Make what you like out of that – ' Sulkily he finished his tea, poured out another cup, looking, Maggy thought, like a ruffled Mrs Tiggywinkle.

She leaned forwards and patted his hand. 'Well, yes, I suppose – look, all that box had in it were papers. Piles of tatty bits of paper to do with the houses we lived in, she and I and those damned boarders, years ago. A pile of newspaper cuttings, there were those, and some photographs. That's all – '

He stared at her. 'Nothing else?'

'Not a bloody thing else. So there's no reason there why anyone should mug me, is there?'

He shook his head, mystification all over his face. 'I don't really – the photographs – what about them? Was there anything there that would explain?'

'I didn't look at them properly. I suddenly felt – I didn't feel good. It was shut in and stuffy – well, not stuffy exactly, but oppressive and – I felt ill, and got the hell out.' She looked down at her hands. She didn't want to tell him just how much that photograph of Dolly had affected her. 'So I don't know what there is in detail. I suppose I'll have to go back and look again.' She said it with distaste. Going back there wouldn't be agreeable.

'Can you go back? Without having that Friese there?' Theo said sharply.

'Yes, of course. I've got the key. Why?'

'Because maybe – he's not a man I like or trust. There was

43

something about the way he rabbitted on to me about Dolly and her affairs and you – I don't trust him.' He stopped then and stared at her. 'The key, you say? What key?'

'The one to the safe deposit box, of course. I've got it here.' She turned in her chair so that she could scrabble in the pocket of her jacket, hanging over the back. 'Here it is – ' She held it out to him, and then, as he reached out to pick it up, almost without thinking closed her hand on it, and put both clenched fists in her lap. He blinked, and then as though he had not noticed the moment of distrust nodded and leaned back in his chair.

'Maybe that's what your mugger was after.' He said it in a conversational way, as the waiter came to put hot plates in front of them and bowls and chopsticks. She served herself greedily and began to eat. It seemed a long time since the fried-egg sandwich.

'The key?' she said, her mouth full. 'How could he be? Who knew I had it?'

'Friese,' Theo said, and watched her, making no attempt to eat himself. 'Maybe he wanted to get whatever was in there. Did he tell you what was in it?'

She shook her head. 'He didn't know. Tried to hang around to be told, but I gave him the push. Have some duck, for God's sake. I'm making a pig of myself.'

He began to eat, fiddling with the pancake and the plum sauce with fastidious fingers. 'Well, maybe he was after the key so that he could go back and see for himself – maybe he got a bloke to do the office for him. And when the bloke couldn't find the key in your bag, because you'd put it in your pocket, he just chucked your bag away. Makes sense?'

'No,' she said, and began on a dish of noodles. 'Friese knows how these places work, that only key-holders can get in. And it isn't enough just to have the key – you have to sign and they compare your signature with the last time – hell of a rigmarole. He'd know there was no use in just the key – '

She stopped eating suddenly and stared at him, her brows snapping together. 'He'd know, but – Oliver mightn't.'

'Oliver?'

'He was waiting there on the pavement when I came out – I told you. He kept asking questions about the box. On and on – ' She shook her head then. 'It couldn't be anything to do with Oliver. I took a taxi and left him there in the Haymarket.'

'Maybe he organized something in advance – '

44

'Oh, this is getting ridiculous!' she said and leaned back in her chair. 'We're talking like a couple of kids playing Dick the Boy Detective. I was mugged by some lout who got scared and ran before he could take anything. That's all there is to it. All this talk about that damned box – stupid.'

'I'm not so sure – '

'Well, I'm not going to talk about it any more. Come on – let's get back. They should have fixed those cans by now.'

She was edgy, anxious not so much to get back to the studio as to get away from him. He sat there looking at her with his eyes round and filled with a look of concern that made her uneasy, almost embarrassed, and she waved at the waiter, gesturing for the bill, and stood up so that Theo had to stand up too.

He paid the bill and in silence they left the restaurant, pushing their way back along the tatty Willesden street towards the studio. He stopped her as they went round the corner to the entrance, holding on to her elbow with a sort of urgency.

'Maggy, I am worried about you, love, I really am. You may shrug it off, but I think – I – I think that box is more important that you realize. I think it's why you were pushed over last night, and I think there's a risk it'll happen again. I'm moving back this afternoon. I'll go to the office, sort out a few things and leave Hal to cope here, but I'll be at the flat when you get home. Okay?'

She looked up at him, standing there with that anxious look on his face, and let warmth for him fill her again. It was damnable the way her feelings veered; one moment solid with suspicion, the next disarmed because he looked at her so caringly.

'All right,' she said brusquely. 'Whatever you like, I don't give a damn either way.'

'Well, I do. So we'll settle for that. Take care coming home, you hear me? Take a cab all the way – '

'I drove here.'

'Where are you parked?'

She jerked her head, and he saw the car then, the old Ford with the souped-up engine and the jazzily painted panels, parked half-way down the little street.

'Let me take it. I'll come back, around six, Okay? I'll pick you up – '

'For Christ's sake, Theo, I can drive myself home! I'm not helpless – '

'Of course you're not. But I think you're – I think there may

45

be risks. No, don't look like that! I'm not just making dramas. I tell you, I'm worried. I'll pick you up, Okay? Six o'clock. Tell Hal he's got to be finished.'

'He'll finish. He won't fancy overtime for the engineers – look, Theo, this is – '

'Yes, I know. See you at home,' and he held out his hand for the car keys and then went striding away towards her car, and waved as he went roaring back down the street towards the High Road. Leaving her confused and more frightened than she had been, even last night, after the police had gone and left her alone in her flat.

5

They went down to Dorset after all, leaving early and driving through the scattered traffic to reach Studland before eleven. Theo hadn't been keen; he'd thought it would be better to stay at the flat, keep an eye on things, he said, but Maggy was determined. The work had gone well in the afternoon, and they had finished in a high good humour, all of them, sure that the reduction session would be an easy one, certain that they had a winning couple of tracks for the new album. Hal had gone so far as to tell her that he reckoned they could be on their way to a gold disc, so satisfied was he with what he'd got, and the effect on Maggy of that sort of praise had been electric. The tension of the past few weeks since Dolly's death seemed to melt away, and she had been relaxed and comfortable all evening, and as eager for a trip to the coast as any child with a bucket and spade.

As for Theo's anxiety about 'keeping an eye on things' – she had scoffed at that. 'Honestly, Theo, you're like an old woman, you really are! As if sitting around all a hot weekend'd make an atom of difference. That kid who pushed me over was just that – a silly kid who got scared and ran before he got anything. There's nothing more to it than that. Forget it and we'll have a great weekend. I've made up my mind to it.'

The weather was perfect, one of those green and blue and gold days that sometimes happen in English summers, and as the car ate the miles through the New Forest she sang, loudly and with great emphasis, the plainchant which was her favourite sound, inventing her own lewd words as she went along, making Theo laugh. As they went through Bournemouth she shouted greetings to passers-by and other drivers, making some of them look affronted and others startled and that made them both laugh absurdly, giggling like a pair of schoolchildren.

They bought cheese and rolls and fruit and a bottle of wine and went down to the beach, finding a hollow between the dunes at the far end of Studland Bay where they could strip off and sunbathe, something that made Theo a little shy, but which he patently enjoyed once she could persuade him out of his clothes. They swam and ate and slept and swam again, and then, as the August sun slanted its hard shadows along the beach, made love, lying side by side. This was something Maggy enjoyed; love-making in a bedroom with the door shut was agreeable enough, but sex out of doors, in broad daylight, where someone might come along and disturb you at any moment; that had a spice that no amount of bed play could ever offer. So she told him, and teased him and touched him until he was too aroused to care either. And they weren't interrupted and it was great, and then they were both lying breathless and relaxed on the sand, staring up at the thick blue of the sky, listening to the distant shouting of children, further down the beach, and the roar of the motor boats dragging water skiers tirelessly about the bay.

'You look about five years old,' he said at length, turning so that he rested his head on his crooked arm, and staring at her. She was lying on her back, her chin tipped up to the sun to catch the heat, her eyes closed.

She laughed. 'Some five years old,' she murmured, not opening her eyes and ran one hand over her breasts and with the other reached out for his crotch and tweaked him, and he pulled away from her hand and laughed too.

'I was looking at your face, ducky. Below the chin, I grant you, you're something else. But your face – five years old. At the outside.'

'Am I supposed to take that as a compliment? Or is it your way of telling me you're kinky for little kids?'

'A compliment, lovey, a compliment. You look smooth and young and happy – five years old.'

'Whoever told you being five years old was happy? You're mad to think it. Being thirty-seven is as near happy as I ever got. Not five years old, that's for sure.'

'What were you like when you were five?'

'Scrawny and carrotty and miserable,' she said. 'Very, very miserable.'

'Were you? Can you remember it so well?'

'You'd be amazed at what I remember.' She opened her eyes then and stared up at the sky. 'I try not to, usually. It makes me so – ' She shook her head, digging a little trough in the sand. 'I don't enjoy it.'

48

There was a sense of intimacy between them now that was so powerful that it seemed to Theo there was no one in the world but themselves. The hollow in the sand dunes, the clumps of coarse grass, the sound of the sea and the distant voices, all built together into walls which lapped them about with security and made him feel that whatever he said, she would understand, whatever question he asked, she would answer. There would be none of that prickly self-defensiveness that she so often displayed when he seemed to come too near.

'Tell me about it,' he said lazily, and perhaps because he was so relaxed himself, so sure of what there was between them at the moment, she was unalarmed by the demand, and began to talk. Easily and comfortably, staring up at the sky as though it were a cinema screen on which she was watching the action of a story, someone else's story and not her own, and telling him about it all.

Going to bed was a lovely time of the day. Dolly would sit her on the table in the kitchen and bring a bowl of warm water, and wash her all over, standing her right in the bowl at the end and squeezing the flannel over her bottom so that the water ran down her legs and made her tickle. Then she would wrap her in a warm towel, the big rather thin old one that covered her all over, and sit her on her lap in front of the kitchen range with its red-hot coals trapped behind the bars of the grate and rub her till she was dry, and then put on the thick nightie with the pictures of sailing boats all over it. The wireless would be on, crooning silly little tunes in the background, tunes that they both loved, and would sing to sometimes; 'You'll never know just how much I love you, you'll never know just how much I care – '; 'You are my sunshine, my only sunshine, you make me happy when skies are grey – '. Happy funny songs that made her laugh, sometimes.

Then Dolly would wrap her in a blanket and give her a cup of Horlicks, because Horlicks was good for little girls, and she would say, 'Story, story, story,' chanting it while Dolly pretended she couldn't hear her, and then suddenly being all surprised and saying, 'Are you asking for a *story*? Really asking for a *story*? What a funny thing to do, to ask me for a *story* – ' She always did that; it was part of the ritual and leaving it out would have been unthinkable.

And then Dolly would tell the story. Sometimes one and sometimes another, but mostly the favourite one.

'Once upon a time there was a brave, brave soldier – '

Oh, but she loved that story. Loved to hear about how handsome he was, and how kind and good, how he had come one day to Dolly's street and seen her, and said, 'You are the most beautiful lady I have ever seen. You will be my wife, you will be Mrs Soldier.' Only of course it was really Mrs Dundas.

She would hear about the presents he had bought for Dolly, the most beautiful lady he had ever seen. The green scarf with black chantilly lace in the middle, very delicate, very rich. The pigskin writing case with the Victory sign in morse code in the corner, three dots and a dash. The photograph album with the thick white satin covers and a real gold clasp, the yellowest reallest gold there ever was. And nylons too, and chocolate, all those things the lovely handsome soldier had bought for the beautiful Dolly.

And then he had to go away, back to the War, back to killing the bad enemy, and Dolly had stayed behind and one day, there had been the baby. 'The most beautiful baby there ever was,' said Dolly. 'As beautiful as the handsome soldier and the most beautiful girl in the world all put together.'

'And what did the soldier say?' she would ask Dolly breathlessly then, staring at her over the rim of her cup. 'What did he say when he found out?'

'He said – he said – ' and Dolly would pause impressively. 'He said, "You must call her Margaret Rose, for she is a princess, our princess, the most lovely princess there is. That is what you must call her – " and that is what the baby's name was, Margaret Rose, for ever and ever amen. And now it's time to go to sleep.'

Oh, those had been good times, those bed-times, just Dolly and Margaret Rose, sitting by the fire, and Margaret Rose sipping as little of the Horlicks as she could, to make it last longer, and teasing Dolly for more and more story. And Dolly would sometimes tell her more, tell her of the handsome soldier and his lovely family, for he had been rich as well as handsome.

'They lived in a big house in the country with a garden with apple trees and pear trees and plum trees, two of each. There were two lavatories in the house, one up and one down, and a separate bedroom for all the people in the house, and the kitchen had so many different dishes that no one had ever counted them – '

50

Dolly would pile on the detail, each night bringing out some new and tiny fact, until Margaret Rose felt she knew it all, had seen it herself. She would go to bed at last and lie thinking about the house in the country with two lavatories, would climb up the stairs on the carpet with the brass holders on each side of it, under the real painted pictures on the walls, past the big bowl of real fruit that was on the table on the upstairs landing, left there in case people got hungry in the night, would wander all over that house.

Sometimes, lying there is bed and nearly falling asleep, she would try to talk to the people in the house, as well, the kind lady with the white hair and the important man with the eyeglass and the moustache, but that wasn't so easy, for she knew that they were dead, that they had died together of grief the day the handsome soldier had died, fighting so bravely to save another soldier's life, far away in France where wars happened. But usually she would think only of the House and thought of it as home, the home they had come from before coming to this one in London, where all the boarders kept wanting things and talking to Dolly when she wanted to talk to her herself. Except at bed-time of course, when Dolly always told anyone who came tapping at the kitchen door that she couldn't stop now, she'd see them later, now was Margaret Rose's bed-time and not to be disturbed –

'It sounds idyllic,' Theo said, and rolled over in the sand, to feel the heat on his belly. 'You sound as though you were happy, not – what was it you said? Scrawny and carrotty and miserable.'

'You reckon?' Maggy said, and now her voice had an edge to it. 'Jesus, man, I was the bastard kid of a tatty boarding-house keeper. The only father I had, the only family I had, were bed-time stories. Big deal. Big bloody deal! You call that idyllic?'

'If you thought so at the time it was,' Theo said. 'I remember when I was at school I thought it was – oh, fantastic. I used to weave great dramas out of everything that happened, from a lousy Latin class to a church parade on Ascension Day. I saw myself as a cross between Stalky and the Best Boy in the Sixth and Gawd knows what else. That school was Eton and Harrow all rolled into one, and I loved it. Now, of course, I know better – it was a tatty, tenth-rate junk joint run by a drunken slob and a couple of half-trained idiots who passed as school-masters and kidded parents they were giving a decent education. I learned bugger all, and it's taken me years to get over the rubbish they filled me with, but while I was there it was fantastic. So it was, wasn't it?'

'Like hell it was,' Maggy said, and sat up and shook her head, running her fingers through her hair to get the sand out. 'I'm getting cold. Let's go back to the pub.'

The intimacy had thinned out, almost disappeared, but he seized at the remnants of it, still lying on his back and staring up at her.

'What went wrong, Maggy? It sounds as though you were really close when you were a child, you and Dolly. What went wrong to make you hate her so much?'

'When you've a year or two to spare I might tell you.' She stood up. and began to climb into her jeans. 'Come on. I'm getting bored with all this. I want to get back. Let's go to Bournemouth tonight. See what's happening in boom town.'

'Nothing. Nothing at all. Let's just stay at the pub, have a meal, talk. You've never talked much about yourself, really, have you? Only about work and – '

'Work's the best thing there is. For talking about and everything else.' She was combing her hair now, holding her head well back so that the sand would fall out, and he stood up and came up behind her and put his arms round her, holding each breast in his cupped hands.

'The best?'

'The best,' she said firmly, and pulled away from him. 'Put something on, for God's sake. The moment's passed for the body beautiful. And it's not as beautiful as it might be, come to that.'

The intimacy finally disappeared, shredding away against the noise of the sea, and they were back where they usually were, she, locked inside her own control, he circling warily around her, seeking a way in past her guard. And he had to admit that that was the way he liked her best. The intimacy had been exciting in its own way, the glimpse into her past full of interest, even dramatic, but it didn't compare with the excitement of chasing after her, the way he nearly always had to do. If they were as close all the time as they had been for just an hour or so there on the beach that afternoon, he's soon be bored. So he told himself as they trudged back up the beach, walking barefoot along the water-line, past the garbage-strewing transistor-playing crowds huddled together at the western end as close as they could get; so he told himself, and almost believed it. What else could he do? Maggy was as she was and he'd have to settle for her as she was. Either that or give her up all together. And one way and another that was the last thing he wanted to do.

They drove inland for dinner, taking the country roads to Sherborne, where they were told they'd find a good restaurant. 'Because of the school, you see,' the barman at the pub had said, earnestly, when they'd asked him. 'People as spends thousands a year to put their kids in those places expect the best when they come down to visit 'em. So you'll get the best, that's for sure – '

'The best' turned out to be expense-account eating of the dreariest kind, all prawn cocktails and steaks flamed in brandy, but it didn't matter. They sat and giggled at the other people there, the sleek polished men and their well-upholstered and heavily diamonded women, and drank a lot of claret. The wine was better than the food and they made the most of it, and slowly the afternoon's closeness returned and Theo, made reckless by the alcohol in him – for he had had three hefty gins while waiting for their food – leaned over the table and looked owlishly at her.

'What are you going to do about the Westpark, Maggy?'

She seemed to pull back a little, like a tortoise going into its carapace. 'What about it?'

'It's yours, isn't it? You'll have to do something with it, won't you?'

'Who told you it's mine?'

'Friese. He talked in circles, sizzled and twisted like a drop of water on a griddle, but I got the impression Dolly had left the place to you.'

There was a little silence. 'If I want it,' she said at length.

'How do you mean?'

'If I don't keep Ida on as a housekeeper and general Queen of the lot, I lose it. She gets it. Great, isn't it? Now you've got it, now you ain't. Just the sort of thing Dolly would do to me to get her own back.'

He blinked. There had been real venom in her voice and he drank some more of his claret and said carefully, 'Her own back for what?'

Maggy shrugged. 'This and that. She'd been trying to do me down for years. Now she's doing it even though she's dead – oh, let's not talk about it. It bores me.'

'You've got to talk about it.' Theo was filled with the stubbornness of the half-drunk. 'Can't just leave the place sitting there. Anyway, it's worth money.'

'Like hell it is. There's so many debts hanging round its neck it's a wonder the place is running at all. It's no bargain of an inheritance, take it from me.'

'Ah, but there's something in the box, isn't there? Something in that fancy shmancy box that'll deal with all that. The slippery Friese said so, and he's a legal man, so he wouldn't tell lies, now, would he?'

Theo was talking just for the sake of hearing his own voice now, and he knew it, and didn't care.

'Friese says that box has got enough in it to pay off all the debts. You say there's nothing in there - mystery! Tell you what, darlin'. Old Dolly's left you a crossword puzzle, that's what. She's left you a clue in that box, and you've got to follow it up and at the end you'll find a bleedin' great pot o' gold.'

'And a rainbow? Promise me a rainbow.'

Maggy was amused now, leaning back in her chair and looking at his flushed face.

'Rainbow. Hmm. Got to think about that.' He thought for a moment, making a special thinking face, staring at her. Then he grinned, and nodded his head. 'Yup. Rainbow. Big rainbow. Rainbow records.'

'Rainbow what?' She stared at him now, quite non-plussed.

'Rainbow records,' he said again, and grinned, a wide glittering grin and leaned forwards and began to whisper in an obviously conspiratorial way.

'Got a plan, you see, Maggy darlin'! 'S'a lovely plan. Make a fortune for us all, and make you the biggest thing in music. 'S'a fact! Biggest thing in music – '

She shook her head at him. 'I think I'd better drive back, don't you? You're pissed out of your mind.'

'No, I'm not. Jus' a bit ambitious, tha's all. Bit ambitious. Rainbow records. Maggy Dundas sole rights, biggest thing in music.'

'Ah!' She nodded now, an understanding came. 'You want to start your own label?'

'There! I always said you were the brightest girl in the business, didn't I tell everyone you were the brightest girl in the business? Tha's it, tha's it in one. I'm goin' to start Rainbow Records, and make you the biggest – '

54

'Yes, I heard you. The biggest thing in music. You make me sound like a bloody tuba. Theo, I'm taking you back to bed. You need to sleep this one off.'

'I'm telling you. All I need is money, you see. Quite a lot, not just a bit. Enough to get off the ground. I'm one of the best A and R men in the business, you're a great performer, great musician, so with you and enough money, I'm tellin' you we could clean up. But money – that's the problem, eh? Unless you sort out what this is all about, this bloody box, and get the cash to clear up the Westpark and sell it, eh? Then we'll have lots of lovely money and I'll have Rainbow Records and you'll be the biggest thing – '

' – in music,' she said, and stared at him, trying to control the feeling that was rising in her again. Oh, Christ, not Theo too, after all? Oliver wanted whatever was in that box. Friese was more curious about it than he had any right to be, and now Theo. How many more people would she have to be careful about?

6

Ida had spent the morning as she usually did; supervising the chambermaids, checking on every room as they finished them, and then working her way through the kitchens, going over the day's buying, the menus, the work schedules, yesterday's leftovers, the lot. They went through a lot of chefs at the Westpark; few of them were willing to tolerage the invasion of their domain by someone from the front of the shop, but she was as adamant as they were. There was no way a single penny was going to be spent at the Westpark, no corner that was going to remain hidden without her being involved, and chefs who complained became out-of-work chefs. The present one was beginning to rumble but she had him in control still. Maybe in a few months' time they'd have to find another, but right now all was going well.

And then there was the office, the accounts to be checked, the banking to be done, the detailed careful work that she most enjoyed. Not that anyone ever knew whether Ida was enjoying herself or not. She went about every job in the same way, whether it was inspecting a blocked lavatory and supervising its cleaning up, or checking the flower arrangements the receptionist had done; straight-faced, quiet and steely sure of herself. But she did enjoy the book-keeping, and when she could spend a little longer at it than was strictly needed. There was pleasure to be found in creating those neat columns of figures, making them check out, comparing them with the figures for this week last year and the years before, looking for signs of waste or inefficiency. And she would sit there with her head bent over the red-covered ledgers, and no one seeing her would think that she was perturbed in the least.

But of course she was. She had watched the debts rise year by year as Dolly spent more and more, raising mortgages, taking loans, wheeling and dealing in spite of Ida's constant warnings. But Dolly was like that; cared nothing for money, never had, She threw it around like water, giving it to wastrels, lending it to people who would never pay her back in a million years, then borrowing more.

In the early days she had kept her money affairs to herself; Ida had been allowed to work only around the bedrooms and in the kitchens, but as she had become more and more efficient, more and more indispensable, she had penetrated into the book-keeping side and eventually taken that over too; but not in time. By then the debts had already been huge, and they had been growing ever since. Looking down at the columns of figures now, Ida tightened her lips and thought: 'They won't wait much longer. She'll have to decide, soon.'

Maggy. Ida put down her pen and folded her hands over the ledger in front of her and stared down at them. Maggy had still been called Margaret Rose when Ida had first seen her. Nine years old, with a great deal of curly red hair over a pale pointed face; and edgy fidgety child, forever demanding something in the way of attention. Ida had looked at her and then at Dolly, soft laughing Dolly, sitting there with the child on her lap with her long legs twined round her mother's and felt a twist of anger that was so sharp she had wanted to shout it aloud. But of course she had not.

She had looked unsmilingly at the child and then said to Dolly, 'Are you sure you want me to stay?'

And Dolly had gazed at her with that silly soft face creased with surprise and said, 'But I told you I did. O' course you must, so long as you like, whatever suits you. Plenty to do around here, one way and another – so long as you like.'

She had a way of speech that was difficult to identify; soft and blurred at the edges, rounded vowels that made her sound comfortable and easy, and it was a long time before Ida, London born and bred, discovered it was Gloucestershire.

Anyway, Ida had stayed. She had moved herself and her one suitcase into the Creffield Road house and put her underwear tidily into the battered chest of drawers in the smallest back room, and hung up her three dresses and her jacket in the equally battered wardrobe, and got to work. She had cooked supper on that first evening; sitting now at the Westpark, looking down at her own hands clasped over the open ledgers she saw herself far away down the corridor of the years, moving about that littered scruffy kitchen, with her sleeves rolled up and a tea towel tied round her waist for an apron. She had been twenty-two; a solidly built silent girl with dark hair club cut and deliberately unattractive over her square face. Now she was iron grey and her hair was neatly shaped by a good hairdresser and her clothes were good and well kept. Not at all like the ugly baggy tweed skirt and yellow twill shirt she had worn that long age evening to cook bubble and squeak for them all.

Remembering, she almost smiled; bubble and squeak. The boarders had come into the dining room and looked suspiciously at the table, because she had laid it carefully, and it looked nice. She had bought some paper serviettes at the shop on the corner and folded them into cornets and set them in the chipped drinking glasses, and then put their food in front of them carefully arranged on the plates, and considering that she had found only cold potatoes and a couple of onions and a dish of left-over cabbage in the kitchen, it was a dammed good supper. The bubble and squeak had been crisp and savoury, spiked as it was with onions to rid the cabbage component of its power, and she had bought some eggs too, and put a fried one in the middle of each portion. Not the most elegant food in the world but the boarders had wolfed it, and asked for second helpings and there had been a mood of sudden cheerfulness in the dusty dining room, with the men laughing and chaffing Dolly and the two women, those dull sisters who worked in a draper's shop in Acton High Road – what were their names? The memory of them had vanished as surely as their thin grey faces – and Dolly saying wonderingly over and over again, 'Well, who'd 'a' thought it, who'd 'a' thought you could make anything so good out o' what I got in the kitchen of a Friday night? Wh'd 'a' thought it?'

Everyone had been cheerful except herself and Margaret Rose. The child had sat and stared sulkily at her plate and refused to eat, while her mother coaxed and exclaimed over her and the men rallied her, until she had burst into tears and had to be given chocolate biscuits from a secret store in her mother's desk, and all the time Idea had quietly eaten her own supper, and given the boarders their second helpings and then the fruit crumble she had put together, again using bits and pieces she had found in that appallingly ill-equipped kitchen, and said nothing. But she had registered the child as spoiled, mulish, difficult, in as bad a state of disorder as the boarding house itself, and had added her to her private plan of reorganization. And if she had wondered fleetingly what sort of child one of her own would have turned out like, she

58

did not allow that thought to reach the front of her mind.

Looking back down the telescope of the years, seeing those figures moving about in tiny but vivid definition so far away, Ida sighed sharply and then switched off the memories as crisply as if she had thrown a switch. Yesterday was over, had no further relevance. It was today and today's debts and Dolly's death and the ownership of the Westpark that mattered now. Something would have to be done.

She made one more tour of the hotel before leaving to do it. The guests were, as usual, all out, except for Mrs Matthews, old and twisted, who sat in her favourite armchair in the corner of the lounge, staring out into the street, avid for any action, whether it be another car coming to park or someone walking a dog. She would have to go soon, Ida thought, nodding and being bright and professional at her as she went by. This wasn't a home for the elderly. The sort of guests they wanted at the Westpark were the sort they mostly had, the tourists who spent every moment they had out in the streets of London, soaking up whatever it was tourists came to London for. The Westpark didn't want people who used it as their home, who found human contact and security and the comfort of permanence in it. That had been what Dolly had enjoyed providing in the old days in Acton, the days when the place had been littered with all sorts of people, all day long. There had been all those men lounging around in their shirt sleeves, sometimes in their vests, in the sitting room, in the dining room, even in the kitchen unless Ida managed to turf them out, listening to the wireless and constantly on the phone with their bets. Ida had told her then, kept on telling her, that there was no profit to be made running a place like that. 'Get them out,' she had told Dolly. 'Get rid of that sort – they just use up heat and light and eat more than they pay for, and expect to be waited on and they're trouble. Go for the sort that are out all day, keep out of your hair – '

But Dolly had just smiled that soft soppy smile of hers and agreed that Ida was absolutely right, and gone on as she always had, getting involved with the people who came as customers, turning them all into friends, almost relations, just as she had with Ida herself. Ida had come to work, so she would remind Dolly fiercely whenever the subject came up, but Dolly would just laugh and say, 'I know, my dear, I know that very well, and glad I am that you did, for where'd we all be without you? But you're more'n just someone as works here, now, aren't you? Part o' the place you are, my dear, an' that's the way we like it – ' Oh, it had been impossible to make Dolly see any sense; but now it would be different. Old women like Mrs Matthews had no place in a hotel like this one, a business-like place that was going to pay off its debts. So Ida told herself. But still did nothing about getting rid of Mrs Matthews. She just nodded at her and was professionally bright, and let her be. Which was, as most people who knew her would have agreed, somewhat out of character for Ida.

She made the journey into town by underground, walking down to Lancaster Gate station in her neat check tweed coat and her highly polished lace-up real leather shoes – no nasty modern plastic for Ida – looking every inch the well-heeled, well-turned-out lady that she was. No one was looking at her would ever doubt for a moment that she was a woman who had her life well held together, who knew good from bad, real from false, right from wrong. She was admirable without being showy, and that was precisely what she wanted to be. No one looking at her could ever know what she had once been, could guess the effect she had once had on people who saw her, the messiness that had been her life – Ida tightened her mouth and lifted her chin, and refused to think about anything but this morning's journey.

She had checked at the office of Jump Records and they had said vaguely that, yes, Maggy would be there and did the caller want to leave a message? Someone would probably get around to giving it to her. But Ida had said coolly that there was no need, she'd call back, and no she wouldn't leave her name, thank you. And had set out unannounced because there was not other way she could actually talk to the girl. It had been a long time since Maggy had willingly faced Ida and there was no reason to suppose she would behave in any other way now. But somehow the matter had to be ironed out, and Ida was the one who could iron it. And would.

She disapproved violently of the office when she found it. It was on the third floor of a tatty house in Denmark Street, and the stairs she had to climb smelled of mice and old shoes and mildew, although an attempt had been made to smarten them a bit with beige coir matting and purple paint on the walls. The outer office was a tiny cubbyhole which reeked of the cheap perfume of the bored-looking girl sitting there behind a small switchboard and when Ida stonily asked for Miss Dundas, the girl stared blankly at her with her mouth hanging lax and open, and then jerked her head sideways at a door on the other side. That led to a larger room, with walls covered with lurid posters advertising pop concerts and discos, and light fittings the shape of huge plastic breasts with vast crimson nipples fashioned in perfect detail stuck over them. One wall was dominated by a painting of a male nude with unbelievably large genitals, and beside it, hanging from a drawing pin by a string tied horribly round its lolling neck, was a rag doll which also was decorated with an outsize phallus, made particularly lewd by the purple colour of the cloth of which it was made.

And beneath it all, at a cluttered desk, sat Theo. She looked at him and nodded briefly and he stared at her, blankly, as though he didn't recognize her.

'Ida?' he said then, and got to his feet, awkwardly, like a child who had been caught by his schoolmaster doing unspeakably wicked things behind the desk lid. 'Ida? What are you doing – I mean, I didn't expect – my dear, do sit down – ' And he looked round for a chair, vaguely, as though he expected one to come up out of the ground like a demon king coming through the trap door in a pantomine.

'I have to talk to Maggy about the Westpark,' she said, not moving. She was holding her heavy leather bag in front of her, as though it were some sort of bulwark, both hands neatly side by side on its wide strap. Her feet were tidily together and her toes turned out at precisely even angles. She looks like an army sergeant, Theo thought and wanted to laugh, suddenly. An army sergeant in drag.

'Maggy? But, my dear, you really can't – I mean, this isn't the place, precisely, is it? Look, do sit down, I'll send for some coffee – Sharlene!' He bawled the name over his shoulder as he came round the desk and brought a chair from the other side of the room, and after a moment the girl from the outer office put her open-mouthed blank face round the door and said, 'Eh? What'cher want?'

'Coffee,' Theo said fussily. 'And put it in a decent cup, for Christ's sake – don't make it yourself, go down to Chubby's and bring some up – black or white, Ida? Want anything with it? A biscuit or a sandwich – '

'I don't want anything,' Ida said composedly, and did not sit down, standing there looking at Theo, who was holding the chair invitingly, and rather awkwardly. 'I came to see Maggy. They told me she would be here this morning.'

'Well, yes.' The girl took her head away and banged the door sulkily, and Theo went back to his own chair behind his desk, seeming more comfortable there, as though he were safe inside his own territory again. 'We've got work to do on the new recordings, you see; we've had one reduction session, but I think we could improve the quality a bit yet, so I wanted Maggy to listen to it – '

'I don't want to interrupt your work.' Ida sounded brisk, like a hospital nurse talking to a silly patient. 'But I don't know any other way to sort this business out. She refuses to answer the letters I've sent her, the solicitor says he can't do anything till she instructs him, and she hasn't, so I decided to come here. The sooner I see her and talk to her, the sooner I'll be able to go away and you can get on with your – reduction session, whatever that may be.' She made it sound like something rather dirty and certainly illicit.

'It's a check on the tapes we've made,' Theo said, almost eagerly. 'It's like editing, you know? We take the best of all of them, meld them together – it's a skilful business. Makes all the difference between a good recording and a smash hit – '

'Really,' Ida said perfunctorily and turned to look at the door on the other side of the office. 'Where is she, then? Will you call her in here, or shall I go and find her?'

'She's in the small recording studio,' Theo said wretchedly. Oh, but this was going to make trouble! Maggy had been uptight enough this morning, one way and another. He had said more than he should about his hopes and plans for their future last night, far more, and it had made her rear away like a frightened horse. And now here was this damned woman coming to talk about *her* future and *her* needs – he pushed his chair back almost pettishly and said loudly, 'Well, I'll tell her you're here. But don't expect much of a welcome. Let's face it, Ida, you aren't one of her favourite people.'

'That's not important,' Ida said, and at last sat down with the air of a woman who has won a small victory. 'She can hate my guts from here to eternity for all it bothers me. I just want a few things sorted out. Go and get her, please. This is wasting time.'

Maggy came in quickly, with Theo behind her, his face crumpled with anxiety, and she stood in the doorway with Theo looking rather absurdly over her shoulder, staring at Ida. She was wearing her favourite black, a long skirt and a loose smock, and her face looked whiter than ever over it.

'Well?' she said harshly. 'And what do you want? I've no time to waste.'

'Nor I.' Ida made no attempt to get up, sitting there with her hands clasped comfortably over her bag, and staring back at her. 'I've wasted enough time already, trying to sort out what's to happen to the Westpark. So, I've come to get a decision from you. Are you taking the place on or are you not?'

'It's none of your business,' Maggy said, sounding bored and cold. 'None at all.'

'Oh, don't be stupid, Maggy.' Ida sounded weary. 'That's sheer self-indulgent nonsense and you know it perfectly well. I know the situation as well as you do. If you take the place, then you have to take me on as well. If you don't, then I get it. Either way we're stuck with each other, so the sooner we sort out the matter, the better. Throwing little tantrums and stamping your feet'll just give you a headache, and bore me. And I've got better things to do than give in to your nonsense, the way Dolly used to. No, don't you look at me like that. I told you, I've got better things to do with my time than argue with you. What are you doing? I've a right to know, one way or the other.'

Maggy was flushed now. The thick white pallor had gone and Ida, staring at her coolly, thought – she looks good. Grew up better looking than she had any right to, the way she used to look, all those years ago.

Maggy came into the room and walked stiffly round Theo's desk, and sat down in his chair, leaning back and putting her feet up on the desk with very deliberate movements. She was wearing high black-leather patent boots and for a moment Ida was amused. Like children dressing up, in all their silly stuff; Maggy in patent boots, and Theo in his pink cheesecloth shirt and dangling chains. What were they trying to prove?

'So,' Maggy said, and clasped both hands behind her head, looking cool and relaxed, though her cheeks were still flushed. 'Couldn't wait any longer, eh? Had to see what you were going to scrape out of Dolly's coffin? How much have you already got your hands on? All her clothes, all her bits and pieces? Stripped her room bare, have you?

'You'll find everything as she left it,' Ida said coolly, and opened her bag, and took out a big bunch of keys, heavy and almost

63

medieval looking, there were so many of them and the ring that held them was so large. 'I locked it as soon as the men from the undertaker's had taken her out, and the bed was cleaned up. Here's the key.'

She was taking it off the ring with neat twisting movements of her wrist. 'Oliver, you see. I thought I'd better keep Oliver out. I'm sure *you'll* understand the need for that.' And the emphasis she put on the *you* was slight but unmistakeable, and this time Maggy went even redder, an ugly colour that looked crude against the brightness of her hair. Ida put the key on the desk at her feet, and nodded, a tight controlled little movement.

'So, there's that sorted out. Now I want to know what's to happen about the Westpark. I've got the daily running organized, the bank'll hold things until they get further instructions from Friese. But you can't go on pretending there's nothing to be done. I've got to have a decision one way or the other, so that we can see where we go from here. Are you taking the place or aren't you? Am I working for you or am I not?'

'Oh, go to – '

'Look, let's not be stupid, shall we? We don't get on. We never have. Let's take that as read, all right? It's less effort. Right. Now, if I work for you, it will be on a basis that will make sure you'll get all that's due to you. Friese told me, the will's as tight and as well worked out as it can be. He didn't draw it up, I gather, but the man who did knew what he was doing. There's no way you can be cheated by me if you do take the place, if that's what's worrying you. Mind you, there's no way you can exploit me, either, which is as it should be. But you've got to make a decision. I need to know just what you're going to do. I can't go sitting in the middle of nowhere much longer.'

'She's right, Maggy,' Theo said, unexpectedly, and came and sat on the corner of his desk. 'I've told you, you can't go on just staying shtoom, and hoping it'll all go away. It won't. There the place is, there the box is, and you've got to do something about it all. There's no dodging it.'

Maggy sat and stared down at the desk. She was sitting up straight now, her feet on the ground, her hands on her lap, and her colour had receded, leaving the whiteness again, and she looked as cool and calm as Ida herself.

There was a little silence and then she said, 'All right. I take the point. Something's got to be done. But I'm pushed for time, all right? There are more important things in my life than some tatty run-down hotel in a back street. Much more important things. So, you'll have to wait – '

For the first time Ida showed a hint of emotion. 'Run down it is not. Considering the debts the place carries, it's in fantastic order. I've decorated rooms myself with my own hands – you know that? – to keep it looking good. I've built your inheritance into something worth having, and never you forget it, Madam! The place'll fetch three hundred thousand of anyone's money, once those damned debts are sorted out, and half of that comes from my labour, now and for the last twenty-odd years. I made that business for Dolly, and she knew it, even if you don't.'

It was as though that hint of warmth in her had melted not only her own cold reserve but something in Maggy. She leaned back now, and grinned, actually grinned, a wide almost happy grimace.

'Okay. So it's the nearest thing to the Bayswater Hilton we'll ever have. Okay. So, you'd like to have it? Go on. Admit it. You'd like to own it.'

There was a little silence and then Ida said, cool again, 'Of course. I'd be mad not to.'

'Well, you can't.' Maggy knew she was sounding like a child, a child who had refused to lend her teddy bear, and she didn't care. It was as though she had scored some vital hit at Ida by making her get excited, and she felt better for it. 'You can't have it, because I'm going to take it. And you can go on as you always have, dogsbodying and sending your accounts to me regularly, through the bank. I want no direct dealings with you, not ever, but you can work all the hours God gives you and a few more besides, and make profits for me. That'll really get up your nose, won't it? You'll have to work to get your own share, and in doing that you'll give me mine. You hated me when I was a child, and you worked and I lived there. You hated me because I was Dolly's daughter and had a right to be there and you didn't. Well, you can go on hating me, you hear me? I don't care – '

'Good. That's settled then. Will you please deal with Friese, then, as soon as possible?' It was as though Maggy hadn't said a word. 'Then, of course, there's the matter of the debts. Let me know what you're doing about them – '

'Dolly left enough to pay them,' Theo said, and his voice coming in so unexpectedly seemed to bring the temperature of the room down. 'Friese said so. In the box.'

Ida glanced at Maggy. 'Have you looked?'

'What business is that of yours?'

'Oh, stop being childish, Maggy, do me a favour! I told you, this is business. Have you looked?'

'Yes.' Maggy sounded sulky, like a child who has been reprimanded by a hated teacher, but hasn't any more courage with which to be cheeky, and Theo looked at her and took a deep breath. She was calming down.

'Was there anyting there?'

'Not that looked money.'

'Papers and photographs? Yes I know about them. She told me they were there. Nothing else?'

Maggy said nothing, and Ida stood up, 'Well,' she said and pulled her coat straight and tweaked at her collar to neaten it. 'It's your affair, of course. But if she said there was something there, enough to pay the place clear, then there is. She's made some sort of private joke out of it. You know what she was like. Nothing she liked better than silly jokes and games – '

Suddenly Maggy seemed to hear Dolly's voice in her ears. 'A story? You're asking for a *story*? What a funny thing to do, to ask me for a *story* – '

'Do you mean that there's something there that might say – that there's money somewhere else?' Theo sounded eager. 'Is that it? A pawn ticket or something? – '

Ida shrugged, and picked up her bag, and dropped the heavy keys which she was still holding into it, so that they jingled a little. She closed the bag with a snap. 'I don't know,' she said. 'She didn't tell me. Only that there were papers there and pictures – all the past, she said. That's all. But I can promise you that if she said there was money there, in some way, then there is. She was a fool, was Dolly, a fool mostly to herself, but she wasn't an idiot. I mean, she was really very clever, in her own peculiar way.' She looked at Maggy then. 'Like you.' And then she walked across the room and opened the door, and turned to look back at them as she went out. 'I'll be hearing from Friese, then, in the next few days. Don't forget to tell him. I don't want to have to make more of a nuisance of myself than I have to, but I will if I must. I could get a solicitor of my own, you see. If I had to. Good morning.'

There was a silence after she'd gone and then Theo said uneasily, 'Well?'

Maggy was still sitting at the desk, staring at her hands, and didn't move, so he tried again. 'Well, love? What are you going to do?'

'Mm? Finish listening to those tapes.' She stood up. 'You can come in about half an hour. I'll have been through them by then and we can go down to Solly's. Finish them off – '

'I meant about the box.'

'Oh. That. I'll have to go back to it, won't I? And look more carefully. Won't I? After all, I've got a lot of responsibilities. What with the Westpark and your Rainbow Records. Haven't I?'

And she was gone, leaving him unsure whether he'd been given the promise he wanted, or a threat.

7

She had been playing for about an hour; arpeggios rippling up and down the keyboard, some of the old childhood pieces she had learned all those years ago, and then some Bach and back to the tinkling arpeggios again, and she was feeling better. The time was a bad time, usually, between recordings, and without any worthwhile gigs lined up. Jump were organizing the American trip, of course, but that wouldn't be for a while yet, and now there was nothing really urgent to do except wait for the launch of the new album, and play three one-nighters, all in London. She could of course, start work on the new arrangements she'd planned for the Purcell stuff; she'd been looking forward to that, because so many people would rear up in fury at the mere idea of jazz and Purcell. But now –

She slid her fingers from one end of the keyboard to the other, relishing the sound, and then twisted on the stool and stared across the room at the table in front of the big low sofa. Her big soft leather bag sat on it, bulky and expectant.

Getting the stuff had been surprisingly easy. She had had to force herself to go back to the safe deposit; it had taken three days of vacillating, three days of being too busy, of having other things to do, somehow not getting round to it, to get her to take a taxi to the Haymarket. But once there, it had been easy. She had simply taken the lift down into the cool basement and signed the form and been led into the little room, and taken everything out methodically and filled her bag with it. And three minutes later, still very relaxed, she had taken the lift back up to the street level, the bag heavy on her shoulder. Only when she had stepped out of the lift had her original fear welled up for a moment, but she controlled it in the easiest, silliest way imaginable, simply by going out the other way, into Regent Street instead of using the Haymarket exit. And there she had called another taxi and quietly gone home. It had been as easy as that.

But now it wasn't so easy. The bag sat there, looking somehow threatening. All those old photographs and pieces of paper seemed to tick in the silent room like a small bomb, waiting to explode into information she didn't want. It would be easy, so very easy, to take the the lot and drop it into the fireplace and set light to it. She could take a candle, one of those thick heavy ones she'd bought on holiday in Italy to use for parties, and set it alight and put the paper all round it, and watch it all burn up, hot wax, old photographs, the lot. It would be like another cremation, sending those pictures up in smoke, like getting rid of Dolly all over again –

The door buzzer made her jump, set her heart thumping painfully in her chest and she went across the room to answer it in a sudden lope; frightened, remembering what had happened the last time she had come home from the safe deposit, and then being angry with herself. Silly bitch, she whispered inside her head. Silly bitch. You're safe inside now –

But for all that she stopped before reaching for the button and then turned and went over to the turret window. She had rigged up a mirror there, long ago, to give her a view of the front step far below so that she could see whoever was there. She had done it because of Komo, who had a tendency to come to her flat when he was in the mood for a party – which was much too often – trailing half a dozen session men with him, all as high as he was. After a couple such episodes when she had ended up with the flat full of din and booze and music she didn't want – for Komo's delight in heavy rock was not one she shared – and flaked-out trumpeters, she had become more circumspect. Now she only answered her buzzer when she knew who it was.

But it wasn't Komo's close-cropped skull that she saw foreshortened in the mirror. Oliver stood there, unmistakeably Oliver, with his balding patch showing clearly, even from this height, through the untidy fuzz of faded brown hair. The buzzer went again and then he took a step back and stared upwards and she shrank back, even though she knew he couldn't see her, and then he waved, a tentative movement from the elbow, and her mouth hardened. The bastard, he knew she was there, knew about her mirror and was trying it on. Again he buzzed and again she didn't move. He was harmless, he wouldn't suddenly start a rock session, but she couldn't risk having him here, not with all that stuff on the table, waiting to be taken out of her bag –

Long after he'd given up and gone away she still stood and

stared in the mirror, frowning slightly. What had happened to her, for God's sake? Was she turning into a complete paranoic? Whoever came, whoever spoke to her, she was suspicious and frightened. She'd been suspicious of Friese who had asked questions about the contents of the box, when she had gone to tell him that she accepted the conditions of Dolly's will, but hadn't he a right to ask? The debts, the problems – as her lawyer he was entitled to ask. But she had dodged him, had left him still talking, almost running out of his office, and then got that mad notion she was being followed. A man in a neat suit, carrying a paper under his arm and with an umbrella hanging over his wrist, a perfectly normal, ordinary city clerk. Yet she'd got it into her head that he was some sort of spy, that he was tracking after her, for she had seen him outside Friese's office as she had come hurrying out into Bedford Row, and then again – or someone very like him – at Holborn underground station as she made her way back to the Jump office. And yet again, or so she thought, at the corner of Royal Crescent when she went home. Mad and paranoid and lunatic, all of it. And yet the doubts had gone on – Theo, for example. To have become so suspicious of him when all he'd done was get a bit drunk and tell her honestly what he wanted – that was crazy. It was a good idea, to have a record company of their own. She'd made enough for Jump, tatty little set-up that it was, and they didn't really appreciate her, and starting something of her own would be infinitely better than being swallowed up by one of the big companies, where they'd just shove her into a category and never let her do her own special thing. And Theo was right, he *was* a good A and R man. As good as any of them. So why back away from him the way she had just because he'd put a proposition to her about a record company? And now there was Oliver –

She moved then, quickly and purposefully, going first to the table in the corner where she kept the drinks and pouring a generous vodka and tonic and then back to the table. Now. There was no more time for all this nonsense. She would now sort out all that rubbish, find whatever it was Dolly had hidden there, pay off the Westpark's debts and sell it and get on with living. Just like that. She whispered it into her drink as she settled herself, cross-legged on the floor in front of the long low table. Just like that. Magical.

The papers, with which she started, still told her nothing. She went through page after page, re-reading some of them several times, but still they revealed nothing. Just bills and records of transactions; none of it significant as far as she could tell. The really important documents, those that related to the Westpark and the money owing on it, were with Friese. He'd told her that, showed her some of them. These seemed to be irrelevant rubbish. But she did not discard them, simply replacing them in their piles, securing them with their original rubber bands, setting them to one side, as the afternoon sun slanted across the floor wheeling slowly from one side of the room to the other. Lunch-time came and went, and she ignored it, not feeling hungry. The phone rang at about two o'clock. Theo probably, calling from Bristol where he'd had to go to see a Country and Western group. She just let it ring, sitting there on the floor and staring at it until it stopped, and then returning to the piles of paper spread around her.

It wasn't until three o'clock that she decided that the papers held nothing of any value. Not as far as she could tell, anyway. Which meant the newspaper cuttings and the photographs. Their turn had come.

She started with the photographs. The one of Dolly that had so upset her the first time she looked at it now sat and stared back at her and had no impact at all. There she sat on her stool, gazing blankly out of the crumbled gloss of the photograph, her mouth in that silly cupid's bow pout, her plucked eyebrows arched in an eternity of surprise, and it did nothing at all to Maggy. She almost laughed aloud, holding it in her hand and staring down at it. Was it this that had made her feel so ill, that afternoon last week? Crazy!

She put it aside and picked up the next, and this one made her mouth crease a little. It was of herself, sitting on a long bench, wrapped in heavy knitted pantaloons and a thick knitted coat, so bundled up that she seemed not to have a neck at all, like one of those potato men she had been used to make out of a box full of plastic noses and hats and crossed eyes and silly mouths. The child in the picture looked anxious and startled as though the camera had frightened her, and as surely as if she could actually remember it happening, Maggy knew she had cried bitterly the moment after the picture was taken. But of course she couldn't remember, for she had been far too young. On the bottom, in Dolly's scrawl, was written, 'Margaret Rose Dundas, September 1942. Weight 23 lbs. Twelve teeth.' A year old. She'd been a year old.

The next pictures were very similar, taken barely three months apart, each with the date carefully noted, her weight, the state of her teeth, and on a couple of them a careful record of the fact that she had had her diphtheria innoculation, and had been vaccinated against smallpox. A loving mother's record of her baby; that was all they were, and Maggy fanned them out in one hand and stared at them and wanted to cry suddenly, wanted to weep for the dead child she held between her fingers.

The next photographs were different. Groups of people, sometimes in front of the house in Brixton, sometimes out in some open place or other, hair blowing in the wind, squinting into the sun. People standing in stiff rows, or in muddled little clusters with their arms about each other. People who looked familiar and yet who meant nothing at all to her now, in their odd clothes, dresses all the wrong lengths, hair styles too fussy, jackets and trousers crumpled and dated.

But she was in all of them; Maggy herself. A child in arms in the first ones, sometimes held by a woman, peering grinningly over her shoulder, sometimes sitting on a broad male shoulder and in each of them she looked the same, laughing, her hair curled and bedecked with bows, her dresses frilled and ridiculous.

And then the Creffield Road house began to appear as background to the groups, the familiar stained glass in the front door and the chipped front path, and now she saw herself standing, usually in the middle of the group, with someone's hand on her shoulder. But she wasn't laughting now. She was scowling or staring straight faced at the camera while everyone around her was grinning and waving.

The people in the pictures were familiar ones now. There were two women in a lot of them, always standing side by side, always as straight-faced as the child Maggy, staring into the distance with wooden expressions, their shoulders very tense and their hands awkwardly by their sides. The Miss Readers, she remembered, and wanted to laugh aloud at the memory of them. They had lived in Creffield Road for years, and never spoke to anyone, going silently through their lives, nodding politely as they passed you on the doorstep, appearing on the dot of time for every meal and wordlessly eating vast quantities of food and then disappearing back to their room at the back of the house. The Miss Readers. She hadn't thought about them for years.

She turned the photographs over and there, on the back, was

more of Dolly's scrawling childish writing. Each one's name was there, in careful order. Miss Mary Reader. Miss Lily Reader. Mr Jim Codling. Mr Ted Hornby. Miss Ida Guthrie. Miss Margaret Rose Dundas. Mr Ivor Baillis –

She turned the photograph over again and stared at the picture of Ida and felt a sharp jolt under her ribs. That face, Ida's? She looked at it again, and shook her head almost as if to clear it. A girl, just a girl, no more than – oh, twenty-three or four, with a heavy fringe over her dark eyes, and a look on her face of – what? She was smiling politely, the way people do for photographs, but there was something behind the smile that Maggy couldn't quite get hold of, and then she thought – watchful. She's watching out for something –

The pictures went on, over and over again the same thing. The people who had lived in Dolly's boarding house, all that time ago, each of them with their names painstakingly spelled out, each with the date noted at the bottom: 1949, 1950, 1951. That was a joky one, 1951; they were holding up a banner, two of the men, with the words 'Festival of Acton' drawn on it in uneven print, and another of them had a placard which read, 'Come to the Dolly Dundas Dome of Discovery!'

It was the 1950 photograph that made her stop. She had passed it over at first, but when she went through the pile again – for they had all been tied together – she spotted it. It was an unusual photograph in that Ida wasn't in it – she was in almost all of the others – and Dolly was. She stood there with her hands tucked into the elbows of two men, and all three of them had their right legs stuck out in an imitation of a high kick. The man on Dolly's right was tall, the tallest of the three, with a lot of thick hair which looked oddly modern because it was quite long, and a face split with a huge grin that showed irregular teeth. He seemed to be very happy, staring gaily into the lens of the camera; and it was hard to tell how old he was. Young? Not really. Old? Definitely not old. Vaguely thirtyish maybe. The one on Dolly's other side was different, though. Also grinning widely, there was something mocking and remote about his expression. Something that said, 'Look at these babies! I'll play the game to amuse them, but don't think I'm enjoying it – ' But he was young, obviously young, barely twenty if that. Smooth face, tight flat muscles, young, young, young –

On the back Dolly had written the names, as usual, very carefully. 'Mort Lang. Dolly Dundas. Andy Kentish.' And the date. August 1950.

Maggy had seen all that the first time she had looked, and thought fleetingly – Mort. That rings a bell – and then passed on. But on this second look she saw there was writing on the front of the photograph as well, and she sat and looked down at the faint characters that were written there, and then, after a moment, got to her feet and went and stood by the window. It was still mid afternoon, and the August sun was strong, flooding the white room with brightness, but she felt the need for more light so pressingly that she wanted to lean out into the open air, and stare at the photograph there.

The writing on the front of the photograph was smaller, much tidier than the words that were on the back and Maggy thought – this is recent. She wrote that only a little while ago. And didn't know how she knew that, but was certain she was right.

'Morty knows a lot,' the words said, written small enough to fit into the part of the picture that was his trouser leg. The words were written one above the other, tidily. 'Morty knows a lot.'

And leaning on the window sill, the hot air on her face and the stink of petrol coming up at her from the Crescent below, Maggy remembered.

Coming home from school on an afternoon when it has been raining is the best sort of coming home there is. The streets smell good, the dry wet smell that comes after the first rain. Or the wet dry smell. She sings inside her head as she walks along. The wet dry, the dry wet. She likes words like that. Like bitter sweet, sorry sad, good naughty. Wet dry, dry wet.

The privet hedges are good too. You take a leaf and fold it in half, carefully so as not to break it, and you tear out little pieces and if you're careful enough, you finish up with a face that smiles at you, or scowls at you, and either way it's good because it's yours and you made it. You can make a whole family, a whole classroom, a whole world of people out of privet leaves, if you're careful.

The house is quiet when she gets there. There is Ida somewhere in the kitchen. Margaret Rose knows that, because Ida is always in the kitchen in the afternoon. She stands in the quiet hall and thinks about Ida. If she asks in the right way Ida will give her a biscuit or a sandwich or something else to tide her over, but she

74

has to ask in the right way. Sometimes Margaret Rose is in the mood for that, but mostly she is not. Ida always on about the right way to ask is Ida complaining about her and about Mummy, and that is not something Margaret Rose likes. Today she will not ask in the right way. 'Cow. Bitch. Mare,' says Margaret Rose under her breath and feels good about Ida. Bad words make good feelings.

The house smells strong. It smells of disinfectant and polish and cooking. Margaret Rose likes the smell but always pretends she does not, because it is a smell that Ida makes. Mummy's smells are the sort she says she likes, the smells of perfume and being hot. But she does really like disinfectant and polish and cooking.

Up the stairs one at a time. Both feet on each step. One at a time. Mummy does not know she is coming because she is early. She remembers suddenly that she is early because of Miss Lichter being ill and the children being sent home early, and this is funny because she will surprise Mummy and that will make her laugh.

The bedroom door is closed. Everybody's door is closed, the Miss Readers' and Mr Willis's and Mr Kentish's, but they are always closed. Mummy's is not supposed to be closed. Another surprise. She will open it softly, softly and jump and shout.

She opens it softly, softly, first putting her leaf people carefully down on the floor, and turns the knob, slowly, slowly and pushes the door slowly, slowly. Then she jumps in and shouts, 'Hooray!' very loudly.

The bed is full of people. Not just Mummy making her bump, which is her with the covers over her and fun to jump on but someone else who is also making a bump under the covers and the bumps are heaving about and seem to be more than two, there is so much heaving about.

Margaret Rose stands still after she shouts and stares and the bumps become small and stop heaving about and Mummy is staring at her with her mouth open, just an open mouth in a head sticking out over the covers and Mort is staring at her with his hair in his eyes and shouting, 'Get the hell out!' and Mummy says something and Margaret Rose can't hear and he shouts again and Margaret Rose turns and runs out of the door and goes into the Miss Readers' room and stays there until she sees them through the window walking up the road, and then she slips out. All the time while she is in the Miss Readers' room she hears Mummy calling her and Mort calling her and she does not answer. When she comes out she goes to look for her leaf family on the floor outside Mummy's door and it is gone, all the leaves are gone and there were five of them. Then she cries a lot and shouts and cries some more and they say she is ill and put her to bed with soup on a tray. No one says anything about Mort and Mummy in bed.

Mort is nice. Mort waits for her coming home from school and gives her chocolate cakes from the baker's shop on the corner, and iced buns and apples to tide her over and who cares about Ida? He tells her stories and plays games with her and is very nice. Mummy says nothing and Ida says nothing and Morty is nice. He is putting her to bed one night. Mummy is out, somewhere out, and Ida is clearing up after supper. The Miss Readers are in their room and the others are in the dining room shouting and laughing and Morty is putting her to bed. She is laughing and rolling about in the bed in her viyella nightie, pulling the covers with her to make it like a sea of covers, sheets and blankets all over the place, and he is chasing her all over the bed as she rolls and kicks her legs and when he catches her he accidentally on purpose tickles her and she shrieks and can hardly breathe and it is wonderful. And then Mummy is there at the door and shouts and now it is Margaret Rose who stares at her with her mouth open, her head sticking out of the covers, and Margaret Rose who shouts, 'Go away!' and then there is a lot more shouting and Mummy is hitting Mort, hitting him with both her hands and kicking him with one foot and shouting and shrieking so that everyone comes running, except the Miss Readers of course who never do anything, and Margaret Rose is crying and so is Mort.

Mort has gone away and Margaret Rose doesn't know where and never asks. And no one says. Andy is still there, though. It used to be Mort and Andy and Mummy, and now it is just Andy and Mummy. Margaret Rose hates Ida more than ever, now.

Maggy closed the window, carefully, leaving just enough room at the top to let some air in, and went back to the table, the photograph in her hand. Her hands were trembling a little, and she moved the photographs about a little, tidying them, trying to stop the shaking that had spread to deep inside her. It was absurd, really absurd, after all this time, to get so agitated just by remembering something. Wasn't it?

Morty knows a lot. What the hell did it mean, anyway? Knows a lot about what? The money, the whatever it was that was going to sort out the Westpark's problems? Maggy looked down at the photograph again, at the happy grinning face under its mop of dark thick hair, the wide uneven teeth. Morty knows.

'I'll have to find him.' She said it aloud and then felt silly, but the words repeated themselves inside her head. I'll have to find him. Ask him. Even though I haven't seen him for almost thirty years, I'll have to find him. Morty – Mortimer, I suppose. Mortimer Lang. But where the hell do I look?

8

The smell in Dolly's room was so heavy that it made her feel that she was absorbing it through her skin, not her nose. Perfume, of course. Lots of that. And old coffee and caramels and a deep mustiness that was old things. Old clean things, clothes that hadn't been worn for years, scarves and gloves rolled up in drawers, handkerchieves and belts and bags.

She was feeling strung up and alert, almost high. Deciding to come here at all had been the first jolting thing she had done. She had sat there in her flat as the long summer day died into its twilight and thought about looking for Morty, finding out what he knew about what she was looking for, why Dolly had sent her to him, and had known all along she'd have to come here. But actually planning – that had come late, while she was eating the cottage cheese her day-long hunger had at last driven her to find in the fridge. Then she'd been able to shower and go to bed and sleep easily, grateful to have made the decision.

And it had stuck next morning, and now, here she was, standing in Dolly's room on the top floor of the Westpark, absorbing the smell and listening to the sounds from the other side of the heavy door.

It had been absurdly easy to get in here unobserved. She had walked in past the milkman, cheerfully clattering his way down the front steps, and gone straight up the stairs, unseen by the night porter who was sitting in the office behind the reception desk, probably sleeping away the last hour of his work shift, and let herself into Dolly's room with the key that Ida had dropped on Theo's desk that morning at the Jump office, and locked the door behind her. Now she could stay here all morning, all day if she liked, and no one would know. Ida no longer had any way of getting in, and anyway, no need to; there was no cleaning to be done, no maintenance work in a dead woman's room.

She took a deep breath and looked around. The curtains were drawn, but enough of the early morning light filtered through to show the contents of the room. It was odd, really odd; she hadn't been in here for the past three years. But it looked exactly the same. There was the bed with its heavy silky counterpane and thickly quilted eiderdown; it had been old fashioned for years, one of Dolly's most prized possessions, and now it looked as modern as tomorrow; mauve satin and thirties design was very in this year.

She moved across the room then and opened the curtains, pulling on them gently so that the rings wouldn't rattle, but they clanked a bit and she stood still, listening hard. She had every right to be here if she chose, but the last thing she wanted was for anyone else to know. Paranoia again, maybe, but that was the way she wanted it.

There was the whine of a vacuum cleaner coming from some-where and a clatter of dishes; breakfast in rooms, now? Ida was changing her tune, she thought sourly; in the old days anything extra of that sort that Dolly had wanted to give her boarders had been stamped on hard by Ida as a waste of money, bad business, stupid. She's probably making them pay for a bomb for it, she thought now, and then irritable with herself, pushed it out of her mind and turned and looked at the room again.

Where to start? That was the problem. Where on earth, in this cluttered overcrowded room with its little tables and cabinets and chests of drawers and boxes piled on wardrobes was she ever to begin looking? It wasn't even as though she really knew what she was looking for; old letters with a return address on them? An address book? What?

She started with the wardrobes, feeling obscurely that they were so big that it would be easier to get through them quickly. An illogical thought, but it gave her a jumping-off point, at least.

There were three of them, two in birdseye maple with fat curves and angled, stepped mirror decorations and one in mahogany with a heavily ornamented front. Dolly had bought that at a junk shop in Ealing, ages ago. She had been so pround of herself, coming home and bubbling over with it. 'Fifteen pounds, my dears!' she had cried, throwing her coat down on the long bench in the hallway and running into the sitting room where the boarders were sitting waiting for their lunch. 'All I went down for was a few bits and pieces, but you know how 'tis on a Saturday morning, all busy and exciting, and there it was, fifteen pounds and solid mahogany, the man said – ' And then when it had been delivered that afternoon by a couple of sweating men in an old van, Ida had looked at it in disgust, and said it was hideous, a waste of fifteen shillings, let alone fifteen pounds, and Maggy had thought the same but would have died rather than let Ida know she agreed with her, and so had said nothing. But she had hated it and thought Dolly a fool to buy it. But now, looking at it, she had to admit she had been wrong. It was a beautiful piece of Victorian craftmanship and would fetch a fat three figures in the Portobello Road and a hell of a lot more in trendy Kensington. Looking at the rest of the furniture with this morning's fresh eyes she realized that a great deal of it was equally good in its own period way. Handsome art deco pieces jostled with well-made Edwardian ones; any antique dealer would dribble at the chance to get his hands on most of it. Maybe that's where the Westpark's future lies, Maggy thought, selling off Dolly's old bargains, and wanted to laugh. Stupid ignorant Dolly with no taste at all, managing to collect money that way!

The mahogany wardrobe breathed lavender at her as she opened it, a great wave of dusty smell and she riffled her hand along the clothes hanging there, and was suddenly sharply embarrassed. They were all men's clothes, every one of them. Suits carefully arranged on heavy wooden hangers with plastic shoulder covers over them; overcoats and raincoats and slacks, and sweaters carefully set on padded hangers to hold their shape. There were shoes ranged tidily on the top shelf and a couple of hats, a grey trilby with a curved brim and a heavy glossy black bowler.

She shut the door sharply on them, and moved quickly to the birdseye maple wardrobes, and there she found Dolly's clothes. Rows and rows of them, dresses and skirts and frilled blouses and long nightdresses with matching negligees in sugary pinks and pallid greens and blues, and they reeked of her usual perfume, that chypre smell that had been so much a part of her.

Maggy worked her way methodically along the rail, flicking each garment away, still not knowing what she expected to find, but knowing she had to touch each one, just in case. But all there was was clothes, clothes, clothes, and she tried to remember Dolly actually wearing them and couldn't. Yet all these were familiar somehow, all part of the fabric of her growing up years. Dolly had loved clothes, had bought something new whenever she could, even when they were waiting for the bailiffs to turn up and make

80

trouble, hadn't been able to resist a pretty scarf in a shop window. There had been some lovely times, long ago, when the two of them, she and Dolly, had gone giggling through the stores, buying, buying, buying, to come home and find Ida tight lipped and furious. And that had been the best part of it –

Both wardrobes were the same, and so were the chests of drawers, filled with piles of clothing that hadn't been worn for years. But no bits of paper, no envelopes or address books; nothing that said anything at all about Morty.

She came back to the big mahogany wardrobe and stood in front of it, and stared at it. Whose clothes were they? Morty's? Not after so many years, surely. Oliver's? Never. He wouldn't have worn those heavy expensive suits, those thick overcoats, and never, never either of those hats. Not Oliver. Anyway, he'd have had them out of there so fast after Dolly's death if they'd been his – and he had a room of his own, besides, and wouldn't need to keep any of his gear in Dolly's wardrobes – the thoughts chased themselves round and round her head and suddenly irritated with herself, she reached forwards and pulled the door open again, so sharply that it swung back and clattered against the side.

It was absurd, really, as though she had expected the sound to coincide with the opening of the bedroom door, because when he came in and closed it behind him and stood there staring at her she stared back coolly, her eyebrows raised, unsurprised.

'Well, Oliver? Was there something you wanted?'

'I knew there was someone in here!' He said it dramatically, standing with his back to the door. 'I said to Ida, there's someone up in Dolly's room and she told me it was impossible, but I knew – I felt the vibes coming at me – you can't fool Oliver, you know. I knew someone was here – '

She held out her hand, palm upwards. 'Give me that key, at once.'

'Key? What key? What are you talking about?' He sounded blustering now, less dramatic.

'The key you let yourself in here with. I've got the only one – Ida gave it to me. So you must have had one cut for yourself. Give it to me at once, or the police'll be called.'

'Police?' He stared at her, his face blank. 'What are you talking about, police? What's it got to do with them? Don't be silly – '

She felt all her suspicions rising again, bubbling up into a thick anger, mixing with the frustration of her fruitless search and her confusion and gave in to the resulting tide of feeling with luxurious abandon. 'It's got everything to do with them, you scrounging, scavenging pig – you'd take anything that wasn't nailed down, you would! You're the sort of sneak thief who'd rob helpless blind old women, you're so – '

He blinked and shook his head and tried to speak, opening his mouth to interrupt, but she couldn't, wouldn't stop, spitting out the harshest words she could lay her tongue to, knowing that most of what she was saying was nonsense, had no basis in fact, but needing to say it, calling him thief and liar and beggar and then thief again, and he stared blankly at her and made no attempt to stop her. Until, at last, her breath ran out and she was standing there with her hand still absurdly out-stretched and shaking in the receding tide of her fury.

There was a little silence and then he said quietly, 'Oh, my dear, did I hurt you that much? I never meant to, you know. I really never meant to – '

The snow was thick, heavy and clotted in the gutters, tight packed and slippery in the middle of the roads where the cars were cautiously slithering by and her hands and the end of her nose were solid with the cold and her boots, clogged with the frozen slush they had picked up, hung on her feet like lumps of dead metal. The physical discomfort was almost the worst she had ever known, and she was desperately, lunatically happy. She clung to his arm as they picked their way over the lumpy pavements, laughing breathlessly when inevitably she slipped and he had to catch her. What more could the world possibly hold for her? What other bliss could there be? Twenty-one, part of the band, in love, and loved back. What more could she ask of life?

Certainty, whispered the silly little voice inside her head as they turned into the entrance to the club, round the corner from Hammersmith Broadway, certainty that he loves you back, and she tugged on his arm again and he stopped and looked down at her.

'Oliver – ' she said, and then smiled, a little tremulously, looking up at him. It was such a joy to look at him, those dark eyes with the heavy shadows underneath and the thick tangled brown hair on his forehead and the long narrow cheeks; they made her melt and made her words come out all wrong.

'It'll be fun, mmm? Lots of fun?'

'Of course,' he said gravely, and looked at her broodingly. 'It's a great practical deal for me, and sure we'll have fun. We'll be into everything – ' He was being a bit American this week, slipping in words and intonations that mixed oddly with his basic London twang. She hoped he wouldn't get tired of it for a while yet, the way he usually got tired of his games. This one was dramatic and exciting. 'We'll get on well, mmm?' she said, trying to say what she really meant, trying to say, 'I love you. Say you love me and that's why you're moving in with me. Please say it.'

'Honey, I go down as easy as pecan pie, believe me. We'll have ourselves a ball, that's for sure – ' and he squeezed her arm against his side and they went on into the club for the rehearsal, and she wanted to burst with it all.

He moved in that night, and she rushed about the flat and cleaned it all over again, although it had shone like a new pin anyway, and she plumped up the gingham cushions she'd bought in that madly smart shop in Brompton Road, and tweaked the mattress-ticking curtains into position and felt she was living on a magazine cover. They's eaten spaghetti she'd cooked with all the care she could muster, and drunk some red wine she'd only paid six and elevenpence for but which tasted all right and then she'd washed up and he'd helped her dry, and it had all been so marvellous.

He's hugged and kissed her cheek when it was midnight and thanked her gravely and then kissed her other cheek and gone to bed in the little room on the other side of her big bedsitter, and she had curled up in her own put-u-up telling herself stoutly that he wasn't like other people, Glory be, he was a caring tender sensitive person and wouldn't dream of pushing himself onto her too soon. Not that she would have thought ill of him if he had –

And she had gone on being happy, even when she realized just how big a problem he had. She had come home one evening after rehearsing all day, having left him in bed because he felt lousy, he's said, tell George he'd be all right for the performances, but he couldn't work today, and found him semi-conscious in a pool of his own vomit, and been frightened out of her mind. She'd got him to hospital somehow, sending for an ambulance in her panic, and they'd told her harshly that drug problems weren't the sort they dealt with and gave her a letter to take him to a specialist – oh, they had been bad times then. But he had been abject, apologized humbly, told her, sitting beside her on the big floor cushions long into the night after they got back from the club at one in the morning, told her how he'd lick the habit, by jeez he would (he went on being American for a long time) and how much he needed her and how much he was grateful to her, and where would he be without her –

So it hadn't been all bad.

And the days had drifted into weeks, and the weeks pleated into months, and he rehearsed less and less and his clarinet sounded – well, not as it should, and George had got mad one night when he zonked out on stage in the middle of a set and told him to bugger off. She'd have gone with him, so red-hot with fury was she as Oliver leaned against the wall in the alleyway outside and retched and George bawled at him, but where could she go? There weren't that many bands in London that'd take a girl on piano, especially one who played her sort of piano, and there was the flat to pay for, and Oliver to look after and the impossible thought of having to go back to Dolly if she didn't earn.

So they went on, for a long time, in the same old way, Oliver cleaning the flat when he felt up to it, and cooking a little, and still, sometimes, sitting close to her on the big floor cushions and talking, talking, talking deep into the small hours. But only sometimes, for now they argued more, usually about money for his stuff, and about not keeping his appointments with the drug dependence clinic, and although she could not, would not, have put it into words, about the way he went, always, into the little bedroom on the other side of her big bedsitter when it came to sleep. He'd hold her close and hug her, and kiss her cheek, sometimes her eyelids and chin, but never more than that, though she clung to him and tried all she knew to show she was ready, that he needn't feel bad about the way she was working to pay all the bills, she didn't mind, he wouldn't be poncing on her or anything like that if they did it.

But he didn't get her message, and she watched him and loved him and needed him and for all her worrying was happy with him, but not as happy as she'd been that day in February when the snow was so thick and he'd been chucked out of his room and she'd offered to put him up at her flat.

And then it was November and the band got the chance to play in Hamburg, the same place the Beatles had played and done so well, and the chance was too much, and she'd gone, even though it meant a week alone for Oliver. 'He'd been marvellous the night she'd told him they were going, fussed over her and packed her

84

case for her and insisted he'd be great on his own, he's paint the kitchenette and really fix the flat up ready for her to come back, maybe even play a little clarinet again for a bit, get his lip back, start a new life style before Christmas –

Christmas. She'd come back, the week after Dallas had happened, when Christmas decorations were appearing in the shop windows, and found he'd gone. She'd walked into the flat, lugging her case and the big box of goodies she'd brought from Germany for him, sausages and jars of sauerkraut and a big sugary apple cake, and she'd known at once he was gone. The flat felt dead and heavy and she'd stood in the middle of the big room and cried and cried, and George, who'd helped her bring her stuff up, had stood and touched her and crooned at her and told her he wasn't worth it, and still she had cried. Until George saw the letter he'd left on the mantalpiece and she thought it was going to be all right.

'Maggy, my own,' he'd written. 'There was a call from your mother, two days after you left. She was ill, pneumonia they said, and she needed you, and I didn't want to send telegrams to Hamburg upsetting everything so I went over there. If this note is still here when you come home, then I'm still there! I hear you had a great time there. The word came back you went over very big – '

She had laughed at George then, laughed in his face when he had read the note and shook his head and said heavily. 'That guy's still trouble, Maggy. Watch him,' and gone away, and she had taken a cab, extravagant after their big Hamburg success, and gone all the way to the Westpark in it, instead of taking the tube the way she should have done. Even ready to be loving to Dolly, to wish her well, and hope she was better, she stopped the cab and bought flowers outside Notting Hill tube, and paid the cabbie a big tip when he dropped her in Bayswater. And ran up the steps, happy and bubbling.

Ida had been sitting at the reception desk, and she'd looked up as Maggy came in, staring at her tight pencil skirt and tiny boxy jacket, the one she'd bought in Hamburg, and Maggy had wanted to laugh, she looked so dowdy. She had opened her mouth to say something but Maggy hadn't waited to hear, but gone running up the stairs, looking for Oliver.

And found him. He was in Dolly's room sprawling at the foot of her bed, reading something to her from a magazine and she

85

was leaning back laughing on her piled-up pillows, her red hair fanned out over the lilac silk and her shoulders a drift of white maribou feathers over a purple frilly nightdress that was tight over her heavy breasts. They had both stared at her as she stood there in the door of the bedroom absurdly clutching her flowers and she had seen them in a golden fog, for lamps had been scattered about the room, and all of them were burning and they created a yellow haze that made her blink, that seemed to wreathe both of their heads with a halo.

And then he'd got to his feet, sliding off the lilac counterpane and patting it tidy again and going to stand beside Dolly to put one hand on her maribou-feathered shoulder. They had stared at her and then they both smiled, wide happy smiles that made her feel cold, very cold and very frightened.

'Maggy darling! Was it a marvellous trip? Did you make marvellous music? I bet you did! And I bet old George raked in millions of shekels and was happy for once. Doesn't your old Mum look great? She's nearly better – she really is. A bit of looking after, that was what she needed, poor old darling, didn't you?' And he bent and kissed Dolly's cheek and Dolly grinned and patted his hand but didn't take her eyes off Maggy.

'Oh, I've missed you, love, I really have!' she said, her eyes wide and very bright. 'I was that ill, and I kept thinking of you, and then when I got so low they were going to put me in hospital, I told Ida I wouldn't go, and made her send a message to you and this darling boy turned up – he's been so good to me, my lovey, you can't imagine – so good – '

'And such a giggle, eh, my old duck?' he said and she looked up at him and they giggled together, shrilly, and. then looked at her again, wide eyed and so pleased with themselves that she wanted to kick them.

But she said nothing, only nodded and smiled, a hard little smile, and looked at Oliver and said tightly, 'It was a great gig. Went great We – they want us after Christmas, January, for three weeks straight. Maybe six. George says you can come and he'll put us both on the payroll. The Germans are paying hotels for all the band, whoever George brings. They liked us.' I can put it right with George separately, she thought, planning it at the back of her mind while she talked, while she stared at Oliver. 'Should be great, eh?'

'Oh, dear heart, me in Hamburg? I ask you! What'd they want

with the likes of me?' He wasn't being American any more, she noticed, and felt frightened again. He was being different, arch and silly and –

'*I* want you,' she said loudly. More loudly than she meant. 'I missed you. A week's a long time. Three weeks'll be even longer. George'll have to know, to make the bookings. Sure he'll want you, the whole band will – '

'Dolly, *darling*, may I be cut in little pieces and boiled for a pudding!' he exclaimed, and patted Dolly's shoulder again. 'It's time for your poison, and here's me nearly missing it. They'll drum me out of the Red Cross Cadets if I go on like this – ' and he came to the door and automatically she made way for him and as he passed her he bent and kissed her cheek, cheerfully, comfortably and with no feeling at all and she had to clench her fists to stop herself putting her arms up and round his neck and holding on hard.

There was a little silence when he'd gone away down the stairs, whistling, and then Maggy said in that same hard little voice, 'So you're all right again?'

'He was so good and kind, lovey, you can't imagine! Made me feel really well, one of the best nurses – Ida was really put out – ' and she giggled, inviting Maggy to join in the dig against Ida. But Maggy stared stonily back and said, 'You're doing it again. Aren't you? You're doing it again.'

'Doing what again? Lovey, what as I doing again?' Dolly's face crumpled, went soft and a little lined. 'I'm not doing anything at all – '

'He's my bloke!' Maggy said loudly, staring at her, not daring to come any further into the room for fear of hitting out at that soft anxious face. 'He's my friend, not yours. He's coming to Hamburg with me!'

'I wouldn't stop him, lovey, if he wants to go! I'd never stop anyone doing what they want, you know that. But – ' She put her hands out towards Maggy, leaning forwards so that the feathers lifted and whispered on her shoulders. 'Not really your fella, you know! Not anyone's fella, not Oliver. You do know that, sweetheart, now, don't you? He's a good friend to you, course he is. Good friend to me too, now, and glad I am of it. But not for your dearie. You're no fag hag – '

'That's not – you can't – it isn't – '

But of course it was. She'd known as soon as she'd seen him

sitting there on the lilac counterpane. She'd always known, perhaps. Somewhere deep inside she'd always known, but she'd hoped she was wrong, that there was still a chance, a possibility. But when he came upstairs again whistling with the medicine and fussed over Dolly and plumped her cushions and then perched on her lilac bedspread at her side and smiled over his shoulder at her, she knew she'd lost.

9

'I'm truly sorry, Maggy. You never said, you see – I thought you were glad to be rid of me – '

'I don't know what the hell you're talking about,' Maggy said loudly. 'I want that key, because everything in this room is my property, and you've no right to it. So do I get it or do I take steps to make you give it to me?'

He shrugged and his face blanked and he threw the key across to her. 'Have it, ducky, for all I care! There's no way I want to take anything out of here. I come in sometimes, just to remember old times, when I'm miserable. It's been a long time, you see. We were together a long time, Dolly and me – fifteen years is a long time – '

'Oh, Jesus, spare me the whining,' she said, and put the key in her pocket and turned back to the wardrobe to close the door. He came and stood behind her and peered over her shoulder at the contents and said conversationally, as though they had been on the most amiable of terms all morning, 'Odd, aren't they?'

'How do you mean?'

'Well, ducks, a wardrobe full of gear no one ever wears – how odd can you get?'

'They're not yours?'

'Mine?' He opened his eyes very wide. 'My dear girl, I ask you! Would I wear the likes of that?' He leaned over her shoulder and took the trilby hat and put it on and posed in the mirror and she almost laughed, he looked so absurd. The anger that had filled her was dissipating now, leaving her tired, almost floppy, not caring much about anything.

'Then whose is it?'

He put the hat back, and slid his hands along the clothes on the rail. 'I don't know. She never said. They were there when I moved in, and they've been there ever since. She'd never say, and I learned not to ask after the first time.'

'Were they – did she ever mention Mortimer Lang to you?'

'Who?'

'A chap we – someone we knew. Used to live in the Creffield Road house.'

'Well, maybe she mentioned him. She used to tell me a lot about the old days, did Dolly. We'd sit for hours and she'd rabbit on – but I can't say she ever mentioned – Mortimer, you say?'

He was looking at her with very sharp bright eyes and suddenly she shrivelled away inside herself. For a moment there she'd been relaxed, off her guard, had forgotten that she had to be careful. She'd been talking to him as though he were just – well, a person to talk to.

'It doesn't matter.'

'But you asked, so of course it does! Now, let me see, let me cast my mind back – ' He struck a little pose, thinking. 'She talked about a lot of people from those days. There was a – now, it was a funny name, to do with toys – damn it, what was it? I said at the time it was like being five years old again – Hornby! That was it! Ted Hornby. A right villain he was, from all accounts. A real one, I mean – and I'll never forget his friend's name because it was so funny – Jim Codling. She talked about them a lot. Even visited one of 'em in prison sometimes.'

She frowned, not wanting to know about that. 'I'm really not interested,' she said as crisply as she could, and moved over to the door. 'I'll see you out. I'd rather be on my own, thanks all the same.'

'But Mortimer Lang. Now that rings not so much as a tiny tinkle. Is he important?'

He was still standing by the wardrobe as though she hadn't spoken, and she opened the door wide and said a little more loudly, 'I'll see you out.'

'To do with the stuff in that box, maybe? Would that be it?'

'Out! Now, Or, by Christ, I really will get the police on to you.'

He sighed, exaggeratedly, and shook his head. 'Oh, come on ducky – such dramas! As if they'd give a shit! But I don't want to be bad friends with you, darling, not after all these years, so out it shall be. Coming for a cuppa? Ida's out – gone to raise hell at the wholesalers. They've been screwing her on the price of lavatory cleaner.' He giggled, and came to the door and stood beside her, and she shrank back a little. Damn memory, damn dead feelings that won't lie down. 'Come on. Maybe I'll remember something useful about this bloke for you. And being suspicious

90

of me isn't worth it, ducky, I mean – me! I couldn't knock the skin off a rice pudding! I'd never be any trouble to anyone, would I? You don't have to mind old Oliver.' And his eyes seemed doggish, now, appealing and apologetic.

'On your way,' she said, but there was no anger in it now. 'I don't want any tea, I don't want any coffee, I just want you out.'

'You coming too?' He hovered outside the door; and she looked back into the room, blank and bright in the morning light, and knew, suddenly, that she couldn't stay, and almost pettishly picked up her bag and followed him out into the corridor, and with a slightly childish emphasis locked it, and put the key away in her pocket.

'There's a good girl!' he said and grinned, and put his hand on her arm. 'Now the cuppa, hmm?'

'No,' she said, and went ahead of him down the stairs, and across the hall, not looking back, feeling obscurely that she had somehow lost a round in a battle, without knowing what the hell the battle was all about. He followed her and stood on the top step, watching her as she went down the street and called after her. 'Try looking that bloke up in the phone book, ducky. I mean, you're not playing cloaks and daggers, are you? No need to go hunting around in Dolly's bits and pieces in secret – unless you're looking for someone naughty – '

She ignored him and quickly went along the street, clutching her bag under her arm and trying not to run.

And there the name was, in the phone book. She resisted the idea all afternoon, going back to the flat, making a few phone calls, picking up her messages from her answer service, and all the time pretending that Oliver and anything he might have to say were a waste of time. But when all the calls were made and there was nothing else she could do she picked up the L to R directory and almost defiantly looked.

And there it was. Mortimer Lang. How many Mortimer Langs could there be, for God's sake? It had to be him, and she stared at the name and address unbelievingly, and then, feeling, foolish, rang directory enquiries and asked them. And they confirmed it. Mortimer Lang, 73 Duplessis Road, Waltham Park, E17. 451 2369. She picked up the phone again, and actually got as far as dialling the exchange before she stopped to think and then crashed the receiver down hard. Phone him? And say what? 'Dolly said you'd know all about it. Kindly tell me at once.' Or, 'Hi there. Just thought I'd get in touch. How have you been? How are things?'

She couldn't phone him. She'd have to go and see him. Find some excuse to go and see him and talk in a vague way about vague things and hope she could get round to what it was she wanted to know, or hope that he would, because she didn't even know what questions to ask –

There was nothing special to do that afternoon. The weather had changed, become sullen and less hot, and sitting there along in the flat was no joy. There was work to do, of course; and she looked across at the piano and pile of manuscript paper and the Purcell stuff and shook her head. The way she was feeling all she'd make of that would be disaster. So why not go and see him? Or at least look at where he lived. There'd be no harm in that. Maybe go into a couple of local shops, find out what he was doing, what sort of chap he'd turned into –

She looked up the address in the street atlas, and ran down the stairs, feeling alert again. Something to *do*. It was what she needed, something concrete to do, and she got into the car and wheeled into the heavy traffic with a lift of excitement that made her feel good.

It was an agreeable drive, working her way through the tangle of shabby Islington streets once she'd left the West End behind, and then along the winding ugly length of the Essex Road as it became shabbier and shabbier and petered out into the Lea Bridge Road. Not until she reached Whipps Cross Hospital on the edge of Epping Forest did she begin to think about where she was going and why, instead of concentrating on the traffic and finding her way through the ill-marked streets.

But by now it was too late to run back. She'd come this far, and she'd at least look; and she wheeled the car left into upper Walthamstow at last, watching carefully for the street name, and trying not to feel frightened.

The house when she found it startled her. It was large, extremely large, the wreck of what had once clearly been a Victorian house of some splendour. It was built of crumbling red brick with peeling stucco additions, and bedecked with so many curlicues over the windows and doors and turrets and gables that it looked like a cakemaker's nightmare.

She parked the car at the kerb and got out and stood there

uncertainly for a moment, staring at it. Did he own a place this size? And then she was annoyed at herself, for wasn't her own flat the top floor of just such an old big house, albeit a rather more elegantly designed one? This place could be subdivided into as many as six or seven separate flats, and obviously he lived in one of them, although it was odd there hadn't been another number as part of his address; Flat 2, 73 Duplessis Road, say.

She was twiddling and she knew it, and with a sharp movement designed to prove to herself how determined and sensible she was, she locked the car and walked through the gateway, up the weed-spattered gravel path which swept from one side of the house front to the other, towards the front door. There must surely be bells with individual names on, or something of that sort, so that she'd know exactly where to write to him; so she told herself and tried to believe.

The front door stood wide open and there were no bells with names underneath then on the jamb, and she stood uncertainly in the porch, looking in. The hallway was large, red-tile floored and extremely shabby. The dull green paint on the walls looked as though it hadn't been washed, let alone replaced, for more than ten years; the staircase, which ran up from the centre, was covered in dull green linoleum, and there was a strong smell of old boots and cooking and machinery in the air, the latter probably coming from the tangle of bicycles which were stacked in a corner of the porch.

It's a bit like a school, she thought uneasily and stepped back to look again at the door jamb, to see if there was any indication at all of names, just as a door on the far side of the hall opened and someone came out. She couldn't see who it was; the light from the door framed the shape and threw details into shadow, but clearly it was a man.

He moved forwards, setting his head to one side, and speaking as he walked. 'Can I help you? Were you looking for someone?'

'I – er – I'm not sure if I've come to the right place – ' she said, and stepped back a little, feeling somehow safer out on the gravel path, instead of in the porch.

He was at the door now, and she could see him clearly. Tall. Thick grey hair untidy over a long face that was sagging, the flesh seeming to be slipping off the bones. He had dark eyes, and looked worried and a little abstracted yet friendly enough, and she stared at him and tried to see the funny man who had made

93

her laugh when he tickled her, all those years ago. He was there all right, but she couldn't see him properly.

'This is Deneside', he said, and his voice was as tired as his face. 'For young people, you know. Waltham Forest Social Services Department.' He peered at her. 'I – we've met before, have we?'

She wanted to giggle then, wanted to tell him that the last time they'd met she'd been wearing her blue viyella nightie and had been deliberately throwing herself around on her bed so that he could see her bottom. But she only raised her eyebrows. 'Possibly.'

'Well, can I help you? I'm the housefather here – what was it you wanted?' He was beginning to sound less tired, more irritable, and looked down at the sheaf of papers he was carrying in one hand and put on an air of busyness. 'I'm rather tied up at the moment, and the youngsters will be in soon, some of them – '

'I – I was looking for Mr Lang,' she said, and stared at him, knowing she'd found him.

'Yes, yes, that's right, my name's Lang,' he said, even more fussily now. 'Housefather here. Are you from the Department? People change so fast these days I never know from one week to the next who's likely to turn up.'

'No,' she said and still stood there staring at him and now he looked at her again, and fumbled against his shirt front, where a pair of glasses were hanging from a cord round his neck, and put them on, and looked at her again, and she smiled. She couldn't help it; he looked such a caricature of a schoolmaster, peering through round spectacles like that.

'We have met before, though, haven't we? I can't quite place – really, I don't – ah!' And now he sounded relieved as someone else came through the open door at the far side of the hallway and came towards them. 'Perhaps my wife will know – Sally – '

She was a square woman, with a square face and square hands and a mouth that opened whenever she spoke into a wide tooth-filled gap that was almost square too, and she had a great deal of untidy grey hair. It made her look absurdly like her husband, for all he was so long and lean next to her solidity.

'You want me?' she said briskly and looked at Maggy. 'Yes? You're not from the Lord Charterman School, are you? I've been worried about young David Midler this past month, and I've told the head I am, so if he's up to his old tricks, you can't say you

94

weren't warned.'

Maggy shook her head. 'I'm a musician,' she said. 'Not a teacher, not a social worker, a musician.' It was important suddenly to establish this, to show these anxious grey people that she was something other than they, something exotic, special. 'I'm a musician,' she said again.

'A musician?' Sally Lang said, and her eyes blanked. 'Oh, how nice. Well, I'm sure Morty can sort out whatever it is – I've got the kitchen to see to. They'll be in any minute, the school lot – and tonight's scouts and then there are the late-night people and they always fuss so – ' Still talking, she went busily away to disappear to one side of the staircase and Maggy looked at Lang again and said, 'A *musician*. Doesn't that help? Or maybe then I hadn't started lessons. Come to think of it, I don't think I had. It wasn't till I started at Fletcher Street School that they found out I had any music in me – '

He blinked, took off his glasses and put them on again and then, tentatively smiled. But his eyes were still very anxious.

'Dolly,' he said, almost to himself. 'Dolly. You're a lot thinner.'

'Dolly's dead,' she said loudly. 'For God's sake, man, she was sixty-two! And I know I'm not a baby – but sixty-two, for Christ's sake!'

'Margaret Rose,' he said, and bent his head to his papers, and fussed with them. 'Margaret Rose.'

'Maggy,' she said, crisply, in control now, all her own anxiety washed away by his. 'Maggy Dundas. You don't listen to jazz, I take it.'

'I do, actually, I really do. Always liked it. But I don't buy records, you know. Not, on my salary! And there's all this – ' He swept his hand around in a comprehensive gesture. 'The council are too damned mean to find me a pennorth of nails, truth to tell, so any real amenities we have to find for ourselves – so no records. But I heard your name a few times. On the wireless – '

She grinned at the word. Wireless. Children's Hour and Saturday Night Theatre and the Ovaltineys, that was wireless. She was feeling better by the moment.

' – and I wondered if you were my – I mean, the girl I'd known, you know. But I thought, well, not really. Not possibly – '

'But I am, as you see!' she said gaily. 'May I come in?'

'In? Oh – er – well, yes, I mean there's no real – well, we could go to the flat, I suppose. We have a place up at the top you know, as houseparents. Not much, but our own, nice view from the bedroom, and a little kitchenette, not that we use it much. Sally says it alienates the young people if they think we live better than they do so we always eat with them, and we watch TV with them and really – well, there's the office of course, less of a climb, you know, and not too uncomfortable, and if Sally wants me – '

He was burbling and she smiled sweetly at him, feeling really good now. Why on earth had she worried? There had been nothing to worry about. It was all going to be a doddle. No messing about, a straight series of questions and answers, and then she'd be on her way.

'Wherever you like,' she said easily. 'I won't keep you long. I just want to know what it is you know all about. Dolly left a message for me, you see, that you know a lot. So I've come to find out what it is.'

And then her new-found self-assurance dissolved and ran out of the ends of her fingers as he went a sick yellowish grey, and his eyes turned upwards and he looked as though he were going to faint.

10

But he didn't. He stood there in the doorway leaning against it and staring at her with his eyes out of focus as slowly the colour came back into his cheeks.

'A message? She left a message?' He tried to smile and she had to glance away for a moment, it looked so painful. 'To do with me?'

'I'd better come in, hadn't I? It's difficult standing out here.'

'Yes. Yes. I suppose you should – the flat – the office – '

She was getting irritable now for he made no move, still standing there leaning against the door jamb. 'I don't mind where, as long as I can talk to you! There's nothing to get into a flap about, is there? Just an old friend, here to talk about old times, that's all.'

He seemed to brighten then. 'Old friend – yes – ' he murmured, and straightened up and turned to walk across the hall, but he was still in some degree of shock, because his knees buckled, and she had to put out a hand to hold on to him.

They walked across the red tiles of the hall, her heels clicking, and his feet shuffling, while she still held his elbow in a supportive grip and she thought absurdly – I must look like some sort of hospital nurse, being kind to an old man. And then, irritably – he's not that old. He was the same as Dolly – only sixty or so – not that old.

The office was as shabby as the hall and the stairs, but much more cluttered. A desk, piled high with paper, a notice board with so much pinned on it that it was impossible to see what point there had been in putting most of the things there in the first place, a couple of chairs stacked with box files, a gas fire hissing dispiritedly over its broken elements. He stood in the doorway as they reached it and looked round, as though he were seeing it for the first time.

'This will do, will it?' He sounded apologetic, less frightened now, and straightened, taking his arm away from her, moving across to the desk. 'Not very glamorous, I'm afraid, but funds are low, and we need all there is to feed the children and – you know how it is with local authorities, I'm sure – don't you?' He peered up at her, pushing the chair towards her. 'Do sit down. I'll ask Sally for some tea. Do sit down – '

'No need for tea, and no need to apologize. I didn't come for a party. Just to talk to you.' She took the chair and sat down firmly, and after a moment he shuffled across the room and took the box files off another chair for himself. He sat with his head down, not looking at her, and there was a little silence broken only by the plopping of the gas fire as she stared at him. Was this the man she had once found so fascinating! The one who could make her shiver inside with such delight when he tickled her, the one who smelled so exciting? She tried to look back down the corridor of almost thirty years to the young man he had once been, but she could see only this old one, this grey-haired frightened creature huddled in a shabby chair.

'I didn't mean to upset you, you know,' she said after a moment, trying to sound friendly and relaxed. 'I just need some information, that's all. Why has it given you such a shock seeing me?'

She felt her puzzlement increase as she watched him; he hadn't been all that alarmed when he had first realized who she was; anxious perhaps, but not really frightened. Not until she'd told him why she'd come had that wave of terror washed over him, leaving him as he was now, shaking and pallid and rather embarrassing.

'Shock? Not at all.' He tried to rally, leaned back in his chair with a movement that was meant to be nonchalent but which was tight and jerky and underlined his tension even more. 'Surprised, of course, – I mean, who wouldn't be? After so many years. You were just a baby, you see, when I knew you, and to find a handsome young woman on my doorstep and to discover she's a well-known person, into the bargain – well, surprised, naturally.'

'Naturally.'

'And a little upset, of course – ' He was trying so hard to be relaxed it almost made her own muscles ache to watch him. ' – to hear of Dolly's death. Dear old Dolly – such a good-hearted soul, your mother – so kind and – '

'We didn't get on,' she said harshly. 'I'm not mourning her death, so there's no need to trot out any platitudes.'

He peered at her over his glasses, and then took them off, dropping them to dangle against his chest with a slightly flamboyant movement that sorted ill with his state of tension, but which was obviously second nature to him.

'Didn't get on? Oh. That's a pity. That really is a pity.' He sounded earnest now, looking at her with that school-masterish expression on his face, and she felt irritation rise in her again. 'Mothers and daughters – such a lovely relationship, such a pity when things go wrong. Do you want to talk about it? Would that help?'

'I'm not one of your kids, you know, not one of the children you housefather here. I didn't come for any sort of – '

'I'm sorry – I didn't mean to pry.' He managed a smile, less of a painful rictus this time. 'But we professionals, you know – we can't help it. I'm good at my job, you know. Very good. The children they send me are always the worst, the most disturbed, the unhappiest, the ones most in need of tenderness and understanding – and I do well with them. I can handle them better than anyone else – '

He was sitting up very straight now and talking more loudly and much more rapidly. ' – even the toughest of them respond to me. I'm doing good worthwhile work here, the sort of work I'm really suited to and it would be a – a wicked waste, it really would, if I couldn't go on doing it. You understand that? It's not just for myself I say it, you must understand. It's for the children. They need me, and the fact that I enjoy what I do, and find great peace of mind and – fulfilment in it is beside the point, though no doubt it contributes to my success. But it's the children who matter, you see. Without me, some of them would have no one, no one at all who cared – '

She stared at him, and opened her mouth to speak but she couldn't for he gave her no chance, going on and on about the children, his work, the importance of it all.

'I'm sure you do,' she said at length, when he had to stop to draw breath. 'I'm sure you're great. And you wife, too – '

'Sally – oh, my God, Sally.' And again his face whitened, and she put out one hand towards him, fearing that this time he really was going to faint, and feeling more mystified than ever.

'She's – she's a marvellous person,' he said, still trying to look relaxed, leaning back in his chair. 'A really marvellous person. Without her I couldn't do a – fraction of what I do. We're a team, you know? To break up our team would be – it would be shattering the whole lives of the children here – '

'Yes, you've said all that.' She tried to sound crisp and business-like. 'And I'm sure it's as you say. Now, look, can I talk to you about what I came for? I don't want to waste your time any more than I have to.' She bent her head to her bag, riffling through it for the photograph. 'It's this I've come about.' And she held it out to him.

He didn't take it, just sitting and staring owlishly at it, and she waggled it at him almost imperiously and at least, unwillingly, he leaned forward and took it. But he didn't look at it, staring at her face.

'I found it among my mother's things in her safe deposit box,' Maggy said.

'Her box? Oh, God, I remember that box. Just like a squirrel she was – hoarded everything.' Still he stared at her, ignoring the photograph between his fingers. 'After all these years – '

Maggy drew a sharp breath, impatient now. 'If you look you'll see it's you and Dolly and another chap. She's written all the names on the back. But there's something else – she's written on you – look at it, will you? You'll be able to read it then.'

Slowly he bent his head, and stared at the square of card in his hand and then, fumbling a little, found his glasses and put them on and went on staring.

'Andy,' he said softly, almost in a whisper. 'Andy.'

'Yes. You and Dolly and Andy. I'm not sure if I remember him. I mean, I do, in the sense I remember he was there in Creffield Road, and lived there quite a while, but there's nothing about him that sticks in my memory. Not as it does about you.' She smiled then, leaning towards him. 'I liked you, when I was a child. You were kind to me. I remember you with great warmth – affection even – '

He shrank back in his chair and glared at her. 'Don't say that! You mustn't say that! I was nothing in your life! Just a boarder in your mother's house, that's all!'

She blinked and drew back. 'Well, yes, I suppose you were,' she said as mildly as she could. 'Nothing to get so agitated about, though, is it?' Again she was puzzled and even a little alarmed. Was he mad? Had the years made him senile before his time, turned him into this up-and-down creature who swung from eager boasting about his prowess as a housefather to a frightened old man huddled in a chair?

'I just don't want any misunderstandings, that's all,' he said,

100

and looked at the picture again. 'No misunderstandings.'

'All right,' she said soothingly. 'There'll be no misunderstandings. Let me just tell you what it is I want to know, and then I'll go away, all right? The thing is, I've – I've inherited my mother's property. In a way – though I've got to keep Ida on – you remember Ida?' Why on earth did I mention her, for God's sake? The thought flicked into her mind, and she pushed it out again. His wackiness is making me wacky too. 'Well, never mind that. But I've inherited the hotel and with it some – financial problems. Now, my mother had a safe deposit box in which she had said, before she died, I'd find the wherewithal to pay off the debts, and sort things out. The thing is, there's nothing in that box but a lot of bits of paper and newspaper cuttings and photographs. I haven't been able to look at all of it yet – but I did find that photograph.'

She held out her hand for it, and he gave it to her. 'You see? The writing on the back – your names – that's obviously old. Faded. But the writing on the front is much clearer, and you can see she wrote it only recently. That's why I'm here. It took me a while to find you – I didn't think to look in the phone book at first – ' and she smiled at him, inviting him to share her self-mockery, but he looked suddenly back at her, and said nothing. ' – and here I am. So, please, Mr Lang – Mort – can you explain? What is that you know all about?'

There was a long silence and he went on staring at her, but now he had moved his head a little so that the light from the window was reflecting on his glasses, giving him a blank Little-Orphan-Annie glare, and for a moment she wondered if he was going to retreat back into fear again. But then she realized that the atmosphere had changed somehow; he was no longer frightened but watchful, very alert, and puzzlement lifted in her again.

'Well?' she said more sharply. 'What the hell is it you know all about?'

He giggled then, a silly high-pitched sound that made her pull back from him.

'Naughty little children,' he said, and giggled again. 'That's what I know all about. Naughty children. I told you.'

'Yes, I remember that. You've told me,' she said, and then with a sudden edge in her voice that surprised even herself went on, 'I was a naughty child. Very naughty. Wasn't I? And you liked me.'

It was as though the atmosphere had altered again; once again he was frightened, his moment of sharpness and self assurance gone as quickly as it had come.

'You weren't naughty,' he said. 'Just a – just a child. That's all. Just a child. They always gets things wrong, forget things, remember things that never happened. Just a child.'

'Let's not waste time any more, please. I've told you what I need to know. What was it Dolly meant when she said you know?'

He looked down at his hands, crossed now on his lap. 'I really can't say.'

'You mean you won't.'

'Not at all – I just don't know – what have such things to do with me? You say your mother left debts? Well, that's not surprising. She was a feckless woman, Dolly, feckless – it was part of her personality – ' His voice dribbled away, and then he said suddenly, 'Mind you, Ida – she was good with money.'

'We all know about Ida,' Maggy said dryly. 'She loathed me when I was a child, and always has. I feel the same about her.'

'Yes – ' He looked at her and for the first time produced a real smile, a gently agreeable twist of his mouth that was suddenly very familiar and endearing. 'Poor child, you did feel shut out, didn't you? And she was so jealous – '

'Jealous? Of me? Yes, I dare say she was. Anyway, there's no way I can get anything out of her – not that I suppose she knows that much. Dolly said *you* did. Why won't you tell me?'

He spread his hands. 'I don't know! Truly, I don't know. We – I went away. I'd been there at Creffield Road a long time and it was a wrench but – I went away. And I never saw any of you again, or heard from you. Till today – ' Again his voice dribbled away.

'There has to be something.' She said it bracingly. 'Or Dolly wouldn't have written what she did. She may have been playing games – she was a damned sight too fond of playing stupid games – but she didn't cheat, I'll give her that. So there has to be something you know that she wants you to tell me. So think about it. Anything to do with money. A lot of money. Because there are a lot of debts, I promise you!'

'Dolly never had a red cent for more than five minutes,' he said, and smiled that gentle smile again, and she found herself relaxing, smiling back. He must really be good at his job, she thought suddenly. He makes me feel quite comfortable, sometimes. 'Poor old Dolly! Good as gold and so generous she didn't

102

know when to stop, and so *silly*.'

'More than silly. She did some – she made me very unhappy.'

'I dare say she did. Women like Dolly try so hard and cause so much damage. And then break their hearts over it. Poor Dolly.'

'I'll cry,' she said. 'When I get round to it. Look, this is getting us nowhere. There must be something you know that will help me. Was there anything going on at the time you were there in Creffield Road, anything that might lead me somewhere?'

He was silent for a moment, and licked his lips and then he said, 'There was Hornby.'

'Hornby?'

'Hornby and Codling. They were staying there too.'

'I don't remember – no, wait a minute, somebody said – ' She sat and stared at him, trying to remember when she'd heard those names before. 'Hornby. Toy trains – Oliver said – '

'Who?'

'No one you know. What about them? Hornby and Codling?'

Again he licked his lips. 'Look, this is none of my business. I really don't want to get involved – none of my business. Leave me out of it.'

'I can't. Dolly, your dear old good-hearted friend Dolly made it your business, when she left that message. Dropped you right in it. So you're stuck with me and my nagging. The easiest thing to do is tell me what I want to know and then I'll go away and leave you in peace. No hassle, no problems. Just tell me.'

He took a sharp breath, sounding irritated for the first time, and she welcomed that in him; the soggy frightened man who had sat and stared at her so woefully had made her deeply uncomfortable. Bad temper and sharpness was something she could understand and handle; it was her own way of reacting to pain and fear, and the only sensible one.

'So let's get on with it. Who were these men? Why might they be useful to me?'

'They lived in the house for years – until they went in prison.'

'Well, well, did they, then? Do you mean they used Dolly's house as some sort of – ' she grinned at the words that came to her lips ' – thieves' kitchen?'

'Well, they certainly lived there. Met people there. Dolly never interfered – she never interfered with anything. At least, she usually didn't.' The flicker of fear came back to his face and voice. 'She didn't care about stealing anyway, and that's what they did.

They went down for robbery. Took a lot of money from a wages clerk. A hell of a lot – it was one of those dress factories in Brixton.'

'And?' She leaned forwards again, eagerly now.

He shrugged. 'That's all I know. They went to prison for robbery, and Dolly went on visiting them, silly good creature. That's all I know. And that's the only thing to do with money I know about. Honestly, the only thing – '

He stood up, sharply, and lifted his chin as a clatter came from the hall outside. 'My little ones are back,' he said, and smiled widely, and took his glasses off with that same flamboyant gesture and turned to the door, expectant and wide-eyed.

She turned to look, expecting to see small children and then blinked as three large youths in black leather jackets came in. They looked like caricatures of Bad Boys, so heavily were the jackets studded with metal, and so spikily cut and dyed was their hair. One had a broad scar running down one cheek of which he was clearly immensely proud, for he kept his head tilted so that it was that side of his face that was most prominent, and all three wore obscenely tight jeans and heavy boots.

'Well, there you are!' Mort said, and the relief in his voice was almost palpable. 'I've been waiting for you – '

The boy with the scar came and stood beside him, staring at Maggy with his face very straight. 'Trouble?'

'No, my dear fella, no trouble. Not at all – is there, Margaret Rose?' Mort turned and looked at her, and the difference in him made him look ten years younger.

'Maggy,' she said, staring at the boy at Mort's side, and very aware of his two companions, one standing across the doorway, the other behind her chair.

'Of course. Maggy. I knew her when she was a child, Dave. Imagine that! Such a brilliant and beautiful girl, and I've known her almost thirty years. She's a famous musician, you know!'

'Yeah?' said the boy at the door. 'What group?'

'My own,' she said sharply. 'If it's any of your business.'

'Where is it in the charts, then?' the boy said, and tipped his chin at David, beside Mort's chair.

She ignored him. 'May we finish our conversation, please, Mort?'

'Oh, I thought we had.' He was becoming more comfortable by the moment, basking in the presence of his three louts, and he smiled at her again, but it no longer seemed so gentle, nor so familiar.

'Not entirely. There are still things we need to discuss – ' She lifted her chin slightly. 'Like what happened the last time we were together.'

She was never to know why she said it, or even what she really meant. That her mother had thrown Mort out because of her, she knew. She'd always known that. But she'd never, until now, thought much about Mort himself, and how he might have felt about that episode, and now, staring at him, she realised that she should have thought about it. And certainly before she had spoken.

'There's no more I can do to help.' He said it loudly. 'Sorry and all that. Now I have a lot to do. The boys will see you out. Good afternoon.'

The boy at the door moved in, closer, and the one behind her took the back of the chair in his hands, tilting it forwards so that she had to stand up and she stood there tight with anger and a great deal of fear. They were so big and so patently enjoying the situation.

'The front door's this way, famous musician what I've never 'eard of,' the boy with the scar said, and moved forwards, and after one more look at Mort's face, blank and empty-eyed again behind his glasses, she turned and went. There was nothing else she could do.

11

'You don't have to count it that way,' Mort said loudly. 'God damn it, man, has it ever been short?'

'There's always a first time,' the man in the neat city suit said, and folded the envelope tidily and stowed it in his wallet. He was feeling better. His tooth had stopped hurting, miraculously, just when he'd reached the point of deciding he'd have to do something about it, go and see a dentist, have it out. He'd slept last night for the first time in a week, and that made him feel perky, energetic, ready for anything.

'You ought to be glad they haven't started taking inflation into account,' he said, and looked at Mort with his eyes very bright. If he could lift the contribution without being told to by New York, that wouldn't only improve his commission; it should make them realize how effective a man he was. They'd look at each other and nod and say, 'Good bloke, that Ernest Gibbs. Good bloke. Knows which way is up – '

'I'm at the end of my rope already.' Mort said the words as if they were new minted. 'At the end of my rope. One more twitch, and I'm – I'm over the top. Finished – ' He threw both arms up in the air awkwardly in a gesture that was both absurd and menacing. 'You hear me? Tell that man from me – if he tries to push me any harder he'll find he's finished me. And what good will that do him?'

'No one's pushing you,' Ernest said, soothingly now. The last thing he wanted was to have this stupid man get all excited. Even the silliest of them got excited sometimes and when they got excited there was no knowing what they mightn't do. Like go over his head, direct to New York. Not that Lang was supposed to know the address or phone number or anything, but you could never be really sure. 'No one's pushing you. I just said, you ought to be glad they aren't taking inflation into account. That's all.'

'So if they're not pushing, why send that girl? Hey? Why send her? I've told you to tell them, I'm doing all I can as it is. I make the most I can out of every penny that comes in here, and there's Sally's money – ' He looked bleak then, tired rather than angry. 'Sally's money – ' His voice dwindled away and the two men sat and stared at each other for a moment. And then he started again, his voice lifting. 'So, you see? There's no sense in pushing me any harder. There's a limit and I'm at it. Tell them that, tell them to keep that girl away, and to lay off. I can cope with you and that's all. No more – '

'What girl?' Ernest was staring at him hard now, his eyes bright and hopeful. 'What girl are you talking about?'

'The Dundas girl, of course. Who bloody else?'

'She's been in touch with *you*?'

'Stop playing silly games with me? I can't be doing with it. Of course she was here and well you know it.'

There was a little silence as Gibbs tried to sort out the information, make it fit into the little he already had. But it wouldn't fit.

'What did she want?'

'I told you, I can't be bothered with silly games! You know as well as I do what she – '

Gibbs shook his head. 'I know nothing about it. Nothing at all. That's why I'm asking.'

Mort blinked and then his face crumpled, like that of a child struggling with a maths lesson he can't comprehend. 'You didn't send her? *They* didn't send her?'

Ernest shook his head, still trying to work it out himself. Had New York been playing both ends against the middle? Were they sending him after the girl when all the time they knew where she was, were using her themselves? But that couldn't be. He'd been very clear on the phone last night, very clear indeed. Find her, or there'd be big trouble, he's said. Find her and watch her and report everywhere she goes – no, they hadn't sent her here. No way.

Mort was staring at him with that same crumpled agonised look on his face. 'Oh, my God. Another of them. I thought she was the same as you. I thought it was him, sending two of you. I never thought – oh, Christ!'

'How much did she ask for?'

'How much? Nothing – never mentioned money – I mean, not from me. Not directly – ' Mort was sounding more distracted by the moment and Ernest lifted his lip at him and shook his head.

'Here we go again,' he said. 'Quivering jelly time – ' and indeed, Mort was sitting curled up in his chair, white-faced and shaking. It took so little to knock this stupid ass off his keel. 'For Christ's sake, man, stop making such a fool of yourself. One of your boys'll come and then where'll you be? Up shit creek – '

Mort straightened, stretched his lips as an attempt to smile. 'Yes – ' he murmured, and took out a handerchief and wiped his mouth.

'So what did she want if she didn't ask for money?'

'She said – she wanted to know something. Told me her mother had died and left her some debts and said I'd know how to pay them off. A lot of rubbish, and I didn't fall for it – '

'What's rubbish? The debts?'

'That I'd know how to pay them off. What do I know about Dolly's money? I've had enough problems over – I've had enough since those days. The last thing I need is to get involved with her debts.'

'Was she asking you to pay them off?'

Mort frowned, staring through him. 'No. Not directly. She just kept on about me knowing something. Never said anything about how much she wanted out of me, or when – but then, I never gave her the chance. The boys came in, and I got rid of her. But she would have. I was sure of that. Sooner or later.'

'What did you tell her?'

'Nothing! How could I? I don't know anything! It was all a load of rubbish.'

'Was she satisfied? Went away satisfied? Or is she coming back?'

Mort shook his head. 'I don't know. I told you, the boys came in, and they frightened her, thank God. If she comes back, I won't see her unless my boys are here – if I had any sense I wouldn't see you unless they were here – '

'Oh, sure! And have me tell what I could tell? That one word from me, and this whole place falls about your ears? One word from me, and the council throws you out on your ear, and puts someone else in who'll keep the place running properly, keep them in control the way they ought to be? I should cocoa! We've been through all that before. I'm not scared of your nasty little bully boys, and don't you ever think I will be. Use them to frighten silly women, if you like, but not for me – now answer a straight question, for Christ's sake! Is she coming back or not?'

'I don't know,' Mort said, sounding sulky now. 'How the hell

108

should I know? I told her I knew nothing about her mother's money. Told her – ' he brightened then. 'I told her about Hornby. Thought that'd get rid of her, send her off on another tack, you know? I thought maybe if she knew there was someone else who had – things that had happened when they were living with her mother, she'd go and try it on them, instead of on me. Oh, I don't know what I thought! I go so confused – I get confused all the time what with you and Sally and worrying about my boys – '

'Who was Hornby?'

'Just another villain – used to live there. In the old house, you know? Got sent down for a wages robbery, him and another bloke there. Codling. Dolly used to visit them in prison, so I told the girl that, and sent her off. Maybe she'll find them, keep off me – ' He looked hopefully at Ernest, child-like and eager.

'I'll be here as usual next week.' Ernest was on his feet, smoothing his jacket. 'Usual time, usual amount. But listen – if she turns up here again meanwhile, you're to call me, you understand? The number I gave you – leave a message on the answerphone, and I'll be here like a shot. Find out where she lives. I haven't been able to yet – '

'Why do you want to know?'

'None of your business. Just do as you're told. I'll get her off your back, see? If she starts being a nuisance I'll deal with her. I can't say fairer than that, can I? I'll get her off your back.'

'Why don't you know where she lives? You told me you were a private detective. Why can't you – '

'She's too bloody fly, that's why,' Ernest said savagely. 'Ex bleeding directory, the lot. But I'll get to her. See if I don't.'

'What do you want her for?'

Ernest was shrugging into his coat. 'None of your bloody business. Just do as you're told, and keep quiet. And tell me when she turns up.' He took a notebook from his pocket. 'Who were those blokes you told her about?'

'Hornby and Codling. Ted Hornby, I think it was. I can't remember the other one's first name. Ordinary it was – Jack? John? I can't remember – '

'Where did they do their porridge?'

'The Scrubs.'

'All right.' Ernest stowed the notebook in his pocket and straightened his coat with pernicketty little movements. 'Don't forget, now.' And he went, leaving Mort sitting in the little pool of light thrown by his desk lamp, looking miserable and frightened and relieved, all at the same time. One of these days, Ernest thought, pulling the front door behind him, and listening to his feet crunching over the gravel path, one of these days that stupid bugger'll crawl right up his own arse, he gets so terrified. Born to be blackmailed, he was. Was the Dundas girl going to play that game with him? Or was she really looking for something else out of her mother's past? Would there be any point in looking out this Hornby bloke? There was a lot to think about, a lot, and he walked away down the lamplit street, smelling the flowers from the dusty gardens and enjoying thinking. This was a bit more like private detecting. Maybe he'd make a go of it yet.

She had done her best to keep herself calm. She'd driven back to the flat, holding the steering wheel so tightly that before she was half-way home she had pins and needles in her right hand; but she'd remained calm on the surface. Parking the car and locking it, walking back round the crescent to the house, climbing the front steps, she managed all that with an air of togetherness that she was proud of. But when she started to reach in her bag for her front-door key, her courage dissolved. She remembered with her body rather than her mind that moment on the top flight when whoever it was had knocked her over; actually felt the thrust against her ribs, the shock and the thick fear it had created in her, and she could go no further. To climb those stairs again would be impossible, and she turned and went back down to the street and after hesitating for a moment on the pavement, began to walk towards Holland Park station.

It was six o'clock, and the rush hour was well under way, and she had to push her way into the station against the home-going mass, and felt fear lift in her again. Could someone be following her in all this hubbub? The little man in the city suit she'd seen – she was surrounded by little men in city suits, all looking the same, anonymous, faceless and infinitely threatening in consequence. Or could one of Mort's horrible boys have followed her here? Everywhere she looked there seemed to be blank-faced youths in metal-studded black leather jackets and punk haircuts. London was full of them, and she was frightened of all of them.

But she got herself on to a West-End-bound train, and sank down in a corner seat, grateful to be going against the traffic; this train was much less crowded than those going the other way, and so she wouldn't feel so threatened.

But she did, finding herself studying every other passenger in the carriage with sidelong glances, trying to see if she recognized any of them, and of course finding every face familiar. It was as though she was paddling at the edge of a sea of panic, could be sucked into it any moment.

She managed to stay put as far as Oxford Circus and then could stand it no longer, feeling claustrophobic, needing to be out and up in the street, and she plunged through the crowded corridors and up the escalators, pushing and shoving and being sworn at and not caring. She had to get out, and when she did at last burst her way through the maelstrom that was Oxford Circus station at quarter past six on a working day she took a deep breath of the diesel fumes and dust and fried onion smells from the hot-dog stalls and felt the panic at last begin to recede.

What was she panicking for, after all? Because Mort had asked the boys he looked after to see her out? Because they were punky kids with sneers on their faces? What would you expect boys who lived in a council hostel to be, for Christ's sake? Eton schoolboys with pretty manners and naice accents?

She was being jostled by the heedless passers-by, pushing any way they could to get into the station, to get home to spend the evening stuporously watching television screens in dreary suburban sitting rooms, and she moved away, turning right, pushing up towards Tottentham Court Road. Quite where she was going she wasn't sure; but home was the last place she wanted to be, that was equally sure. She'd go somewhere to eat; that would be a good idea. She hadn't eaten a proper meal since – she couldn't quite remember. She'd go to Joe Allen's, have a steak and a spinach salad, see a few friends, maybe play the piano for them a little. That would be fun.

With a goal now she felt better and began to walk, slipping into the easy dodging stride of the native Londoner, weaving her way through the purposeful pushing crowds like a dodgem car in a fairground, not having to think about it. And began to think, instead, of what had come of her afternoon visit.

Mort. That tired old man, so frightened and bewildered, was Mort. She tried to mesh the memories that she had had all these years with the man she had seen but the memories had softened at the edges, lost their old sharpness. Now she had seen old Mort as he was she couldn't see young Mort any more. And she felt a

111

sudden stab of pain, as though she had lost something. And forced herself to order her thoughts more usefully, deliberately pushing away any emotion the afternoon had dredged out of her past.

He had said he didn't know what the message on the photograph meant, and she believed him. She couldn't have said why but she believed him. He hadn't been trying to hide anything, hadn't been prevaricating in any way. He truly hadn't known. That he's been frightened about something was obvious, but that had nothing to do with the core of the situation. He really didn't know.

She contemplated that fact bleakly, turning left into Soho Square, making her way across the dusty grass towards Greek Street. Which meant either that Dolly had been playing stupid jokes or whatever it was that Mort knew, he didn't know he knew it.

Like me, she thought suddenly, stopping on the corner of Greek Street, and staring blindly down its bustling food-scented length, watching the early diners parking their cars, hurrying into their restaurants, but not really seeing them. He was frightened of me because I know something about him that he doesn't want me to know, and I don't know what it is. At least, I don't think I know – and she shied away from the sharp vision she had of herself, rolling on her bed in her blue nightie and shrieking and laughing and displaying her bottom. What I know doesn't matter. It's what he knows.

She began to walk again, heading towards Cambridge Circus, still weaving her way expertly along the crowded pavements. It's what he knows that matters. Was what he said about Hornby important? Hornby and Codling. That was the only thing he'd said that might be of any use. Oliver had mentioned them too.

It began to come back then. Memory again began to move in her head, odd snatches of pictures. She saw herself sitting at the table in the kitchen, playing with crayons. Dolly was there fiddling at the stove, cooking something. She could smell it suddenly, the scent of macaroni cooking in milk. Dolly was making a pudding for Margaret Rose because it was her favourite pudding, with spoonfuls of lemon curd on it. The kitchen was warm and happy as well as good smelling because Ida wasn't there. Ida had gone somewhere. Ida wasn't there, and Margaret Rose was singing under her breath, pushing the crayons about over the paper to make thick smudgy lines and liking them, and being happy.

But someone else was there. Someone leaning against the

112

cooker and talking to Dolly, laughing sometimes, a thick soft laugh that made Dolly laugh too.

'Stop it, Jim, do,' Dolly said. 'Give over. I've work to do, m'dear. You'm enough to drive a woman mad – '

'That's why I do it,' he said, and laughed the thick laugh again. 'I like you when you're mad – '

'Not now.' Dolly's voice was sharper now, more definite. 'I told you, I got my little one's supper to do – Margaret Rose, my duck, will you have it with honey for a change?'

'Honey's rotten, honey stinks,' sang Margaret Rose. 'Honey comes out of bees' bums, honey's rotten, honey stinks – '

'Oh, where does she get it from, young limb o' Satan!' Dolly's voice was warm and loving and admiring and only pretending to be shocked. 'Such things as she says – Jim, give me that plate, no, not that one, lummox! The one with the cat on it – that's the one – '

'You can have a hundred plates with cats on soon,' Jim's voice said. Why can't I see him? Maggy thought, walking down Greek Street, staring ahead of her at the cars and the taxis and the lights of the strip joints. Why can I only hear his voice behind me? What did he look like? 'You can have anything you want, Dolly, my love. Just got to ask, an' Jim Hornby'll provide it. Just got to ask – '

'Piano maybe?' Dolly's voice was laughing, teasing, but underneath it was real, and Margaret Rose stopped pushing the crayons over the paper and listened.

'Piano maybe?'

'Sure, if you want one. What you want a piano for?'

'Margaret Rose. They told me at school she's got a natural way with a piano. She can just sit down an' pick out any tune you fancies, can't you, my little love?'

Dolly was kissing the back of her neck now, pushing her paper and crayons to one side, putting the big plate full of macaroni and milk and lemon curd in front of her. Margaret Rose began to eat, blowing on it first because it was hot, seeing the cat peer out for a moment every time she dragged her spoon across the bottom of the plate.

'Lessons too, if you like.' Jim was sounding louder now, and Maggy, walking down Greek Street, nearly at Cambridge Circus, heard his voice over and over again above the traffic noises and the tinny pop music coming from the strip joints. 'Lessons too,

113

lessons too, lessons too – '

So that was where they had come from, Maggy thought, and stood still in the middle of the pavement, so that people had to eddy and twist to pass her; that was how it all happened. Oh, Christ, why didn't I ever know that before?

12

Autumn leaves in the gutters, drifting across a wide road. A hill to climb that made her breathless. Odd houses, all looking different, and hardly any people. A quiet easy sort of place that made her feel funny, because it wasn't the way places she knew were like. She knew roads where the houses marched on each side in exactly matching pairs, roads where people walked quickly with their heads down, not strolling like here, with dogs beside them. She knew roads with buses and crowded shops and lights and stalls on corners, not this sort of quiet politeness where the shops looked as empty and dull as the houses.

'I don't like it here,' she announced, and stopped and stood still, looking down at her feet on the pavement, and then was entranced. She was wearing her new shoes and she'd forgotten. Red ankle strap shoes over socks with a frilly edge. Her feet looked beautiful.

'We're not there yet, my duck. Give 'un a chance!' Dolly said, a little breathlessly, and happier now that she'd looked at her shoes, Margaret Rose started to walk again.

'When will we be there?'

Dolly shook her head. 'Next on the right, I think. Then left, then right again, the man said. 'Tis a climb from that station, a climb and a half! Haven't walked so much since I were a girl!'

'Where did you walk?' Margaret Rose demanded immediately, hoping for a story, but the time wasn't right. Dolly shook her head and walked on, tugging her by one hand. Margaret Rose sighed and stroked Dolly's hand. She was wearing her blue nylon gloves, smooth and silky to touch yet with an edginess under the smoothness that she liked. Sometimes the edginess turned into sparks, real yellow sparks, when Dolly rubbed her fingers over something rough, like a sofa cushion. Lovely gloves.

The place, when they found it, was too big. A wall, high with great stone balls on each side of the gateway in the middle, and a notice board beside the gate. 'The Thomas Tallis School.' That was all it said. 'The Thomas Tallis School.'

Dolly didn't stop to look and whisper with her the way she wanted her to. She just walked straight in and up to the door and rang the bell even before Margaret Rose could say she didn't want to go there, and then there was someone at the door and they had to go in, and it got dark and bewildering.

But there was a piano. That was the next bit. A big room with a floor of polished wood, not lino, and a huge piano, not a flat-backed one like the one at school, or the one that Dolly had brought home and put in Margaret Rose's bedroom, but a great spreading one, with curves in its side, and a lid that was propped up on a thick stick. A great shining, singing thing, and someone (who was the someone? That memory had gone) pulling out the stool and lifting her on to it so that she sat there with her feet dangling even higher above the pedals than they did on her piano at home or the one at school. And she reached out and touched the keys and played some notes.

And oh, but it was lovely! Maggy standing thirty years away at Greek Street listened to the piano and felt again the surge of sheer pleasure it had given her then. The notes, so clear, so round, as perfect in their pitch. None of that twanging ugliness that she had to put up with at school, none of that wrongness in the pitch that on the piano in her bedroom made her stomach feel bad. Clean, clear round notes that sang the same on the piano as they did in her head.

'Play it,' someone said behind her. 'Play whatever you like.'

'Margaret *Rose*,' said Dolly's voice from somewhere, and the began to play. Nothing special. Just notes and chords, going up and down the keyboard, those lovely pale cream-coloured slivers of ivory, those plump black fingers with their plump black sounds, singing inside her head to match the piano. It was the best way she had felt for as long as she could remember.

'What was that, Margaret?' the voice said.

'Music.'

'Whose music?'

'Mine. Can we go home now? I think I want to go home now.' She was frightened suddenly. The music had been good, the piano had been beautiful, but now she was frightened, and she tried to get down from the stool, pushing away the hand that came on to her shoulder, holding her there.

'Would you like to play this piano again, Margaret? Any time

116

you wanted to?'

'No. Yes. No. I want to go home.' Margaret Rose was beginning to feel stick, now, the feeling pushing up from her stomach, into her chest, horribly close to her throat. 'Home – '

'She's very young Mrs – ah – Dundas.' The voice sounded dubious. 'Too young, I suspect. Nine, you say – but young for her age. Some nine-year-olds cope better than others – '

The sick feeling got into her throat, and pushed out, and changed into crying on the way. 'I want to go home!'

'I'm sure you do,' the voice said briskly. 'It's been a difficult day for you, I'm sure. Come along, Margaret, and we'll see about some lemonade for you while your mother and I talk – '

And that was all. A memory starting in a void, ending in blankness. Why? Maggy stared deep into her own mind and couldn't find out why. She remembered being at T T; how could she not? She'd started there at ten, and stayed until she was fifteen and they had been the most – well, they'd been important years. Desperately important. But had she gone there a year earlier, with *Dolly*? That was crazy. It had to be crazy. She'd started there after Miss Lucas from school had taken her there to play a test piece. She had sat in that big room, as though she'd never been there before and played 'Für Elise' by Beethoven and 'Rondo Alla Turca' by Mozart, easy baby stuff and they'd said she was good, fine, she could start at the school, and they'd be glad to have her, and Miss Lucas had smiled her wide gummy smile, the one that always made Margaret Rose look away, and patted her shoulder and said how pleased the school would be. And on the way back to the train, she'd told Margaret Rose that she should be very proud, she'd got a scholarship to the best music school any little girl could hope to go to, ever, and to be worthy of it.

Maggy creased her forehead and began to walk again. I got a scholarship. Everything I got in the way of an education I got on my own. She had nothing to do with it, nothing at all. Dolly had nothing to do with it.

And yet, and yet – the memory refused to be erased. It clung on stubbornly, filling her head with its authenticity, convincing her that somehow Dolly had been part of her years at Thomas Tallis, where everyone was so much better than Dolly could ever be, where Dolly never came.

And behind that, the memory of the thick laughing voice in the kitchen. 'Lessons too, if you like – ' repeating over and over again. 'Lessons too, if you like.'

It had been an expensive school, T. T. She'd discovered that early. Very early. Sitting in the cloakroom, changing her shoes.

'I like your shoes, the ones you go home in.' A high clear voice, very clipped and tidy.

Margaret looked up. A neat child with very thick dark hair, cut in a pretty fringe, and curling over her ears. Dark brown eyes with absurdly long lashes, an enchantingly pretty child. Margaret Rose had noticed her from the first day there. She had laughed a lot and chattered a lot and the other children liked her, talked to her a lot, not ignoring her the way they ignored Margaret Rose.

'I've been watching you,' the pretty child said, in her high confident voice. She sounds like someone talking on the wireless Margaret Rose thought, and blinked at her. 'You're interesting.'

'Interesting? Me?' Margaret Rose stared at her, her mouth half open. Me with red hair and all the wrong clothes and talking the wrong way? 'What do you mean?'

'Oh, they're all half dead here.' The dark child tossed her head, making her curls bounce over her ears. Margaret Rose was bewitched by that, and wished she'd do it again, and as though she'd heard her thoughts, the pretty child did, and then smiled. A nice friendly smile. 'What's your name?'

'Margaret – ' and then she stopped. Mrs Cornelius always lifted her lip a little when she used both the names, and Margaret knew now. It was common to have two names and use them both. Especially when you were named after a princess. That was *very* common. Vulgar, even.

'Margaret,' she said again, and smiled, carefully, not too much, not wanting to frighten the pretty child away.

'I'm Susannah Goldman. I'm eleven. I'm a weekly boarder and my father's a conductor.'

'Conductor?' Margaret thought hazily about buses and trams, seeing a man with curly hair that bounced over his ears putting tickets in his pinger.

'The Westminster Philharmonic,' Susannah said, and shook her curls again. 'You've heard them on the wireless.'

'Oh, of course,' Margaret lied. 'Lots of times.' Dolly only ever had Radio Luxembourg on, or one of the cheerful popular programmes on the Light Programme. Philharmonics? Never. Though Margaret knew about Philharmonics; Miss Lucas at her other school had told her about them. Taken her to a concert

118

once, even, so Margaret knew all she needed to know about Philharmonics and about conductors.

'Where do you live?'

'Creffield Road.'

'Where's that?'

'Ealing.'

'I live in Suffolk. Not far from Aldeburgh. So convenient for the music, you know, and Papa – we always call him Papa, isn't that sweet? Everyone says so – he likes us to have the best of the country while we're young. My brother's at the Conservatoire, in Paris, you know. Daniel. He's a genius, of course. Me, I'm just immensely gifted. Are you?'

They were sitting side by side now on the narrow bench beneath the coat hangers, and Margaret fluffed her skirt out over her ankles. It was her favourite dress, black and white and red checked organdie, with frilly petticoats under it, and she wore with it black patent shoes with a cuban heel. She wasn't surprised Susannah liked it, having to wear uniform all the time. A yellow blouse with a green gymslip couldn't compare with checked organdie.

'I don't know.'

'You're piano, aren't you?'

'Yes.'

'Me too. Better than violin, I think. More elegant. As for 'cello – ' She shuddered prettily. 'Papa thought of 'cello for me, but Muvver said no – we always caller her Muvver, people like that as well. She put her foot down with a *very* firm hand.' She splayed her knees wide in mockery of the cello-playing stance and laughed, and Margaret, obediently, laughed too.

'Of course this place is *wickedly* expensive, so we were able to bully them a bit. They wanted me to do violin like Daniel. But Papa being a conductor, of course – ' again the flicking head, the bounce of those lovely curls. 'So we won, and piano I am.' She looked sideways at Margaret, her eyes bright and knowing. 'Does your father complain about the fees? Papa never *stops*.'

Reddening a little Margaret said, 'I don't have a father. He's dead. Killed in the war.'

'Oh, my dear Margaret, I'm *so-o-o* sorry.' Susannah put one hand over Margaret's. 'You poor darling. A war orphan!'

'I've got a mother,' Margaret said, ungraciously, hating to admit that she wasn't as interesting as she appeared.

'But your father dead in the war – too awful for *words* – '

Susannah was clearly delighted with her new friend and Margaret blossomed, lifting her head, enjoying the warmth.

'So who pays for you here? It can't be easy for a mother alone.' Bright-eyed, probing, curl-bouncing Susannah, thought Maggy, crossing Cambridge Circus. What a little bitch she was. And how I loved her.

'I don't know,' Margaret said after a moment. 'I never thought.'

'Don't say never. It's bad grammar. Say I don't know, I haven't thought – I expect you've got a scholarship or something.'

'Yes. That's right. A scholarship.' Margaret frowned, ashamed of her own ignorance but needing to know. 'How much does it cost to come here without one?'

'About seventy-five pounds a term,' Susannah said, airily. 'Papa complains like mad but of course he can afford it. It must be awful for – would you like to be my friend? I could look after you when the others are nasty. Some of them are awful snobs.' Her eyes shone liquid with compassion and Margaret bobbed her head and said thank you humbly and that was that. From then on she belonged to Susannah.

Joe Allen's was quiet when she got there, early as it was, and she tucked herself into a corner behind one of the small tables and ordered a vodka martini and a steak and sat and brooded.

Now what? For the past few weeks I've been in a flat spin. There I was, perfectly happy, getting on with my own life. I'd got rid of Dolly. I'd stop caring, I was free and on my own. And then she goes and dies and ties me up in knots all over again.

Free? Were you? How can you be free when you're eaten up with fury? How can you be free of someone when you hate them so much? It's as bad as loving. It keeps breaking in –

The thought came as a revelation, so sharp that she put down her glass with a little thump, splashing some of the vodka on to the gingham tablecloth. Hating someone is as bad as loving them. It's probably the same thing really.

But I *did* hate her. How could I have loved her when she did such things to me? When everything I wanted she took away?

But what did she take away from you? Think about it. What did she actually take away?

Everything. People. The right sort of home. Respectability.

Susannah again, saying casually, 'Muvver says I'm to bring you home for the next weekend. Just a toothbrush and that in a bag. Papa will pick us both up on Friday.' And Margaret alight with excitement, telling Dolly.

'Away for the weekend? Oh, my dear, you don't want to do that, now, do you? Bad enough you got to be away at school for such a long day. I miss you from the time you goes in the morning till you gets home at night – and then all that practising. Oh, my ducks, you don't want to go away all the weekend, sure-*lee*?'

'I do, I do, I *do*,' Margaret said passionately. I've *got* to go. Susannah's fixed it all up – '

'Oh, Susannah!' Dolly laughed. She was sitting up in bed, a cup of tea on her lap and her hair tied up in curlers and the room smelled of scent and sweat. It was untidy, clothes strewn around, magazines all over the floor together with empty chocolate wrappers. Margaret, sitting on the edge of the bed, pulled her skirts in fastidiously. 'Susannah's a funnical man, man, tiddeley dan, Susannah's a funnical man! You don't want to spend no weekends with a funnical man, my love. Do you, my Margaret Rose?'

'Margaret! I hate being called Margaret *Rose*. It's stupid. *Margaret*. And I do want to go, and I will, and so there – '

Dolly's face, crumpled and puzzled, shaking her head, stubborn, hurt. 'Not for the whole weekend, my love. Not to see you all day Friday or Saturday or Sunday or Monday – oh, no, lovey – '

And so it had been, a weekend of fury and misery, imagining Susannah at her house, imagining herself there with her, the awfulness of not being with her. The even worse awfulness of Susannah being remote, her voice tinkling with ice, at school on Monday morning. 'Oh, there you are – yes I had a *lovely* weekend – there's Jenny – excuse me – Jenny, what are you doing next Friday?' Oh, the pain of that rejection!

But thank God, she'd got over it, and asked her again, casually, looking at her sideways, and this time Margaret swore she'd go, no matter what Dolly said, and started asking about it as soon as she got home from school, following Dolly about the house, nagging, whining, refusing to eat. She had to buy chocolate from the corner shop to make it possible to sit at the table for meal after meal and stare at her plate tight-lipped while Dolly cajoled and bullied and coaxed and at last, unwillingly, had given in.

That weekend. Maggy finished her drink and started on her steak, trying not to remember that weekend with the Goldmans, but it wouldn't go away.

13

The car had been the first marvel. It was big and the seats were wide and soft and the windows whispered up and down when you pressed a button. There was even a little cupboard with bottles and glasses in it.

Papa was tall and white-faced and talked a great deal, scooping up the two girls with loud cries of welcome, being immensely affable with Mrs Cornelius, who bridled and laughed and bridled again, and behaving in a way that, were he a child, would have been labelled as showing off. Since he was a grown-up, of course, it wasn't. It was just Susannah's Papa, a very satisfying answer to her weeks of wondering what he would be like.

Once they were in the car and driving out of London, equipped with bars of chocolate and fruit 'to stay your vitals until we reach the haven of our own hearth and home, my beloved!' Susannah settled down to chatter the journey away. She talked about so many things that Margaret knew nothing about; holidays, for example, holidays abroad, going on the cross-channel ferry, staying in hotels in the South of France, taking taxis to restaurants; a world of glamour and marvels that left her wide-eyed and enchanted, and she listened and asked questions and could feel Papa in the front seat somehow approving. He seemed to bask in his daughter's chatter, reminding her sometimes of small details she had forgotten about a particular journey, adding his own share of tinsel to the decoration Susannah was weaving round her life.

The house, when they arrived, frightened Margaret at first. It was so very like T T, with a red-brick wall in front of it, even a couple of huge stone balls flanking the gateway. She whispered as much to Susannah, who looked at her in some surprise. 'Oh, most houses like this have *those*,' she said. 'Didn't you know that?'

She didn't, and there was a lot more she didn't know, but by now she knew enough to keep quiet about her ignorance. To hold on to Susannah's esteem was important; more than important, it was essential. A life in which Susannah did not figure, a world in

122

which she did not stand where Margaret could circle round her was unimaginable. So, she kept quiet, as much as she could, and watched and listened and learned.

She learned about Muvver, first. Tall and thin and with dark hair, as dark as Susannah's own, pulled to the back of her neck into a thick knot, not a bit like Dolly's fuzz of wild redness, she wore clothes that at first Margaret thought were very dull. Soft smudgy colours and no frills at all, quite unlike Dolly's extravagant satiny dresses with their bright colours and brooches and necklaces of diamante. But after a while they didn't look so dull. They seemed to move on her when she moved to look different, changing their colours, making surprises. It was like the difference between that Sousa march she had learned once and the Fauré piece she was working on now. Delicate and quiet, and very, very clever.

And then she learned about eating. About not picking and choosing or talking about the food you were given – though it was different enough and exciting enough for Margaret to want to talk about it – and not letting the top of your fork show when you held it, and not holding your knife like a pen, but hiding the handle in the palm of your hand, and not making sounds with your mouth as you chewed, and not starting your food as soon as the plate was put in front of you but waiting for everyone else. A lot to learn about in just two days, but she learned fast. She had to, because Susannah told her, laughing as though it didn't matter, that things like that were worth getting right, it made it so much easier all round, didn't it?

She learned about living in a house so big that she couldn't remember where all the rooms were. The Creffield Road house had always seemed enormous, with its tangle of little rooms for the boarders, but now she knew it was cramped and crowded in a way that this house could never be. It had high wide rooms with low soft furniture in them, and great expanses of shining glass windows looking out on to trees and grass and more trees. It had broad shallow stairs, not a steep narrow climb like the one at Creffield Road. It had a big kitchen which was tidy and shining with pots and pans hanging on hooks, and an empty draining board, not the cluttered mess that was the Creffield Road kitchen where even Ida couldn't prevent the draining board from always being piled with dishes because the kitchen was so small for all that had to be done in it. This house was peace and comfort and music – for someone was always playing an instrument somewhere

123

– and felt to Margaret to be the most right place she had ever been in. She was bedazzled by it almost as much as she had been bedazzled by Susannah.

And then Daniel had come home, arriving from Paris on Saturday morning for the half-term break, they said, coming in a clutter of cases and presents and bottles of wine for his parents and laughter and noise. Susannah squealed and leaped at him, but he fended her off, lordly in his seniority, and Margaret stood and watched and fell even more deeply in love with Susannah and all her appurtenances.

Daniel was thirteen and as good-looking as the rest of his family, and kept lapsing into French and then translating himself with a casual ease in a way that was very impressive indeed. Margaret was happy to be impressed.

In the afternoon, after playing with Susannah in the garden with a croquet set Margaret was left alone for a while, because Papa and Muvver called Susannah in to play for them. 'Not an assessment, dear heart, just the joy of hearing you!' Papa said with loud bonhomie, winking at Margaret. 'Your young friend here will forgive you for a while, I'm certain, hey, little Margaret?'

'Oh, yes,' she said, and watched them go, feeling bleak suddenly. It was a very big garden, and the house looked huge and unwelcoming from where she was standing and for one brief moment – the only one in the entire weekend – she wished she was at home in Creffield Road.

'Well, let's hear all about you, then.' Daniel seemed to appear from nowhere, standing there with his hands in his pockets and looking down on her. 'Where did young Soos find you then?'

'I'm at school,' she said, after a moment of puzzlement. She hadn't been lost, so how could she be found?

'Are you, then! *Sacré bleu*, but the place must have changed! You're not precisely like the others who go there, are you? A right little cockney, hey?'

'Pardon?'

'Pardon!' he mimicked. '*Ma chérie*, do not, I plead with you sully the air with such an expression. It is not *comme il faut* – '

She stared at him, saying nothing, thinking how like his Papa he sounded, and he made a face and shook his head.

'*Nom d'un nom*, but you really are – tell me, what do you and Susannah *do* together? You've hardly much in common.'

She thought for a moment, not understanding, but holding on

124

to what she could pick out of his tangle of words.

'Do? Talk. Play games, things like that.'

'Fings like that – ' he said, mocking again. 'Dear heart, you can't have been at dear old Thomas Tallis long. Not sounding like *that*. How long?'

'How long what?'

'How-long-have-you-been-at-school-with-Susannah?' he said, enuciating each word as though she were an idiot, and she felt her face go red.

'Since September.'

'Six weeks – hmm. Well, I dare say you'll improve. Mind you, silk purses and all that.'

'Pardon? I mean – what?'

'I'm not sure what isn't worse than pardon,' he said, and moved closer, taking his hands out of his pockets, and folding his arms over his chest. He seemed taller suddenly. 'You're a right little cocksparrer, ain't yer?'

She knew she was being mocked, knew he was laughing at her, and couldn't work out quite why. Then other girls at school said things about the way she talked, and she knew she didn't speak as they did, but still she couldn't understand why, and she tried to do what she could to protect herself and could only do as Susannah would; she tossed her head as though she had curls to bounce around her ears and it seemed to work because he laughed, and unfolded his arms and took her chin in one hand.

'There's a pretty little girl then!' he said, and bent his head and kissed her, pushing his tongue between her lips in a way that first startled and then excited her. He closed his eyes, but she didn't, staring at his face as close to hers that it seemed to be distorted. This was kissing. This was what the girls at her other school had been on and on about. This was kissing.

She finished her steak and asked for coffee and leaned back in her chair. Daniel Goldman. Odd to remember him, after all this time. What had happened to him? For all his supposed genius he hadn't ever made any name for himself as far as she knew. Violinists – she cast her mind across the list of those whose names mattered, and his was nowhere. One of these days she'd find out, perhaps, if it mattered. If she ever played a gig in Israel, maybe she'd look up Susannah, living there with her husband and three children. She'd written to her a couple of years ago, a gushing

125

letter full of chat and exclamations, as though they'd never lost touch, being oh-so-casual about the fact that she'd seen reviews of Maggy's big London concert, the one that had got all the attention, pretending she hadn't been impressed.

Maggy's lips curved, remembering that letter. Still trying to put her down, after all this time, poor Susannah. Going on and on about her marvellous children, how clever they were, little Rivka's genius on the piano, young Adi, already composing, even the baby Uri positively crying in tune; how *satisfying* motherhood was, compared with a mere career. . . .

You're playing silly games, she told herself, stop it. Think straight. You've got into an orgy of nostalgia. Stop it.

Not nostalgia, another corner of her mind argued. Nostalgia is pleasant. Nostalgia is the Good Old Days, Wasn't It All Lovely?, but this is hurting. This is new, this is finding about what I was, how things were. Not wallowing in the familiar, the comfortable. This is a journey to my mother.

'No.' She whispered it aloud and then looked up, embarrassed. The place was filling up now, and she looked round for familiar faces, an old friend to share a drink with. Anyone would do to get her out of this flat sick mood she'd fallen into.

There was no one. Her eyes flicked over the tables, straining a little to see, for Joe Allen's basement was always dimly lit. And saw just the usual tight-trousered boys from the boutiques, the heavy men in crumpled sweaters from Bush House, talking interminably about Bulgarian broadcasts and the African service, a few early journalists, sour and tired at the end of another Fleet Street day, a man in a city suit, tidily eating a hamburger –

Her mind jerked then and she stared at him, almost furtively. Oh, God, is it that man again, the one who was following me? But then she relaxed and breathed more deeply, because she saw now that this man had a beard and was extremely tall; that his city suit was tacked on to a far from average person. This man was one she'd never seen before. But, Christ, she was getting uptight! Imagining trouble all the time. Mad.

Not so mad, really. She *had* been mugged, she *had* been followed, and those boys this afternoon at Mortimer Lang's house *had* been threatening. Ever since Dolly's death there had been real cause for her tension; she wasn't imagining it all, she wasn't. No one could say she was. Tonight, maybe, she'd got worried for nothing, but she was entitled, damn it.

126

Moving sharply, she pushed her coffee cup to one side and began to rifle in her bag, looking for a pen and paper. Writing things down had always helped her, making lists of things to do, problems to consider. And it would be something to do now.

She found an old envelope, and after a moment drew a line to make two columns and headed one 'Pros' and the other 'Cons'. And then sat and chewed her pencil end thought.

What was she getting from this search she'd started on? A lot of memories she didn't want, wasn't enjoying much. A lot of worrying about people following her. A dig at Ida, who wanted to get the Westpark to herself. The chance of money.

Money. She wrote the word in the column headed 'Pros' and contemplated it. Money. She'd never cared much about it, oddly enough, considering the sort of pinched childhood she'd had, the constant awareness of money problems that Dolly had carried round with her like an aura. She'd been dazzled by the Goldmans, all right, by their big house, their big car, the sheer luxury of their life, but it wasn't because of money. It was their self-assurance, the knowing-how of everything that was as much a part of them all as their riches. That was what had mattered.

And all through her career she had shrugged her shoulders at money. There had been offers of all sorts that would have made her big cash – like writing those jingles for catfood commercials. They'd offered her thousands for that, what with the repeat fees, but she'd refused, because it was such a tatty job they wanted. She'd chosen every job she'd done, every record producer she'd worked with, on the same basis; was it worth doing for the work's sake? Interesting? Satisfying? The money came last, always had.

So why was money important now? it must be, or why else would I be putting myself through all this instead of giving the Westpark to Ida and letting her have the headaches?

Because of Dolly. She knew that, now. At first, when all this had started – was it such a short time ago? It seemed to have been going on for months – she hadn't known what had motivated her, but now it was crystallizing in her mind. Now she knew she was looking for Dolly, for the reasons for all the things that had gone wrong, the source of the anger and pain that still filled her when she thought of her. Even in this past few days she had begun to get a different picture, a murky confused one, but one painted in softer more blurred shades than the one she'd been carrying in her head for so long. That picture was of a hard Dolly, all sharp

127

edges and violent colours and contrasts. The one she was finding, deep in her own memory as she replayed the course of their lives together, was different.

That's what I'm looking for. And I won't find it till I find out what it was she wanted me to know. So, where do I go from here? Where do I look? She said Morty would know, but he didn't.

Concentrate on what Morty did know rather than on what he didn't. He had said that two men who'd lived with Dolly for years, had ended up in prison. They'd stolen a lot of money.

Oh, God, she thought, as her memories pleated themselves together, does that mean that Dolly was a thief, too? She was stupid and careless of her feelings and –

Stop that. Was she a *thief*? She tried to visualize Dolly stealing, tried to see her taking things from shop counters, taking money out of a bank at the point of a gun, and wanted to laugh, then. Dolly? It was a ludicrous picture. Feckless, casual, off hand about money, yes, but the cold calculation needed to be a thief? Never. Not Dolly. Running up debts with an insouciance that by the time she was fifteen or so Maggy had found infuriating, being casual about her responsibilities in a way that seemed positively childish to the mature person Maggy believed herself to .be as an adolescent; but that did not mean she was also a real thief.

'Hornby,' Maggy whispered the name again, and wrote it down on the other side of her envelope. He was the key. There was no point in talking to Morty again, not at present anyway. Not unless she found out something else he could explain. The only lead she had to money at the moment was Hornby's name. So she'd have to find him. See where she went from there.

Miss Lucas. Why she thought of Miss Lucas then, she couldn't be quite sure. The school teacher who had taken her to Thomas Tallis and then told her she'd got a scholarship, the one who had come every year to the Open Days, had been so excited when she passed all her exams. Miss Lucas from Fletcher Street school, where it had all started. Why think of her?

Because she might know about that first journey to Thomas Tallis with Dolly. Did Hornby pay for my lessons? Did he send Dolly and me to T. T.? And if he did, what money did he use?

She began to laugh then, leaning back in her chair, alone at her table at Joe Allen's and laughing like a child, because of the ridiculous, terrible thought that her career, her whole career, had been based on someone else's stolen money.

14

She needed to get home now as urgently as she'd needed to get away earlier, and she paid her bill quickly and made for the door. On the way out she met Dan and Chalky coming in, and they greeted her loudly, wanting to buy her a drink, wanting her to turn round and come back in again. But her mood had changed, and she shook her head and at last they let her go, and she found a taxi in the Aldwych and sat and brooded heavily all the way to Royal Crescent. This thinking back, this remembering, was getting to be a habit, a small portion of her mind told her dispassionately. It's getting to be more important than the here and now.

No, it isn't, she argued back, staring out at the strolling tourists in Trafalgar Square and the pigeons who strutted, fat and scornful, among them. It's because of the here and now that I've got to do all the remembering. I'll never sort things out if I don't make myself remember.

The Crescent was quiet in the late evening sunlight, and she unlocked the front door and started to climb the first flight of stairs; and then, almost ashamed of herself, went back and propped the front door open, thinking – if there's anyone up there who jumps me, I'll scream and people out in the street will hear – and then unpropped it, realizing how much more dangerous it could be to give any passer-by easy access to the house.

But no one jumped her, and she let herself into the flat with a deep sigh of relief, and then almost leaped out of her skin as the bedroom door banged, and he said loudly, 'And where the hell have you been? I've been worried sick about you!'

'Theo,' she said after a moment and went into the living room and dropped her bag onto the coffee table. 'You frightened me. I didn't expect you back yet – '

'I frightened *you*!' He was wearing just a towel tied round his waist, and his hair was damp from the shower. He looked flushed and his face was tight. 'How the bloody hell do you think I've been feeling? I've been phoning you from Bristol every hour, and leaving Christ knows how many messages with the answering service and not a damned peep do I get out of you. What the hell have you been doing?'

'And what goddamned business is it of yours?' She turned on him, giving in to the luxury of losing her temper, putting on a show of being more angry than she was. 'Jesus Christ, you don't own me! I'm not a baby, you know, to be watched all the time! I was out, all right? O-U-T. *Out*. Dealing with my own affairs. Doing my own thing. None of your business!'

'None of my – listen, Maggy. I live here, right? With you, right? What's more I work with you, so I know what you're doing, usually, and where and who with. And I happen, fool that I probably am, to care about your welfare. All right? From where I stand that adds up to a perfect right to ask you where the hell you've been this past two days, when I've been trying to get hold of you. I know the only work you had to do was here, that you weren't due anywhere else, and when I couldn't get any answers I got worried, what with everything that's been going on. I should have stayed in Bristol another two days, but I couldn't – I had to come back and find out what was happening – '

She pulled off her jacket and walked past him into the bedroom. 'Oh, yes! I can tell how worried you were. I mean, first thing you do when you get here is take a shower, make yourself comfortable. Just the way to start a search for a missing person – '

He shot across the room behind her and took her shoulder in one hand and pulled her round and she stared at him, her chin up, feeling a wave of stubborn silliness rising in her. It was like being a small child again, deliberately being outrageous, deliberately sulking and being hateful when all Dolly wanted was for her to be nice and loving and warm, when most of her own self really wanted to be nice and loving and warm. But the stubborn silliness was more important and much more powerful, and she said tightly, 'Take your bloody hands off me,' and pulled away from him.

It wasn't deliberate; at least she didn't think so, but in pulling away she moved her foot and her high-heeled boot came down hard on his bare toes and his face whitened with the pain and almost as a reflex movement his hand came round and hit her face, hard, so that her head snapped back on her neck and her eyes filled with tears of pain and shock.

130

'You lousy bitch!' he shouted and hit her again, the other side of her face, so that her head snapped back the other way, and she lost her balance and fell against him and he held on to her tightly, trying to stay upright. And then they were both falling, tied together in a knot, landing heavily on the floor, she on top of him. They lay there breathless, both crying, and holding on to each other so tightly that she could feel his fingers pinching into her arm, causing a pain that was greater than the stinging on her cheeks or the aching of her neck. But she was glad of it, wanting to feel the hurt, because it made her feel right again, made her feel she was alive now, in the present, a separate living person, rather than just someone standing at the end of a long line of past experiences, looking backwards at old feelings.

'Oh, Christ, I'm sorry – ' he gasped and his fingers eased on her arm, and he tried to sit up, but she was still holding him down.

'Me too – ' she said, equally breathless, and turned her head so that her face was over his, and kissed him, more eagerly and hungrily than she could ever remember doing.

It had never been quite like this before. They'd been sleeping together now for over three years, but never had it been quite like this. She pulled at her own clothes, ripping them and not caring, sweating heavily as she twisted against him, and he was so urgent, so aroused, that she couldn't remember ever feeling so much pain; or liking it and needing it so much either. He seemed to be all sex, nothing but sex, as though his whole body had been converted into the huge pushing that filled her. It felt so good, so agonizing, that when she did come, bursting over the top into an explosion of feeling, it was more like anticlimax than climax; the least part of the whole experience.

And for him too the end seemed less important than what had gone before and they lay there, panting a little, not moving, eyes half-closed.

After a while he spoke, heavily, his voice sounding thick in his throat. 'I took a shower because it was something to do. There was nothing else I could do, was there? Just be here and wait and hope you'd come in.'

'It doesn't matter,' she said, and rolled a little, so that they separated at last and she stood up, gathering her torn clothes about her and got to her feet and went to the bathroom, still steamy and scented and littered with damp towels and his shaving gear. But it didn't irritate her, as sometimes evidences of his

131

occupation irritated her. It was comforting, reassuring, to see his razor beside her talcum poweder and bath oil, and she found herself whistling the theme from Lalo's Symphonie espagnole between her teeth, the way she always did when she was particularly content. She didn't whistle it very often.

He appeared at the door while she was in the shower; she could see him over the top of the glass screen as she stood there, letting the water run over her head, plastering her hair to her cheeks, and revelling in it, and she grinned at him through the water.

'You've got cream on your whiskers.'

'Eh?'

'Cat that got the cream. Pleased with yourself. Why does getting violent with sex make a man look pleased with himself?'

'You don't look precisely upset yourself. Very creamy in fact. Did I hurt you?

'Yes.'

'Should I apologize?'

'You dare. Next time the same. Please.'

'I'll tell him.'

'Without the fury, though – ' She turned off the water, and stepped out and he unhooked her robe from the wall and gave it to her. 'I don't need the fury. Just the violence.'

He grinned then, leaning against the door jamb, looking very relaxed and comfortable. He'd put on the black shirt again, over white drill trousers, and looked good and knew it.

'Any other orders?'

'I'll let you know. Dry my back for me – ' He did, and then rubbed in her afterbath lotion and she pushed and twisted herself against his hand like a happy cat, almost purring, and he slapped her buttocks lightly and pushed her away.

'Come on, get dressed. I'm starving. We'll go to that Greek place – at Notting Hill Gate. Andrea's.'

She shook her head, walking past him back to the bedroom and throwing herself down on the bed, enjoying the feeling of the fake fur spread against her moist skin.

'I've eaten.' She yawned then, and rolled over on to her side. 'Joe Allen's. Go get something from the fridge, hmm?'

'I've looked there, and it's damn near empty. Nothing but cottage cheese and yoghurt and that I can do without. I'll go over to Notting Hill and get a doner kebab, then. And some baklava. Do you want some?'

132

'Not a thing,' she said and yawned again, and her eyes closed and he laughed and kissed her, and she heard his footsteps going across the living room, and the front door of the flat close behind him as she fell asleep.

How long she slept she didn't know. Her eyes opened suddenly and her pulse beat heavily in her throat as she lay there startled, staring at the wall, and then it came again – the shrilling of the front door bell', far below.

He's forgotten his key, silly ass, she thought sleepily and rolled off the bed and went across the room, pulling her shoulders back into a small stretch as she walked. Her neck still hurt, and for a moment she forgot why, and then, remembering, grinned. The bell rang again and she pressed the button beside the door and muttered, 'Idiot! Come on then – ' into the intercom, and switched on the living-room light, because it was getting dark now, and went back to the bedroom.

But she didn't fall asleep again, and as the moments went by she found herself tightening. He ought to be up by now, for God's sake. It is a bit of a climb, but he's used to it after all –

And suddenly all her fears were out on spikes all over her so that she felt like a porcupine and she was tumbling off the bed, trying to run to the door of the flat to barricade it somehow, to keep whoever it was out. Oh, Christ, why didn't I look in the mirror? Why did I just press the damned button –

And then the door began to open, and suddenly aware of the fact that she was completely naked she turned and ran again, back to the bathroom this time, more frantic about being seen like this than about who might do the seeing.

Behind her the living-room light went out as someone flicked the switch and she stumbled, trying to move faster, reaching for her robe which was lying crumpled on the bathroom floor. But she wasn't fast enough; she felt the weight behind her of some-thing, and didn't know what she was feeling. Because she wasn't feeling anyting at all.

She opened her eyes to a painful brightness and closed them again, screwing up her face, and then felt the nausea huge and imperative in her belly and retched, and then someone was hold-ing her head and she was dreadfully, agonizingly sick, heaving and spitting and hurting abominably.

'All right, love, all right – hold on – there's someone coming

– ' Theo's voice very loud, very frantic, and again she was sick, and then let her head roll back as the nausea went, and she lay panting on the floor. It was as though time had slipped backwards and they'd been screwing on the floor and she had burst over the top again, and –

'Someone came in,' she said suddenly, creasing her eyes so that only the minimum of light could get in, staring up, looking for Theo's face. 'Oh, Christ, someone got in – rang the bell and I thought it was you without your key and pressed the button and then – '

'I know, love. Hold on. I know. No need to wear yourself out – oh, thank God!' Someone else was there, a man beside her, touching her head, making it hurt again, and she winced and said, 'What the hell – who – where – '

'Doctor, love. I took one look at you and called a doctor.' Theo said, and his voice was thick with anxiety. 'I should never have left her, I know I shouldn't have. I just didn't think – damn it. I should have thought – '

The doctor was shining a torch in her eyes, making her wince again, and then telling her to look at his finger, follow his finger, this way and that, and peering in her ears and her nose, and she felt suddenly as though she were on display in front of a huge jeering audience and tried to turn her head away from him, but he was relentless and went on and on, and Theo's voice in the background went on and on too, castigating himself, thick with fury and shame.

'She's all right,' the doctor said, and stood up. 'Here, help me and we'll get her to bed. Just a bit concussed – skin's a bit bruised, is all. No laceration. He didn't hit her all that hard, whoever he was – '

They were pulling on her shoulders and her legs and again she was dreadfully, shamingly aware of her nakedness and began to cry helplessly, and Theo murmured, 'It's all right, sweetie, all right. You've had a bad shock – easy does it – ' and then, at last, blessedly, she was in bed, under the covers, and could be a person again.

'Will she be all right? Should she be in hospital? Should I get a nurse?' Theo said anxiously, and she tried to shake her head at him, but it hurt too much.

'It'll take me half the night to get her a hospital bed. You know how it is these days,' the doctor said. 'As for a nurse – no, I don't

134

think so. Keep an eye on her, wake her up every hour or so to make sure you can – if she's sick again, or hard to rouse, call me. I'll fix a hospital bed for her then. Right now, I don't think it'll be necessary. She's got a hard head – '

She could see him more clearly now, a big shabby-looking man, and he looked down at her and said curiously, 'What did he want?'

'What?'

'The guy who did this. Not sex, obviously – ' He grinned at her, cheerfully, not in the least offensively. 'I mean, stark mother naked, and very nice too, and all you got was a bash on the head. Didn't you?'

She closed her eyes, trying to think. Sex? Oh, God, had he, whoever he was? Could that have happened? She moved her body experimentally and felt a terror deep inside, but whether that was a real sensation or just a memory of what had happened with Theo she couldn't be sure.

'Yes,' she said loudly, opening her eyes. 'Yes. That was all. I'd know if – it was just my head.'

'If you say so, then it was,' the doctor said and grinned. 'Women always know about these things, even if they've been knocked out. I don't think you were out for long anyway. Did you see anything when you came back?'

He was looking up at Theo now and Maggy turned her head and looked at him too. He was standing beside her, one hand protectively on her shoulder and looking wretchedly anxious, and she tried to smile at him, to resassure him. But it was too much of an effort; she was feeling incredibly weary now.

'I didn't look,' Theo said, his voice rather high and tight. 'I mean, I just came in, let myself in the front door – the street was fairly full of people, and I never looked at them – '

He stopped suddenly and wrinkled his eyes, thinking. 'Oh, shit! I heard someone go down as I came up, I'm sure I did. I passed the second floor and the light had blown – it's always blowing, that bloody light – and it was dark, and when I was halfway up the next flight I heard someone going down, but I didn't think anything of it. I mean, there're so many comings and goings in this house. The people who live in the flats, the people who visit – I didn't hear a door shut though, just someong going down. It must have been – oh, Christ, if I'd known! I'd have been after him like a – '

'Well, you didn't,' the doctor said practically. 'So no point going

135

on about it. Tell the police when they come. You've called them?'

'I didn't stop. Just called your number. If you hadn't been there I'd have dialled 999, I suppose – I was just frantic about Maggy – ' He looked down at her, squeezed her shoulder reassuringly. 'You're sure she's okay?'

'She's a strong healthy girl. It'd take more than tap on the bonce to hurt her for long. Go call the police, man. I'll wait here till they come, in case they need evidence. Less trouble than being called out again.' There was something almost avid about his interest, Maggy thought somewhere deep in her fatigue. He's too bloody interested. Maybe it was really he who came and hit me? Oh, Christ, here I go again. Suspecting everybody.

'Theo,' she said effortfully, and was almost surprised to find that her voice sounded normal. 'Theo, did he do anything else?'

'Anything else? Christ, Maggy, wasn't it enough?'

'I mean, take anything – ' She moved then, lifting herself up in bed. She was beginning to feel better. A lot better. 'He must have wanted something. Anything gone? There's the radio and the record player – have they gone?' Please say yes they have. Please let it be just a tatty little robbery. Then I can forget about it.

'I haven't looked.' He squeezed her shoulder again and went away and she could hear him moving about in the sitting room. The doctor sat beside her on the bed and put his hand on her wrist, checking her pulse.

'Nothing, as far as I can see.' Theo came back, standing beside the bed and looking down at her, his face creased. 'Everything looks fine. But he wasn't interrupted or anything – I mean, he must have already been half way down as I unlocked the front door downstairs, if it was the chap I heard – '

'Give me my dressing gown.'

'Now, Maggy, don't be silly! You've had a nasty wallop, for God's sake. Stay where you are – there's nothing to get up for, nothing at all. I've told you, there's nothing missing, and – '

'My dressing gown!' She was sitting upright now, holding on to the counterpane to cover her nakedness and glaring at Theo. 'I'm feeling better now, and there's something I've got to check. If you won't give it to me, I'll just pull the sheet off and use that.' And she began to tug at the sheet.

'Won't do her any harm,' the doctor said and stood up. 'I always reckon you can leave it to the patient. If she feels all right and wants to see something, let her, man. She'll rest better afterwards.

136

Where's your dressing gown, hmm? I'll get it.'

'I will,' Theo said furiously and did, and then helped her put it on, refusing to let the doctor help.

She felt a bit shaky when she stood up, but only for a moment, and then, holding her head in a gingerly fashion to prevent excessive movement that she knew would make it hurt again, she went into the living room, and over to the coffee table, and stood there looking down at it, knowing it had all gone. All except – and then she began to laugh weakly, holding on to the edge of the coffee table, bending almost double to reach it.

'What is it?' Theo was all anxiety again, and came and took her by the shoulders and led her back to bed, and she still laughed and the doctor watched from the bedroom door, fascinated.

'Get my jacket,' she said at length, when she was sitting on the edge of the bed. 'I dropped it in here when I came in – '

He looked, and found it where it had been kicked under the bed during their furious love-making on the floor and their glances locked for a moment as he brought it to her, both remembering at the same moment.

She put her hand in the pockets, riffling from one to the other, and then she found it and pulled it out.

'There, you see? That's all that's left. He's got all the rest. But this was in my pocket. Just like the key was the last time he tried – ' and she held up the photograph of Morty and Dolly and Andy.

'Just like the last time,' she said, and laughed again. And then cried, as suddenly as a baby, the tears rolling down her cheeks as she looked at Theo and the doctor, and they stared back.

15

She slept badly, waking, it seemed, every few minutes
and then feeling she hadn't been asleep at all, really. She thought
and dreamed and remembered and dreamed again, and couldn't
tell one from the other as images tangled themselves behind her
closed hot eyes.

Beside her Theo slept, infuriatingly, and at one point she lay
on her back, listening to him breathe and thinking sulkily, I could
be dead. The doctor told him to keep waking me up to make sure
I was all right, not unconscious or anything, and there he is,
sleeping like a pig, I could be dead. And then rolled over and
tried to sleep again, knowing herself to be absurd because
obviously she wasn't dead, so why be angry with him?

They had sat squabbling interminably after the doctor had at
last gone, about her refusal to let him call the police.

'What's the point?' she had said wearily. 'What can they do?
What did they do last time? Nothing, nothing at all. It's not even
as though it was a real robbery. All that's gone is a pile of old
papers and photographs and rubbish – why have the police prowl-
ing around over that? I couldn't be doing with it. No.'

'But for Christ's sake, Maggy, you can't go on being pushed
around like this! You've got to have some protection – '

'Protection? A fat lot of protection I'll get! They've got better
things to do, the police, than send a copper following me around
all day to keep off muggers. Even if they'd do it – which you
know damned well they wouldn't – can you imagine what life'd
be like being body-guarded? It's bad enough being jumped – I
couldn't stand being shadowed by a policeman as well – '

He'd given in at last out of sheer weariness, unhappily, and
swearing he'd have to act the protector himself if she refused to
get the professional kind. 'I'll go everywhere with you,' he had
promised, and yawned hugely, and patted her shoulder as she lay
with her back to him.

'No you won't,' she muttered into her pillow. 'I told you – I couldn't stand being shadowed by a policeman, so why should I put up with you?' But he'd fallen asleep, suddenly, too worn out to argue any longer.

And she had lain awake, trying to make some sort of sense out of the cat's cradle of events and memories and feeling a dull ache at the back of her head and in her neck and occasionally deep in her pelvis and not knowing which bothered her most. It's never like this in films, she thought at one point; people get bashed about and then jump up and they're fine, and I just had a little tap, the doctor said and I feel lousy, lousy, lousy –

I won't think about it, I won't think about the way I feel. I'll think about something else. Who was it? Who took that silly stuff from Dolly's safe deposit box? Who'd want it? Someone who knows about the money she's left. Someone who knows it's there somewhere, but doesn't know exactly where and wants to find it before I do. That's who. That's why they took the stuff. They're looking for my money.

Who wants my money? No, not mine, Dolly's. Who wants Dolly's lolly? That made her giggle, lying there with her pillow bunched under her head, the hot linen against her damp cheek. Dolly's lolly, Dolly's lolly, Dolly's lolly, and she crooned it silently over and over, using it as a lullaby, hoping it would send her to sleep. But sharply the spell was broken as Oliver's face seemed to come looming out of the red blackness behind her eyes and she snapped her lids open and stared at the luminous clock face on her bedside table.

Oliver? Would he have bashed her on the head to get that stuff? Maybe. He's never really been the violent type, as far as I know, but if he wants something badly enough, who knows what he mightn't do? Oliver. Just the sort of man who could knock out a naked woman and turn his back on her and not be interested –

Rubbish. Not Oliver, wet weak Oliver. Ida then. A woman could ignore another woman's nakedness easily enough, and she wanted the Westpark, didn't she? And that meant she'd want Dolly's lolly.

Maybe. What about Theo? Now you're really being mad, paranoid screaming mad. He didn't have to knock you over to get that stuff. It was on the coffee table when he came in. He could have taken the lot any time he fancied. Looked through it, got the information he wanted, whatever it was, and left it all there, and you none the wiser.

Hardly Theo. So who else? Mort and his bully boys? They don't even know where you live. How could they? They could have followed you. Seen you come to the house, worked out that your flat was the only one without a name over the bell. And the man in the city suit, what about him? Could he have –

You're a fool. You're not a policeman. What do you know about detecting? Stop trying, think about something else. Think about something else –

Think about Susannah. That'll do. Go on remembering, can't do any harm. That'll send you to sleep. Maybe.

Daniel following her all over the place, finding her whenever she was alone, kissing her. It had been weird, really weird, for she had found it exciting even though she didn't like him. He was as nasty as the girls at school, in lots of ways, talking at her instead of to her, laughing at her in that sneering way, yet whenever she was anywhere in the house on her own, there he was, waiting for her to come out of the lavatory, standing by her bedroom door whenever she went there to get something, his hands ready to hold her shoulders and her face, his busy red tongue alert to push itself wetly into her mouth. She didn't like it, felt his grip painfully hard on her skin, and yet he excited her, so that she began to find reasons to wander away from Susannah, went to the lavatory more often –

And then it was Sunday morning, and she had been there for half the weekend, though it felt as though she'd been there for years and years, in a sort of way. Sunday morning and the weather had changed. Rain pushed itself noisily down the wide windows, and a fire was lit in the biggest room with the lowest softest furniture and there was a drift of newspapers everywhere and they ate breakfast from a long low table in front of the fire. It's like a magazine, she thought at one point, sitting awkwardly on a sofa with her feet neatly side by side, trying not to look at Daniel sprawled in his pyjamas on the hearthrug, a plate of toast and smoked salmon in front of him. She didn't want to look at him because his pyjamas were thin and his skin seemed to shine through them, and that made her remember his kissing. It's like one of Dolly's film magazines with pictures of people eating biscuits or drinking hot chocolate, she thought, and experimentally ate some of her smoked salmon. It was salty and slippery and she

140

didn't like it much.

'Margaret, dear, after breakfast, I've got a plan for you,' Susannah's mother said and smiled at her, a small neat smile that didn't move her face very much. She was wearing a long yellowish-coloured dressing gown that looked soft enough to eat. Margaret found herself wanting to pick up a fold and chew it.

'Oh,' Margaret said, a little blankly. What was she supposed to say? 'Thank you.'

'You're a slender child, and there should be no problems,' Mrs Goldman murmured and smiled at Susannah who looked complacent. She was wearing a bright red dressing gown and very fluffy slippers that looked like bundles of feathers. Margaret, carefully dressed in her checked organdie, felt awkward, looking at them all. Papa was wrapped in a great shaggy green dressing gown with a hood on the back, with white pyjama legs sticking out underneath. Checked organdie. Oh dear.

'I'm sure your mother won't mind,' Mrs Goldman said serenly. 'These days, after all, it can be such a help to find a child marginally larger than one's own, don't you agree?'

'Oh, yes, of course,' Margaret said, and tried the salmon again. It seemed rude not to when they were all eating it, but it still tasted nasty. 'I'm sure too,' and didn't know what she was supposed to be sure about. Only that she was having a marvellous time. 'I'm having a marvellous time,' she whispered to herself, because she had to be sure about that.

The plan turned out to be a session in Susannah's room, going through her wardrobe. Susannah changed, put on trousers and a sweater, looking very daring, Margaret thought, for she had never worn trousers, and sprawled on her bed while her mother stood in front of the big wardrobe, taking out garment after garment.

'That should fit you, my dear,' she murmured, taking from its hanger a green plaid dress with a wide belt and white collar. 'Slip it on, there's a good child, and we'll see what we can do – '

Puzzlied and deeply embarrassed because of showing herself in her vest and knickers, but feeling obscurely it would be rude to refuse, Margaret obeyed.

'Yes, that's fine. Tell your mother it could do with being let down an inch, perhaps. There's plenty of hem. Now there's this one – it was always a little small for Susannah, so I'm sure it will be splendid for you – ' This one was a purple dress in a heavy material with ribs in it. Margaret hated it at sight.

'That's charming on you, dear,' Mrs Goldman said, standing back and looking at her with her eyes slightly crinkled, as though she were a painting. 'Don't you think so?'

'Oh yes,' Margaret said fervently. 'Lovely.'

And then there were skirts and jumpers, rather skimpy ones that were tight round her middle and made her chest itch, but she couldn't scratch and stood there miserably smiling while Mrs Goldman tweaked at them and nodded and Susannah watched, her lips curved into a contented line.

'What about the pink, Muvver?' Susannah said then, stretching out on the bed and lying with her arms behind her head. 'I've always loathed it – '

'Darling, that one cost a fortune! Surely you can – '

'I won't wear it,' Susannah said and grinned at Margaret. 'Not ever.'

'Oh well – ' Mrs Goldman sighed and took out the dress, a confection of deep pink silk, with tight long sleeves and a stand-up collar. Against Margaret's red hair it looked sickly and for a moment after she'd put it on Mrs Goldman looked at her doubt-fully, turning her to the mirror and staring at their reflections over Margaret's shoulder as Margaret too stared, trying not to let the colour upset her.

'It looked so lovely on Susannah, with her dark hair – ' she murmured. 'Darling, are you sure – '

'Positive,' Susannah said firmly. 'You have it, Margaret. It's nice. Cost a fortune.'

'I – ' Margaret began, not looking at the dress, feeling worse and worse. 'It's – thank you.'

'There, dear,' Mrs Goldman said expansively. 'I'm sure that will help at home. Talk to your mother about some shoes to go with them, won't you? Patent leather – not quite right at your age – ' and she drifted out of the room, leaving Margaret standing there in the pink dress feeling as though she'd been punished for doing something unspeakable. Which was an odd way to feel when you'd just been given things.

'There!' Susannah said and got to her feet. 'Isn't that nice for you? And won't your mother be pleased? Muvver says it must be frightful to cope as a woman alone – she's going to let you have all my things when I'm finished with them. Say you're pleased.'

Margaret took the dress off, pulling it over her head, trying to hold on to the fact that she'd been given presents, but it didn't

142

work. She felt the tears pushing out of her eyes and her nose running and she couldn't stop it happening. It was dreadful.

'There!' Susannah said, delightedly. 'I knew you'd be grateful. But you don't have to cry – put the green one one, now, and we'll go and play with Daniel. He's changed ever such a lot since he went to France, but I suppose that was inevitable. I think I'm going to ask if I can go, later. It seems madly sophisticated, doesn't it?'

'Madly,' Margaret said obediently, and put on the green plaid dress. What else could she do?

Dolly looked at the things spread on the bed, and picked up the purple corduroy between two fingers, distastefully, and let it go.

'She gave them to you? Why?'

Margaret shrugged, not looking at her. 'I don't know. She just said I was to have them.'

'What does she think you are, for God's sake? Some sort of workhouse brat?' Dolly said, and Margaret had to look at her now, for she sounded different. Her voice was blurred, the words coming out more countrified than usual. The London sound that was usually there, and which was so much part of Margaret's own speech, seemed to have gone. 'I don't take no hand-outs from some Lady Bountiful, and never let it be thought I do! Who does the bloody woman think she is, then, givin' you her cast-offs? You just take them back an' tell her she can take 'em down the church jumble sale and not go treatin' you as though – '.

'I can't,' Margaret said flatly.

'You can and you will, my duck! I'm not havin' you made some sort o' charity object by these damned – '

'It would be rude to take them back. Unsophisticated.' Margaret said, wanting to shout, sick about the whole affair. She didn't want the dresses either, hated them, felt the humiliation of the Goldman's lazy generosity as sharply as she had ever felt anything, but it was her friend, her Susannah, and no one, no one at all, was going to spoil things with Susannah.

'Un – what did you say? My God, but they've taught you some strange things at that damned school o' yours! You were better off at Fletcher Street, that you were. Them an' their fancy ideas and fancy talk an' bloody insults. I never ever heard o' such a thing – '

It was rare that Dolly was angry and looking at her now Margaret was suddenly afraid. Her face was blotchy, and her eyes were wide and staring so that Margaret could see the whites at the top as well as at the bottom of the pupils and it gave her a mad look that made Margaret want to cry, made her want to run and throw her arms round her neck and hide her face in her shoulders, so that she couldn't see that furious glare. But then she'd have to take the dresses back and be rude to Susannah and that wasn't to be thought of –

'I shan't take them back, I shan't! And she's right, Mrs Goldman, she's right! I wear all the wrong things and I talk wrong and the other people laugh at me and I hate you, I hate you. I won't take them back – '

It wasn't the first time she'd found refuge in shrieking and she began to shriek now, stamping and shouting until, suddenly, Dolly hit her and the shock was so profound, for Dolly never hit anyone, that she was silent at once, not even sobbing or panting, just standing and staring back at her.

'Now, there, see what you made me do!' Dolly was all contrition, her soft overwhelming self again, all widespread arms and crumpled face, but this time Margaret wasn't going to let herself be swept up and hugged and fed on hot milk and cake. She pulled back, folding her arms across her narrow chest and staring at Dolly with her face twisted and tight.

'I didn't make you do nothing – anything.' Even as she corrected herself she could hear Susannah's light high laugh. 'You might as well get it right, Margaret. One just doesn't say *do nothing* that way – ' and she scowled even more. 'All I did was tell you I can't take these back. I don't want to take them back. I've got to have something better to wear than I've got – they all laugh at me at school when I change to come home. All of them. It's horrible. My shoes are wrong too – '

'Such fancy notions – ' Dolly said, but she sounded uncertain now, and Margaret pushed home.

'I want new shoes, and a new coat, and better dresses of my own. I want to be like the others. They don't like me because I'm not like them.'

'I knew it! I knew as it'd be like that!' Dolly threw herself down on the bed and sat with her knees hunched up, staring at Margaret over her folded arms. 'I said when it all started as it'd be all wrong for you. Piano lessons fine, I says, she's got a talent o' course, piano lessons. It was my idea, but why such a fancy school an'

144

all? Can't she have her piano-playing lessons separate like? I said. But no, he would have it it was the best – '

'Who did?'

'Eh? Oh, it don't make no never mind! Listen, my duck, wouldn't it be better to go back to Fletcher Street and we'll ask Miss Lucas to arrange for separate lessons for you? Eh? Won't that be better than all this traipsin' off across half London an' having all these horrible girls givin' you notions and – '

'Who made me to to Thomas Tallis? Miss Lucas said I got a scholarship.'

'And so you did, my duck, so you did, clever girl that you are an' all. You got a scholarship to that fancy school like Miss Lucas said, but I don't know – it's not workin' out like I thought it would. I wanted you to get your piano-playing an' all, it was all my idea at first, that bit of it, but now, I don't know – it just isn't working right, is it? Goin' away weekends an' coming home all shook up like this, and people treatin' you like a measly charity child – '

She sat and stared at Margaret, broodingly, her face still crumpled, and Margaret stared back, silently. She's not talking about the dresses now, she thought. I won't have to take them back. I wish I did. I hate them. But Susannah – '

'I want to stay at T T,' Margaret said flatly. 'It isn't fancy, and the music is very good and I'm learning a lot. Mrs Cornelius says I'm very good indeed.'

'I know. They've said all along as you're exceptional an' all that, but I don't know – it's making it different with you. You used to be my girl, my lovely girl, but now you're all – '

'I'm not anything,' Margaret said. 'I'm all right. It's everyone else who makes fusses. I'm all right.' And she picked up the pink dress and went to the wardrobe and took out a hanger. Dolly said nothing, sitting there and watching her and she knew she had won. She'd keep the dresses, and she'd keep on going to the school. But there was something that wasn't all right, and she didn't know what it was, and she felt very tired inside, tired and flat.

Maggy, opening her eyes to look again at the clock, thought drearily, bloody Susannah. She really did put the mockers on me, one way and another. Poor Dolly! It must have been hell having me come home and trot out all that snobbish stupid rubbish. But

145

she let me, and said nothing. Why?

Because she loved you, whispered the clock back at her. Its hands were set at ten to two, and looked like a long sad smile, like Dolly's face. She thought it was what you wanted, so she let you sneer at her and be ashamed of her and didn't say a word.

She cried for a while then, not sure why she was crying. The pain in her head? Probably. But after a while the tears stopped and she slept, heavily, till next morning.

16

And woke full of certainty. She knew what she was going to do, even how she was going to do it.

She moved, experimentally, and her back ached a little, was stiff and felt bruised, but her headache was gone. There was just a sore spot there when she touched her scalp gingerly, and she slid her legs out of bed, quietly so as not to wake Theo, and padded to the shower. Her backache was due to yesterday afternoon's thrash, she decided; that had left more evidence on her than the tap on the head, and she grinned a little as she soaped herself, looking forward to telling Theo that.

He came rushing into the bathroom as she dried herself, standing swaying a little in the doorway and blinking at her. 'Maggy! you frightened me – for heaven's sake, come back to bed at once! You need to rest – '

'Oh, balls,' she said cheerfully. 'I'm fine. Just got a sore patch under my hair, that's all. I've got more bruises from you than I ever got from him! Give me an aspirin and make some coffe, there's a good chap. And put some clothes on, for pity's sake. You make me feel cold to look at you – '

He tried to object, fussing over her until she had to snap at him, but he gave in at last, washing and shaving and dressing with his usual speed and then making breakfast. She was happy to sit in the living room staring out at the summer morning sky and let him get on with it; it gave him something to do and now she was dressed she did feel a little shakier than she would have admitted to him.

But coffee and hot toast and honey helped and she ate a lot more than she usually did and they listened to the radio for the news, and Theo too seemed to relax, believing at last that she was all right.

'Theo, love, I've not been to the studio all this week, and I think someone ought to, don't you? You know how they are – all sorts of cock-ups happen unless you make a nuisance of yourself

– will you go in and see how they're doing? You might have to go over to the factory, too, if the master's already gone there. I'd feel happier if it was checked before they went right into production – '

He looked at her doubtfull. 'Will you be all right on your own? I hate to leave you – '

'Now, let's not be daft! I'm safe enough as long as I only answer the bell to people I know, right? I'll look every time, I promise.' And I'll keep the promise, she told herself. If I'm here.

'You'll rest? You've had more of a shock than you know – '

'You heard what the doctor said last night. Trust the patient. I'll do only what I feel like, not a bit more, I promise.' And I feel like doing a lot.

'I ought to go, I suppose. I mean, there's tapes I've brought back from Bristol – there's a group there, got a good heavy sound. If I don't line 'em up fast someone else'll be in there. There was a Decca man at the concert the last night – I really should go in – ' He looked at her, his expression uncertain. 'I just don't want to think of you alone here and someone – '

'I told you. I'll only answer the door to people I know. There's nothing to fret over – you're being a bit of an old woman, you know – '

'Yes. I know. And I'm going to go on being. I do love you, Maggy.'

'Do you?' she said lightly. 'There's a comfort. After yesterday afternoon – '

He grinned, his eyes brightening. 'It really was something, wasn't it? Fan-tas-tic – ' He was silent for a moment, looking at her. 'I love you a lot.'

'I know.' She smiled then, putting out a hand, touching his sleeve. 'I know.' And I think I love you. Some of the time, anyway. I think I do. But she said nothing, just smiling and after a moment he nodded and stood up.

'I'll be back as soon as I can. No later than three or so.'

'Great.' I can be there and back by then, and he'll know nothing about it. Not that I care if he does, really. It's just that –

That it could, just possibly, have been Theo who walloped you last night, couldn't it? Until you know for sure who it was, you can't take any risks with anyone.

Leaving the flat took all the courage she had. She looked out of the window first, twisting her neck to see the street below, looking for loafers, watchers, anyone unusual, but there was no one who seemed at all odd; only passers-by, hurrying along, patently uninterested in anything but their own affairs.

She ran down the stairs, singing loudly, feeling foolish, but wanting to be heard, feeling obscurely that if anyone did hit her again and the singing stopped suddenly as a result, the neighbours would hear and come out to investigate –

But there was no need, for she reached the street and stood on the top step, breathing fast and pulling her jacket about her. For all it was summer the air was cool, and anyway she felt safer with her clothes fastened firmly about her. Absurd, but that was how she felt.

She looked at the car and nearly took it, and then decided against it. If it was gone, they'd know she was out, might try to get into the flat again.

Who would? Who would know which was her car, after all? The silly questions pushed against her ears as she walked to the corner and waited, watching for a taxi. Silly questions with no answers.

When she arrived she stood outside for a moment, staring up at the building. It looked the same, just as it always had, but in half scale. It had shrunk to a miniature of the vast palace of a building she had remembered to become an ordinary London primary school, red brick, arched entrances to the playgrounds with 'Boys' and 'Girls' carved on the lintels in self-important lettering, battered grey dustbins clustered round the caretaker's entrance at the side.

Inside it was even more familiar; the long polished wood-floored corridors with their green and cream painted walls no longer stretched into infinity but otherwise they looked the same and certainly smelled the same; plimsolls and Jeyes fluid and chalk and sick. Comfortingly, frighteningly, familiar.

There were sounds coming from all directions; a piano being played badly somewhere, thump, thump, *thump*, and children's voices chanting and a man's voice shouting. Outside there was traffic, heavy roaring traffic. She'd forgotten how close to the main road the school was, how much a part of her time here that traffic din had been, and she felt better, knowing that the same buses and the same lorries were grinding past now as had done nearly thirty years ago. Nearly thirty years. Oh, my God.

She walked along the corridors, turned left, went up the stairs, then right and along that corridor, knowing exactly which way, and then there the door was. 'Staff Common Room,' it said on a battered panel, just as it always had.

She tapped, and someone called faintly, 'Yes?' and she walked in, feeling that little surge of terror that had always seized her when she passed this threshold. There was something sinful about being in here, even when you were told to come in, something special and exotic and, in a way, dangerous. Would they ever let you out again, once they got you there? Would they all sit and stare at you and strike you blind and dumb and deaf? It used to make her shiver nearly thirty years ago, and she shivered again now.

'I'm looking for Miss Lucas,' she said, standing in the doorway, looking round. Small, of course; she was getting used to that effect. And cluttered, with walls covered with notices and posters and chairs scattered about and tables piled high with exercise books and magazines and stained coffee cups.

There was only one person, a thin girl in jeans and a heavy sweater, her lank hair hanging greasily over her face.

'Oh. Miss Lucas – yes – ' She pushed the hair away from her eyes and stared at Maggy, and Maggy stared back, puzzled for a moment. Is this what teachers looked like now? The people she remembered were all grey, all over grey. Grey hair, grey dresses, grey legs, grey faces. And old, old, old. Like Miss Lucas was old.

'Are you a mother? Because you know, the staff *do* like parents to make appointments – it does help so – '

'No, I'm not a mother.' She grinned at the thought, and shoved her hands more deeply into her pockets. She was looking good and was suddenly aware of the fact as the girl stared at her. She'd put on her Bill Gibb alpaca jacket over the dress Ossie Clark had made for her, and her hair was brushed up and shiny. I must look incredibly exotic to someone so dreary, she thought, childishly pleased with herself, and grinned again. 'I'm an old girl, actually.'

'Oh.' The girl in jeans looked unimpressed. 'Is that why you want to see Miss Lucas?' And Maggy was deflated sharply. How absurd to be a grown woman and come visiting the primary school you once went to. She must think I'm mad, she thought, and felt her face redden slightly.

'In a way. I mean, there's some information I need – '

But the bejeaned girl had lost all interest in her. 'Her room's down the hall, fifth door on the left. The bell'll go in about five minutes. Wait outside and see if you can catch her – ' She had her head down over a pile of exercise books and didn't look up when Maggy said, 'Thanks,' and went out. She slammed the door behind her, not loudly, but a slam all the same; cocky madam! Just because she was a teacher, she didn't have to make her feel as though she'd crawled out from under a stone.

Waiting outside the classroom door, hearing the soft buzz of children's voices from inside, was the oddest part of the morning so far. For the first time the building enlarged again, became as big and as enveloping as it had been all those years ago when she had been nine years old; it was as though her own stature had dwindled and she was Margaret Rose again, small and vulnerable and always worried about something, not grown up sophisticated Maggy.

Grown-up and still worried, she whispered to herself, and then straightened her shoulders. She was being absurd, quite absurd. Last night's experience must have addled her brains, for what was there to worry about here? She'd come for information, confirmation of something she suspected, a something which might lead her to find her mother's money. That was all. Just information.

The bell when it rang made her jump, and the door burst open and children came out in a cataract, small, noisy and exhaustingly energetic. Was I like that? she wondered, watching them leap along the corridor, thumping each other, bouncing and clattering. Was I ever such a powerhouse?

She went into the classroom hesitantly and stood looking at the woman behind the desk, watching her writing. Tall, rather bulky, with thin mousy-coloured hair frizzed up to look as though it were thick, and wearing glasses. Otherwise she looked much as Maggy remembered her, and that came as a shock. Because after nearly thirty years, surely she ought to be apple-cheeked and white-haired, a doddery old woman using a stick? This woman looked about sixty or so, which meant that when Maggy had known her first she was little more than a girl. Younger than I am now, Maggy thought. Yet I remember her as being so *old*.

And suddenly she realized how absurd she had been to expect to find her at all after so long. And how much greater was the absurdity of the fact that she *had*.

Miss Lucas looked up, peering through her glasses and smiling

151

thinly.

'Yes? Can I help you?'

'Hello, Miss Lucas.'

'Er – hello. Were you looking for your child? They've all gone now. I'm afraid – ' And she looked round the room a little vaguely, as though a child might be hiding under a desk somewhere.

'No. I'm looking for you. How are you?'

'I beg your pardon?'

'How are you? You're looking – well. Hardly any different.'

Miss Lucas took off her glasses, and put them on again, a wide distracted movement that clearly had nothing to do with her ability to see, and then stood up.

'Oh dear. You must be one of my old girls, I suppose. Oh dear, oh dear? This keeps on happening, and I always feel so bad about it, but really, it's not my fault! I have a new class every year, you know, forty children every year and I've been here for – well, it's ridiculous, it's so long! I can't possibly *remember* everyone, can I? And of course, bless you, you will all go and grow up!' She laughed then, a pleasant fat laugh that lifted her face and made her look quite young. 'Now, let me see. How old are you? That will help me – if you don't mind my asking! Come and sit down and let me have a good look at you!' And she pushed her own chair towards Maggy and perched on the edge of her desk.

'I'm Maggy Dundas. You knew me as Margaret Rose. I play the piano,' Maggy said flatly, watching her face and Miss Lucas sat and stared at her, blankly at first and then, remembering, began to nod, slowly, her head bobbing up and down like a mandarin.

'Margaret. Margaret Dundas who played the piano. Oh, dear me, but I wondered about you! So often I wondered about you, but there, it's been a long time and I haven't thought for years – well, well. Margaret Dundas. My dear girl, whatever happened? Why didn't you – I mean, I always expected great things of you, great things! I used to watch the concert reviews, you know, and the advertisements for the various halls and I never saw your name – I wondered if you'd changed it, perhaps! Have you given up music?'

Maggy wanted to laugh then. 'No, I haven't given up. In fact, I'm doing very well. I'm off the to the States soon for a series of big concerts, and I've just made a new album – I'm really doing

152

very well indeed.'

Miss Lucas looked blank.

'I play jazz,' Maggy said gently, and then smiled even more widely at the look of surprised disappointment that moved across the other woman's face.

'Oh,' she said, opening her eyes rather widely. 'Well, well. Jazz you say? How very nice.'

'You said that as though it were an attack of the measles. It's quite respectable, you know.'

'Oh, dear, I'm sorry! It's just that – well, I'm old-fashioned, I suppose, but at my age I'm entitled to be! You were good, you see, had such classical potential. But I suppose one has to make a living – '

'Not at all,' Maggy said, nettled now. 'I could have made just as much money out of the Chopin and Beethoven circuit. More, maybe. It's just that jazz is my kind of music. It excites me. I can – I can get inside it, myself. Chopin makes you play Chopin. Jazz lets you play what you are, when you are. Music ought to be personal. I'm more than just a damned craftsman, you know! Anyone can be taught to play the great classics – me, I play *me*, I build on the composers – Stravinsky and Purcell and – '

'I'm sure you do,' Miss Lucas said mildly and Maggy laughed again, after a moment.

'I'm sorry. I do get a bit heated, I suppose. You're not the first to be offhand about my stuff, you see, so – well, I'm sorry.'

'I'd like to hear you some time,' Miss Lucas said politely. 'Perhaps you can educate me.'

'I'll send you a record.'

'That would be very kind.'

There was a little silence and then Maggy said abruptly, 'I need your help, Miss Lucas. I'm trying to find out something. You can help me.'

'I? My dear girl, I can't imagine – '

'It's about me at Thomas Tallis School. Can you remember about what happened when I went there?'

Miss Lucas stared at her, her eyes opaque behind her heavy glasses and then her gaze slid away over Maggy's shoulder so that she seemed to be looking at something small and very far away.

'Remember? I can't say, really. I mean, it must be – how long since you went there?'

'I was ten. 1951.'

'1951 – my dear girl, that's getting on for – '

'Yes. Getting on for thirty years ago. Still and all, I thought you might remember. I mean not many children from this school went to T. T., did they?'

'No. Not many.'

'Only me, in fact.'

'No. There was another. About twenty years ago, that was. She was violin. A splendid talent, splendid. She – well, she never achieved much, either – oh, I'm sorry! I didn't mean that the way it sounded. But I'd always hoped, you know, to find myself a little Myra Hess or a Harriet Cohen, a great concert performer – '

'You took me there. I remember that. And you told me I'd got a scholarship,' Maggy leaned forwards, watching the older woman closely. She hadn't the most expressive face in the world, but still she was worth watching. 'Was that true?'

'Ture? I don't – how do you mean?'

'Did I really get a scholarship? Or was someone else paying for me, and not wanting that known? That's what I need to know. Did someone else pay my fees there? It was a very expensive place – '

Miss Lucas bent her head, looking down on her hands in her lap. 'Really, my dear, after so long – you do ask a lot – '

'No. Not a lot. Just some information. You see – my mother's dead. She died a few weeks ago. I'm trying to – '

'Dead?' Miss Lucas looked up, her face smoothing, making her look young again. 'Oh. Oh, I see. I'm sorry. And I suppose that does – well – '

'She left me a lot of problems. Financial ones. But she also left information that would solve those problems. I really can't explain properly – you see, she didn't give me all the information I need. I have to find some of it for myself. And I have an idea that – '

'She wanted you to know what happened, you mean?'

'Wanted me to know? Well, yes, I think she did. We – I have to tell you we weren't on very good terms. We – I didn't spend much time with her in the last few years. There were reasons – I won't bother you with them now. But she left a will, you see, and a safe deposit box – but, oh, this sounds all so confusing – '

'Your mother.' Miss Lucas was staring out of the window now, her lips curved into a faint smile. 'Oh, but I liked her! I was the only one here who did, you know! The headmistress then, I remember her well, told me the woman was no more than a – oh, there I go again! I'm sorry, my dear, I don't mean to be so rude but – '

'You're not being rude. And she was. Dolly was – awful. Noisy and vulgar and – '

'She was fun,' Miss Lucas said. 'She made me laugh. I liked her.'

'Yes. People did. But you didn't have to live with her, did you?'

'No, I suppose not. But – she did try so hard for you, you know.'

'Please, Miss Lucas, will you tell me what happened? *Did* I have a scholarship?'

Miss Lucas shook her head. 'No. You were put in for one, but they said you had the wrong temperament. Talent, they said, but not the temperament to make a first-flight performer, and scholarships only went to those who had – well, who could be sure to do well for the school. That's what they said. But I knew you could do it and I told your mother so. Told her you ought to be there, and to try again. But she came back, with – with a friend.'

Her voice changed and her gaze slid away, so that she was looking out of the window again.

'A friend, she said, wanted to pay the fees for you. They asked me if I could persuade the school to take you as a fee-paying pupil, so I did. But they wanted you always to think you had a scholarship – '

She turned her head and looked at Maggy again then. 'I'm afraid, my dear, that the scholarship was refused not because of you but because of your mother. She was so – well, she wasn't their sort of parent, you know!' She laughed then. 'Oh, but they were full of themselves at Thomas Tallis School. They could get away with it of course, because they were so very good – they really were the best music school there was then, so they could pick and choose, and they didn't choose your mother. And she knew it. That's why she said you were to be told it was a scholarship, and why I took you for your entrance exam and why she never used to come to the concerts and end of terms. I went for her. She was a very sensible woman, your mother, you know. Had no illusions at all.'

Maggy said nothing, staring at her, trying to see Dolly as she was that day they had first gone to T. T. She could remember her own new shoes, could remember her own clothes, the blue coat, the matching hat, but Dolly – what was it about her that had

155

made them refuse to accept her child? Suddenly her eyes felt hot and dry. It's anger, she told herself, anger. I'm not upset. I don't want to cry, I'm just *angry*.

'And her friend – well, he wanted to do whatever she wanted, he said. So there it was. I paid the fees for you with money they gave me. And you were told you had a scholarship. I would never have said anything, you know, if your mother were still alive – but now she's dead – it's good for you to know, don't you think? She was really – '

'Yes, I know. She was really – ' Maggy said. 'Really something. Who was he?'

'I beg your pardon?'

'The friend. Who was he?'

Again Miss Lucas looked blank and Maggy leaned forwards. That look, she was learning, only appeared when Miss Lucas was trying to decide whether to answer or not. 'She wanted me to know, really she did. She left me a message to say there was money available to sort out the financial problems she left, but didn't say where. But she wanted me to know.'

There was a long silence and then Miss Lucas sighed, a soft, tired sound. 'Oh, well, after all this time – and they're – well, he was not a very nice man, I'm afraid. Hornby, his name was.'

'Jim Hornby. I rather thought so.'

'Yes. Well, afterwards, I mean, once you'd started there at Thomas Tallis, there was a great fuss because, you see – well, he – ' Her voice dropped. 'He went to prison.'

'A wages robbery.'

'My dear, you know! Then why ask – '

'Because I don't know all of it. I don't know what happened to him after he went to prison.'

Miss Lucas shrugged. 'I don't know either. You'd left here by then, of course, being at Thomas Tallis, and your mother came to see me one day at my flat and gave me – oh, a lot of money. Enough to pay your fees for the next five years. She trusted me, you see – I appreciated that. And I paid your fees, and that was that. I never saw her again, or you, after you left Thomas Tallis. All such a long time ago – '

'I'm sorry,' Maggy said after a moment. 'I suppose I should have kept in touch.'

'Yes, I suppose you should.' Miss Lucas smiled. 'But people of fifteen or so are never quite as – well, you're grown-up now, and

156

here you are. And very nice too. It's so pleasant to see what happens to one's children over the years. So many of them, you know. Forty a year, for thirty-five years. I'm retiring soon, I'm afraid. Got to. I thought I'd teach piano privately, instead of just here at Fletcher Street. Not that parents care as much as they used to. Your mother cared. She was one who wanted the best for you, always – '

'Hornby – please, Miss Lucas, Hornby.'

'Well? What about him?'

'What happened to him? After prison, I mean?'

She shook her head. 'Oh, my dear, I'm afraid I haven't the least idea! None at all. I never saw them again, you see.' She looked mournfully at Maggy, clearly saddened at her own inability to help, and then her face lifted a little. 'I can remember one thing, though – one thing that might help. He came from my own home city, you know. We made a joke about it, even though I didn't like him. He said the town was always said to be poor, proud and pretty, and I could have the pretty bit and the proud bit, but he was going to do away with the poor bit – a silly joke, really.'

'Where – '

'Cheltenham, my dear. They call it the poor, proud and pretty city. Didn't you ever hear that? In Gloucestershire.'

Maggy felt it lifting in her again, the cold anger that Dolly used to make her feel, the sick fury, the – 'No.' She said it aloud very hard and sharp. 'No – '

'Yes – indeed, not far from where your mother came from. We made quite a thing about it, all three, being from the same sort of area. Only she came from Cirencester. But then, I'm sure you knew that, didn't you?'

17

    Cirencester. The very sound of the town's name made her feel sick. She thought she'd got over it, long ago, thought she'd come through the whole silly business and out the other side, because after all, who cared, these days? What did it matter where you came from, who your parents were? It hadn't really mattered then, if she were to be honest.

It mattered to me. It mattered dreadfully to me.

'I – thank you. I really shouldn't have bothered you.' She was on her feet now and Miss Lucas was blinking up at her, mild behind her heavy glasses.

'It's been so pleasant to see you again. I hope I've been of some help?'

'Oh, yes. A lot of help. A great deal. I'm very grateful. It was good of you to spare the time.' Stop gabbling, you fool. Shut up and get out. Stop gabbling.

'You musn't *mind*, dear, really you mustn't. I mean, the way things were about your poor dear mother. She was a happy soul, and *she* didn't care. She knew the people at Thomas Tallis looked down on her, but she didn't think it was important, any more than I did. It made it – oh, much more fun to beat them, you know? We were all so amused, afterwards, that they hadn't remembered you, when I took you back the next year. It really was quite funny, wasn't it, when you think about it? And as for Mr Hornby – well – ' She stood up, shrugged. 'Anyone can make a mistake, can't they? I never thought it was so dreadful, prison and so on. They did here, of course, you know how people talk, but I said to them then, and I meant it, his only fault was being found out. The world's full of people everyone looks up to and admires and kowtows to, as long as they don't get found out for what they really are. He just got caught – '

'I'd forgotten how much she talked, Maggy thought, as the words went on and on, and she moved slowly towards the door. She talked a lot then, and I'd quite forgotten.

158

' – and as for who paid your fees – well, there again, what does it matter? I mean, dear, the important thing is your talent was recognized and you were taught, that's really the *important* thing, isn't it? And I'm glad you're enjoying what you're doing now, and I'm sorry I didn't know about the jazz, but there, I've always been classical, you see, my wireless is positively rusted on to the Third Programme!' She laughed then, and held out her hand. 'You'll come and see me again? It's so nice to hear from my old children, and I'm retiring soon, you know, going to teach piano privately if I can – '

'Yes, of course I'll keep in touch, I really will.' Let me get out now. Please let me get out now and think a bit, will you? Do stop talking –

'And I hope you find what it is you're looking for. This financial thing – fortunate I never cared much for money – which is just as well, seeing I never made any!' She laughed merrily, and her glasses glinted in the sunlight.

A bell rang somewhere and the noise began again, children thumping, shouting, rushing in the corridors. Gratefully Maggy pulled the door open.

'They're back, I see – play-time over? Yes – thanks so much – very kind of you, thanks so much – ' and at last she was away, hurrying along the corridors, smelling the Jeyes' fluid and the plimsolls and feeling the tight feeling in her throat the way she had when she'd first found out.

Coming back to London from Deal, sitting in the train, watching the soft Kent countryside dribble away past the windows, thinking how it will be when she gets there, not knowing how awful it's going to be.

Thinking about Gerald. Gerald who had been so exciting and handsome and *special*. And old. At least thirty-five. Gerald who had been chosen to be The One. Gerald who had come to the Little Theatre under the railway arches at Gunnersbury and been so sweet to her, and made her laugh and took her out to buy her coffee and cheesecake –

But that was all over. *She'd* ruined all that, and sixteen-year-old Maggy, sitting in the train chattering its way across Kent to London broods heavily on what she's suffered. Plans how she'll be when she sees her, practises the cool stare, the uncaring lift of the chin, the offhand way she'll be. She'll have to give up then,

159

she'll have to let me do what I like then, I'll make her. I'll be so horrible to her she won't be able to make me stay there. She'll have to let me go.

But it wasn't like that. It wasn't like that at all.

I don't want to go through all this again, do I? Why do I have to remember all this? Maggy sat in the Wimpy Bar, the only place she could find near the school where she could sit down, and stirred the muddy lukewarm coffee the bored waitress put in front of her and tried to keep her mind firmly fixed on the present, staring at the traffic outside the windows, concentrating on the todayness of today, the immediacy of now. But it didn't help. Twenty years slid away and exposed it all, the confusion and the pain and the sheer *silliness*.

It had all started absurdly, in that tatty place under the arches. They'd called it a theatre but it was little more than a grubby girly show, with tired, thirty-five-year old women with stretch-marked bellies and incipient varicose veins posing in grubby chiffon while she played the piano, watching them, making sure her rhythm matched their movements because they were all totally incapable of following her beat, however hard she tried to show them. She'd told herself it was really Art, that she was on the first rung of a great career, but sometimes when she was tired and when Dolly had again been asking questions about her job it was difficult to believe. Had all the years at Thomas Tallis, the practising, the studying, the hour after hour of gruelling effort, been for this? To play sugary tunes for worn-out women to wobble their breasts to, while even wearier men watched them and tried to get some sort of excitement from it?

But then Gerald had turned up. Financial Director, Mary Duffy who owned the place had called him, grandly. 'Going to sort us out, my dear, put us on our feet, probably get us into the West End – ' she'd said, and Maggy had looked at him and thought he was marvellous. Square and stocky with fair hair cut close to his head and a smile that always looked as though it was meant for her and absolutely no one else at all. And he saw me, daft and young and the only one there likely to be of any use to him, Maggy thought bleakly, stirring her muddy coffee, watching the bored waitress leaning against the counter in the Wimpy Bar, and I was stupid enough to think it was all real.

160

The coffee-bar visits that were replaced by lunches in the local pub, the gins and tonics that made her feel giddy and a bit sick, but oh-so-adult, the desperate kisses and gropings backstage when Mary was trying to fix those awful costumes and the performers dozed in the front row, waiting till the afternoon punters came in, how marvellous it had all seemed! She'd gone through her days in a haze of excitement, taut with her own sexuality, constantly aware of her breasts in front, her buttocks pertly rounded behind, so conscious of her own body that it was as though she could feel every inch of skin, all the time. And then she'd made up her mind. Just like that. He was to be the one who'd do it, and it would be marvellous, and then – well, afterwards, who cared anyway? Anything could happen, and probably would.

So when he'd said it to her, leaning close towards her over the bar at the King's Head, breathing into her face, when he'd said it she'd lifted her chin and smiled and said cheekily, 'My dear, I thought you'd never ask!' and felt immensely proud of her sophistication. He'd looked startled for a moment, his eyes flickering oddly but then he'd grinned and leaned closer and taken the lobe of her ear between his lips so that she'd shivered all the way through to the soles of her feet.

'My place, or yours?' she'd said then, feeling her sophistication growing by the moment, wishing desperately that Susannah were here to hear her, that'd show Susannah and her damned French chic, because she hadn't got *this* far yet, that was for sure. She'd have been talking about it interminably if she had, so obviously she hadn't.

'Yours,' he said, his voice low in his throat, smiling at her. 'I have – tiresome neighbours. Yours, my dear.'

And that had brought her down with a thump, hadn't it? Maggy, drinking some of her coffee now, and wishing she hadn't, almost smiled as she remembered. What on earth was she to tell him? How could she possibly take him to horrible Creffield Road? And what about Dolly? Oh, God, why did I say it, why did I say it? thought young Maggy, pushing her face into her glass of gin, planning feverishly, trying to wriggle out of it.

'Where do you live?' he'd asked then, and she'd said, as lightly as she could, 'Oh, it's rather a dump, I'm afraid. One of those awful private hotels, you know. Ealing way.'

'Darling, how clever of you! Much better than digs with landladies with noses as long as monkey's tails. Private and peaceful

161

– how absolutely marvellous of you!'

So that had been that. She'd made it a day when Dolly went buying. Wednesday it was, usually, though you could never be sure. She was so disorganized, so woolly that you never really knew what she'd do next, but Ida was usually able to get her there, nagging about supplies, going on at her about running out of lavatory paper, so Wednesday it was, and that morning she made up her bed with clean sheets and managed to get some flowers in, and put on her fanciest underwear, the trimmed lace panties she'd been given for Christmas, not the sensible stretch briefs she usually wore, and, daringly, didn't put on a brassiere. Getting out of it could be a problem, and now she'd made up her mind, she wanted it to be good, to be dignified, no struggling with hooks and eyes.

Asking Ida, casually, were they going buying, hadn't been easy because she hardly ever talked to Ida these days, she was so boring, but she'd managed it, and then gone to Gunnersbury to do the first show, almost shaking with the excitement of what was to come.

And up to a point it had gone marvellously. She could still remember the afternoon show, with hardly any customers at all and the way Gerald had said easily, 'For Christ's sake, Mary, give the buggers their money back. It's not worth the girls' pay or the electrics to put the show on for 'em. Tell 'em the star's gone down with rabies or something and they can come in half price next time. I'll absorb it in the books, don't you fret. Give us all an afternoon off, can't do us any harm – ' And Mary agreeing and then the way they'd left separately with loud and obvious farewells and met again at the corner, and gone back to Acton in the almost empty bus, sitting at the back of the top deck necking all the way – oh, it had been marvellous.

Until they got to Creffield Road. The house had been quiet, someone's radio playing somewhere, but quiet otherwise, and she'd let herself in with her key and said as casually as she could, 'I did tell you it was a dump, darling, didn't I? But what can you do, these days? Rents are so horrendous – ' drawling it, sounding madly relaxed, very effective.

'My dear, not bad at all as such places go!' he'd said, looking round. 'When I remember my first digs my blood runs cold! You could be much worse off. Decent people run it?'

'Tolerable,' she'd said, and took a deep breath and began to

162

walk upstairs, not waiting to see if he'd follow her, unbuttoning her coat as she went and feeling her fingers shake. And he had followed her, right into her room and as soon as the door was shut he'd put his arms round her and gone into a marvellous kiss, a real standing-on-one-leg, head-thrown-back-in-ecstasy film-star sort of kiss, and she'd wished she could watch it happening as well as be in there feeling it.

And they'd gone across the room to her bed, and he'd said something, his voice deep and heavy, but she couldn't do anything about what he'd said, because suddenly there was her door wide open and Dolly was there staring at them, her hair on end and her face looking a mess because she'd been putting her make-up on and hadn't finished, and then shouting and carrying on and generally being –

Oh, God, Maggy thought. Oh, God, it must have been funny! But she didn't laugh, dropping money on the table to pay for her coffee, going out into the street, walking towards the underground station. What a bloody fool I was! But it mattered to me, silly though it must have looked to them, it mattered dreadfully to me, and she shouldn't have done it, she really shouldn't.

Gerald being sent away, the fights, the arguments between Dolly and herself, the tears and the fury when she told Mary that Maggy was only sixteen, not twenty, as she'd pretended, and getting her sacked. And after that being sent off to spend a few weeks at the seaside with Dolly's old friend Minnie, as virginal as she had been all her life and sick with fury and disappointment, although she told herself it was love, Real Love that was causing her pain. Not that she had really believed it, even then, but at sixteen you have to have something to be dramatic about.

And then the message to go back. No, Minnie didn't know why. No, she didn't think Dolly was ill, anyway Ida'd never said she was. Just that Maggy was to go home to Creffield Road, that Dolly wanted her. And the journey back from Deal, sitting in the train watching the soft Kent country side dribble away past the windows, not knowing what she was going back to.

Walking down past Fletcher Street, towards Ealing Common, deliberately going the long way round so that she wouldn't have to go along Creffield Road, not wanting to see it again after all these years, Maggy felt tired, and her head began to ache. Yesterday had been pretty awful, after all. It wasn't every day you

163

got knocked out; she was entitled to have a headache. But she knew her headache wasn't really due to being knocked out. It was all the old pain coming back as the memories moved from the absurd to the really hateful.

Dolly was sitting in the kitchen, crying, when she came in, dropping her case in the hall and walking through to the back with dragging feet and a deliberately sulky expression on her face. I'll show her she can't make me do what she wants, she thought, pushing the kitchen door open. I'll show her I'm an Individual, that I've Got My Own Life to Live. She formed the words in her mind, seeing them written up, almost hearing them. I'll Show Her.

But Dolly in floods of tears, her face blotched and swollen was so shocking a sight that she forgot the sulky expression and stood in the doorway staring, her mouth half open, frightened, because sometimes Dolly got angry and sometimes wept easy comfortable tears, but she had never, not ever, looked like this. Desperate and bleak as though she'd been totally abandoned.

'What's the matter?' she'd said, staring at Dolly, not able to come any further into the room. 'What's happened?'

Ida's voice then, from the other side of the kitchen, coming out from the corner where the fridge was, walking towards her, jerking her head at Dolly.

'She's had bad news and she's upset. Been like this for two days. She wants you.'

'But what's the matter?' Still standing by the door, too frightened to come in any further, too alarmed by the sight of Dolly being so strange to risk coming near her.

'She'll tell you. She wants to – go on, girl – for God's sake, don't stand there like a stuffed dummy!' And she'd given her shoulder a push so that she had to come in, and she'd walked over to the table awkwardly and said, 'Mum?'

Which was odd, really, because she hadn't called her that for years and years, hardly ever called her anything directly, always thought of her, spoke of her as Dolly, never as Mum.

Dolly lifted her head, peered at her through half closed puffy lids and her face folded, became saggy and shaky and she said thickly, 'Is that my baby? Is that my little one? Oh, Margaret Rose, my lovey, what shall I do? She's dead, an' I never said I was sorry nor anythin' an' now I never can – oh, Margaret Rose,

164

what shall I do now she's dead?'

'Who's dead?' She wanted to back away, to get out of reach of the hands Dolly was holding out to her, but she couldn't, and just stood there staring and Dolly took hold of her, her hands feeling hot through the cloth of her coat sleeves, and pulled her closer. 'She's dead, my darlin' an' I never saw her, nor said what I ought, nor did what I ought – '

'Oh, for God's sake, Dolly, tell the girl properly! You're just maudling on – you wanted her back, and now you've got her, so make a job of it!' Ida's voice was sharp and loud, but there was a warmth in it, a deep compassion that made Maggy look at her sideways, surprised.

Dolly seemed to shiver a little and then let go of Maggy's arms and stood up, heavily, and leaned forwards and kissed her, and again Maggy wanted to pull away, for her face was wet and unbearably hot against her cheek, for she was still cold from the outside air. But she didn't, feeling the need that was in Dolly and after a moment, she put her hands out, touching Dolly's shoulders.

'What is it? What's happened? Who's dead?

'It's my Mam, my little love, my old Mam. She's dead of a stroke, an' I never knew it till it was too late. I swear I never knew – '

'Your – who?' Maggy stared, and then turned and looked at Ida. 'What does she mean?'

'Your grandmother,' Ida said shortly and came and took Dolly by the shoulders and sat her down again, and taking a handkerchief from her apron pocket wiped her face, mopping at her eyes and nose, and Dolly sat with her face tilted upwards, and let her, like a baby.

'My – but I haven't got a grandmother.'

'Not now you haven't,' Ida said shortly. 'Oh, come on, Dolly! She must have been an old woman, for God's sake, and she gave you a hell of a life, one way and another, as far as I can tell. No need to get into this sort of taking, is there? Life has to go on, you know.'

'I wanted Margaret Rose, because she's my girl. You can understand that, can't you Ida? I lost my Mam so I need my girl. You can see what I mean?' Dolly still had her face tilted up, staring at Ida, her eyes more open now, looking appealingly at her.

'Me? I wouldn't know any such thing,' Ida said. 'How could I?

What do I know of what a mother feels like?' and she moved away, went to the stove and put on the kettle.

'You said they were all dead,' Maggy said, confusion building in her. 'You said that you were an orphan and that after my father died his family all died and – how can I have a grandmother?'

That was when the door opened again and she turned to look to see who it was, and Gerald came in. Gerald, in pyjama trousers, yawning and obviously just out of bed.

18

After all this time why does it matter? Why should you beat your brains out over someone you only thought you cared about and who certainly never gave a tuppenny damn about you, who used you and your mother as he would have used a box of paper tissues? One wipe and chuck it away –

It mattered then, that was the thing. Even now, thirty-seven, poised, adult, sophisticated, successful, big name in her own world; Maggy reeled off the words inside her head, working at convincing herself; even now, I can still feel the hot thick feeling that I got when I realized what had happened and why he was there. He'd stood there in the kitchen door looking at her with his gritty unwashed eyes under his tousled hair and grinned, a wide-eyed self-congratulatory sort of grin, and said, 'Hello, my dear! Fancy seeing you! We can't go on meeting like this!'

It had been Ida who had saved it, who had moved in and prevented Maggy from disgracing herself by crying or shouting or throwing herself at him or something.

'Shut up, you,' she'd said and her voice was as gritty as his eyes. 'You're the last thing any of us need. Lay off. And get the bloody hell out of here – '

'No, Ida, don't – leave him be. He don't mean no harm,' Dolly had said, her eyes still wet, her face still horribly puffy but, not, thank God, crying now. 'You don't have to go away, Gerry. But don't go upsetting no one – ' and she'd looked at Maggy sideways and then smiled, a silly soft smile, and standing on the underground platform, waiting for a train to take her back to Holland Park, Maggy saw the smile again and tried to understand the message in it. Had she been saying I'm sorry? Saying – I just tried to make everyone comfortable, I never meant to hurt you, but you didn't really give a damn about him, and anyway the man was a shit, just a nasty little user and you know me and users, I always let them get away with it, it was the only way I knew how to be, whatever people wanted, I always let them have it, because I didn't know any other way to be –

Maybe. Maybe that was what she meant, Maggy thought now, thirty-seven poised etcetera Maggy. But I was sixteen then and I couldn't unerstand the message. All I knew was she'd robbed me, destroyed all my fantasies about the first man I'd fallen in love with, the first one I'd imagined sex with, the one I'd planned to be the first. It had hurt dreadfully, *dreadfully*, and as the train came into the station and she moved forwards to get on to it, she felt the tears she hadn't shed twenty years ago behind her eyes, making them feel bulging and hot.

And as if that hadn't been enough, there had been the whole bloody business about her grandmother. Her dead grandmother.

In a way, Gerald had acted as the plug to Dolly's cascade of tears. From the time he had appeared in the kitchen her crying had stopped. She seemed to slide back into being her usual self, albeit a woebegone version, but still her usual self, relaxed, easy, thinking only of the pleasure of now and the pains of now.

'It's lovely to have you home, my little love,' she'd said when Gerald had taken himself off with a cup of tea in one hand and a plate of toast in the other to go back to bed. 'I've missed you somethin' chronic. I'm that glad to have you back.'

'It was you sent me to that stinking place,' Margaret had said tightly, leaning against the dresser, staring at her. 'Is *that* why you wanted to get rid of me?' And she'd jerked her head towards the kitchen door through which Gerald had gone. 'So's you could get yourself all – '

'Oh, don't mind him!' Dolly had said. 'He's a soft thing, no use to anyone. All talk and show he is. Wind and water like the miller's cat. Him and that stupid cow as you got that fancy job with! I told you, tell me what's going' on and what you're up to, an' I'll know if it's all right, but there, you would have it you knew better'n anyone, wouldn't tell me nothin' – '

'Anyone who tells you anything has to be out of their minds,' she'd said then, still sick with rage and hurt and shame. That he could treat her like that, stay here with the woman who'd torn them asunder, that he could so demean himself as to drink her tea and eat her toast – and whatever else it was he'd got from her, a deeply hidden voice in her mind whispered – that he could be so easily deceived; the fancy words had twisted themselves in her head, in and out between her eyes, making her face feel stiff and making her words come out thick and sulky. 'I'll never tell you anything ever. You'll only use it against me.'

'Oh, my love, as if I would! Didn't I always want the best for you, didn't I? Didn't I try all I knew how to – '

'What's this about a grandmother?' she'd said then, very loudly. 'You told me they were all dead. Said we were alone in the world. What's all this about me having a grandmother?'

Dolly's eyes had filled with tears again, then. 'Oh, my love, I didn't want to upset you, did I? I don't want ever to upset you! An' I thought, I always thought, least said soonest mended. And my old Mam, she – ' She shook her head then, and looked at Ida. 'It was better I never told you, weren't it, Ida? Tell her it was better.'

'It was better. Now can we shut up about it? You've got the girl back, you've cried Lake Windermere, now shut up about it. She'll have to get a job, now she's back, won't she? What are you going to do about that? The way this place eats money you can't afford not to have her working – and paying something to her keep – '

'She don't have to pay nothin', nor never will!' Dolly had said loudly. 'I told you before, Ida, I'm glad to have you lookin' after business an' that, but I don't have my own child paying' anythin' to me, not now, nor never. It wouldn't be right.'

'Then you'll be in Carey Street and good luck to you,' Ida had said shortly. 'I'm sick of it. You let anyone put their feet under your table as wants to, and to hell with everything else. Him and her and – I've had enough of it, I'm getting out.' But she went on crashing the pans as she always did, organizing the next meal, and they all knew it was just talk. She was as much a part of Creffield Road as they were, as she had always been and always would be.

'We'll talk about it tomorrow,' Dolly said vaguely and stood up. 'I'm feeling poorly, my love, I truly am. I don't often feel poorly but I – I'm that glad you're back, really I am. I should never have sent you down to Minnie, but it seemed the best thing at the time – '

She stood at the door, looking at Margaret. 'It'll be all right now. We'll just go on as we always have, eh, love? Yes, that we shall. I want a bath – '

And she'd gone wandering out of the room, leaving Margaret standing with her back to the dresser, her arms folded tightly over her chest, her head sizzling with different feelings and thoughts and confusions.

It was Ida who had started her off again. Did she do it on purpose, I wonder? Maggy, staring out of the train window at the swooping black pipes on the blacker tunnel walls, tried to work than one out. Did she want me to do what I did, go shooting off to Cirencester like that? Silly childish thing it had been to do –

'Well, now, what are you going to do?' she'd asked, not looking at Margaret, mashing potatoes with a heavy wooden mallet, banging the pan on the table.

'Do? I don't know,' Margaret had said and stared down at her feet. Gerald and grandmothers – it was all too much.

'Well, well! And you the one that always knows her own mind! You amaze me!' Ida had put milk and margarine in the potatoes and was mashing them harder than ever now and Margaret watched her, liking the way the yellow of the fat disappeared into the white of the potatoes. 'I didn't think you'd give up that easily.'

At which point the idea had come into her mind. Had Ida meant it to? Possibly. But why should she? What difference would it make to her whether I found out or not? And what the hell does it matter now, anyway? Forget it. Don't think about Cirencester. You'll only get yourself all stirred up –

But of course, she did think about it, all the way home to Holland Park.

Getting the money to go had been easy. She'd walked into Dolly's room while she was in the bath, and gone to her bag and taken out all she could find in the way of cash. Not a lot, just seven pounds fifteen shillings, but it would do. And then, deeply aware of her daring, full of her own sense of will, she'd gone out of the house and taken the bus to Paddington. Just like that. She was going to Cirencester to find out about her grandmother. Just like that.

She'd thought first of all about hitch-hiking. She had no idea where Cirencester was, only that you went there from Paddington, Dolly had told her that long ago, when she had told her all the stories of the handsome soldier from the big house and the pretty girl and all that had happened to them. Paddington, she'd said, change at Swindon Junction. But how could you hitch-hike that way, not knowing exactly where it was? So it had to be a train – but there was no need to spend good money on it. Margaret was pleased with herself, planning how to travel free, buying a platform ticket at Paddington, getting the information she needed

170

about the trains at the information desk, and then getting on the train and watching out for the guard. She knew how to do it, even though she'd never tried it, because Gerald had told her once, laughing about it, describing the way he'd travelled all over the country when he'd been very young and cheeky, hiding in the loo, getting right behind the door so that when the guard opened it he thought it was empty and went on his way collecting other people's tickets.

'It's easy if you're small, and I was thin, pitifully thin and half-starved,' he'd told Maggy, laughing at the idea of successful Gerald being underfed and thin enough to hide behind lavatory doors on trains. 'And if you're cheeky enough – '

So she'd done it on the train, watching to see the man come along the corridor, slipping out and into the lav, and then hearing him go away, shouting, 'Tickets per*lease*,' above the noise of the train. It had been fun, that, made her feel she was really living in a big way.

Until she had arrived at Cirencester and had the awful business of having to pretend she'd lost her ticket because you couldn't get past the barrier with just a tuppenny platform ticket from Paddington, and having to give a name and address. She'd given them Dolly's, taking a malicious pleasure in that. She'll have to pay for it when they get on to her, she'd thought, marching out into the road, dark and shadowy and smelling of dead leaves. Then she'll be sorry.

It had been worse at the hotel. She'd walked into the middle of the town, trying to discover what it was like but failing to see more than blank house fronts in the lamplight and feeling the quietness of it like a blanket. Some of the houses had lights in the windows but mostly they did not, showing blind shuttered fronts to her as she went hurrying by, and she was filled with a vast loneliness, a feeling of being the only person alive in all this dead town. But at least there had been a hotel, a small place, little more than a pub, and she'd walked in, casual, supercilious, and asked for a single room, and had been rapidly deflated by the cold fish-like stare of the man behind the desk, finishing up almost pleading with him to let her have a room, agreeing to pay in advance as she had no luggage. A horrible experience.

And now the memory faded, blurred at the edges into nothing. Maggy, concentrating in today's train on the way to Holland Park, tried to see what she had done next. She could remember walking

171

up the stairs of the little hotel towards her room, but that was all. What had it been like? Had she had a meal? Gone straight to bed? What had she *done*? But the memory had blanked out completely. There was nothing until the shop, that horrible dingy smelly shop.

She could see herself there, all right. Greengrocery on all sides, piles of earthy turnips and sagging carrots and onions and a few sad cabbages, and some apples, too, bruised and yellowish in a box by the door, giving out a faint smell of rotting, but not strong enough to overwhelm the stink of paraffin from the stove in the corner.

There had been the old woman sitting there on a box with a sack over it, wearing an old overcoat that had obviously once belonged to a man, with the worn cuffs turned back to show the stained lining, and mittens, heavy woollen mittens out of which her fingers poked rough and red and as knobbed as the potatoes piled behind her.

'Wotcherwant?' the old woman had said, not getting up, holding her newspaper folded into a tight wad between her fingers. 'Wotcherwant?'

'Someone – I asked – I was told – ' Margaret had begun and the old woman had stared at her and sniffed, horribly, the dew-drop that had been hanging on her nose disappearing into it and then, disgustingly, oozing out again.

'Wotcher*want*?' she'd said again, and stared up at her, and Margaret had to look away, for the pupils, pale as boiled goose-berries, had white rings round them and somehow that frightened her, made her feel sick.

'I was told that you knew Mrs Dundas,' she said then, and was pleased with herself for getting the words out properly. 'I wanted to ask about Mrs Dundas.'

'What abour 'er? She's dead,' the old woman said, and then laughed. 'Dead and layin' down now. She'm been dead for years but wouldn't lie down – '

'I know she's dead, but – ' Margaret had swallowed and looked desperately out of the window into the street. A dingy narrow street with a few shops as dreary and miserable looking as this one. This was the dingy part of the town, obviously the worst part, the wrong side of the tracks, she had thought and then, absurdly, tried to remember where the railway station was, as though it really mattered.

172

'The thing is, she – I think she might have been a relation of mine.'

The old woman was suddenly alert and not laughing at all. She stared at Margaret with her eyes wide and now she had to look at her, boiled gooseberries or not.

'It was a proper will. I made sure o' that, I did, long time ago. It were a proper will and there's no one can say otherwise. I got the lawyer to prove it an' all – '

'Will?' Margaret had said, puzzled. 'What will?'

'She left me what there was, fair 'n square. No strings, she said, no strings. I looked after 'er all those years, kep' this place goin' an' she left it me fair 'n square. It's mine and no one can say otherwise.'

'No, of course not,' Margaret had said, and frowned. And then understood. 'I don't *want* anything of hers, you know. Just some information, that's all. You see – I never even knew she existed. I mean, I thought she was dead. I mean, I thought she was dead a long time before she was, you see – '

The old woman was still staring at her, her eyes as wide and horrible as ever and suddenly she said, 'Your 'air natural like? Or does yer dye it?'

'What?'

'Does yer dye it? Like them tarts do?'

Margaret reddened. 'Of course I don't. Anyway, what's it got to do with – '

'She had 'air that colour. Once. When she was young, like. Bin bald, almost, this last ten years, but once she 'ad red 'air.'

At once Margaret was on edge, ready. 'That's the thing, you see. I – my mother came from here. And I understand that she – that her parents had died when she was young – and – well, then I was told that my – that her mother had died only recently and I thought – well, that was the thing, you see. It was just that I wondered – '

The old woman bobbed her head, folded her newspaper into an even smaller wad and then looked up at Margaret, grinning. 'Well, well! 'Oo'd a' thought it? 'Ow old are you, then? Would you be about – let me see now – sixteen, I reckon it'd be. Eh? Sixteen, are you? Be seventeen come next November?'

Margaret stared at her, her mouth dry now. She'd found something and now she didn't want it. She didn't want horrible smelly old women in men's overcoats and mittens staring at her out of

173

boiled gooseberry eyes and telling her when she'd be having her birthday. She didn't want that, no matter what else she did want, she didn't want that –

'Well, 'oo'd a' thought it! Dorothy's brat come back! Eee, but wait till I tell 'em, just you wait! Won't they be in a takin'! Won't they just!' And she rocked on her box a little, laughing, holding her wad of newspaper in both hands and banging it on her lap in an ecstasy of private delight.

Margaret turned, began to fumble with the door of the shop but now the old woman was on her feet.

'No need to go runnin' off, my dear, no call to make strange! You'll be Ruby Dundas's granddaughter, clear as you like, and it'd ill behoove me to let you go off without a sup o'tea. Or somethin' stronger. Yer ma always liked somethin' stronger, even when she was just a girl, poor cow!'

Margaret turned back, not looking at the old woman, her face stiff and awkward. 'No, really, it doesn't matter. I'm sorry to have bothered you. I really didn't mean to – '

'It's no bother, it don't make no nevermind,' the old woman said, and at that, Margaret gave in. The sound of her mother's familiar phrase on this woman's lips was like a leash tied round her neck. She could no more have run away now than flown through the roof. She had to stay now.

And so she had, sitting on another upturned box, holding a tin mug of thick yellow tea which she couldn't drink, for the old woman had put a dessertspoonful of thick sugary condensed milk in it, listening to her talk. A couple of customers had come to buy pennorths of carrots and onions, staring at her curiously, and she had sat with her head down over the mug of disgusting tea, pretending not to know they were there, grateful when they went away and the old woman was back beside her, talking, talking, talking.

'Looked after 'er all those years I did, after 'er old man died, like. Went to pieces she did. Never 'ad more'n the one, you see, that Dorothy, an' spoiled 'er somethin' rotten, not that 'er dad did, I'll tell you that. He was a right tartar, took 'is belt to 'er soon as look at 'er, 'e did, and that was often enough, because she was a right piece, was that Dorothy – a right piece – '

Another customer, another scrutiny, another moment of wondering whether she could just get up and run while the old woman fiddled in her pocket for change. Could she get out? Hear no more? It was hateful, hateful, hateful –

' – an' then o' course, after 'e died, she went right soft in the 'ead, an' what was I to do? 'Er with no kin, like, wouldn't never see Dorothy again, so someone 'ad to take 'er on, di'nt they?' She looked sideways at Margaret, drank some of her tea, making a slurping noise that made Margaret want to retch, hearing it. 'So I did. All this time, an' never got nothin' for it, only she made 'er will, fair an' square, left me this shop, proper like, so there's no call to go thinkin' – '

'I'm not thinking anything,' Margaret had said desperately. 'Really I'm not. Tell me, why did – I mean, why did she – why didn't my mother – oh – ' and she floundered and stopped, staring again at those awful white rimmed eyes.

'Well, natural, wasn't it?' The old woman seemed to understand. 'I mean there she was, respectable woman, respectable family you might say, because 'e drank a bit, yer know 'ow men is, but respectable enough, worked for the Carters on the side 'e did, kept a decent enough place down in Watermoor Road, never no talk about them or anythin'. And then young Dorothy goes and gets 'erself into trouble – well, natural enough, wasn't it? Neighbours can be right nasty, some of 'em – anyway it was a respectable neighbour'ood, one way or another. But me, I didn't. I mean, I just went on like I always 'ad, being a friend, you know. That will, it's all square and proper – '

'Got herself into trouble?' Margaret stared at her, not seeing the white lined eyes now, only seeing confusion and unhappiness. 'Into trouble?' But she knew, really, for how could it be otherwise? Ruby Dundas, Dolly Dundas, Margaret Dundas –'

'Well, it was you, weren't it? Funny when you think of it, really, takin' to you now, I mean, a real laugh – ' And she did laugh, heartily, wiping her nose on the back of one of the mittens.

'But – my father – I mean. There was his family. The war and everything – '

'His family? Well, that'd be a puzzle to know about, eh? Red Indians for all we knew! Though lookin' at you now, they weren't. But Gawd knows. Gawd knows.'

'But they lived near here. Had a big house – flowers and fruit in bowls and – ' Margaret said it loudly, as though that would make it more obvious, would make this stupid woman understand how wrong she was being. Would convince Margaret herself that it was true.

'Lived near 'ere? I should cocoa! No nearer'n t'other side o' the world, my duck! One o' they soldiers, I was told. One o' they soldiers. Picked 'im up down the Fleece where she always 'ung out, when she could get away from her dad, and there 'e was. Never knew 'is name, so far as I could understand it, let alone anythin' else! Oh, a right tart was Dorothy Dundas. One o' they alley girls, down the back o' the Fleece. Everyone knew that!'

19

One good thing about being so obsessed with the past, she realized as she poured herself vodka and tonic, is that it takes the fear out of the present. She'd let herself into the house and climbed the stairs to the flat without giving a thought to the possibility of danger, so absorbed was she in her memories. Something to be grateful for, perhaps?

She threw herself into a chair and sat there with her drink cradled in her hands, wanting to think about other things, but knowing she had to see this morning and all it had brought back to her through to the bitter end. Finding out that Jim Hornby had been from her mother's part of the world had both shocked and reassured her. Shocked her into remembering that past misery, that sense of having been abandoned, of struggling to survive in an alien world; but comforted her because maybe it meant that he was old friend, someone from the happy days, and possibly had helped Dolly not because he was just another of the pieces of human detritus who got themselves washed up in her sleazy boarding house, but a real, *bona fide* honest-to-goodness friend.

What bloody difference does it make to me if he was? she asked herself then. If your music was based on stolen money – which it is now very obvious it was – what the hell difference does it make if the thief was a casual pick-up or an old friend?

All the difference in the world. She whispered it into her glass. All the difference in the world. You do things for friends, take things from friends that you never take from or do for casual pick-ups. Casual pick-ups are for babies. Oh, Christ, casual pick-ups are for Margaret Roses. That's how you get little princesses. That's how you –

It doesn't *matter*. You're you, now and here. You're a talented capable person. What the hell does it matter how you started out? Can't you take yourself for what you are now, rather than for what *they* were?

But she couldn't, still couldn't, despite all the years of trying.

Ever since that day twenty years ago when she has found out what she was, how the special uniqueness that was herself, that was Maggy, had started out she had been consumed with rage and fury. Against Dolly who had done it to her.

She remembered, now, the way Dolly had looked when she'd told her. The way she had sat there at the kitchen table, her head bent as she looked at her hands lying lax in front of her, and let Maggy's fury burst over her like a breached dam.

'You were a tart – a stinking lousy tart! You were just a filthy pick-up – they told me, that horrible woman told me, you were talked about everywhere – they all knew you – I hate you, I hate you – '

Ida had stood there too, behind Dolly, watching her, her face tight and closed. Ida silent and watchful and unmoving.

'You robbed me, you know that? You go on and on about what you want to do for me, how I've got to have everything you can give me, how me learning music is so important and – and all the time you're robbing me and killing the people I care about and – I hate you, I hate you – '

'I never killed no one,' Dolly said piteously, seizing on to it somehow, looking for something she could deny. 'I never hurt no one, my love, I just wanted the best for you, that's all, that's why I never said – '

'Yes you did, you did, you did, you did!' She shrieked it, wildly, luxuriously, enjoying the fury and the feeling of letting go. It was like the times when you were little and needed to go to the lavatory, were bursting with it, and then you got there and you could let go. She was letting go now, bursting all the filth that was in her all over Dolly's head. 'You did, you killed my dad, you killed him, you – '

It was Ida who stopped it, leaning over almost casually and hitting her face hard with the back of her hand so that her cheek stung. Maggy could feel it still, the pain and shame of that blow.

'Stupid bitch!' she'd said dispassionately. 'Stupid, spoiled, selfish bitch! She's spent her whole life worrying over you, put herself into a business she's no good at, always in trouble with, all for you, so that you could have a home. Spoiled rotten you are, spoiled rotten.'

'Leave her be, Ida. She don't mean no harm. She doesn't understand, poor little love, how can she understand? I told her such tales – such tales I told her – ' Dolly, crying again. 'I meant

178

no harm, my lovely, I meant no harm. I never meant no harm, but it never comes out right.'

It never comes out right. It never did. Poor Dolly, Maggy throught, and was startled at the thought. Poor *Dolly*? After all these years, she could think that?

Yes, poor Dolly. I don't know why, yet, but it's there inside me somewhere. I'll work it out yet. Poor Dolly.

Forget it now, for God's sake forget it! She got up and went to the piano and opened it, lifting the heavy lid and balancing it on the stick and sitting herself down and then letting herself go on it. She played everything and anything; exam pieces from the old T T days, the new tracks she'd just finished recording, the stuff she was going to use in the States and then, at last, she loosened, came free, and the music began by itself, the improvisations that would come upon her sometimes, the notes pleating themselves into perfect patterns under her fingers, coming out of her hands like a fountain, bypassing her head, just leaping up out of her guts, rippling, banging, sharply dissonant music. Somewhere a small dispassionate Maggy thought – pity the tape recorder isn't on. There's some marvellous stuff here and I'm going to lose it all – but that didn't matter. Just play, let it happen, let the piano sing, let her belly sing, let her head sing. Ripple, run, leap and die, form and reform. Music.

She didn't hear Theo's key in the door, didn't know he was there until at last, sweating, her head hurting a little with the pressure she'd allowed to build up inside her and her legs trembling, she stopped, splaying her fingers over the dead keyboard, and looked up and saw him.

'Christ, but that was – what happened? Did you record it? For God's sake say you recorded it!'

'No,' she said dully and stood up, and smiled at him vaguely and wiped the heel of her hand over her forehead. It was wet. 'No. It just – I just felt like it.'

'It was bloody incredible,' Theo said, and stood and stared at her, his face a little blank. He seemed suddenly like one of the fans, standing and staring and not daring to ask for an autograph. 'That was incredible.'

'Yes,' she said, and went back to the armchair and fell into it, stretching out, pulling on her muscles, enjoying the sensation. She was drained and exhausted and it was marvellous. Better than sex, better than sleep, better than breathing. Music.

179

'Are you all right? Don't feel ill? How's your head?' He was fussing round her now, sitting on the arm of her chair, and touching her forehead, and she wanted to put her arms up round his neck and lie against him. She was feeling good now, marvellous in fact, and she opened her eyes and smiled at him.

'I'm fine, really I am. I'll sort it all out, you see if I don't.'

'Sort out what? The music? Can you remember it? It sounded fantastic. Fan-tas-tic – '

'What? Oh. No. Maybe. I don't know. One day. It's all there somewhere. No, this other business. It'll be all right.'

He looked doubtful. 'How d'you mean?'

She closed her eyes again. 'I'll work it out. It's all got to be linked together, somehow, hasn't it? Jim Hornby and Cirencester and everything. I'll go there, find out. I can manage it now – '

'Are you sure you're all right?' His voice sharpened. 'Maggy? Have you got a headache or anything? Maybe we ought to see the doctor again after all – '

She remembered then, and sat up. 'Mmm? I'm sorry, love, I was half asleep, I think, for a second. Ignore it. How'd it go at the office? Are the tapes all right? What did they say about your stuff from Bristol?'

Fool, she told herself, smiling up at him. You nearly gave it all away then. Be careful, be careful. It could have been him, after all. I wish I could fee safe with you, Theo. I wish I could, be careful, be careful.

'Fine,' he said, doubtful still, staring down at her, his hand on her forehead. 'You feel hot, you know. Maybe you're a bit feverish – '

'Oh, balls. I just started playing and I got took – you know what it is when that happens. I get all worked up. Marvellous.'

'I wish you'd taped it,' he said and stood up and went over to get a drink for himself. 'It sounded – well, it was good. Bloody good. One of these days, Maggy, they're all going to go mad over you. You've got your following now, I know, but one of these days – '

'Yes, one of these days. How was it at the office? You haven't said.'

'The album sounds terrific. Fantastic. I heard it through from the top and I have to tell you it's great. They've given me a white to take over to the States with us. If I use it properly we'll get some good advance publicity on it. Can't wait for the sleeve – '

180

'The States.' She sat staring at him, thinking hard. She'd almost forgotten, and yet she hadn't. 'I've lost track a bit. When do I go?'

'Friday.' He came and sat beside her again. 'I've got the itinerary here – five gigs all in and around New York and Washington this time, thank God, so you won't have to travel too much. But I've told 'em, you're not too well, you might have to postpone, no – don't worry, I didn't tell 'em why. Didn't think it'd be a good idea. You know how they are on publicity. If this one gets out – mind you, it'll be a problem if we postpone. The trade press stuff is already out, and they're advertising. It worries me, love. I'll tell you. After last night – '

'I'm fine,' she said, abstractedly. 'Theo – ' and then stopped.

'Hmm?' He slid one arm around her, cupping his hand over her breast. Cosy.

'I want to go on my own.'

His hand tightened, almost painfully, and then let go. 'What? Why?'

She turned and looked at him, trying to keep her face blank. 'To – to get my nerve back.' She was improvising now, just as she had on the piano. Let it happen. Let the words come out the way they want to. Then it'll be all right. Just like the piano.

'If you get scared you don't work at getting over it, you can be stuck like it for life. People fall off horses, never get on again. Or fall in a swimming pool and never swim again. I don't want to get like that. And if I don't go on my own, this time, I'll never go anywhere on my own again.'

'Now, Maggy, for God's sake, don't be daft! Of course I've got to go with you! I always go on these trips – it's what I'm for. As for being alone – what about the others? Dan and Komo and Chalky. Are you going without them as well?'

She grinned at that. 'Oh, come on, Theo! Those three? I look after *them*! They just get stoned and stay that way – anyway – ' She leaned forwards, as earnest as she knew how to be. 'They're different. We're together, but not really *together*. Not the way we are, you know? When you're with me – I lean, I don't bother about things, I leave it to you. It's too easy.'

'It's what I'm for,' he said, and there was a note of stubbornness in his voice that told her she'd won, almost, she just had to push it home.

'I know, love. You're marvellous. And leaning on you is great.

Some of the time. This time, though, I've got to lean on myself. Because if I don't I'll never manage it again. I want to go on my own. I've got to.'

His face was closed now and he stood up, went over to the piano and started to close it, carefully blowing dust off the keys, using his handkerchief to rub a mark from the case. She watched him and wanted to cry, suddenly, wanted to hold out her arms and say, 'It's all right! Of course I trust you – of course we'll go together.' But she didn't. Because much as she wanted to, somewhere dragging deep, was the lingering suspicion and fear still there.

He was punctilious in everything he said and did for the rest of the week, making no comments about her decision, behaving as though it were the most normal thing in the world. The office booked the plane tickets, arranging she should go to Washington the day before the others to meet the tour manager and look the scene over, and still he said nothing, even when the people at the office showed surprise that he wasn't going along. He'd gone along on every concert she'd done ever since they'd been together; no wonder they were surprised. The girls in the typing pool giggled and guessed, whispering about them to Sharlene from reception and they both knew it, and both ignored it. What did they care about stupid gossip?

But he looked tight-lipped and withdrawn and that worried her more than she would have thought it could. Had he nagged, fussed, tried to insist on coming with it would have been easier; then she could have been angry with him. As it was she was filled with guilt and that made her tense and remote.

They were polite to each other all week, cool and polite, and though they made love once or twice there was no passion in it, no real involvement. She began to feel lonely again, the way she had been long ago, before Theo, living alone in the flat. Was I lonely like this when I first left Dolly? she asked herself, sorting through clothes, planning what to take. I moved into that dismal little room in Shepherds Bush, all by myself; was I lonely like this then? But she couldn't remember and didn't want to try, and thank heaven, had enough to keep her busy so that she was able to control this maddening new tendency of hers to go scrabbling in the past.

He drove her to Heathrow on Friday morning to catch her

plane; he'd insisted on that, for the first time showing a flash of the way he was feeling about her refusal to let him go with her, and she hadn't argued. There was no need to slap him in the face after all, and she let him check her in, see her as far as passport control on the way to the departure lounge.

'Take care, now,' he said, and took her face between both hands and kissed her. 'You hear me? Take care.'

'I'll be fine, really I will. It's here there are problems, so there's no need to worry. I mean, whatever's going on with break-ins and all has nothing to do with this tour. If anyone's at risk, it's you – I mean, maybe whoever it is'll break in again – '

'I wish he would,' Theo said grimly. 'Christ, but I wish he would! Then maybe we'd begin to get somewhere. I'd have the arse off him – '

'Well, *you* take care. And I'll be back in a week – and I'll call you – '

'Yes – call me tomorrow, hey? Whatever time, it doesn't matter. I'll be waiting. Go on – they'll be calling your flight – ' And he pushed her gently and she grinned and went through passport control, smiling back at him over her shoulder as she did. He looked as lonely as she felt, standing there, his hands in his coat pockets.

'She's starting in Washington. Two concerts there and then one in Long Island, and two more in Manhattan.'

'Where's she staying?'

'I haven't found out yet. But no hassle – there'll be someone meeting the plane. We'll know soon enough.'

'Okay. But no pushing, you hear me? I want to see this one through myself. It'll be interesting, apart from anything else. After so long – and call Gibbs, will you? Tell him he's fired. From now on I'll deal direct.'

Bloody Americans. Bastards, every one of them. He'd done them proud, hadn't he? All this time he'd done them proud. Why give him the push now? All right, so he hadn't managed to keep as close an eye on the girl as they'd wanted to, but what did they expect for tuppence ha'penny? If they'd paid him enough to run his own proper transport it'd be different. As it was, rattling around the way he had to, was it any wonder he hadn't done so well? They wanted Starsky and Hutch for fivepence, they did.

But there was still Lang, wasn't there? They'd told him enough about that situation to make it an interesting one. Anything they can do, I can do better. They don't want me to collect from him any more? Great. I'll do it for myself. Set up in business on my own account –

Whistling softly to himself, he scrabbled in his pocket for a twopence piece to make a phone call.

20

She liked the States. She always had, ever since that
first visit nine years ago, coming as part of an all-girl band playing
a dozen one-night stands around the Eastern seaboard. It was the
sheer verve of it all, the screaming signs and the reek of hambur-
gers, the pot-holed streets and the eternally hooting traffic, and
the people, the startling incredible mix of people. There were
fatter and thinner and taller and shorter and uglier and more
beautiful people here than anywhere else, certainly than in
London. It excited her, made her feel more awake, and made her
music bubble nearer the surface.

Washington went fine. The concerts were sell-outs, and the
boys were happy, even Komo going along with the general
euphoria and not losing his temper more than twice in three days.
There was a lot of attention from the press, and that pleased Josh,
the tour manager, who beamed and sweated and rushed her from
interview to TV station to radio show, obviously loving every self-
important minute.

'We're doing well, incredibly well, sweetie,' he told her, leaning
back in the car as they went back to the airport for the hop to
New York. 'There's some big stories around right now, some big
stories, Sinatra at Radio City, Rice and Lloyd Webber are in
town, Lancaster came in yesterday, got a big one at Madison
Square Garden – that'll really grab 'em – so you're getting great
coverage, considering – '

'Lancaster?' she said idly, not really caring, watching the houses
rush pas the car windows, staring at the advertising hoardings, the
traffic going the wrong way, all the exotic foreignness that was
America. 'What's he? Should I know?'

He laughed. 'No reason you should know. Not a musician –
revivalist. Got a big following back on the West Coast – '

'Oh,' she said. 'That chap who's going to Wembley next month?
I've read about him at home. Another of those Billy Graham
types, isn't he? Is he so big here?'

'Is he ever!' Josh said shaking his head in admiration. 'Real gut stuff he throws out, and they come, and they pay. Must be making a bomb – '

'Sooner him than me,' she said, bored. 'Are the boys ahead of us? I tend to worry about Komo – he's a bit on the unreliable side sometimes – '

'I sent Dave with them. They're behind us – ' He peered through the rear window. 'Yeah – there they are. No sweat. We'll be in New York in a few hours and then we'll wake 'em up! You're getting great coverage, great – '

She grinned. 'I'll tell them in London. Don't worry, they'll be told,' and he grinned too. This is a stinking business, she thought, stinking. Constant back-scratching, all the time. You help me, I'll help you, what's in it for me?

And sharply, her mind shifted and she was back in the maelstrom of confusion that had been such hell to live with ever since Dolly's death. For the past three days here in Washington she'd been caught up in the excitement of work, had rushed about, played her music, been on a high, but now she came down as suddenly as though the high had been drug-induced. She'd tried pot a few times, not because she was particularly into drugs, but because the boys did, and it seemed silly not to see for herself, and the same thing had happened. It was why she'd stopped using it. One minute buzzing along on the top deck, the next hitting the ground with an almost physical thump. That was how it was sitting here in the car, going to the airport in Washington.

Dolly and Hornby and Gerald and Morty Lang and Andy and Ida and Oliver and Theo – the names swirled around in her head, coming between her eyes and the passing scenery at which she was staring, and she felt her neck muscles tighten. Why did it have to be like this, damn it? All this because of a tatty debt-encrusted hotel she didn't really want. Why did she have to go digging up a lot of ancient history, just to quality for the ownership of a burden? It was absurd.

But it's not. It's part of a search for myself. I'm sitting here in a car in Washington on the way to New York, on top of a lot of dead people. There's the child Margaret Rose, long since dead, and you're still mourning for her; there's the adolescent gawky Margaret, posing and yearning and stamping her feet and she's dead too, and yet you cry for her; and there's the almost adult Maggy in there somewhere, still in the process of dying, still

186

pushing you – the now Maggy, the real living Maggy – to the top of the heap with her last gasps. All of them sitting in a car on its way to Washington airport.

'I'll go to Cheltenham as soon as I get back,' she said aloud, staring out of the window as the car curved, turning into the airport road. 'As soon as I get back. Get it over and done with.'

'What?' Josh was fussing with tickets, fiddling with pieces of paper in his wallet. 'What's that you say, sweetie?'

'Nothing. Just sorting out a few ideas. I've got my passport here. I'd better take my own ticket, hadn't I? Thanks – no, I'll take this bag. It's got the music – '

It was raining in New York, the water swirling in the gutters, carrying garbage and taxis out of sight and the line for taxis at La Guardia was long and Josh began to fuss, trying to get VIP treatment for her and the boys, and not getting far.

She stood in the taxi line, calm and quiet; she'd learned long ago to pace herself, not to expend previous energy on fussing and anger, leaving it to someone else. But she was tired and wanted a shower and found herself wishing, suddenly, that Theo was here. He never had trouble with taxis.

'Ma'am – may I be of service?' She turned her head to see a tall quiet young man in a neat black suit and blue shirt and quiet dark tie standing behind her. His hair was glossy, short and neat, and his teeth – he was smiling to show them – as white and even as a toothpaste advertisement. She almost expected a shaft of reflected light to come off them, they always did on TV commercials.

'I beg your pardon?'

'I understand you're having problems with transport? I have my car here, and I'd deem it an honour, ma'am, if you'd allow me to take you wherever you want to go.'

She frowned for a moment and then looked over his shoulder to where Josh was standing expostulating with someone with a peaked cap and a bored expression.

'Well, I don't know – that's very kind. But someone's – '

Josh came hurrying over. 'Goddamned fool! It's like talking to a – listen, honey, I'm sorry, there's no way we can do a thing. Just got to wait in line, I guess – I've done my best – '

'We've been offered a lift, Josh,' she said, and smiled at the tall young man. He was looking glossier by the second. 'I don't know who – '

The young man smiled even more widely. 'My name is Greening, Gregory Greening, ma'am. Glad to be of service to you.'

Josh beamed, became expansive. 'Well, now, Maggy, fans everywhere! That's great, really great. There's quite a crew of us, though. Greg! There's myself of course, and the band – three guys, their luggage – and the sound man, Dave – are you sure you can – '

'My pleasure,' said Greening. 'I have a friend here – ' and he turned his head and out of the hubbub of people milling around them came another glossy young man, blond this time, but just as highly polished and healthy-looking. Maggy wanted to giggle suddenly. They looked too good to be true. Fans? Such well-soaped shining young men fans of *hers*? They looked as though they never listened to anything much more exciting than Laurence Whelk, or Mantovani if they were feeling really daring.

'This is Hartford Salmon, ma'am, and he'll be happy to help take your party. If the porters will just follow us – '

Smoothly the two young men scooped them up, led them away, and luggage was piled in the back of one car and somehow, the rest of them, the band, and Josh and Dave, all got into the other station wagon leaving Maggy to go with Greening and the luggage.

He settled her comfortably in the seat beside him, even offering her a rug, which piece of old-world concern amused her, and then slid into the driving seat beside her and pulled out into the traffic with a smooth easy movement. He drove carefully and quickly.

'Well, now, we'll have you there in no time, ma'am. Have you stayed at the Waldorf before?'

'Yes,' she said, studying his profile. 'Tell me, what were you doing at the airport that you can take time to help out a stranger like this?'

He smiled, gently, so that his cheeks dimpled. He really is absurdly pretty, she thought. It's as though he were cut out of the back of a cornflake box. Make your very own All-American Boy.

'Well, now, ma'am, I was rather looking for you, you might say.'

She turned her head sharply then, to look over her shoulder at the car following. She could see them, Josh in the front seat, his hands waving and his jaw moving rhythmically as he talked across Dave to the driver. All round her there were cars, cars, more cars. Why was she so suddenly frightened?

'Looking for me? You knew I'd be there? How can that be?'

'You've had a lot of publicity, Miss Dundas. Papers, and all that. Lots of advertising, going to be a big concert, they tell me, this one. Lincoln Center? Yes.'

'Reading ads about concerts is one thing. Recognizing the person who's going to be giving the concern in a taxi queue is something else.' All her nerves were on edge now, and she found herself sitting very upright, staring at his reflection in the windscreen as the car moved into the heavy traffic heading for the tunnel into Manhattan.

'My, that's very unassuming to you, Miss Dundas. I always thought pop stars expected everyone to recognize them all the time.'

'I'm not a pop star. I play jazz. Good jazz. Do you like it?'

'Well, now, ma'am, you must forgive me, but to say the truth I've never actually – '

'No, I didn't think you had. You don't look the sort to be interested in my sort of music.' She was sounding offensive now, and she knew it, and at a deep level was ashamed. After all, he was helping her, doing her a favour. Why be so hostile?

He laughed aloud at that. 'You're right, ma'am, indeed you are. I'm not interested in music at all, any kind. I always was an oddball that way. My folks could never understand it. They all played records all the time, you know? But there, I just never took to it. I read a lot, and I like to concentrate on the words. Music gets in the way, I think, so – '

'You're getting off the point,' she said sharply. 'I'm still puzzled about why you picked us up.' She could still see the other car right behind them, reflected in the wing mirror on her side, and that helped keep the sense of alarm in her under control. They could hardly kidnap six of them – at which thought she relaxed a little. Crazy notion, kidnapping. Why should anyone want to –

'What do you want?' She said it loudly, and he looked at her, turning his head briefly and then looking back at the road quickly, too careful a driver to be distracted for long.

'Why, Miss Dundas, just to take you to the Waldorf. That's all.'

The car slowed down for the toll booths and he opened the window and reached for coins from the dashboard and she put her hand on the door, thinking confusedly, 'I'll get out, run for it – Josh will see and realize, and they'll get out too – '

'No need to worry, ma'am, I locked the door. No risk of falling

189

out, I promise you,' he said and smiled again as the car picked up speed.

'Look, it was kind of you to offer a lift, but I've changed my mind. I want you to stop, please, and let me out. Do you hear? I want you to stop and let me out – '

'Here? On the freeway? Why ma'am, then what would you do? I guess you must be tired and nervous, huh, after your flight? Why not lean back, close your eyes? We'll be around another twenty minutes or so, I guess, traffic being what it is – '

'No! I want out. *Now* – you hear me?'

He shook his head smilingly, and she turned in her seat, and waved furiously at Josh behind. He was still talking across Dave, who looked lugubrious and it was a moment or two before he saw her, and then waved back, grinning, happy, monkey-stupid.

'Now, Miss Dundas, you really should relax, you know,' Greening said. 'You'll get yourself all worn out before this evening – and you with a concert to play – you need all your energy, surely!'

He was all sweet reason, and underneath her panic she felt common sense stirring. She must be mad to get into such a state; all he was doing was giving her a lift. He showed no signs of trying anything odd, he was taking the right and fastest route into the city – she remembered enough of that from her last trip – and behaving in a perfectly normal way. She was the one being stupid, wasn't she?

She sat back in her seat and tried to loosen her shoulders, but never took her eyes from his mirrored reflection in the windscreen, seeing the shadowy dimpled face through the passing buildings.

And when they arrived at the Waldorf, sliding down the side street and in under the building into the car bays she wanted to cry, she was so relieved and so ashamed.

'I'm sorry,' she said, not moving, as he switched off the engine and the doorman moved towards them. 'I was rather foolish there, I think.'

'Like I said, Miss Dundas, tired and nervous. Flying makes a lot of people that way. We'll have you settled in no time.'

He was out, fussing with luggage, helping her out and then the other car arrived and the bustle was on as Komo bawled at the doorman who manhandled his big double bass with less reverence than Komo demanded and Josh soothed him and all was hubbub. She was swept into the hotel and the lift and up to the check-in desk in a welter of noise and Komo's loud expostulations and Dan

190

laughing, and it wasn't until they were walking through the big ridiculous Disneyland lobby that she realized that Greening and Salmon were gone.

'Where are they?' She stopped in the middle of the lobby, looking round. 'Josh, where did they go?'

'Who? Oh, those guys? Left 'em downstairs.'

'I should have said – '

'Don't worry, don't worry. I gave them tickets for tonight.' He was all expansive generosity. 'Good seats. Told 'em we've got a sell-out, but they could have these two. Come on – check-in time. Then you'll need a rest, huh? I've got to go check at the Center that everything's OK, but it should be, it should be, they've been told just what's what – '

He bustled her through the checking-in procedures and saw her to her room on the seventeenth floor, tipping the bellhop who brought her luggage, ringing down for room service for her, but she told him as politely as she could she didn't want a thing, please, just to rest, no, not a thing and at last he was gone, and she stood alone in the hotel room, her luggage piled on the stand by the door and stared out of her window into the well at the rows of more windows on the other side of the building.

The traffic noise came muted and blurred, taxi horns and police sirens and the squeal of brakes merging into an almost pleasant din, and she began to unlock her bags, wanting to unpack. But she was restless and edgy and after a moment made for the door and went down to the lobby again.

The place still looked Disneyesque and she stood for a moment staring at the inverted cupolas over Peacock Alley and listened to the tinkle of Cole Porter's piano and smelled the richness of cigars and cream cakes and gin and then, irritated, made for the coffee shop. She ordered a club sandwich and then couldn't eat it, but pretending to gave her something to do, and after a quarter of an hour she went upstairs again, feeling more relaxed, though not knowing why.

The red light on her telephone was flashing as she let herself in and she picked up the handset and dialled the number for messages. Trouble at the Center? Was Josh ringing her about problems already? Only four more days to go, and home again. Three more concerts and home again –

'You have a message for me? Maggy Dundas, in 17 Y.'

'Miss Dundas, one moment, please – will you please call 737

191

8765.'

'Who is that?'

'We do not have that information, Miss Dundas. Just the message you should call this number, 737 8765. Have a good day.' And the phone went dead.

She dialled for a line, automatically, and when it buzzed, dialled the number she had been given and then, as the first burr of the ringing tone hit her ear hung up again, sharply. Who the hell was she calling, anyway? Why should she call a number she'd been given just because someone told her to? I don't talk to anyone unless I know who I'm talking to, she told herself and after a moment, dialled for a line again, and rang the Lincoln Center number. It took a while to track Josh down, but she found him at last and told him succinctly to call the number she'd been given.

'I don't know who it is or why, and no way do I call people unless I know who they are. But I'm curious – '

'It might be press,' Josh said fussily. 'Might be a publicity thing – I'll get on to it right away – I'll call you – right away – '

She unpacked the bare essentials she'd need that night, shaking out the silver lurex dress and hanging it up. It looked good on her, fitting tightly, shimmering over hips and breasts, lighting her hair to a richer-than-ever red, and she scrabbled in her make-up bag, looking for the silver eyeshadow that went with it. She'd show 'em tonight! The day's tension, the moments of panic there on the freeway hadn't tired her after all. She was wound up now, feeling a mainspring of energy radiating from her hands deep into her belly. She'd knock them for a million tonight.

She showered, and then rolled herself in the counterpane and fell asleep, and woke, sharply, when the phone bell trilled. It was dark now and she reached for the light sleepily before answering.

'Maggy? Josh. This call – it's some guy says he knows you. Old friend, he says.'

'Hmm? Oh, the message – yes. What's his name?'

'Wouldn't say. Wants to surprise you, he says. You're to call him.'

'Like hell I will. Some goddamned nut, probably.'

'Well, maybe, though he sounded OK. Still, it's up to you. Listen, honey, you're OK? Resting and all?'

'I was.'

'Go back to sleep, get a real rest there, you hear me? We've got a sell-out here, no question, a sell-out. And the TV people

192

are here – NBC. I tell you they're setting up for a live extract! It's some documentary they're doing, but I told 'em, you want my lady on a documentary, great, but you see to it she gets exposure on the programmes where it matters, right? And they said sure, they said and it's all fixed – '

'You said to rest, Josh.'

'Oh, Jesus, yeah – look, hon, you sleep, OK? I'll have the desk call you at six. That'll be soon enough to get dressed, down here for seven? Great, great – '

To her surprise she did manage to sleep again and woke just before the phone rang with her alarm call, and dressed and made up quickly, feeling good. Even her false lashes went on at first try, and she felt obscurely that that was a good omen. It would a good night, she knew it in her bones.

Walking across the lobby from the lifts, wrapped in her silver dress, trailing her silver bomber jacket over her shoulder, she felt heads turn to look at her, and for once enjoyed it. Usually the staring aspect of being a performer irritated her. It was her music that mattered, not her clothes or her looks, but at other times, like now, it all came together, the excitement of having music hovering on the edge of performance and looking and feeling good, making the whole world seem to sparkle and shimmer about her. Tonight it shimmered double and she swept out into Park Avenue and into a taxi feeling like the greatest performer New York would ever see.

21

And for a while, she was. The audience, huge, lifting and heaving like a single vast creature, murmuring and muttering and smelling of tobacco and, somewhere, a hint of charred grass, good-humoured and asking to be entertained, sent out a wave of welcome and interest that wrapped her warmly as though in a fur rug, and her skin felt moist and alive as though it were sending out sparks.

The boys had picked it up too, and stood in the wings jigging a little, Komo softly whistling between his teeth, Chalky grinning inanely at the lights, Dan relaxed and peaceable, and they turned as she joined them, smiled, touching her, murmuring a little. Four such different characters, not even particularly liking each other very often, when they made music they merged into a whole, just as the audience did, forming a unit that communicated within itself without any effort, no words, occasional looks and touches, that was all. Usually they didn't reach that stage of union until they were on the stage, maybe halfway into the first set, but tonight it was there already. Even Josh, fluttering and jabbering on the periphery, fussing over details with Dave, couldn't touch them, couldn't get inside the enchanted bubble that was the Dundas Band ready to make music.

And such music they made; it was better than it had ever been. The sounds rose and fell, tangled and untangled, created worlds of their own and then destroyed them ready to be built up again, and the audience swayed and went with it and almost dreamily she watched her fingers dancing on the keyboard, saw the glitter of the lights leaping off her dress and reflecting in the polished wood of the Steinway, and felt whole and good and right. It was marvellous and when the audience exploded into applause she just sat there, looking at them, grinning, her head up, feeling every bit of herself responding as though each hair on her head was standing and cheering back at them.

And the next set and the next – it built and built until she was floating, almost, and Dan caught it and went off into one of his soaring drum experiences and she let him go and then followed him and twisted in and out with him and the audience screamed its excitement and adoration and Komo roared and laughed and twirled his bass and Chalky just smiled peaceably and blew his clarinet like an angel. Oh it was great music, the greatest ever, and Maggy, entranced, lifted her head and walked off stage three inches off the ground and left the boys to take the rest of the applause. She had the next half to get ready for; she had to hide in her dressing-room and protect this fragile bubble of perfection, to make it last until the end of this unique and glorious evening.

'You didn't call that number, Miss Dundas.' The voice was soft, and she turned her head, blinking in the dim light backstage, peering.

'What? Is that you, Josh?'

There were people everywhere, bustling, calling, and above the noise there was the din of the audience lifting its vast corporate voice in worship, but she couldn't see clearly, for her eyes were glazed with the lights of the stage.

'Why, no, Miss Dundas. Not Josh. It's such a pity you didn't call that number, Miss Dundas. I know you got the message, because your friend Josh called there, and he couldn't have done that if you hadn't given him the number. Could he?'

'Who the hell is that?' The bubble was bending, losing its perfect roundness, threatening to explode and she tried to hold on to it, turning to go away, back to her dressing-room.

A hand reached out of the dimness and took her elbow. 'Miss Dundas, you have time to call now, I think. There's fifteen minutes break, and if you choose to stretch it, no one can object, I reckon. They seem to like you – ' He cocked his head to hear the audience, still shouting, though with less noise now, and his face came into a shaft of light. The All-American boy.

'Greening?' she said, and the bubble burst, splattering shards of joy around, making them turn into sourness in her mouth as they landed. She felt flat and a little bit sick. I wish I'd eaten that sandwich, I feel empty.

'That's right, Miss Dundas. Now, can I find you a phone?'

'No, you bloody well can't!' Anger moved in now, filling the emptiness, and she was glad of it and encouraged it, fanning her rage to a blaze. 'Who the fucking hell do you think you are, coming back here? Jesus God, is there no way I – '

195

'Why, Miss Dundas, there's no need to get so – ' He shook his head reproachfully. 'I just came to give you a message, is all! From an old friend.'

'I have no old friends. No one I want to talk to now or ever. Now get the bloody hell out of my way. I'm going to my dressing-room – '

'But a phone call takes only a moment or two, you know. No more – ' He was still smiling, still full of dimpled charm, and she threw her head back and bawled, 'Josh!' at the top of her voice and at last he was there, coming out of the horde of people in the wings, bustling and blessedly ordinary.

'Maggy, Maggy, Maggy, that was unbelievable, unbelievable! I've never heard anything like it. I tell you, you were the greatest – you made me cry – ' And indeed his face was streaked with tears. ' – and they're going to eat you in the next half, eat you. I've never heard anything like it, you were – '

'Josh, get this bastard out of here, will you?' she said, her voice loud and hard. 'He's pestering me. Get him off my back – '

'Eh?' Josh turned, peered, and then grinned. 'Oh, it's OK, Maggy! It's that guy picked picked us up at the airport – Green or something – hi there, George – '

'Gregory,' the young man said, still looking at Maggy. 'Gregory Greening.'

'He's pestering me. Get rid of him' she said again and turned and went, pushing through the crowds into her dressing-room, throwing herself down on the couch.

But the damage had been done. The magic of the evening had gone, that special quality that had filled her as well as the music had melted away and when she went back it was as a showman, a performer, not a musician eaten with the glory of her own sounds. The boys were still good, the audience still screamed, an intoxicated as ever, but it was different and she knew it. She felt as edgy and flat as if she'd been making love and was on the point of exploding over the top, only to find it fizzing out in a series of tired twinges. A sneeze in the loins, no more. No glory, no glitter, nothing. Just a sneeze.

They were besieged afterwards, newspaper people, fans wanting autographs, other musicians, and she couldn't get off the stage. The concert had been a fantastic hit, had had an impact that the first half had deserved, and the second half hadn't. Not that the beseiging crowds seemed to have noticed the difference; for them

196

the magic she had woven was still there, and faces came and went, beaming, excited, bright-eyed, and she nodded and smiled back, but inside her the weariness built and built until she felt like a lump of lead. Whatever had happened to the bubbles? A lead bubble, she thought absurdly and then – if I don't get away soon I shall scream –

The crowds at last began to drift away, and the scene men came on, began to clean up, shifting the drums and covering the piano, and Josh came back, grinning from ear to ear.

'There's a chat show, Maggy, we've got it all set up – '

'Not now, Josh. Please, not now. Tell me later. Tomorrow. I'm bushed.'

He was all solicitude at once. 'Of course you are. Jesus, of course you are. You were fantastic, great – of course you are – '

'It was great, Maggy.' Dan stopped on his way out and stood beside her grinning, but there was an undertow of grimness in him. 'Not much longer now, eh?'

'Not much – I how do you mean?'

'You're a solo lady, Maggy. Every inch a solo lady. You need the really big stuff now. We made a good noise tonight, but you – you took off.'

'I did, didn't I?' She looked up at him, smiling, almost shy. Whatever anyone else said, it was people like Dan who mattered. Professionals like herself.

'Next time you'll be able to hold it all through. Not just the first half. Then you'll be on your own. You won't need us then – oh, well. That's this stinking business all over.' He grinned even more widely, and bent and kissed her, noisily. 'You're a great girl, Mags. See you at the party?'

'Party?' she said vaguely, wanting to argue with him, wanting to tell him not to worry, they'd always be together, but knowing that he was right. Soon, now, very soon, she'd be on her own.

Josh patted her shoulder. 'At a new place on Seventh Avenue. There's a singer there – great – I'll take you over – '

'No – not yet. I – give me some time, OK? Where is it? I'll come on myself. No need for you to wait.'

He looked doubtful, yet eager to go, knowing nothing would go right at the party unless he was there to supervise. 'Seventh at Forty-Fifth. Noah's Ark, it's called. Good place, easy to find – '

'Then I'll find you – let me go back to the hotel, change – you know? I'll see you there – '

197

She went back into the hotel through the Madison Avenue entrance, hurrying up in the lift, scrabbling in her bag for her key. She needed to be alone, just for a little while, to think and sort out her feelings. Then, maybe, the party. She'd need that, need to come down before she could go to bed and get any sleep.

Even as she turned the key in her door she knew. There was someone in there, and for a moment she stood poised, as though there were time to turn away, go downstairs, call the hotel detective. But it wasn't possible, for she had turned the key and pushed open the door and was inside, the door closed behind her, even as the thought slid through her mind.

The two men sitting on her bed stood up, politely, as she came in.

'I thought it would be easier to pick you up here than in the Center, Miss Dundas,' Greening said gently, and smiled so that dimples appeared in both cheeks this time. 'That was quite a welcome you got, wasn't it? You are a very popular lady, indeed you are.'

'Get out. Get out or I call the police, you hear me? I'm not going to be – '

He shook his head gently. 'But there's no need to get excited Miss Dundas! No one's going to force you to do anything! No one's going to force you to do anything at all. No one at all! Are they, Harty? No, of course not – '

The blond man said nothing, just nodding and smiling. I've never heard him say anything at all, come to think of it, Maggy thought wildly. Maybe he's a robot.

' – we just want you to talk to this old friend of yours. Just – ' And he moved from the side of the bed, and she shrank away, back towards the door, and he smiled yet again. 'No need to be anxious! No one is going to hurt you, you know. My, you are a nervous lady, aren't you?'

Somehow Hartford had managed to get behind her while she wasn't looking and she turned and stared at him, her eyes dilated with fear as he leaned against the door, and Greening picked up the phone and dialled for a line and then a number. He listened for a moment and then said, 'She's here. Just hold the line a moment, will you?' and held the phone out to her.

There was nothing else she could do; she stood and stared at him and then, slowly, moved across the room and took the phone from him.

'Miss Dundas? Margaret Rose?'

The voice was warm and soothing, even through the distortion of the phone and she listened, saying nothing, breathing deeply.

'It is Margaret Rose, isn't it? It's been a long time, Margaret Rose.' His voice sounded comfortable, familiar, yet at the same time there was an exotic quality to it and she thought absurdly, 'He's English – no, he isn't – he's American, he's both, he's neither – '

'Who are you? she said harshly. 'What the bloody hell is going on here?'

'I'm an old friend, Margaret. It's been hard to get hold of you, one way or another. I sent my friends to meet you at the airport, just to make sure it was you, and it was, so I called. But why didn't you call me back?' The voice was reproachful, hurt, and for a mad moment she felt she should apologize. There was something so very warm, so very confiding about him.

'I don't call people I don't know. Are you going to tell me who you are, or do I hang up on you?' She looked at Greening, leaning against the bed and at Salmon by the door, and lifted her chin and repeated it more loudly. 'Do I hang up on you and throw these yobs of yours out?'

'Yobs? My friends yobs? My dear girl, have you *looked* at them?' He laughed, a bubbling rich sound and she almost laughed too. It *was* absurd to call that polished pair yobs. 'As for who I am – well, it's obvious you don't remember me yet, so I'll tell you. Don't say anything. Just listen. Andy. Andy Kentish. Remember now?'

She stood there with the phone in her hand staring at Greening, who smiled gently back.

Andy Kentish. The name slipped in and out of the memories in her head, and she tried to catch it, tried to pin it to a face, a person, and then the picture lifted itself in front of her eyes. The three of them standing in front of the Creffield Road house, their arms linked, their right legs stuck out in imitation of a high kick. Dolly in the middle, Morty Lang on her right, grinning happily into the lens from under his mop of thick hair. And on her left, the smooth young face, the boy who looked so mocking and remote.

'You're – ' she began and the voice cut in sharply, peremptorily.

'Don't repeat it. Just say after me, Adam Lancaster.'

'Adam Lancaster?'

199

'That's right,' he purred now, soft and easy again. 'That's my name now. But you knew me all those years ago as Andy Kentish. But that's a secret between us, just you and me I don't want anyone else to know that. Not my yobs – ' And his voice invited her to laugh.

'And why the hell should I – '

'Keep a secret for me? A very good question. But I think you will when I tell you what it is that we have to discuss. Now, do you want time to change? Or are you ready to come now?'

'Come where?'

'The boys will bring you. I wouldn't bother to change. I thought you looked marvellous tonight, simply marvellous – almost as good as the music. You've come on a long way since you were that sulky little girl I knew so long ago, hmm? So come now.'

'I'm not going anywhere.' She said it flatly, mulishly.

'But of course you are! Here am I, an old friend of yours. And Morty's and Dolly's. Here I am with all these memories to share with you – how can you possibly not come?'

He'd won, of course. As soon as she'd first heard his name she'd known it, really. Somehow this man was part of her search, part of the past that she was trying to relive, to exorcise, and she had to talk to him. They both knew it.

They took her across town, settling her in the car with great solicitude, Greening checking that the heater was at just the level she liked, again offering her a rug. Salmon, as silent as ever, sat in the back of the car and she watched the streets flick past, trying to relax, trying to sort out the confusion in her head.

She should have called Josh, told him where she was going, so that in case of trouble they could come and fetch her. Stupid idea; as if they would have let her. All right then, she should have stopped in the middle of the crowded foyer on their way through, loudly called a bellhop, given him a message to send to Josh, told someone, somehow, so that she was protected. Too late now. Too late.

They were leaving the mid-town parts of the city behind and the East River lifted its spangled blackness ahead of them as the car crossed Fifth Avenue and went on towards Sutton Place. She could feel almost as much as see the bulk of the United Nations Building rising on her right, and she leaned forwards, suddenly frightened again.

'Where are we going?'

'Don't worry, Miss Dundas. We'll stop before we hit the water!' Greening said and laughed and she leaned back, feeling anger rise in her because he had so accurately picked up her momentary madness. What would be the point of trying to kill her, for heaven's sake? Whatever this was about, there'd be no sense in that –

They stopped, pulling off the road into an empty lot and Greening switched off the engine.

'It's a little difficult to see the way here – I'll take your arm – ' he said as he helped her out, and she let him. The moment had long since passed to be dignified, to refuse anything. They were in charge now, and passively she let herself be swept along.

The building was dark and looked far from elegant on the outside, but as they came in through the heavy main doors, she blinked. Inside it looked like the most expensive of Park Avenue apartment blocks, thickly carpeted, walls covered in heavy wild silk, cut glass crystal chandeliers. The lift was also walled in wild silk, and purred upwards so quietly it was almost as though it weren't moving at all. And at the top, she stepped out on to an even thicker carpet, and stood still, staring. Behind her the lift doors slid closed and she turned her head sharply, to see that Greening and Hartford had gone.

There seemed to be no one there. A vast room, clearly the penthouse of the building, the far wall was all glass and looked out on to the river. She could see the lights of Queens on the far side and there, far away to the left, the Queensborough bridge lifted its spans against the black sky. It was beautiful and quiet and she felt her tight muscles loosen as she looked at the rest of the room, the thick white carpet, the black and crimson walls, the low black furniture, the great swathe of white net curtain that hung each side of the vast windows.

'Well, well! After all this time! How are you, my dear? It's lovely to see you.' He seemed to appear from nowhere, somewhere on the right side of the room and she moved sharply, turning on her heel to face him. And blinked because it was as though time had jerked backwards, and she was a child again, looking at Andy standing in the dining room at Creffield Road, smiling at her.

She took a deep breath and the illusion passed and she looked again and could see why it had happened; he still looked so young, so incredibly young. On that photograph he'd looked about twenty and looking at him now, the smooth face, the sleek hair, the faintly mocking smile, he seemed to be no more than twenty-five, if that. Yet he must be – she worked it out, counting in her head; he must be close on fifty. Forty-eight at least.

He moved forwards, coming nearer to one of the big lamps on the low tables and now she could see him more clearly, and the illusion faded, but only a little. There was a soft crêpiness about his eyes and a faint line running from each side of his nose to the corners of his mouth, but his skin was taut and smooth everywhere else, and his jawline clean and sharp. Thirty maybe? Thirty-five if you wanted to be uncharitable.

'I'm Adam Lancaster,' he said and held out one hand, and automatically she lifted her own and he took it, and then closed the other on it, so that he was standing close, holding her, looking down into her eyes. Tall. She'd forgotten how tall. But then everyone was tall when she was nine.

'We've got a lot to talk about haven't we? Such a lot to talk about. Come and sit down, Margaret Rose.'

22

'I'm going to need a lot of explanations for this – this hijacking,' she said, sitting very upright. He had been busy with glasses and a soda siphon on the far side of the room, and came towards her, carrying two tall glasses frosted with ice and with long straws emerging from the frothy white mixture in them.

'Hi-jacking? Dear child, what an expression! You're much prettier than an aeroplane.' The word sounded oddly English on his tongue, for his American accent was much more obvious now than it had been on the telephone. 'This should comfort you. It's non-alcoholic of course – we never touch alcohol here – but agreeable. Pineapple juice and coconut milk – no, don't jump to conclusions. Try it.'

She did, suddenly aware of how empty she was. The mixture tasted pleasant and soothing and agreeably sweet, and she drank it thirstily.

'I still want explanations.'

'Of course you do!' He was sitting on the low couch next to her now but not too near. There was nothing threatening at all in anything he was doing and slowly some of her tension oozed away. 'Of course you do. And you shall have it.'

'And an apology.'

'You want an apology? Then you shall have that too. I apologize. Quite for what, I'm not sure – '

'You're – God damn it, man, you frighten the shit out of me, sending your – your characters to follow me around, pick me up like – like I'm being kidnapped – '

'Please, Margaret Rose – there's no need for such language! I know it is difficult for you, living the life you do, but here – please do moderate your speech, a little.'

She stared at him, feeling grubby, like a child who has been reprimanded, and he smiled gently at her. 'You find it odd that I should object?'

She shook her head. 'I'm trying to remember – '

'What I was like when you first knew me?' He sat up straighter now. 'I don't think you should bother to do that, my dear. It isn't relevant. I have been born again, you see.'

She said nothing, almost gawping at him.

'I'm sure you *are* surprised. Most people are when they meet someone to whom it has happened. Even more surprised – and delighted – when it happens to them.' He put one hand on hers and it felt warm, but somehow remote, as though he were wearing invisible gloves; there was no real contact there. 'Perhaps it will happen to you.'

'What the hell are you talking about?'

'I told you, didn't I, that my name here is Adam Lancaster?'

'Yes – you said something – what is it? An alias? Are the police interested in Andy Kentish?' She grinned then, a knowing little grin. 'A lot of my mother's friends used to arouse police interest, I've discovered. Are you another of 'em?'

'Clearly you haven't taken time to put yourself as much in touch as you might be with the American scene. And what will soon be the British scene. Perhaps I'd better show you.'

He got up and crossed the room and went behind the bar and began to handle some invisible equipment, and after a moment a panel lifted on the wall beside him, folding itself away to reveal a big shimmering white screen, and at the same moment the lights in the room started to dim as a faint burring sound began.

He came back and sat beside her again as the picture appeared on the screen in rich colour, sharply defined, as perfect as any she had ever seen in a cinema and she watched, too surprised to say anything.

'Born Again!' the screen announced in huge letters as music lifted heavily, organ music with a lilt to it; beguiling, she thought, latching on the sound at once with her musician's ear. Clever stuff, like cheap Bach with overtones of Bacharach, churchy yet tuneful, dripping with emotion. Sickening and bloody, bloody clever.

The screen filled with pictures of people as the music became heavier, duller; men and women hurrying purposefully through rush-hour crowds, spilling out of buses, pushing each other on pavements, faces drawn and tired and angry and despairing and blank. They made her feel tired to look at them.

'Life today,' the voice-over said, a deep comforting voice, 'is a wearisome business. We work, we eat, we sleep, we work again.

A never-ending cycle of effort and worry and pain. And for what? What lies at the end of it?'

The pictures on the screen dissolved, became more people, old people sitting blank and hopeless in rows in what was clearly an institution of some sort; and shuffling helplessly along slum streets, shabby, obviously hungry, abandoned.

The voice went on, lower now. 'For what?' Above the music came another sound, of shrieking ambulance sirens, and then pictures of a white ambulance, its light revolving hysterically, arriving at a hospital, white coated figures rushing round to pull out a trolley. The camera closed in on the face of the figure on the trolley – eyes half open, the old face twisted, mouth lax, obviously dead. A hand came into shot, pulled a sheet over the face. 'For what?' repeated the voice. 'Oblivion? Nothingness? The end of everything?'

The screen lifted into bright colours, swirling reds and yellows and oranges and the music changed, became softer, more reverent. Rather more Bach and Bacharach now, she thought, staring, fascinated.

'Not if you hear this message – '

And ther he was. Andy Kentish, the man sitting quietly beside her, appeared on the screen in close up. She looked at the face, stared at the lines, trying to see the boy she had once known, the face from the photograph, and it was there, it was there all right, and yet it wasn't. That smooth sleekness, that smiling gentleness that gazed out at her seemed to mask the original; it was as though a perfect replica had been made of the real face and stuck on the top. It was real and yet it was hidden.

He began to speak, the voice coming from the screen softly as the music swelled and then sank to a faint humming, a high soft and undulating sound, and again her musician's ear was alerted and she thought; Nabucco –

Quite what he was saying she wasn't sure, for the voice rose and fell gently, beating on her ears like the waves of a quiet sea, firmly yet without aggression, almost stroking her. But although she could not have repeated the phrases he was using the message was coming clearly enough. He talked of redemption, letting the word slide sweetly from his lips like a curling little wavelet in a runnel of sun-warmed sand. He talked of eternity, of peace and joy and fearlessness, the end of pain and the satisfaction of all hungers. Over and over again.

After a while the image on the screen changed, though the voice and the distant strumming sound went on, and she saw a vast stadium, tier upon tier of benches rising in a great curving ellipse, people cramming every inch of them. The camera moved across the rows, showing faces in close-up, rapt, happy, wide-eyed smooth faces. Some were young, many were old, others were indeterminate and they all looked the same; remote and enchanted, totally inaccessible. She felt that even if she had been sitting next to them, she could not have got near them, couldn't have made them listen to her, respond to her, hear anything except that smooth undulating voice and its counterpoint of smooth undulating music.

The camera lifted, dipped and went down the rows of faces, closing in on the space in the centre of the ellipse. A tall red draped object, and on top of it a sleek white figure; standing very still, head up, hands gently crossed in front of him, he seemed to be surrounded by a nimbus of light as slowly the camera moved in, filling the screen once again with Andy Kentish's face.

His voice rose, became more urgent as the music too lifted and became more rhythmic and less tuneful, a broken syncopated beat that got inside her head, ticking away like a demented clock. It was a remarkable rhythm, almost hypnotic in its effect, and she felt her tongue move in her mouth, clicking softly against her teeth; ta-ta-ta-t-t-t-ta –

And now the camera came back to watch the tiers, and they seemed to be moving, lifting and rippling as the people began to spill out of the tidy rows into the aisles, tumbling, running, leaping down the steps to the central area, and now the scale of the place could be more easily seen. There must be hundreds of thousands of them there, she thought, hundreds of thousands -ta-ta-ta-t-t-t-ta –

The voice went on and on, relentlessly soft, relentlessly beautiful, and the people she was watching were crying, tears running down their cheeks, and throwing their arms up towards the figure in the red pulpit who still stood there, white and remote and slender in the bright lights thrown on him. More music, more sweeps of the cameras, showing the hordes of happy beautiful people, laughing now as well as crying, hugging each other, looking as though fires had been lit inside them, as if they were translucent and light could shine right through their skins.

'Born again,' The voice sank, softly, almost to a whisper. '*We*

206

are. Will you be, too?'

Slowly the screen blanked and the lights in the room came up to their former level as the wall panel unfolded and covered the screen. She sat there, silent, looking down at her hands.

'You see?' he said after a moment. 'You see who Adam Lancaster is?'

'Someone told me – ' She lifted her head and looked at him. 'You're very popular in California, I gather.'

He laughed. 'Popular? My dear child, what a word to describe my Western crusade! I *am* California! Soon I shall be New York as well. And London. And everywhere else in between – '

She shook her head, amused suddenly. 'How does it feel to be a continent?'

For the first time there was a sharpness in him. 'Oh, you can laugh. You English – so supercilious, so clever, so cynical! You can laugh!'

'*We* English? As I remember it, you were as English as I am! Come off it, man! I may have been only nine when I last saw you, but I wasn't stupid! And there are things I remember that mayn't have made sense then but are beginning to now – '

He looked at her, seeming to be as relaxed as he had been when she first arrived but there was a watchfulness in him now.

'What do you remember?'

'That you and my mother were – close friends.' It was a lie and she knew it. He'd been just one of the boarders, no one special. Not a Gerald or a Morty –

Her eyes widened as the thought came into her head. Morty. Morty in bed with Dolly, the bump heaving and lifting as she stood at the door and watched them. Morty and Dolly.

And Morty and *Andy*, standing close together in the kitchen as she came in, and jumping apart. Morty and Andy sitting close together in the dark in the dining room and someone coming and telling Dolly he'd seen them there, and Dolly shrugging and saying, 'Listen, love, if they likes bread-and-bread sandwiches, it's no skin off my nose. Live and let live, that's my motto – '

'And you and Morty Lang,' she added, softly, watching him. 'You and Morty Lang. I'm beginning to understand, I think. Just beginning – ' She frowned, working away at her memories, picking at the knots in an effort to untangle them. 'He was scared out of his mind, Morty. And his bully boys, the way they – is that what the stupid man was so scared about?' She was talking almost more

207

to herself than to him. 'Scared about what I remembered? Scared I'd tell people? No, it couldn't have been that. Could it? I never saw anyone so – '

'I see I'm going to have to be fairly firm with you.' He was on his feet now, standing looking down on her. 'I really must be firm with you. This can't go on, you know. I can't have all this time-wasting nonsense going on.'

'Time-wasting? Who the hell brought me here in the first place, damn it? *I* don't want to waste your time, believe me! It's too much waste of my own.'

'You've been making a nuisance of yourself, young woman,' he said and she grinned. She was feeling more in command of the situation than she would have believed possible. It was shadowy still, a lot of it, but things were beginning to slot into place. Just beginning.

'How?' she said perkily.

'Bothering Morty. He doesn't want to be bothered, and I don't want him bothered. Do you understand? I really don't want him bothered. You will stop pestering him.'

She laughed aloud at that. 'You are funny, you know! You stand there lecturing me like a schoolgirl and – I'm a big grown-up lady, you know that? No one tells me what to do or not to do, no one.'

'You came here, didn't you? Because I told you to.' The mood changed, sharply. He seemed to have shifted his ground and regained some control over himself. It was only now that he had returned to his previous urbanity that she realized just how rattled he had been. 'My dear, we really must stop being so silly, mustn't we? All I wanted was to meet you as an old friend, tell you what I was doing, and share some happy memories. When I heard you were coming to the States I thought – how splendid! What a lovely opportunity! That's all.'

'Oh, how natural! How reasonable! What could be more – more *normal*·than to send a couple of – of special constables in your private force to pick me up at the airport, hang around me at Lincoln Center and then bloody near kidnap me! What could be a more reasonable way of greeting an old friend!'

'My dear, I meant only to make our meeting easier! This is a hard place to find and you're a stranger in New York. I didn't want to put you to any trouble. That's all! I do assure you – '

'Then let me go now. If that's all it was, let me go. Right now.'

'By all means.' He smiled and went back to the bar where his equipment for the film was and pressed a button. A voice came, disembodied and tinny, into the room.

'Sir?'

'In ten minutes, Gregory, please, the car for Miss Dundas.'

'Sir.'

He came back and stood beside her, still smiling. 'You see? It was just to be friendly. That's all.'

She was back where she had been, tense, her muscles knotting at the back of her neck. In this state he was much more menacing than he had been, and she stared at him, trying to understand.

'I'm sorry to hear of Dolly's death,' he said, and sat down again. 'A good soul, your mother.'

'A good soul? To you, who never drinks and who gets upset by bad language? *Dolly*, a good soul?'

He produced a smile of infinite loving-kindness. 'Her sins shall be forgiven her. Tell me, my dear, did she die – in penury?'

'What's it to do with you?'

'Nothing at all. I was just – I remembered that old house, you see, and then I remembered that she had moved on, gone to a bigger place. I've heard all about it. A big hotel in Bayswater. A far cry from Acton.'

'You know a lot about what's happened, don't you? How come?' She was beyond trying to fence with him. All she could manage now were bald questions, blurted out. She was beginning to feel very tired.

'I like to keep in touch. I have my – old friends there still, you know.'

'Morty?' She shot it at him, wanting to see if he would react as he had before, but he just lifted one eyebrow and smiled.

'I have my old friends,' he said again. 'They keep an eye on things. They told me she'd died, you know. Told me you'd inherited her hotel. And her debts.'

He was watching her closely and she screwed up her eyes to clear her vision. She was getting more and more exhausted, and it made it difficult to think clearly.

'What's that to do with you?'

'I'm interested in anything that happens to old friends! Tell me, have you managed to find what you are looking for?'

'What? I don't understand – '

'Oh, dear, Margaret Rose, of course you do!'

'Don't call me that!'

'Hornby did.'

She sat there staring at him, her eyes no longer sandy with fatigue, strung up and taut.

'What did you say?'

'Hornby called you Margaret Rose. So did Codling and the Reader sisters – so did everyone. All the good old people from the good old days – '

He was smiling gently and she stood up, shaking her head.

'I'm tired. I want to go. Where's this car you promised me?'

'On its way, my dear child, on its way. You're still looking for him, then?'

'Yes. No. I mean, I don't know – it's none of your bloody concern – '

'Of course it isn't.' He stood up too and looked down at her and she stood as still as she could, feeling that any movement in her now would make her vulnerable, encourage him to hit her; a ridiculous, crazy idea, because he was the quietest, gentlest – '

'Well, we'll just keep an eye on things, shall we? My friends will tell me what happens. But I thought you might be interested to know that I'm interested. After all, I'm a very important person, now.'

'Really? How nice for you.'

'It's tens of thousands now, but soon – ' He smiled again, his chin lifting and once more the years slid from him and he looked as young as he did on the photograph. ' – soon it will be everyone. Everyone who matters. And then – well, you'll see. And I really can't have anthing spoiling that, can I?'

'I don't know what you're talking about.' She turned her head to look at the lift doors in the far wall. Had she heard a faint hum? Was he really going to let her out?

'It's expensive, of course. A lot comes in, but a lot goes out. Expensive. I need all the contributions that come to me. I need them for God.'

He's mad. That's why he looks so young. That's why all the cloak and dagger nonsense, all this – he's mad. Fatigue was clamping down on her again, thickening her mind, making it difficult to think clearly.

'Think about my message, Margaret Rose. Think about it. If you are born again, it will make it all so much simpler. Then you will be part of us, and share with us, and it will all be so much

210

simpler – '

His smile was wide again, gentle, warm, enveloping, and she looked up at him and thought muzzily, Born again – born better. Not Dolly's daughter. Better –

Behind her the lift doors slid open, and Greening was there and some of her exhaustion lifted, gave her enough energy to turn and walk towards him.

'We shall talk again, before you go home, shall we, Margaret Rose? Gregory will come and fetch you, bring you to our rally. Tomorrow – being born again will be a wonderful experience for you. Won't it, Gregory?'

'Oh, yes, sir,' Greening said, and smiled and looked at Maggy, and she shook her head. 'Oh, yes,' he said again. 'You'll love being at our rally. Tomorrow night. I'll come and fetch you.'

23

'I've got to get away.' She whispered it to herself, sitting on the edge of the bed, staring at the wall. I've got to get away. Right now. If they come back, take me to their rally, it will be the end. I'll fall into the middle of it, right down the middle, and that will be the end of everything. The end of music, the end of –

You can't. You've got another concert the day after tomorrow and then Long Island – you can't.

If I were ill they'd have to let me go. Wouldn't they? If I were ill –

She moved across the room then, first checking that her door was locked and angry with herself that she felt the need. She'd locked it as soon as she'd got there, and yet she'd become so jittery that she had to check again. This way lies madness. I read it in a book, obsessive checking of things you know need no checking is a sign of madness.

When she picked up the phone she didn't know for certain who she was going to call. It was as though someone else was making the decisions, organizing her, and she heard her own voice almost with surprise, talking to the operator, giving her the number.

'Hold the line please, I'll try to connect you right away,' the operator said chattily. 'The lines are good right now, just tried a London call – '

And then, blessedly, Theo's voice after an eternity of listening to the double ringing tone.

'Hello? Hello?' he mumbled, and three thousand miles away she could see him, up on one elbow in bed, holding the phone to his rumpled head, his eyes closed as he tried to hold on to sleep. 'Hello? Whassamatter – '

'Theo. It's Maggy. Darling, I'm coming home.'

'What? Maggy?' His voice sharpened and she felt his eyes snap open. 'Maggy! Christ, what is it? What's the matter? What's the time? Are you ill?'

'It's way past one o'clock – ' She laughed then, absurdly. 'Nearly seven in the morning, my dear. Time you got up anyway.'

'Seven – Maggy did you say you were coming home? You've got another three days yet – '

'I know, but there's something – I can't explain now, but I can't finish. Can you get another band out to fill those dates? I just can't finish – '

'Are you ill? Oh, Christ, I knew I should have come with – '

'Yes, I'm ill. Say I'm ill. The incapacity clause – I'll see a quack as soon as I'm home, get a certificate, we'll be OK with the contract. Just get another band out here for the day after tomorrow and then for the Long Island date. I'm taking the first plane I can get on.'

'But what is it? What's happened? For Christ's sake tell me, Maggy!' His voice sounded almost despairing and she shook her head, wanting to tell him but too weary.

'Darling, I can't. I'm OK, really and I'll be on the next available plane. Just contact Josh, sort it all out – '

She packed her bag with all the speed she could, but still tidily, still organized, changing first into jeans and a shirt and boots and then quietly carried her luggage out of the room, leaving the light on and the 'Do Not Disturb' sign on the handle. Maybe, if they come, they'll believe I'm still in there –

The clerk at the cashier's desk was remote and matter of fact, behaving as though Waldorf guests routinely checked out at almost two o'clock in the morning, and she paid her bill with a traveller's cheque, trying to keep her fingers from trembling, trying not to look over her shoulder at the still-busy lobby, trying not to show how tense she was. And succeeded very well, because as she left the cashier's desk, still carrying her own bag, making for the lift that would take her down to the garage, she heard her name being called as a bellboy went through the lobby, paging her. 'Miss Dundas, call for Miss Dundas – ' And she didn't show any hint of reaction that she'd heard him.

It wasn't till she was in the cab on the way to Kennedy that she realized that the call had probably been Josh or one of the boys, over there at their Seventh Avenue party, wondering what the hell had happened to her. Maybe she'd call from the airport. Maybe –

But she didn't. She went through the formalities of talking to the clerk on the desk, explaining with limpid dewy-eyed honesty

213

about the urgent call she'd had to go home, her father was dying – and that was a nice one, she thought wryly – she simply had to get on the first available flight, and being treated with all the sympathy and help there was in the whole world. Sure, they'd get her on the first flight in the morning, somehow. Not to worry, Miss Dundas, we're here to serve you, we'll get you out on the seven a.m. –

'Nothing before that?' She said it almost in a wail.

The clerk shook his head. 'Gee, no, I'm sorry, Miss Dundas, but there's a hold on all flights out, you know? We can't fly anything until the weather men give us the go-ahead. Like, there's some fog – but they reckon to be clear by morning, so we'll have you on that first London flight – seven a.m. You go to the coffee shop, huh? I'll call you if we have any problems but I don't reckon on any. And maybe you can get a little shut-eye there, stretch out on one of the benches maybe – '

But she didn't feel sleepy. Tired, God, yes, tired all the way through to her middle. But sleep, no. She sat in the almost deserted coffee shop, drinking thick black coffee and watching the few people there were, wondering idly why there was anyone here at all when there were no flights out till morning, listening to the woman with the broom moving desultorily between the tables singing with a high soft undulating sound –

It hit her suddenly as the woman came abreast of her and her singing changed to a broken syncopated rhythm, and she said, almost without thinking, 'Are you born again?'

The broom stopped moving and the woman turned and stared at her, her eyes wide and bright. She was a big woman, sagging and lumpy, in a blue checked overall, with thin greying hair pulled back into a thin bun at the back of her neck. She had big rough hands, clutching the broom like lumps of old dried meat, and every inch of her bespoke the years of work and struggle and sheer misery that had shaped her. Yet her face was serene and happy and her eyes wide and beaming and she looked at Maggy with a joyousness that would have looked remarkable in a bride.

'Oh, sister, and aren't we the happy ones!' She came forward and leaned close and kissed her cheek, all in one easy smooth movement and Maggy stared at her, startled. She smelled of frying and dust and cheap soap. 'Glory, glory, aren't we the happy ones!'

'Not me,' Maggy said. 'I mean, I don't know – tell me about it. Will you tell me about it?'

'But you know! That's why you asked me, because you know.'

'I don't know enough,' Maggy said, trying to sound humble. 'Will you tell me?'

'I surely will – ' The woman looked over her shoulder to the self-service counter, and then began to move her broom to and fro, as though she were sweeping, but staying in the same place. 'God wants us to tell the truth to all who will hear it.'

'Are there many people born again?' Maggy said, watching her, and the woman smiled, her face lifting even more.

'Oh, sister, there are, there are. In California, he tells us, 'most everyone is hearin' the word and running and flocking and leaping to come to the good life! And here in New York, well there's some of us, but after tomorrow – tonight, I should say – after tonight there'll be more and more and more! God will take New York to be his own, and Adam Lancaster will lead us safe over the river to the peace of bein' born again!'

'Over the East River? Or the Hudson?' Maggy said it sharply, needing to pull her down, and the woman looked at her and shook her head sadly.

'Oh, sister, you can sneer and you can scorn, but I tell you that when they hear him tomorrow – tonight – when they hear his word, they'll all succumb. You come and hear him and you will too. You'll know the peace and the loveliness of – '

'How much does it cost to be born again?' She could see the penthouse imprinting itself as a shadow on the coffee bar, could see crimson and black walls and thick white carpets where reality was garish yellow plastic chairs and green formica-topped tables with ketchup bottles shaped like tomatoes. 'It must cost a hell of a lot to be born again.'

'What's money?' the woman said swaying over her broom. 'The Lord provides, the Lord decides. I push my broom for God, and the money is nothing – nothing at all. It goes to the Lord to get more souls for the Lord. All I ask is to eat and sleep sometimes – and even that I would give up for the Lord and for *him*.'

Still she rocked to and fro and Maggy stared up at the round sagging face with its bright eyed stare and felt fear stir in her, somewhere deep inside. To look like that, to feel like that, to push a broom and feel like that – how must it feel to be like that all the time, just pushing a broom? I get it sometimes with music, go leaping and soaring away beyond everyone and everything, just sometimes, once in a blue moon; but she gets it all the time, with a broom.

And she remembered last night, remembered the first half, heard the music move in her belly and wanted to be like it all the time. Would Adam Lancaster, old friend Andy Kentish, do that for her? She must be mad, running out like this. Stay for the rally, let them collect me and take me to Madison Square Garden, let me be born again –

She had actually put her hand on her bag, was almost on her feet when she realized she was moving at all, and sat down again, staring at the big woman who looked contentedly back at her. God, this is mad, crazy mad. I'm halfway there. I'm right to try to get away. Oh, God, let it be morning soon, let me get home and safely away. He'll steal me too, if I don't get away from him.

She slept on the plane awkwardly, her legs twisted against the seat in front, her head lolling painfully against the backrest, but at least she slept, and at last stood blinking in the hubbub of the baggage reclaim hall, shivering a little with reaction. Three thousand miles ago, six hours away, he had nearly had her. She had sat at a green formica-topped table in Kennedy Airport and almost tumbled over the edge into madness, and now she was safe. It made her feel light-headed.

Outside customs, standing close to the rope rail, Theo was waiting, looking strained and white-faced in the middle of the chattering crowds and the stolid men holding aloft placards with names on them, and as she came through the door he ducked under the barrier and came to her with long easy strides and the sight of him brought tears to her eyes.

'Oh, Christ, Theo, but I'm glad to see you! I nearly got hooked, would you believe it? I nearly got hooked, there's this guy – he was the other one on the photograph, he's there now, got another name, calls himself Lancaster, runs a revivalist thing, and he nearly got me hooked. I tell you it was awful. He'd been after Morty Lang – said I was to leave him alone, and he was after me too of course. I know that now. I understand so much about it all now – '

'Darling, I've arranged for you to see a doctor right away – ' He was soothing, taking her luggage in one hand, holding her elbow warm and close with the other. 'At home, as soon as we get there. I arranged it all. Come on, darling, don't talk. You need a rest – come on, love – '

216

'You got another band out there? Was there time? Did you get hold of Josh? I should have told you, he was at a party at Seventh Avenue, I should have told you, and the contract – but the doctor'll fix that, won't he? An incapacity certificate, the contract'll be fine – Theo, he was awful. And I'm sorry. I'm truly sorry. I thought it might be you, but I know now, it couldn't have been. Could it? It must have been him, because he said he knew what happened here, had friends, he said, so one of them must have, though I'm not sure why – well, of course, I'm a fool! To find Hornby, of course. That's why they hit me, took all the stuff from the box. It's all money, really, all money. I'm sure of that. I talked to this woman in the coffee shop, poor devil, he's got her so hooked – she gives almost every penny she gets to him! To Lancaster, only really he's Andy Kentish. He's bad, really bad, and I thought it was you, and I'm so sorry. But you can understand, can't you, just a bit? With all that was happening – '

'Maggy, stop it, for God's sake, stop it! You're scaring me silly!'

They had reached the outside of the Terminal Three building now, heading for the car park and she stopped and blinked up at the late evening sunshine and then looked at him.

'What? Scaring you – '

'Darling, you're talking nonsense, just talking nonsense. Do stop – just take it easy, doze in the car. I'll have you home as fast as I can, get the doctor to see you – '

Fatigue clamped down and she nodded dumbly. 'Yes. I must have – I'm sorry. But I wanted to explain – '

'Later, sweetheart, later. There's plenty of time. Later – '

The doctor had gone, leaving a handful of sedatives behind, and she lay back on her sofa, her eyes half-closed, as normality at last moved in again. Across the room she could see her piano standing quiet and ready in the bay of the turret, the light slanting across it from the windows, and beyond that her mirror, tilted to get a view of the street below. Around her she could feel the ordinariness of it all; the familiar smells of coffee and furniture polish and her bath oil and it wrapped her in the first sense of peace and security she had known for weeks.

She could hear Theo's voice quietly at the door, and the doctor's heavier burr, and then the door closed and Theo came back, moving quietly, to stand in front of her and she looked up at him and smiled, lazily.

217

'He says there's no harm done,' he said. 'It's not your head or anything. I was so frightened it was – that you'd got a fracture or something that was making you so – but he says it's just tension and stress and all that. Take it easy a few days, you'll be fine.'

'I know,' she said, and stretched, feeling the tranquillizer the doctor had made her swallow move easily through her limbs. It was a good feeling. 'I know. I'm sorry if I – '

'There's nothing to apologize for. I was the wrong one, letting you go alone.'

'You couldn't have stopped me, you know that.'

'I could, somehow.' He sounded grim. 'But I chose to stand on my dignity. Christ, but I chose to – '

'You were right. I'd never have found out if you hadn't'.'

'Found out what?'

'That I was being – stupid to think it was you. The robbery – the papers – '

There was a little silence and then he said stiffly, 'You thought that I – '

'I'm sorry, Theo. But I was so damned confused – twice, you see, twice someone had hit me and the second time, you were – well, you were around, you know? And you'd talked about Rainbow Records.'

He was sitting down now, on the armchair facing her, very upright, his face still and hard.

'You thought that because I want my own record company, I'd try to hurt you? That I'd try and get hold of whatever this money is that Dolly's left you for *myself*? You really thought that?'

She closed her eyes, feeling the warm wave of tranquillizer recede a little and anxiety come moving back.

'See it my way, for God's sake, see it my way! There I was, in a tangle of Dolly's silly mysteries, trying to – and all of you so damned *interested*. Oliver and Friese and Ida – and yes, you. How could I be sure? How could I? I still don't know for sure that – well, I'm almost sure. I think it was Andy Kentish. I really do. He's the sort who makes things happen, even when he's not there.'

'You'll have to explain more. I still don't understand. I'm still not sure that – '

She explained as carefully as she could, trying somehow to get across to him the smooth silkiness of that voice, the effect that presence had had on her, the way the film had made her feel, the woman in the coffee shop, all of it, and he watched her and

218

listened and said nothing.

'And he's bad, Theo, he is, he really is. I know it as sure as I've ever known anything. And you should be grateful to him, because without him I might never have been quite certain about you – and I am. I really am, I think – '

And suddenly he grinned, leaning back in his chair and shaking his head and grinning, but there was no pleasure in it.

'You think. You still suspect that maybe, just maybe – oh, Maggy, why the hell do I put up with you? Do you know what you do to me?' He had stopped grinning now and she could see the hurt in him and wanted to put her arms up to him, to show him she didn't mean it. But that wouldn't work. He had to find his way through this for himself, just as she was doing.

There was a silence and then he said. 'Well? And now what? Where do you go from here? Or is it *verboten* to ask?'

'Don't get suspicious with me, Theo, please, plase don't! I've had a hell of a time – please, don't. I don't think I can – '

But he didn't move, didn't come and sit on the arm of her chair and soothe her as she'd suspected he would. He just sat and looked at her and then said in a hard tight voice, 'I mustn't show my feelings. Mustn't show my reactions – God, but Dolly spoiled you, Maggy! You were the middle of her whole damned world, so that she fretted over you and planned for you even for after she'd be dead, and you take it all for granted, don't you? You expect to be the middle of everybody's world. But there are other people, a lot of other people around! Think about it! Maggy matters, but so do Oliver and Ida and – we're people too! And me, God help me, I love you. D'you have any idea of what that means? Or are you so used to being the one who gets all the love that you don't know how to give it back? It's a two way experience, in case you hadn't noticed.'

This time she did put her arms up to him, and her face twisted as she began to cry, and he looked at her and then after a moment shook his head almost wearily, and came and held her close.

They made love then, there on the sofa, and it was gentle and quiet and much much better than it had ever been before, even better than it had been that afternoon that had ended in the attack from wherever it had been. And that surprised her because this time and for the first time she had been much more concerned about him and his needs and his reactions than she had about her own.

24

She woke to a dull sky outside the bedroom windows, but a clear mind inside her head. Lying in bed curled up with Theo, her bottom thrust backwards so that she was virtually sitting in his lap and his arm thrown heavily across her, she revelled in the way she felt. No panic, no anger, no confusion, just herself and Theo, happy in bed.

I shall start again today. I shall get this whole damned business sorted out once and for all today, and then I can forget all about it, and get on with work and with living and Theo. And Rainbow Records. She liked that idea, hugging it to herself with Theo's heavy arm, and then, made restless by the excitement of the thought, slid out of bed and into the shower.

They shared breakfast in a companionable silence with the papers and then he said, 'What will you do today? Come to the office? You're OK, now, aren't you?'

'Yes. How can you tell?' She smiled at him, feeling the life in her veins, enjoying the sense of well-being that filled her.

'You're different. After all this time with you I know the way you feel. And today you're different from yesterday.'

'I feel great. That was some knock-out stuff the quack gave me.'

'Yes. He said it was good. So, will you come to the office?'

'Did you get another band out for tonight – I suppose it is tonight, I get so lost with times – did you manage it?'

He nodded. 'Hot Quince went. Glad of the chance.'

'Then I'd better not show, had I? I'm supposed to be incapacitated.'

He grimaced. 'Damn it, yes. I'm a bloody fool. I'd actually forgotten that – you'll have to keep a low profile for a couple of days. Mind you, it was a true bill. You should have seen what you looked like when you got off that plane.'

'Half demented?'

'Three-quarters.'

'I was. It's only now I feel normal I know now – '

'Yeah, well, forget it. It's over now – '

'I'm not sure it is – ' she said slowly and put down her coffee cup.

'How do you mean?'

'He told me that – he seemed to know everything that was going on here. All about Dolly dying, and that I'd been to see Morty Lang – '

'You keep talking about this Morty.' He said it almost petulantly. 'I don't know who the hell you're on about, you know that?'

'I'm sorry.' She came and sat on the floor beside him, resting her arms on his lap, and staring up at him. 'I've been horribly secretive, and I'm sorry. But – '

'Yes I know. You weren't sure.'

'Well, no more. Listen. I found a photograph in that box of stuff – the one that was left behind in my pocket, you know, after I was walloped? Right. That was a photograph of Dolly and two men who used to live with us in Creffield Road – Morty Lang and Andy Kentish. And she'd written on Mort's picture that he knew. So I went to see him.'

'Knew what?'

'I don't know. That's why I went to see him. And – he was odd. He works in some home or other for delinquents in Walthamstow. That's what they looked like, anyway. Bully boys in leather with studs and nasty sideways stares.' She shivered a little. 'I thought they were following me, that it might have been them who got to me that night. Anyway, he was scared, absolutely shit scared and I couldn't work it out. I can now, of course. It's Andy. It's that damned Andy – '

'Did he have the information you wanted?'

She looked up at him, waiting for the small lift of suspicion that once would have come in response to that question, but it didn't and she breathed deeply and took his hand in hers and smiled, wide and brilliant. 'No – at least he didn't seem to. But he talked about someone Dolly used to know, who had some money. He was a thief.' She looked at him solemnly. 'A tea leaf, a villain, a crook. Went to prison for robbery.'

He laughed then. 'You sound like a tuppenny ha'penny thriller!'

'I know. That's what I – well, anyway, I managed to find out from Miss Lucas – oh, God you don't know about her either, do you? She used to teach me when I was a kid. When I first went to Thomas Tallis School, you know?'

'I don't, but keep on. Maybe I'll get some of it clear in my head eventually.' He was smiling down at her, seeming uninterested in all she was trying to explain, and she knew that he too had passed a moment of truth. He had known she had expected suspicion and that none had come. They were through that patch and out the other side.

'Well, she told me that Hornby, this thief chap – used to live in Cheltenham. Or near by, anyway, not far from where Dolly came from. So, I thought I'd better go there, see if I could find him. But then I had to go to the States. So that's my next step. I'd better go to Cheltenham, see if I can find this Hornby bloke, see if he knows what Dolly was on about.'

'Why should he? I thought Dolly said that this Mort knew?'

'That was what she wrote on his picture but he said he didn't. Maybe he didn't know what she meant. Maybe she knew he'd tell me about Hornby.'

'You said he was scared. Maybe if you go and tell him you've met this Andy of his and lived to tell the tale he won't be so scared and'll remember something else.' He bent and kissed her lightly and then began to clear the breakfast things and she got to her feet after a moment and helped him.

'Listen, Maggy. I've been thinking – about this whole damned business. Why not let Ida have the place, hmm? The headaches and the fuss – it just doesn't seem worth it. And you don't need it. You've got an incredible future ahead of you, my love. I had to phone New York, sort things out while I was waiting for you to get in, and they told me. You were pretty incredible at Lincoln Center.'

'I was,' she said soberly. 'Best I've ever been.' And she stood still, a milk jug in her hands, looking back at herself at the Lincolns Center. 'Dan said I'm ready to go solo.'

'Yes. So why bother? Why give yourself all this hassle for – let Ida have it.'

'No,' she said and bent her head and looked down into the depths of the milk. She could see her face reflected in it, pale and a long way away. 'No.'

'What did she ever do to you to make you so – '

'It isn't because of Ida. Not any more. It was, at first. And maybe the money, too, a bit. I thought of all I could do if I had it, and – and I was mean. Hateful. I didn't want her to have the place because – oh, I don't even know why because! Just a lot of left-over fury and – but that was at the start of all this. Now it's different. It's Dolly now, you see.'

'Dolly?'

'She wanted me to have it.' She looked up at him, leaving her reflection to drown in the milk. 'It was important to her. It must have been to have hidden it so – '

'That matters to you?' He was standing beside the sink, drying his hands, and mechanically she turned and put the jug in the little fridge and then started to dry the dishes.

'I don't know. I suppose so. Maybe. I just don't know.'

'It's a reason I can cope with. Better than hating Ida. Better than just wanting money.'

'Yes.'

They finished the dishes in silence, tidying the kitchen and then going into the bedroom to make the bed, going through their usual daily chores, for they were both neat people, needing order around them, and as she straightened sheets and then went into the bathroom to hang up towels and wipe away soap traces from the basin she tried to think, tried to see herself and Dolly together, tried to work out just what it all was that was now driving her to go on with this search.

But she couldn't see her, and when they were both back in the living room she said abruptly. 'So, what do you think? Cheltenham today? Or should I leave it for a while? Honestly, Theo, I'll do as you say. 'I want you to tell me.'

'Gloucestershire. It's a bit of a drive – look, love, I know you're feeling better today but – no, not today. Give it a rest. I've got to go in to the office – there'll be things to sort out over Hot Quince, and you and the boys – I've got to go in. But – '

'I'll go spare here on my own all day.'

'I know. Why not try this Mort again? Walthamstow's not too far. And like I said, maybe he's remembered something more by now.'

She thought for a moment, remembering that frightened quivering man crumpled in a chair in his cluttered office. Mort, scared silly. And his young men –

'I think I will. I'll tell him he needn't be – that I won't say anything about anything – and maybe he'll be better this time. You never know – '

The journey seemed incredibly familiar, considering she had only done it twice before. Each corner she had to turn beckoned her as she reached it and familiar buildings and landmarks kept appearing as the car swept through the acres of London streets, heading east. So that she arrived relaxed and pleased with herself, like a child who has just found her way to the middle of a maze.

There was a big van outside the house, and she looked at it curiously as she went up the path, her feet crunching on the old gravel. A removal van?

The hall was bustling with men carrying furniture and a couple of black-suited civil servants being busy with sheets of paper on clipboards, and she stood on the doorstep for a while watching, trying to work out what was going on, and then, as the furniture men went pushing past her, went across to the nearest of the black-suited civil servants.

'Seventeen, Boone? Is that all? Are you sure? Oh, but this is going to take a lot of – yes, what is it? I'm afraid we're *very* busy. Any queries really must be taken to the Town Hall. Phone them if you like – '

'I'm looking for Mr Lang,' she said and the man looked up, his face suddenly avid with interest.

'What?'

'Mr Lang, Mortimer Lang. He – oh, he's an old friend, you see. I'm not here on business of any kind. It's just that he's an old friend and – '

'Oh. Well, yes. Oh.' the man said, and his eyes flicked sideways at his partner. 'This lady, Boone, says she's a *friend* of Mr Lang – not here on business – an old *friend*.'

'Oh. An old friend?' The other man looked at her and frowned portentously. 'Oh, dear me. Well, now, this is really very difficult. Very difficult – '

'Where is he? What's happened?' She could feel herself sharpening with tension, and her source of relaxation began to harden in her muscles. 'Is there something wrong?'

The first of the men shook his head, heavily, clearly finding a good deal of satisfaction in what he was doing. 'I think you'd better sit down, my dear, while I explain, don't you Boone? I mean. I really don't think – '

'Oh, for heaven's sake, man!' She said it sharply, drawing away fastidiously, for he had put one hand on her arm. 'What on earth

224

are you – '

'I'm afraid Mr Lang has passed on,' the man Boone said, more portentous than ever, and looking at her with a deeply mournful expression. 'I fear we must be the givers of bad tidings. I *am* so sorry. That was why Mr Ellis here wanted you to sit down. He was afraid – there you see? You *do* feel out of sorts! Quick, Ellis, a chair – '

'I'm all right,' she said curtly. 'Just – surprised.' She pulled away again, for once more the man had taken hold of her arm. 'What happened?'

'Oh, I don't think we're at liberty to divulge – ' Boone began but the other man shook his head and said quickly, 'Well, why not? I mean, it was in all the papers, the local ones, I mean. There was even a photograph on the front page of the *Evening Standard* – you know, the 'News in Brief' column. It's not exactly a secret – '

There was a sound on the stairs, even above the noise the furniture men were making, and she looked up and saw the shape of a woman there. She moved then, coming further down the stairs and now Maggy could see her more clearly.

It was Sally Lang, the square dumpy woman she had met briefly that afternoon when she had last come here to see Morty, but the change in her was startling. She seemed to have collapsed in on herself and her squareness had dissolved into a heavy shambling shapelessness that made Maggy suddenly want to cry.

'Mrs Lang,' she said quickly and moved across the hall towards her, her hand out. 'I'm so sorry. I just heard – I had no idea – I'm so sorry.'

'Who is it?' The woman peered up at her, frowning, and then nodded, slowly. 'Oh, yes. I remember. He said he'd know you when – what do you want?'

'I didn't know. I'm so sorry. I just came to see him. I had no idea – '

Maggy stopped, staring at the woman on the staircase who stared back at her with dull heavy eyes. She shouldn't ask, she knew she shouldn't ask, but she had to.

'Mrs Lang, what happened? Can you tell me? We – I did know him a long time ago and – '

Sally Lang nodded, heavily. 'Yes,' she said. 'It was an accident. A car accident – '

'A *car* – ' She saw it in front of her eyes, like a scene from a

225

bad cops and robbers thriller on television. A car being chased, pushed off the road, going over and over down a hillside –

'Well, not exactly an accident, eh, Mrs Lang?' The man Ellis said, his eyes suddenly avid again. 'I mean, the papers said – no other car was involved, was it?'

'No. But it was still an accident.' She lifted her chin and some of the shape seemed to come back to her sagging body. 'He was a very hard-working man, and I believe he was tired, quite desperately tired, and he just – he fell asleep, and the car went off the road and into that tree – that was what it was. He told me as much himself – '

'He *told* you?' Maggy said sharply, trying to hold on to reality.

'He didn't die at once. The other one did, but he didn't. He was in intensive care at the hospital for three days, and he was quite lucid. Some of the time.' Sally Lang said dully. 'He told me some of it.'

'I – is there somewhere we can talk, Mrs Lang. On our own?' Maggy looked at the men with distaste. 'In confidence? I knew him so long ago, you see and – '

'The back kitchen hasn't been started yet,' Ellis said fussily and Boone nodded, like a mandarin, his eyes glued to Sally Lang's face. 'We'll be in there later, of course, but we've got all these other rooms to finish first. Why not go there? No one'll disturb you there – '

the back kitchen turned out to be a scullery, stone-floored and smelling of potatoes and mildew and dirty washing, and Sally Lang sat down heavily at the wooden table in the middle of it and looked up at Maggy, trying to smile.

'I'm sorry I can't look after you better, but you know how it is – ' She waved her hand vaguely in the direction of the two men outside. 'The council here and all – '

'They aren't throwing you out, are they? My God, how could they be so – '

She shook her head. 'It doesn't matter. It was Mort who was employed here, really, you see, not me. I did a lot, of course, but I was just his wife. It was his place. His job. So I've got to get my stuff out of the flat – that's what the removal men are doing, clearing my flat – and there has to be this inventory, you see, before I can get Mort's last pay cheque.' She grinned then, a thin grimace. 'Not that it matters. We spent every penny we had on this place and on the boys. His pay cheques and my money. My

226

father's money. That was how Mort wanted it, so we did. Every penny. They could have had his last pay cheque as well, for all I care. I shan't bother with it – '

'But where will you go? What will you do?' I hardly know her, Maggy thought, but it matters, it really matters. The poor creature – 'Where will you go?'

Sally Lang shrugged, looking down at her hands on the table. 'I don't know. Don't care very much.'

'But my dear, you've got to – I mean, when they've cleared your furniture – where are they taking it?'

She shrugged again, and was silent.

'Is there anything I can do?' Maggy said, and came closer, and after a moment touched the other woman's arm. She had never used physical contact much in any of her relationships, but she felt a need to reach out to this woman, and it expressed itself in a light touch on her shoulder. But then she pulled her hand away and said again, 'Is there anything I can do?'

'No. Thanks all the same. I'll be all right. I can manage. Don't fret over me. I'll be all right.'

Outside a man's voice was raised in a shout and then someone else expostulated and the shouting sank to a low rumble, and Maggy looked up and round the narrow bleak little room almost in desperation. Oh, God, now what? Here I am stuck with a woman who doesn't seem to want to say anything and I said I wanted to talk to her, and now what do I do?

She tried again, almost despairingly. Please, Mrs Lang – Sally, isn't it? Please, Sally, what can I do? I knew Mort, you see. He was – he was quite kind to me when I was a child and – '

Sally looked up and very slowly nodded her head. 'Yes, I'm sure he was. He was always kind to children. He liked children.'

'Yes. So let me help you, if I can. I can't do much, I know that, but – '

'You know how he died, then?' Sally said and looked up at her, her eyes bright and yet heavy, like polished pebbles. 'You know how he died?'

'You said – a car accident – falling asleep at the wheel – '

Sally Lang shook her head, as heavily as just before she had nodded it.

'He killed himself. That was what he did. He committed suicide. How can anyone help me after that?'

25

Beyond the room the sounds went on; footsteps on the stairs, men's voices, and from further away the traffic in the road outside and Maggy looked at the heavy shape sitting there at the table and shook her head.

'Suicide? But how – what – '

Sally took a sharp little breath, almost irritated, and then spoke in a clear careful voice as though she were talking to a child. 'He deliberately went off the road. Aimed at the tree. He meant to kill both of them. But the other one was luckier. He didn't have that week of – it took him seven days to die, Mort. You know that? Seven days. That's a long time when you're – when you don't want to be alive. And you hurt.'

Maggy swallowed. 'Who was the other man?' She didn't really want to know. She really couldn't have cared less but she could see all too clearly the picture of Mort, in pain, in hospital, that Sally was staring at with her dead shining eyes. 'Was he a friend?'

Sally grinned then, a wide incredible grimace that made Maggy look away; it was too painful to see it. 'A friend? No. He was – his name was Ernest Gibbs. He was a private investigator. Isn't that ridiculous? A private investigator. A nasty little man in a pin-striped suit. I didn't know people like that existed. I thought they were just invented for television. Nasty little men who look so ordinary they can't be real. Whoever could have thought such things were real? But he was real. And he was with Mort.'

'In a pin – Oh God!' Maggy whispered, and needed to sit down, and pulled the chair out from the other side of the table. 'A little man who looked like a city clerk? I thought I'd imagined him.'

Sally looked at her, her face taking on some sort of expression for the first time.

'What?' She frowned sharply. 'What do you mean?'

'I kept seeing someone like that, following me. I thought – I thought I was imagining it. Getting paranoid. He looked the same but somehow different every time. A little man with hair that you

228

know isn't really growing on the top of his head the way it pretends to be. It's sort of pulled over from the back – '

'Why should he have followed you? What – did *you* have something to do with all this? With Mort dying? Did you? You came here and then – it was after that – '

'No!' Maggy almost shouted it. 'It was nothing to do with me! He was frightened when I came but I didn't know why, I really didn't know why. But then he frightened *me*. Those boys – he sent those boys to see me off, and – '

'Mort's boys.' Sally bent her head again, to look down at her clasped hands, quiet again. 'I knew, of course, I pretended I didn't, but I knew. I just kept hoping it would be all right. That – but there was no point in saying anything, was there?'

She lifted her head again, looking at Maggy. 'Was there? If I'd said anything he'd have got all upset, and tried to stop, but it would have been no use. He'd have just started again. He thought I didn't know but I did. I'm not as silly as I look. So I said nothing and hoped for the best. It suited the boys so they wouldn't have said anything – and it suited me. I can't lie about it. It suited me.'

'What did? I don't understand. I'm so – Sally, it was nothing to do with me – what happened. It couldn't have been. How could it?'

Sally sighed, a tired heaving of her shoulders. 'He was gay, you see. Isn't that a stupid word? Gay – when it made him so miserable, so – all his life it drove him nearly mad, when it came on him. He never said, we never talked about it, but I knew. They were the times he wouldn't leave me alone, you see. No sooner in bed but he was – then I knew it had come again. The way it did sometimes. Then there'd be the in-between times when he was just working and working and left me alone. And that was awful. Then it was me who felt bad. But I knew it'd be all right again, when the need got to him.'

She lifted her chin. 'Silly, wasn't it? The only time he loved me properly was when he wanted boys. So I had to say nothing, didn't I? If I'd fussed, tried to change him, I'd never have had any part of him. So I never said anything. And he thought it was a secret and that was why they could do it to him.'

'Do what?' Maggy said it almost despairingly, floundering, but just beginning, dimly, to see what the woman was saying, just beginning to glimpse, far away and in a blur the pattern of their lives together. The hunger of this square dull woman for a man

229

who hungered for sleek boys with narrow flanks and flat bellies, when all she had to offer was wide hips and heavy breasts and a vast, patient, uncritical love. The trap she had twisted and turned in, finding her own needs satisfied only when his guilt about his own drove him to seek the warmth of that burgeoning female flesh. 'Do what to him? I don't understand.'

'He used to come and get money from Mort. This Gibbs. Every week he came and got money, and Mort used to make entries in the books, such clumsy silly entries and then I had to tidy them up, in case the council realized – but it was all right. We managed well enough. I'm a good manager. But then it all changed. After you came – ' She shook her head, weary again. 'What does it matter, anyway? He's dead. What does it matter?'

'It matters a lot. I can't let it seem it was because of me – that I had anything to do with his dying! You can't expect me to live with that – '

Sally looked at her and again that wide painful grin filled her face. 'Poor you. Oh, poor you,' she said, and Maggy felt her own face darken as blood rushed up from the well of shame that suddenly filled her belly.

'Oh, I'm sorry! I didn't mean to sound so – but I do want to know. Please? And I want you to know.'

'All right. You want to know. I'll tell you. This man, this Gibbs, after you came he was here more often. Mort said to me he was an old friend, and then he said he was in trouble and could we put him up and I said – well, what could I say? Mort looked dreadful, as though someone had – well, dreadful, anyway, and he was so loving, so very loving, over and over again. It was awful, it was marvellous – oh, God!' And she bent her head again, so that Maggy couldn't see her face.

There was a silence and then Maggy said, 'And he came to live here?'

'Yes. And Mort gave him more and more. Before, at least it had been different. The same every week, steady, you know? But now it was different – '

'Do you know why?'

'Yes. He told me.' She stretched then, lifting her shoulders and said unexpectedly, 'I'm thirsty. I'll make some tea,' and got up and moved about the scullery, fetching chipped beakers and tea bags and putting on the kettle. She made the tea by pouring hot water over the bags and leaving them in the beakers, so that the

230

brew became heavy and black, and then she thrust one of the beakers at Maggy, offering her neither milk nor sugar, and they sat facing each other, sipping, silent, each locked in her own thoughts.

'You see, the whole situation had changed.' Sally spoke suddenly, as though there had been no break in the talk. 'Gibbs used to come for money for someone else. That was what Mort said. There was someone in America, who knew all about him. Knew about the boys, everything. I think he and Mort, once – well, anyway. There was this Andy and – '

'Andy.' Maggy put her beaker down so sharply that it splashed tea onto the table. 'What did you say?'

'Andy. A man in America call Andy. It was him Gibbs got the money for. But then he suddenly started to get it from Mort by himself. He sent him telegrams.' She shook her head, almost smiling, reminiscent. 'Mort tried to hide them from me, said it was just messages from the council, but I knew they never sent telegrams. But what did it matter to me? There was nothing I could do. So I just said all right, and went on with what I had to do, didn't I? Making beds. Meals. The washing – '

'So this man Gibbs – '

'That was the trouble. He'd started to get money from Mort as well, you see. Mort talked and talked there in the hospital. He was all strung up, like – it made me think of cat's cradle. Did you play cat's cradle when you were little?'

She put down her beaker, and began to make complicated movements with her hands, twisting and turning them, concentrating.

'It was like that, cat's cradle. And Mort looked like that with ropes and pulleys on his legs and all those tubes going everywhere, even up his nose, and he talked and talked and they said not to stop him, so I just listened and he told me. There were the telegrams from America and Gibbs asking for more and more and all because of something that didn't matter all that much. I mean, I suppose if they'd found out at the council about Mort and the boys – they're all under twenty-one, you see, and that makes it illegal – I suppose there'd have been trouble. But me, I wouldn't have said anything, would I? And we'd have managed somehow because I'm a good manager. But he thought I'd have left him too, and it was that that was the worst, he said. So he put Gibbs in his car and they went for a drive and he drove the car at the

231

tree. But he did tell me it would have been the worst if I'd left him, so I suppose – '

She picked up her beaker and began to drink again, the tea bag bobbing against her upper lip and leaving a stain there.

'He loved you a lot, didn't he?' Maggy said, gently, trying to sound right, not silly, not sentimental, just right.

'Do you think so?' She put the beaker down again, and looked at Maggy with her head on one side. 'Do you think so?'

'It sounds like it.' Be careful. Don't go over the top. 'I mean, if he said the worst would have been you finding out – he must have.'

Again a silence and then Maggy said, still careful, 'I can't see that my coming here had anything to do with it all. Can you?'

Sally shrugged. 'I don't know. It was just at that time so I suppose I wondered – I hadn't thought of it till you came here, this morning. And then, just for a bit, I did wonder. But it doesn't matter. Does it?'

'No,' Maggy said. 'No, I suppose not. Sally, I'm sorry. About Mort. I remember him from so long ago, when he was kind to me.' And didn't just like boys with sleek flanks and women with wide hips and heavy breasts but little girls as well. Poor bastard. Poor hungry bewildered bastard. 'He was really very kind to me.'

'He was a very kind person. He always tried so hard to please people, you see. That was all he ever really wanted. To keep everyone happy. Silly, really. It was all I could do to make one man happy, and he wanted to make everyone happy!' She laughed then, an odd ringing little sound in the cold scullery, bouncing off the stone floor. 'And he wanted to make everyone happy! Well, you can't say he didn't try. And he did love me, didn't he?'

'Yes,' Maggy said and stood up. 'No one could love anyone more, to do what he did for fear of losing you. It must be very good to be loved like that.'

'I'll think about that. I'll think about it a lot. I'm glad you came now. I wasn't at first.'

'I'm glad too. Is there anything I can – '

Sally shook her head. 'No. I'll manage well enough. I've always been a good manager.'

It wasn't till she was nearly home that it hit her. Andy black-mailing *Mort*? Because they'd been homosexual together all that time ago? But it was mad. Andy was Adam Lancaster now. Born again. Handsome and polished and looking so young and vibrant, obviously as clean and perfect inside as he was outside. If all those eager people she had seen on the film knew that once he had – what would they say?

And the woman with the broom at the airport; would she work so hard for money to give him if she knew?

So why should Andy blackmail poor Mort until he died in a cat's cradle of ropes and pulleys and tubes in the clinical stink of a hospital intensive-care unit? Hadn't he more to lose than Mort had? Mort had only a dreary job in a council home for delinquents to lose, and a lumpy square wife who was a good manager. But Andy – he had California and New York and the whole of his heaven to lose.

'And all the broom-pusher's money,' she whispered, as she drove the last few yards back to the flat. All the broom-pusher's money. How many broom-pushers in California and New York? How many dollars could they bring to Adam Lancaster's heaven? Dollars, dollars, dollars – is that why he tormented Mort? As a way to stop Mort from tormenting him? So tortuous, so twisted – how can anyone be so twisted? Andy is, she thought. Adam Andy Kentish Lancaster is.

And now he knows that I know about him. I told him so. The thought exploded between her eyes as she parked the car and switched off the engine. He knows I know. Will he start to blackmail me? But how can he? What have I got to lose? It is I who could blackmail him –

Which makes me dangerous. Obviously he tried to keep Mort quiet by frightening him. Blackmailing Mort was the best way of keeping him quiet, wasn't it? They do that in bridge. She remembered Susannah trying to teach her to play bridge. 'Pre-emptive bidding, dear heart,' Susannah's clear tones rang in her head. 'You bid what they've got and then they can't – '

Stop being so silly. Think. You know something about Andy that could, surely, damage him. Don't you? Which makes you dangerous. He drove another dangerous part of his past to death. Couldn't he do the same to you?

Maybe he actually killed Mort? Maybe it was this man Gibbs, who was working for Andy, who drove the car and killed Mort?

Don't be crazy. That would have meant getting the man to kill himself. 'Just pop along and drive that man Lang into a tree, will you? Of course you'll be killed too, but you won't mind that – '

Maybe a Born Again Gibbs? Could that have been it?

No. Of course not. Gibbs was just a seedy little go-between who had decided to do his own blackmailing. He stopped doing it for Andy which was why Andy had to start doing it himself, sending Mort telegrams. And Gibbs starting too, getting money for himself.

'Poor bastard.' She said it aloud, sitting in her car and staring ahead at her at the familiar Crescent. 'Poor bastard.' Both of them on his back. What else could he do but drive at a tree?

And now what? Will Andy start on me? Try to find a way to drive me into a tree? He'd be better off if I were dead.

But if that were true, why did he let me go in New York? He could have killed me then and there, dropped me in an alleyway somewhere nearby and I'd have been just another police statistic. Mugging goes on all the time in New York, doesn't it? What's another body in an alley down near the spangled waters of the East River? Just a silly tourist wandering where she had no right to be –

Because of Hornby.

The idea slid into her mind slowly, almost insinuatingly, and behind it she could hear his voice as the lift came whispering up to his penthouse. 'It's expensive, of course. A lot comes in but a lot goes out. Expensive. I need all the contributions that come to me. I need them for God.'

He wants Dolly's money. Hornby's money. He knew about Dolly leaving me the hotel and the debts, and knew I was looking for Hornby, as part of looking for the answer to those debts. It could be a lot of money; I know that, and it's obvious he does too.

So that was why he let me go. He wants me to find the answer to Dolly's silly riddle and then he'll come and get it from me. And then what? Will he just say thank you and tip his hat and go back to New York?

This is mad, absolutely mad. You're getting more and more embroiled in a nonsense. Telling youself silly stories.

Dolly stories.

She shook her head angrily and turned to open the car door. And then she saw them. Two tall young men, walking down the steps of the next house but one to her own. They were wearing dark suits and sparkling white shirts, and firmly knotted dark ties and their shoes shone smooth and bright on the dusty pavement as they came to street level and then turned sharply right to climb the next little flight of steps to knock on the next door.

I'm getting worse and worse. I thought they were Greening and Salmon, but they're not. They're just a pair of neat and tidy young men doing a market survey or something. Market-survey people are always coming, making pests of themselves. Housewives earning pin money.

But these are young *men*. Glossy young men who could have been cut out of the backs of cornflake packets. The sort of young men Lancaster would use to collect people for his Wembley rallies when he gets here. The papers are full of it. Everyone knows he's coming, the New Voice of America they're calling him –

She turned back then, fumbling to get the key back into the ignition and started the engine and revved it so that it roared, and one of the young men on the doorstep turned and looked at her. Smooth-faced and young, he looked at her for a moment, and then turned away apparently uninterested, as the door opened. It was the last thing she saw as she drove away round the Crescent, heading back for the main road, and shaking so much that she could hardly keep her feet on the controls.

26

'You think they were this Andy's people?' Theo's voice came thin and tinny through the phone. 'Did they try anything? Try to follow you when you drove away?'

'No.' She could see her face in the grimy mirror over the phone, see the street outside reflected behind it, cars and buses grinding by, a flower-seller, people hurrying past. No one there who looked at all threatening.

'No. I looked back when I got to the other end of the Crescent and I could just see them standing on the doorstep talking to someone. They didn't try to follow me. But Theo – I think I understand it all now. I really do. It's Mort you see – though he's dead.'

'Dead?' The tinny voice sharpened. 'What happened? I mean, was it a funny death? Or – '

'Suicide. Drove into a tree. But he had someone with him, and he was a blackmailer and used to collect money from Mort for Andy. And I think he was the one who used to follow me – oh, Theo, it's all so bloody complicated. I can't tell you all about it now – but I thought – look, I am being stupid, aren't I? I mean, there hasn't been time for Andy to get anyone over here, from the time he'd have discovered I'd gone? He thought I'd be in New York longer, you see, was going to make me go to one of his rallies. Well, has there been time? Was I imagining those chaps? Could they have been salesmen or something? It was just that they looked so damned *sleek*. Like the ones who picked us up at the airport – '

'I don't know – Maggy, will you stay there? Pretend to make calls or something. Anything. I'll leave now, get to you as fast as I can – '

'Don't be daft. I'm at Marble Arch. It'll take you ages to get here. And the traffic's like soup – I – actually I feel better now.'

'I'm damned if I do. This is getting mad. You stay there. I'll be there as fast as I can and we'll go to the police – '

236

'No!' She shouted it. 'No! What for? To tell them I'm having paranoid nightmares? That there's this revivalist character who scares me? I can just see it – and anyway, I don't want to – I've got a feeling I can see a way through this – '

'What sort of way? There isn't any other way but to get the law involved – '

'No. I'm going to Cheltenham. It's obvious that that's where this money is that Dolly was on about. Morty talked about him and so did Andy – I'm going there.'

'Then I'll come with you. At least let me do that! You can't stop me from – '

'No, and I don't want to. Can you get away now? I can be at Paddington in fifteen minutes by underground. Meet you at the ticket office?'

It was really extraordinary how alive she was feeling. The morning's confused emotion had given way to a taut alertness that was very like the way she felt before a big concert. There was a sureness in her, a total conviction that she could make everything come out the way she wanted, just as she had at Lincoln Center a couple of nights ago. A couple of nights ago? Crazy, crazy, only a couple of nights ago.

'Do you see, Theo? It's all to do with this money. And it's *mine*. Dolly wanted me to have it, so it's *mine*.'

Theo was leaning back in the corner of the compartment, watching her as she sat on the edge of her seat, her face alight and her hands restlessly gesticulating.

'But you didn't want it, did you? To start with? You said – '

'I know what I said!' She leaned back now, and turned her head to stare out at the passing landscape. It was bucolic and charming, all the tight organized prettiness that was Gloucestershire, but she wasn't seeing it; her eyes were wide and staring far beyond it. 'I was confused and I didn't know – I've found out a lot this past few weeks, Theo.'

'You've done incredibly well. I doubt if I could have worked it out as you have. If you're right about it all, of course.'

'Oh, I'm sure I'm right. Absolutely sure. But I don't mean about Andy and the money. I mean about Dolly. And me.'

'Well? What have you found out?'

'I don't want to talk about it. Not yet. But I've found out a lot.'

237

He said nothing, just watching her, and her eyes remained fixed on the passing scenery, and her face was smooth and almost serene, and he sighed softly and closed his eyes. She never looked like that with him. Shut away in her private world she looked like that, but never with him.

She didn't mean it, ever, Maggy was thinking. Never meant anything to work out the way it did. She was just Dolly, doing what she wanted the moment she wanted to, and trying in her own way to make it what I wanted. I wish it could have worked right. I wish I could go back to the top and play the whole score again. Dolly and me, Dolly and her stories. I'd make her tell me true ones, if I rewrote the score. No romantic soldier hero for a father, no rich country house owners for grandparents. I'd just play a clean and straight score for Dolly, without any of her grace notes. That was really all it was. She wanted to play the pretty music, not the real raw stuff. Poor dear Dolly.

Dear Dolly?

Yes. She hurt me, and I thought I hated her, but I didn't really. It was the other side of the same penny, loving her and needing her, and then hating and rejecting her. I've never sorted it out, before. Now I'm beginning to.

And when I've got the money, and I've sorted out the debts and all the hotel stuff, I'm going to do what she really knew she ought to do. I'm going to give it to Ida. I'll earn what I need. All of it. Ida can have what she's earned.

Ida. Think about her, too. All those years of resentment and hate, and for what? Because of her, or because of me? What it my fault or her fault that we loathe each other so much?

I can't think about that now, I can't. But I'm going to give the hotel to Ida, all the same. It ought to be hers. She did the work, made it all happen, Dolly just – Dolly was just Dolly. Indolent and slaphappy and doing it all wrong. Without Ida we'd have all been out on the street, time and again. It was Ida who kept the place together, and Ida who ought to have it. But I'm going to find that damned money first. I am, I am, I am.

But she still couldn't really understand why it mattered so much.

They started with the local telephone book. There were quite a few Hornbys in and around the town and she rang them all, as Theo sat beside her on the hotel bed and read out number after number.

'I wonder if you can help me?' The words got easier and easier, coming out like a script she'd learned by heart. 'I'm trying to find an old friend of my father's. He'd be in his sixties now. James Hornby – they called him Jim. Lived in London, for a while, in Acton – '

Blank after blank after blank. Terse denials of anyone ever called James or Jim in the family alternated with garrulous accounts of every cousin, uncle and nephew who had ever graced a particular family tree. There were the suspicious ones who wanted to know all about her father – and she told a complex tale of shared army services – and the uninterested ones who weren't even remotely concerned about why a stranger should call them out of the blue asking for a relation they didn't have. And as the afternoon wore on she became more and more dispirited.

It was Theo who said suddenly, 'The local paper.'

'What?'

'Newspaper. He must have been written about, surely? Local villain? Went to prison? I would have thought – '

'Where? Where is it?' She took the phone book from him, leafing through it almost feverishly. 'Oh, Christ, what's the bloody thing *called*?'

Theo picked up the phone again and the operator, obviously fascinated by the strange behaviour of the couple in seventeen, answered at once.

'Local paper, sir? The *Gazette* you mean?'

'Call them,' Maggy said, when she found the number. 'Ask them – no, we'll go there. Look for ourselves – '

'Now? It's gone four! They'll never let us just wander in like that, go through the back numbers, will they? We'll have to wait till tomorrow, make an appointment. We'll have to stay a few days, that's all. It's worth it, and it'll be a rest for you – '

'Like hell. I'm going now.' And she reached for her jacket and went, and wearily he followed her. There was little else he could do; she had become almost white-hot with enthusiasm, as eager and as excited as he'd ever seen her in their three years together, and it depressed him. All this for money that she said she didn't want? All this for Dolly, whom she'd always hated so much? It hurt to see her like it.

'Back numbers?' the girl at the reception desk said, dubious and bored at the same time. 'No, not 'ere. 'Tisn't somethin' we does, I don't think – '

'Of course you do,' Maggy said briskly. 'Every newspaper does. Fetch me someone who knows a little more about the place, please. Go on now! You're obviously not the person who can help us, and this is important! Fetch your boss, whoever he is.'

He turned out to be a small woman with very black hair set in tight ripples on each side of her narrow head from a centre parting, and tied in a knot at the back. Her face was bony, with the skin stretched over her cheeks and her teeth very white and even. She looked like a plastic version of Mrs Simpson, the sort of doll tasteless entrepreneurs might have produced to make money out of the Abdication crisis forty years ago.

'Well, now, can I help you?' she said, looking at Theo, her teeth very evident in a wide smile, and Maggy thought, 'She sounds just like Dolly. That soft blurred sound – '

'We're trying to find some information about – about an old friend of my father's.' Maggy said quickly and the small woman turned her head and looked at her, the smile fading a little. 'He – er – my father died, you see, and left a few mementos of the war and he wanted them to go this chap he was in the army with. A James Hornby. He said – well, he said, to tell the truth, that he wasn't as good a citizen as he'd been a soldier, and blotted his copy book more than somewhat but still he wanted him to have these things you see, so – we can't find him, that's the trouble. So we thought if we came to Cheltenham, where he came from you might be able to help – I mean, he ended up in prison, I'm afraid, for armed robbery, though he'd been a very brave soldier – ' And she beamed at the little woman who was listening with her mouth half open. ' – and you have to forgive people, don't you? And my poor old father was so anxious his medals should go to this old friend – '

'Oh, my dear, o' course we'll help if we can, gladly.'. The little woman looked ferociously at the girl who stood hovering behind her. 'Dawn, you keep an eye on the phone now. I'm goin' down to the cellar, see? Just keep an eye on the phone and don't do nothin' daft – '

'Yes Miss Stapleton,' the girl said, and watched in dim fascination as the little woman lifted the flap of the counter that stretched across the reception room and made way for Theo and Maggy to go through.

'We keep a few, like, of the old papers,' she said chattily. 'Not all of them, mind, because we bin goin' a long time here, that we have. Why, do you know, the Gazette reported news of the Great Exhibition, it did! We got that edition on account of it was a big one, an' they must ha' been main proud of it, but we don't have a lot as far back as that.' She was leading them along a corridor and down stairs at the far end, chattering busily all the way. 'Mind you, we got a clear run for the last few years, like up to the war and all – '

'The war? So you'll have them for say – forty-nine, fifty or so?'

'Oh, yes, my dear! I meant we got 'em back to the *War* – fourteen eighteen! So if this chap o' yours was writ about then we should find 'im! Went to prison you say? For armed robbery. Around 1950? Well, now, that rings a little bell with me. We don't get that many armed robberies, you know – that does ring a little bell, indeed. I've been here thirty years now, since I was little more'n a girl, and there's not much I don't know about the Gazette, or the town either, come to that. So we'll have a little look – and we'll see what I can remember for you – ' She chatted all the way down to a dusty cellar smelling faintly of mice and old paper and with walls lined with broad slatted shelves on which leather bindings were piled, the month and the year stamped on their narrow spines.

It was ridiculously easy to find him. It was in an early May edition for 1951. 'Cheltenham Man Gets Twenty-Year Sentence,' the headline read and there were several close-printed columns about the trial at the Old Bailey. Hornby and Codling had made quite a showing at their trial, for they had been pert in the witness box, had shouted back at the counsel throughout the trial, and several times been threatened by the judge because of their behaviour. Clearly the press had thoroughly enjoyed it all, not least the *Gazette* reporter who took a gloating satisfaction in detailing virtually every word Hornby had spoken. Clearly Local Boy Making Bad had been as important as Local Boy Making Good, back in 1951.

Maggy read every word of it, with Theo reading over her shoulder, while Miss Stapleton chattered on and on and leafed through later editions of the paper, and then, when Maggy had finished she said cheerfully, 'So there you are! That's what you wanted, isn't it? I told you we had a good run here – and that I'd a good memory – '

'Well, not exactly,' Maggy said carefully. 'I mean, this says where he used to live, but not where he lives now, of course – '

Miss Stapleton beamed at her, her teeth gleaming joyously. 'Oh, my dear, but you wouldn't find that there, would you? No, o' course not! That was when he went to prison, wasn't it? Oh, I remember all about that case you know. I remember so well! You seek, he had an old Mum, he did. Lived over to the other side of the town – over to Charlton Kings. And she were ill at the time. I well remember because you see there was such a fuss, on account the Vicar said as it's be all wrong to make a public spectacle of her for nothing she done, only that her wicked son had done, when she was so ill. So the address was never put in. I remember that – '

'Remember it?' Maggy stared. 'After all this time?'

'Well, I should say I do! There's not a lot happens you know, like that, in Cheltenham! Most people are quiet enough – and a big case like that, it got everyone goin', that it did! I mean, it was in all the papers, all over the country, so o' course we was extra interested. I'd misremembered his name, I don't deny, but I remember it all now, because I was in the office when the Vicar came in and made all that fuss about this old woman, the feller's mother, you see – '

'What else do you remember?'

'Well, let's see now – ' The little woman settled herself on a stool and folded her arms, watching Maggy with bright little eyes. 'It's been a main long time, o' course – but I know there was a lot o' fuss because the police got a search warrant for his mother's house, and the Vicar, he said as they couldn't come in, because it wasn't right, with her so ill, and the police started a great fuss – ' She leaned over and picked up another of the old newspapers. 'It's all in here – how they got in to search at last, but only after the old lady died and the Vicar said it was because she'd been harried by the police – oh, the trouble went on and on in the paper for weeks! But of course they never found it.'

'Found what?' Theo said, as Maggy took the paper from Miss Stapleton, and began to read the columns she pointed out.

Miss Stapleton opened her eyes very wide. 'Why, the money, o' course! The money they stole. It was never found, you see. The police never found it, and if the man's mother had known, she wasn't in no situation to say, bein' dead, and there it was! Never been found, and there it sits to this day, wherever it is.'

Maggy looked up, and stared at her, her eyes wide and blank. 'Never been found – and it was a lot, wasn't it?' She turned back

242

to the first paper they had read, and ran her finger down the columns, looking for the information. 'A hell of a lot – here it is. Five hundred thousand, they said – '

'And never found,' Miss Stapleton said triumphantly. 'So he never got nothin' for his trouble, did he?'

'Well, he's not in prison, now, is he?' Theo said. 'He got twenty years, it said here – he must have come out of prison several years ago, what with time for good behaviour and all that sort of thing – '

Miss Stapleton laughed, a cheery little sound, and shook her head. 'No, that he isn't. Not in prison now. Because he never got out in a manner o' speaking. Died, he did, both of 'em did – '

'Both – who? How do you – '

'There was two of them, you see. Look – ' And again she went riffling through the paper, looking for the right place. 'See? Codling, that was the name o' the other one. And he and this Hornby got into a fight in the prison yard seemingly – it was in another paper – now, let me see, I found it a moment or two back – here it is! In 1961 it was. They were in the same prison, and got into a fight with knives and there was three people died. And there were two of 'em – '

There was a little silence and then Maggy said blankly, 'Dead? Hornby? Dead? I've been looking all this time for a dead man?'

''Tis a pity at that, my dear!' Miss Stapleton said, cheery as ever. 'Now your Dad's medals'll have to stay with you, I dare say! Still, if they're all dead, I suppose no harm done. I mean, none of 'em know, so they won't be upset, will they? 'Tis only the living gets upset, after all.'

'And the money was never found,' Theo said. 'The money they stole was never found.'

'Mr Geary always said they had a minder.' Miss Stapleton began to tidy away her old newspapers. 'That's what he said, and that whoever it was had done nicely, once the two of them were dead. There it was to hold on to and no questions asked.'

'A minder?' Maggy said, watching her stack the papers neatly back in their worn leather folders, trying to organise her confused thoughts.

'That's right, my dear. Someone to look after it, you see, until they were out of prison and could collect it. Mr Geary told me – you learn a lot about life on a newspaper, you know, and he was our reporter for years, went to all the courts and knew everything

243

that went on, did Mr Geary. And he said as someone looked after that money for 'em because that was what thieves always did, had minders. But there, the mills o' God grind slow, don't they? Both dead, and never got nothing for their evil ways. It only goes to show doesn't it? I'm sorry you couldn't give your dad's medals the way he wanted, my dear, but like I says, once folks are in their graves it don't make no nevermind, do it?'

'No,' Maggy said. 'It makes no nevermind at all.'

27

Ida sat behind the desk and stared at her, and Maggy stared back, her face very still, and then, feeling awkward and embarrassed, she nodded.

'Hello, Ida.'

'Well, this is a surprise! Slumming, are we? Or coming to keep an eye on the wage slaves?'

'May I sit down?' Maggy said quietly and Ida shrugged, making no other move, and Maggy brought a chair from the other side of the office and sat down in front of Ida's desk.

'I need to talk to you, Ida,' she said, after a moment. 'There's a lot I have to – '

'I'm in no mood for arguments,' Ida said harshly. 'And I've no time for 'em either. There's a lot of work to be done here, whoever owns the place, and keeping heads above water doesn't happen by accident. I've no time to – '

'Please, Ida. I know we – it's been difficult in the past. But there have been changes. Things are different.'

'Changes?' Ida looked at her sharply and Maggy stared back, determined to hold her gaze. I wish I could like her, I really wish I could. But after so long –

'First of all, I have to thank you.' She said it steadily, still holding her gaze, and Ida stared back, blankly.

'Thank me?' she said, her voice expressionless.

'Yes. You've coped with a difficult situation since Dolly died – and I was no help.'

'That you weren't,' Ida said, her voice still harsh, but she seemed to relax a little, leaning back in her chair instead of sitting ramrod straight.

'I had a lot to cope with too. Dolly and I – it wasn't easy.'

'No.' Ida said. 'It never was. She was such a fool with you, always was. Told you such lies, led you such a dance – '

'Why, Ida?' Maggy leaned forwards. 'Ever since she died, I've been trying to find out – I've found out a lot. Such extraordinary

245

things. Incredible things. She was – some of the people she had there in Creffield Road were – they were trouble, weren't they?'

Ida laughed then, a sharp little sound that echoed in the small room. 'Trouble? My God, you don't know the half of it! She was such a fool, Dolly! Too soft for her own good, such a fool.'

'Can you explain? I don't think I ever really knew. I saw it all – '

'You saw it through your eyes and no one else's,' Ida said dispassionately. 'Spoiled rotten you were. I used to try, tried to make you see there were other people in the world apart from you, because I knew you'd have a bad time of it later on if you went on being as spoiled as she wanted – but it made it worse, I suppose. I was young, then, and foolish. Thought I knew better than anyone else – and – ' She bent her head sharply, deliberately cutting off what she had intended to say and Maggy said, 'What?'

'It doesn't matter.'

'It does. It's why I've come this evening. Well, one of the reasons. I need to know. I really do. About you, and why I got so – why we never got on – '

'Why *we* never got on?' Ida looked up and Maggy stared at her, trying to see her as she really was, not as just the smooth hard-faced woman she'd always loathed so much. A clean skin, only sagging a little with age, lightly powdered. A little rouge. Narrow eyes under straight brows, a hint of mascara, just enough for a face of that age. Neat hair, well-cut, agreeably arranged. But was that all? Was there a real woman behind that veneer of under-stated business-like rightness? There had to be somewhere –

'Well, if we're going in for the all-girls-together bit, and trying a bit of honesty – though I can't imagine why we should, after all this time – '

'I told you. I need to know.'

'All right. The reason you didn't like me – that was what I was for. It was what Dolly wanted me to do, so I did it. The way everyone always did what Dolly wanted. She couldn't bear to be the nasty one, you see, not ever. So that was what I was for. We played it all the time we were together. I'm the bastard, she's the nice one.'

'I'm not sure I understand – '

Ida sighed, sharply. 'Oh, for God's sake, Maggy! Just think! How often did she ever say no to you? How often did she ever make you do things you didn't want to do? Once or twice, maybe – I remember the way she tried to stop you going to that Susan-

246

nah's place – and how upset she was that you were miserable about it, and she never stopped you again, did she? That was what I was for. The miserable things. I was the one who made you – oh, brush your teeth and get to school on time and – all the dreary things. It was the same with the hotel. She was the kind one, the nice one, the warm and loving one, and I was the one who made them pay their bills and toe the line. Of course you hated me, of course all the boarders hated me! It was what I was for – '

Staring at her Maggy thought, she's right. My God, but she's right. Why did I never see it before? Ida always did the dirty work, every single scrap of it. No wonder I loathed her. Oh, poor Ida. You poor, poor –

'Ida, why? Why on earth did you do it? Why did you put up with it?'

'Why?' She laughed her little bark again. 'That's another story. The stupid thing really is that it didn't work properly. She could never understand it, you know. Why you got so – why you didn't just adore her all the time. She couldn't understand it, after that man Gerald, and after Oliver she still couldn't understand it. She didn't even realize what she'd done. But I did – I was sorry for you. And angry too.'

'Angry?'

'Because you let it happen. You let her just – just *absorb* people to herself, take all the love and attention she could get, and you never hit back. Not till too late.'

'Hit back? How could I? There was no way I could – I'm not sure I always understood anyway – '

'Understood?' Ida smiled then, a tight little grin. 'She was impossible to understand because she was so – there was nothing there, you see. No bones. Just marshmallow.'

'Then *why*? Why in God's name did you stay around and – why did you put up with it? You've got bones! You're strong. Why should you do all you did, and get so little back? That's even more impossible to understand.'

There was a silence between them then and Maggy could hear the faint buzz of voices from the other side of the office wall as someone in reception talked to the girl there, and people in the foyer talked and laughed. It was the busy time of the evening, half past eight, with dinner over, the card-players not yet settled down and the television-watchers just beginning to decide which pap they were going to swallow tonight. She was tired, aware of the weight of the day behind her; it had been a hell of a day; first Sally and then the afternoon in Cheltenham and now Ida, sitting and staring at her with her blank face and opaque eyes, saying nothing.

'Ida,' she tried again. 'Please. It's been a bad few weeks for me. I've had to go back over so much of the past, remember more than I wanted to, and it's not been easy. And there have been things – things have happened because of it all that I'll have to explain to you, sometime. You might as well know, because you were a part of it, too, in a way. Weren't you? But tell me, first, *why*. What made you stay? What was it about Dolly that made you put up with so much?'

'I suppose I loved her,' Ida said at length and then tried to smile, a twisted little shape that made her mouth look very soft. 'She was kind to me when I needed kindness, and I felt – the stupid thing is that even after I realized it was such *mindless* kindness, it went on mattering. She did for me what she'd have done for a dog that had been run over or a starving kitten. Took me in and stroked me and then – ' She shrugged. 'Then I was part of her furniture. Just like everyone else. Except you. You she always went on caring about. But everyone else – once she'd taken 'em in, and been kind to them, they were part of the furniture. But I was still grateful.'

'You must have needed her very much at the time.'

'You're determined to find out, aren't you? Digging and digging – all right!' Ida spoke loudly, for the first time lifting her voice and not seeming to care whether the girl outside could hear or not. 'All right! If it matters that much!'

'Look, I don't want to – oh, damn it. Ida, you really don't have to – '

'Yes I do!' Her voice dropped again now, and the faint lift of colour that had come into her cheeks faded. 'Now I've got this far – I had a baby. All right? He'd have been nearly thirty now. He *is*, I suppose. I had him adopted. In 1950 there was nothing else you could do. No abortions then – '

Maggy sat silent, her head bent, too embarrassed to look at her.

'I was pregnant and chucked out at home and where the hell else could I go? She gave me a job and somewhere to live and when I went away and the baby was born she was – she came to

248

see me and let me cry after he'd been taken away and then she took me back. And I stayed on with her. What else could I do? And you – sitting there on her lap, all over her, and she was – I suppose I hated you for that. I couldn't hate her because she'd been kind, but I hated you because she'd kept you. Mine had to be taken away, but she'd kept you.'

'I'm sorry,' Maggy said, and made herself lift her head to look at her.

'Sorry? Because she was stronger than me? Because she, the marshmallow one, was strong enough to keep you, and me, the tough one, was too weak to keep mine? It's something to be sorry for, that is.'

'Yes,' Maggy said, and didn't know what else to say.

'So there you are,' Ida said after a moment. Her voice was normal now, its usual quiet hard self, and Maggy looked at her trying to see the emotion that had filled her for a few seconds but seeing nothing. Just that firm, powdered, lightly rouged and understated face. 'Does it help you any?'

'Yes, I think it does. It's made me – I think I ought to apologize to you too. I came to say thank you, but maybe I should apologize too.'

'I wouldn't bother,' Ida said. 'I'm coping well enough. I'm not one for digging around feelings the way you are. The way she was. I've told you a bit tonight because you nagged. Now can we forget it? Get on with the here and now?'

'Yes – the here and now – ' Maggy took a deep breath, and then, baldly, plunged in. 'I think I might have found the source of the money Dolly said was available to pay off the hotel's debts.'

'Have you, now?' Ida said softly, and looked at her sitting upright in her chair with her hands folded neatly over the open ledger in front of her. 'Have you?'

'Hornby. Do you remember Hornby?'

'Yes. I remember him.' Ida smiled again, the same twisted little smile, but there was nothing vulnerable about it now. It was hard and knowing. 'A stupid swaggering man. All shout and mouth and – threw his money around, talked big. And then went and got himself knifed in a prison riot. Stupid creature.'

'He stole a lot of money. Five hundred thousand.'

'I dare say. I never counted it.'

'I think Dolly did,' Maggy said softly. 'I think Dolly knew all about the money. I think she had it.'

Ida frowned. 'Dolly had it?'

'I think she looked after it for him, when he went to prison. A minder, that's what she was. For a consideration, she took care of his money – '

Ida shook her head, firmly. 'Impossible. The police were all over Creffield Road after they got him and Codling. Turned the place upside down.' She laughed then. 'The only thing she cared about was that they shouldn't come when you were there. Begged 'em do their searching in school hours. And because she was Dolly they did. They bloody well did. And much good it did them because they didn't find a thing. She knew they wouldn't, she was so offhand and laughing about it, so it couldn't have been there.'

'But she knew where it was. I'm certain of that. She hid it somewhere and then – she wanted me to have it and she couldn't leave it properly, in a bank or wherever, because the police would have been down on it, wouldn't they? So she hid it somewhere. That's why she left that message in the safe deposit.'

'Message?'

'There was a photograph. Herself and Morty Lang and Andy Kentish – '

Ida was silent, staring at her, searching back through her memory and then she nodded. 'I remember. A nasty character. Slippery as they came. Always sneaking about and watching and prying – but as smooth as silk. Could charm the birds off the trees.'

'He's hateful!' Maggy said violently and Ida lifted her brows.

'I saw him – in New York. He's – he's very bad. He's trying to – I think he's trying to get the money Dolly left. Hornby's money.'

Ida shook her head, her eyes watchful now. 'I don't understand all this. You're not making sense.'

Maggy sighed, tired now. 'I only just understand it myself. Look, Dolly had this money that Hornby had given her to look after. He died in prison, his mother died, Codling died. So there was no one else who knew about it, and Dolly decided to keep it. For me – ' She grimaced then. 'A hell of a legacy. But she – well, she was Dolly. And that was what she left. But she had to keep it hidden because of where it came from, which is why all that business about leaving a message on a photograph. But when I went to Morty he didn't know. I don't know what it was he was supposed to tell me, what Dolly meant him to tell me, and now I never will. He's dead – and I'll never know. But he mentioned

250

Hornby, which was a start, and that was how I found out. From him and someone who used to teach me, years ago. The thing now is, where the hell is the money? Is it here?'

'Here?' Ida shook her head. 'You know all that's here. In her room. Enough rubbish there, God knows, but I haven't been through it. That's your affair. You've got the key. No one else has – only you – '

'Not Oliver?'

'Oh, him!' Ida said, with a withering scorn. 'Stupid creature! Not him. He managed it once, getting a key from me, and copying it. I heard about that. But no more. Never again.'

She reached into her desk and took out the bunch of keys and put it on the ledger in front of her. 'It never leaves me, this bunch. The only key to Dolly's room is the one you've got. If there's any money there, it's yours. But I'll be surprised if there is, because the world and his wife have been in and out of that room, over the years. Oliver wasn't the only daft feller she had dancing attendance on her. There were always other people she'd been kind to, you know. That stupid empty kindness of hers. Plenty of 'em – '

'It's got to be somewhere,' Maggy said, almost despairingly. 'She's had me dancing all over the bloody country after it, finding people, nagging people, driving myself mad with memories and – it's got to be somewhere, this money she's left.'

'Well, go and look. And if you find anything apart from those men's clothes and her own bits of rubbish. I'll eat my hat.'

'Those clothes – ' Maggy said sharply. 'Do you know who they belonged to?'

'No. She just said she was looking after them for someone – '

'A minder!' Maggy said triumphantly. 'I knew it – I *am* right. They must be his! She looked after everything for him, clothes and money – '

'So go and look and see if there's anything there,' Ida said calmly. 'And I'll get on with my work. I've too much to do to waste much more time over this. Go and look.'

So she looked. She went back up the stairs, and into that dead silent room, and switched on the lights and stood there and looked at the blank bed with its absurd lilac satin eiderdown and the tables and cabinets and chests of drawers, and tried not to think of Dolly, sitting in that bed with her feathers round her shoulders and her shock of mad orange hair and her soft silly grin –

The wardrobe doors swung open easily and she moved fast, taking everything out, hanger after hanger, concentrating on what she was doing, trying not to think of anything else. Ida breaking her heart over a baby she had to give away. Dolly being kind to dogs and kittens. Ida being the bastard, Dolly being the nice one – not to be thought of.

There was nothing there. Just suits and overcoats and hats and shoes. Clothes, smelling faintly and mustily of the human body that had once occupied them. Nothing but clothes.

She left them where she'd piled them, on the bed, and went, locking the door behind her, running down the stairs and through the now empty lobby and back to Ida.

'Nothing,' she said, standing in the doorway and staring at her, a little breathless. 'Nothing there but clothes.'

Ida's lips moved as she finished adding up the column of figures she was working on and calmly she made an entry and then looked up. 'I'm not at all surprised. I told you there wouldn't be.'

'But there's got to be – it's got to be *somewhere*. And I've got to find it for you – '

'For me? What's is got to do with me?'

'I want to give you the hotel. Afterwards. When I've found the money. It's for you. I don't want it, and it belongs to you anyway. After all this time, and all you've done, I want you to – '

Ida shook her head, her face as expressionless as it had ever been. 'No thanks.'

'But – '

'No buts. I'll work here as long as it's necessary. But I don't want it if I have to get it with the sort of money you're looking for.' She lifted her head then, with an almost child-like pride. 'I don't want it that way.'

'I've still got to find it,' Maggy said, stubbornly. 'Dolly wanted me to find it, and I've got to – '

'So go and look,' Ida said almost contemptuously. 'But don't involve me – ' and she bent her head to her books again.

'But isn't there anywhere else in the hotel? Another room she kept things in? Kept locked? Didn't let anyone into?'

Ida didn't lift her head, but pointed at the bunch of keys that still lay in front of her.

'There you are. All her keys, just as she left them. I put them on my bunch. Go and help yourself. Try every lock in the place if you want to. It's yours, so why shouldn't you?'

Maggy leaned over the desk and picked up the keys, staring at them. A big bunch, with a leather tag, worn and unreadable, but that had once had the name of the hotel embossed on it in gold letters. She remembered that, from a long time ago. But she remembered nothing else about any of the keys on the ring. Just a collection of pieces of metal, some in dull grey, and some shining and silvery and some yellowish and heavy. Just keys.

She turned them over in her hand, sliding each one through her fingers. Yale keys, lots of them. Little flat luggage keys, several of them. Two or three heavier ring-headed keys with 'Chubb' engraved on them. A couple of small cashbox keys with hollow stems. A small silvery key with a number engraved on it. B 9. Another Yale key –

She stopped and fumbled, trying to get back to the engraved key, and the bunch fell from her clumsy hand on to the desk with a silvery rattle and Ida took a sharp irritated breath.

'Ida! This one – what key is that? This one here – the one with a number of it. Look. It says B 9. That key – where did that come from?'

Ida looked at it, the bunch on the table between them, and Maggy looked too, not wanting to touch them, not wanting to pick them up.

'I don't know. I told you, when she died. I just put the lot of her keys in with mine. It seemed the only sensible thing to do. I gave you the one for her bedroom. I brought it to that office of yours, remember? The rest are there. That's all I know.'

'That one – it's – ' Maggy said and then stopped. Was it? She hadn't got the other one with her. She kept it in her small locked desk at the flat. But it looked the same, exactly the same, except for the number. That was different.

'It looks,' she said carefully, 'like the key to a safe deposit box. Not the one I've already opened. Another one.'

28

Theo was sitting on the top step outside, leaning against one of the pillars, his face in shadow, and as she came out into the heavy September night he got to his feet and said anxiously, 'Maggy?'

'Yes,' she said, wearily. 'I'm here. It's all right.'

'There's someone there. No, don't get into the light. Come here.' He put his arm round her and held her close, talking into her right ear. 'I thought I saw them when we got here, but I wasn't sure. Now I am. They've been there all the time – over an hour. Two of 'em. Look like missionaries.'

'That's the sort,' she said and began to shake, feeling the fear deep inside her. 'Oh, Christ, that's them. What – '

'No need to get frightened. We can get rid of them. Come back inside.'

They walked back into the hotel and Theo, one arm still protectively round her shoulders led her to the desk.

'We need a taxi, in a hurry. Not a black cab – a mini-cab. Phone one, will you? And can we get out the back way? There's someone we're trying to dodge – you know how it is, fans – ' And he raised his eyebrows comically.

Ida came out of her office and stopped as she caught sight of them.

'I thought you'd gone.'

'I had,' Maggy said. 'I mean – there's someone – Andy – '

'Andy?'

'It'll take too long to explain now,' Theo said, crisply. 'Tell this girl to call us a mini-cab, Ida, for heaven's sake. Maggy's whacked and I want to get her home. Can we get out the back way?'

'Of course,' Ida said, as though it were the most natural question in the world, and nodded at the girl who picked up the phone obediently and Maggy looked over her shoulder at the entrance, nervous, still shaking inside and not knowing what there was to be so scared about. What could they do, after all? Rush in through

254

the glass doors and gun her down? Hit her over the head with all these people standing around? It was nonsensical to be so frightened when she was so well protected – and Theo's arm felt good across her back – yet she couldn't control it.

And even after they were in the mini-cab, a battered old Peugeot with a young driver who agreed with alacrity to drive as fast as he could to Holland Park, and had slipped out of the back way and left the watchers still at the front, she shook, and Theo sat beside her holding her close and saying nothing. And slowly, she relaxed, recovered her equilibrium and when the car screeched to a stop outside the flat, leaned forwards ready to get out. It was Theo who held her back, getting out first, looking round casually as he paid the driver.

'OK. No one here, as far as I can see. Though there may be someone in the shadows on the other side – ' He led the way towards the house, and then, after a moment, called back over his shoulder to the cab driver.

'Hey, squire – do me a favour? We've had some break-ins – come up with us, just in case there's someone there who tries to jump us?'

'Sure,' said the driver cheerfully and got out of the car and came up the steps, and with a man on each side of her, Maggy climbed the stairs, feeling more foolish now than frightened.

'This is mad,' she said to Theo as he pushed her back against the cab driver before, very gingerly, putting his key in the lock of the flat door. 'We can't go on like this, jumping like cats at every shadow – '

'It's all right.' Theo had put the light on, and moved quickly through the rooms, checking there was no one there. 'It's fine. Thanks, squire – ' and he gave the driver an extra pound note and the man grinned and nodded and went whistling away down the stairs.

'He probably thinks we're dodging a jealous husband or something,' Maggy said, and threw her jacket on to one end of the sofa and sank on to it with a deep sigh of relief. 'It's the most childish cops-and-robbers stuff – '

'Childish it may be. Real it certainly is, Maggy. We're going to have to call the police, you know that, don't you? We can't go on putting up with this sort of thing. Being followed and – '

'I've found what it is they're after,' Maggy said, and Theo, who had been pouring vodka and tonic into glasses, lifted his head

255

sharply.

'What did you say?'

'I think I've found Dolly's money. Hornby's money. My money, damn it. Not that I want it. Ida says she doesn't either – '

Theo ignored that. 'Where? How much?'

'It's the maddest thing, it really is.' She began to giggle as she took her drink from him. 'All these weeks and all this fuss, and she had the damn thing the whole time. Did Mort know she had it? He couldn't have. But Dolly sent me to him, and not to Ida – it just doesn't make any sort of sense – ' and she drank again, and giggled again. 'It's the maddest thing.'

'*You're* not making sense,' Theo said, and sat beside her, watching her as he too drank. 'Who had what the whole time?'

'This.' She put her hand in her skirt pocket and took out the key and held it out to him in the flat of her hand. 'This.'

He stared at it.

'It's a key to a safe deposit box. Not the one I've already got – that's over there, in the desk – ' She got up and went over to the desk and took its key from the little cleft in the side where she always hid it, and unlocked it, and fumbled around, looking for the other key.

'You see?' She sat down beside him again. 'They are the same, aren't they?'

He picked them up, turning them over and over in his fingers. 'They look it.'

'Different numbers. See? This one, the one I already had, is B 11. This other one is B 9. The same, only very, very different.' Again she laughed. 'Stupid, isn't it?'

'Where did you get it?'

'Ida. It was on her bunch. She put it there with Dolly's other keys, after she died.'

They were silent for a while and then Theo said carefully. 'And you think that the box that key belongs to – '

' – is in the same safe deposit that the first box was in.'

'And that it's got – ' He stopped, and stared at the key.

'It's got five hundred thousand pounds in it. Or at least, what's left of it. He probably spent quite a lot before he went to prison. On my schooling, for a start.'

She laughed then, trying to be insouciant about it, but it hurt all the same. 'And of course there was the other man, Codling, I suppose he had his share and that's – well, that could be any-

256

where. But at the very least there's got to be a couple of hundred thousand pounds there, hasn't there?'

'It's a hell of a lot of money, Maggy. Enough to – enough for almost anything.'

'Rainbow Records?' she said, and knew her voice was hard, and wished it weren't.

He lifted his head and looked at her. 'I'm never going to be allowed to forget that, am I?'

'I'll try,' she said. 'I will try. It was – it still is, I suppose. I'm more screwed up about Dolly and all the things that happened than I knew. Though – I don't know. Maybe it's not as bad as it was. I've found out a lot, haven't I? See things more clearly, maybe.'

'From a different angle, perhaps. But you're still pretty screwy.' He smiled, rather thinly, and impulsively she leaned forwards and kissed him.

'I'll get better, love, really I will. Let me finish this business off, get it out of the way, and then we'll see where we go from here, hmm? It will get better – '

'I'll keep you to that.'

He got up after a while and went over to the window, peering out into the dark street far below.

'Anyone there?' She tried to sound casual, and was pleased with how successful she was.

'I don't think so. Not that I can see, anyway. Tomorrow, we go to the police. Quietly. No fuss, but we'll tell them, ask for a bit of help. I've made up my mind to that.'

'After I've been to the Haymarket.'

'The Haymarket?'

'To get the money, Theo. I've got the key, haven't I? I've got to go.'

'Yes. You've got the key – Maggy, why do you suppose Dolly sent you to Mort? Have you thought about that?'

She closed her eyes, leaning back on the sofa. 'A lot. I just don't know. Unless – '

'Unless what?'

'This'll sound silly, but – well, to make me love her again. To feel sorry for all the things that happened.'

'You never stopped loving her. I've always known that. Even when you were at your most vitriolic, I knew that. You were angry with her, and hurt by her, but you never stopped loving her.'

'Didn't I? I don't know any more. I just don't know. One thing's sure. *She* didn't know. All she knew was that I was – I made strange. Wouldn't go to see her, was always – It was because of Oliver. That's what I used to think. But not now. He was just an excuse.'

He was leaning against the window now, watching her, his arms folded across his chest.

'Oliver.' He said it quietly. 'I always thought there was something about him and you. Not that I could understand it. You and that – '

'He wasn't always the way he is now,' she said swiftly. 'Not always. He was a good musician once. He really was. But then – oh, well, I was young and so bloody ignorant it makes me feel sick when I remember it. I thought I could save him, or something. I didn't even realize he was the way he is, do you know that? Christ, how dim can you be? I didn't even know he was gay – Theo, isn't it extraordinary how much people being gay has mattered in all this? I mean Oliver, and Dolly scooping him up, and then Mort and Andy. And Dolly – '

'She felt safe with them,' Theo said sapiently. 'There are lots of women like that. Scared of their own feelings, scared of their own sex. So they only feel really safe with ambiguous people. That's all it was with Dolly.'

She looked up at him standing there with his arms folded and smiled, comfortable suddenly. 'You're a very knowing bloke Theo, sometimes, aren't you?'

'Given the chance,' he said, lightly. 'You've always kept me at arms' length, though, haven't you? Never given me the whisper of a chance. But now – Maggy, get this bloody money tomorrow, will you? And then – oh, give it to Ida, get rid of the Westpark, and we'll get married.'

'Just like that?'

'Just like that.'

She laughed, hearing the sound in her own ears, warm and friendly. 'I'll think about it, love. It sounds a bit wacky, at our time of life and all that, but I'll think about it.'

She dreamed about it. Saw herself in a great haze of white on the stage of the Lincoln Center and people whizzing around her and playing trumpets and double basses and flutes and shouting, 'Here

258

come de Bride, here come de Bride – ' and all she could do was
laugh, and then Theo was there and he was laughing too. It was
a nice dream, a comfortably mad dream and she woke feeling
relaxed and happy to lie looking at Theo lying with his mouth half
open in unlovely slumber and liking what she saw. Married? It
could be fun at that. Get a house, maybe, with a real music room,
instead of a flat with stairs people could hide on to mug you. It
could be fun at that.

It was while they were having breakfast that her answering
service called. They had three messages for her from the day
before, the thin clacking voice reported. Jump Records had called
and wanted Mr Cordery, please would he call in first chance he
had. The dentist had called to ask her to change her appointment
from the nineteenth to the twenty-sixth, and Adam called to say
he was so sorry to have missed her in New York, but he'd keep
in touch through his friends, who will be around, and he'd see
her in London very soon.

'What did you say?' she said, catching her breath sharply.

'Adam is sorry to have missed you in New York but he'll keep
in touch through his friends who'll be around and he'll see you in
London very soon,' the girl repeated glibly.

'Thank you,' she said mechanically and hung up, feeling all the
tension of the day before build in her again, all the comfort of the
night's dreaming shattered into sharp little points of anxiety.

'Theo – ' She told him and he listened, his face hardening.

'It's enough!' he said loudly. 'It's more than enough. No one's
going to go on threatening you like this. I won't have it. I'm
calling the – '

'Not yet.' She took his hand, pulling him away from the phone.
'Listen, love, let me get this money out first, will you? If you call
the police you've got to tell them all about it, and that means the
money'll have to be given up, won't it? It was stolen, remember?
And I want Ida to have it.'

'But – '

'No. No buts. You said it last night. Get the money, give it to
Ida, get rid of the Westpark, and then we'll – then we'll get on
with whatever we want to do. Right?'

He stood uncertainly for a moment and then said unwillingly.
'Well, I suppose – '

'You know I'm right. Look, it's almost ten. If we go now, we
can have the whole thing over and done with before lunch. Will

259

you come?'

'If you're going, I've got to. Don't be stupid, Maggy? There's no way you're going anywhere on your own while all this is going on.'

'All right,' she said peaceably. 'Great. Fine. Anything you say. I'll get dressed.'

They decided to go by taxi. 'If anyone's out there and following us, train will be too easy. Taxis aren't that thick on the ground, and with a bit of luck we'll leave 'em behind, if they're down there,' Theo said.

They were. As Maggy came down the steps of the house she saw them. Two smooth young men in neat suits standing side by side on the other side of the street. Not the same ones she had seen on the steps of the next door house the day before, but very like them, and she pulled back against Theo as he closed the door behind them, and he reacted fast, following her gaze and seeing them.

They stood there poised on the steps for a moment, looking at them and the two young men stared back and then after a moment they turned with an almost comical precision and walked down the street towards the main Holland Park Road, not looking back.

'Cheeky bastards!' Theo muttered furiously. 'God damn their guts – they know we've got to go that way and they're playing stupid games with us – for two pins I'd go after them and knock their bloody heads together – '

'We could go round the Crescent the other way,' Maggy said. 'Maybe they won't think of that – '

'Oh, do me a favour, Maggy! It's obvious they know exactly what they're doing. If we do that, they'll be at the other end waiting for us. Come on. We'll just brazen them out. And pray that we get the only taxi there is – '

But prayer was pointless. They waited on the corner, watching for a cab with its 'For Hire' light on, and when one came bumbling up from Notting Hill Gate Maggy almost wanted to jump up and down in excitement, for it was the only one. They were going to get away with it –

The two young men were nowhere to be seen, and she looked round as the taxi came abreast of them, hunting. But there were just the usual morning hurriers-by, the desultory shoppers going to the little supermarket, the buses, the vans – and then she saw the car.

Parked insolently on a double yellow line, just a few yards up the road, a narrow blue coupé, shining absurdly clean among the shabby London traffic. The two men sitting in it, side by side, neat and unsmiling, and as she climbed into the taxi, and peered through the back window and watched with a sense of almost helpless fury as the car pulled out into the traffic behind them.

'There they are,' she said to Theo and he looked too, and swore softly, and leaned forward to speak to the driver.

'There's a car following us,' he said. 'A blue coupé. Can you get rid of it? This lady is Maggy Dundas, jazz player, you know? And these two are journalists trying to pester her – '

'Who?' said the taxi driver, not turning his head. 'Never, 'eard of 'er.'

'Well, never mind that – but can you get rid of them?'

'I'm not on the bloody telly, mate,' the driver said, and hunched his shoulders. 'Can't stop a geezer from followin' if that's what he wants to do. None o' my business – '

But for all that he seemed to pick up the challenge and moved fast, cutting across traffic lights just as they turned red, so that the following car was forced to stop, and then twisting off into side streets instead of going straight up the Bayswater Road. But it made no difference. Within minutes, the blue car was there again, bobbing about in the rear window, and Maggy watched it, her rage growing and hardening into a hard lump in the middle of her chest.

'They'll have parking trouble, won't they?' she said suddenly as the taxi cut into the traffic heading into Oxford Street. 'And won't they be picked up here in Oxford Street? Only taxis and buses are supposed to come down here.'

'Whatever they're supposed to do they still come, bleedin' private cars do,' the taxi driver said sourly. 'Bleedin' police make their bleedin' rules and no one takes no bleedin' notice. There! What'd I tell you? There the buggers are again.' He seemed to be taking a melancholy pleasure in the chase now. 'You ain't goin' to get rid o' them that easy, lady, that's for sure – '

'Listen,' Theo said suddenly. 'Take us to Piccadilly underground, will you? At the end of Regent Street. Then we can dodge into the subways, come up in the Haymarket.'

'Anythin' you say,' the driver said, and sniffed unappetizingly. 'S'no skin off my nose. But you won't get rid o' them that easy.

Right cunning buggers they are. Drive like bleedin' cabmen, and you can't say worse than that – ' and he laughed, pleased with his joke.

He was right. They paid him while they were still in the cab, and then ran from it down into the underground just as the blue car came up behind the taxi, and Maggy had a mad desire to turn and stick her tongue out at them, or thumb her nose.

But her triumph was short-lived. The car just pulled over to the kerb, apparently oblivious of the no parking signs and both the men left it there and came running over the Circus, weaving their way through the hooting traffic. The leader of the two was less than a dozen yards behind them as they went running up the stairs on the far side of the Piccadilly concourse to the Haymarket exit.

And as they turned into the building, he was so close behind them that he caught the swing of the door as Theo let it go.

Theo was white with tension and anger now, and she felt his arm tighten under her hand as he turned and stared the man in the face.

'Maggy, go ahead. I'll wait here for you,' he said curtly. 'Now you, you bastard. What the hell do you mean by making such a bloody pest of yourself?'

Maggy ran, obediently, heading for the bank of lifts, and as one opened its doors with a hiss she ran in and pressed the button for the basement, still watching Theo and the man in the neat deark suit.

The last thing she saw as the doors closed was the young man smiling at Theo, and bending his head politely, and actually holding out his hand as though to shake Theo's. He looked as affable as it was possible for any man to look.

29

She came out of the lift with a firm step, her head up and her arms held protectively round her jacket, which was tied into a bundle, and her lips quirked a little. Theo, standing on the far side of the lobby, with the two young men on each side of him watched her come and was puzzled, trying to read something into her expression. But she looked happy and, incredibly, a little amused.

She walked steadily across the lobby directly towards them and he moved forwards a step, wanting to fend her off, but she just shook her head at him slightly, and came and stood in front of them.

'Well, now,' she said coolly. 'Who are our friends, Theo? Have you managed to find out? And have they apologized for behaving in such a stupid fashion?'

'Why, Miss Dundas!' one of them said, and smiled. He was tall, even taller than Theo, and had very blue eyes. A good-looking square-shouldered young man. 'Miss Dundas, the last thing we'd ever want to do is upset you! And if we have we surely do apologize. But I just don't understand what all the fuss is about. I mean, I just came in here about my business this morning, and this gentleman here – well, I have to say it, ma'am. He attacked me! Just turned on me and accused me of all sorts of things. As if I would ever follow people or hurt them in any way! Do I *look* as though I would?' And he smiled at her disarmingly.

'Yet you know my name. If you haven't been following us and – and all the rest of it, how do you know my name?'

He opened his eyes to an ever richer blue. 'Your friend here told us, ma'am! And – '

'Do you know, George, I don't think there's any need any more to make any pretences.'

The other man was quieter, less physically big, altogether a more nondescript figure, though just as neat and clean, but there was a menacing air about him that made her shoulders tighten.

263

'It's clear Miss Dundas know we've been looking for her and I don't think we serve anyone's purpose by prevaricating. Do you, Miss Dundas?'

'None at all,' she said crisply.

'So let's talk sensibly, shall we?' He turned to Theo. 'We really must introduce ourselves properly, sir. My name is Fowler, Wendell Fowler, and my friend here is George Porteous.'

'And you're both friends of Andy Kentish. Or should I use his alias? Adam Lancaster. Are you two Born Again, Fowler?' Maggy said, putting all the scorn she could into the words, 'Have you two joined the great Crusade to get sweeping women to work their guts out to make Lancaster rich?'

Fowler turned his head to look at her again, and his mild eyes looked reproachful.

'Why, Miss Dundas, I would never have thought you the sort of crass person who would deride a man for his religious beliefs. I'm very surprised.'

'Are you? Well you needn't be. I don't deride religious beliefs, when that's what they are. But I deride cheats and nasty little con men and – '

'I think that will do, Miss Dundas,' Fowler said as mildly as ever, but there was a note in his voice that made the back of her neck tingle suddenly and she jerked her chin up and said hotly, 'Like hell it will! That man, that Andy – he's a liar and a cheat and a – '

'I think we should talk some place else, don't you?' Porteous said. 'No peace here at all – I know it's a shade early, but how about a little lunch, hmm?'

'I don't want any lunch,' she said icily. 'I just want to get something sorted out. Right here and now.'

'I want to go to the police right here and now.' Theo spoke for the first time, and his voice was shaking a little. 'I've controlled myself for as long as I – '

'Theo, it's all right. Leave it to me.' Maggy looked at him, her eyes wide, trying to get the message across to him. 'Believe me, there's no need for police. Not now and not ever, unless these two make fools of themselves. I don't think they will, though, when I tell them what I'm going to do.'

She turned back to them and looked at them, moving her head slowly from one side to the other, staring at their smooth young faces and their neat round heads and then she laughed, softly.

264

'You want my money, don't you? That's what Andy sent you for, didn't he? He wants the money my mother left me. Did he tell you about that money?'

Fowler smiled, gently. 'He told us all we need to know, Miss Dundas.'

'And how much was that? It's worth telling me, because you know – ' And she lifted her arms slightly, so that the bundled jacket could be more clearly seen. ' – it might be worth your while.'

Porteous's eyes flickered as he looked at the jacket and then at Fowler and Maggy laughed again.

'Oh, no, George! Never think you can hit me on the head and help yourself this time. Last time I was alone in my flat and it was easy, wasn't it? Just a naked woman alone in a room – ' Porteous's eyes again flickered and his neck reddened and Maggy grinned, triumphantly. 'It was you, then! Yes, I thought it was! And much good that stuff did you, didn't it? Just a load of old newspaper cuttings and not a penny to be found. You poor sap! As if it would be that easy!'

'Miss Dundas, can we keep to the point?' Fowler said softly. 'You have that money there in your jacket?'

'Money? In my jacket?' she said sweetly and looked down at it, as though in surprise. 'Is that what's in here?'

'Maggy, for Christ's sake, stop it!' Theo said urgently. 'I don't know what you're doing but – '

'Don't worry, Theo!' Maggy said, and grinned at him again. 'Oh, believe me, there's not a thing to worry about. Not a thing – I just want to know from Mr Fowler here, and Mr Porteous – if he can keep his mind off the fact that he hit me over the head when I was alone and naked – ' and she threw a wicked glance at him, ' – what their charming boss told them about my money.'

'It isn't your money, Miss Dundas,' Fowler said, and moved a little closer to her, and Maggy became aware suddenly of how few people were moving in and out of the lobby now. Earlier it had been busy, with plenty of traffic, but now at not long after half past eleven there was a lull, with few people coming in from the doors that led to the street on each side to wait for lifts. And there were two of them and they did look strong, particularly Porteous. But she lifted her chin and said sharply, 'If it isn't mine, then who does it belong to?'

'To God, ma'am,' Porteous said, and he too moved closer. 'We know that this was ill-gotten money. That it was stolen by a bad man and held on to by a bad woman. But she's dead now, and it's time the money came to God, because God will wash it clean.'

'You really believe that,' Maggy said, staring at him. 'You really believe all that, don't you? You believe that Kentish is a truly religious man? You actually *believe* what he tells you.'

'I believe the truth, Miss Dundas,' Porteous said, and now his eyes were so blue that they seemed to bulge outwards. 'God has his ways of working and he has led our leader to this money. There's a lot of it, we know, and God can use it to good purpose and make it clean again. So – ' and he reached out one hand towards the jacket.

'No!' Theo shouted and hit his hand upwards and Porteous turned with the sharpness of a trained soldier and lifted his arm sideways to make a hard chop, but Fowler was faster than he was. He grabbed Porteous's shoulder and twisted him round so hard that he almost lost his balance as Maggy shrank back and away from them. Theo was fast too, and came out from between them and over to Maggy and grabbed her and shouted, 'Run!'

But she pulled away from him, grinning from ear to ear.

'No, love. No! I'm going to give it to them. They can take it to their leader and much good may it do 'em!'

And she crouched down and put the bundle that was her jacket on the floor and untied the sleeves.

Theo watched her, his mouth half open in amazement and it seemed to him that she moved slowly, almost like a slow-motion film as she pulled on the sleeves and the jacket opened up and he saw the piles of banknotes. And then, still with sickening slowness, she lifted the jacket at each side and tossed it high in the air and the notes went up, twisting and turning lazily in the dim light of the lobby to fall in scattered heaps at their feet. 'There you are!' she crowed. 'There's nothing for you to follow me for any more, is there? Nothing to hit me on the head for. It's all there, every last bloody scrap of it!'

And she took Theo's wrist in one hand and pulled him towards the door, and he, as bemused as though he had been struck, let her take him as the two men fell to their knees and began to scrabble among the heaps of paper at their feet.

'All of it?' Ida said. 'Every bit of it?'

'Every bloody bit of it,' Maggy said. 'I'm sorry, Ida. The Westpark is as lumbered as it ever was. There's nothing there to pay the debts with, and – '

She stopped, staring, because Ida was leaning back in her chair and laughing, her tight smooth face twisted and wrinkled into lines of genuine mirth and her head thrown back as tears ran down her powdered cheeks and left runnels there.

'What's so bloody funny?' Oliver said from the doorway and Maggy turned her head and looked at him.

'Hellow, Maggy. I didn't know you were here. Nice to see you, ducks. How are things? What's got into Ida, then? Never saw her laugh like that. Someone tickled her fancy at last?'

'It's about the money,' Theo said, and suddenly he grinned too. 'And she's right. It is funny, very funny, if you can stand sick jokes, that is – '

Ida had caught her breath now. 'Bloody Dolly,' she said, but she was still grinning. 'Bloody Dolly! If that isn't just the sort of thing she wouldn't think of! It doesn't seem possible anyone could be so cunning and so daft at the same time.' And she took a handkerchief from her sleeve and began to wipe her eyes.

'I wish someone would tell me what the hell this is all about,' Oliver said petulantly. 'You sit here shrieking like the witch of Endor and – '

'I'm not sure it's any of your business, Oliver,' Maggy said coolly. 'Is it, Ida?'

'I shouldn't think so,' Ida said and lifted her brows at Oliver, still grinning.

'You two are very thick all of a sudden,' he said, still petulant. 'Since when did you share girlish jokes?'

'Since Maggy told me what she found at the safe deposit.' Ida said and Oliver lifted his head sharply.

'Ida! For Christ's sake – '

'Oh, don't be so twitchy!' The laughter had gone from her face now, and she sounded scornful. 'It's all over and done with now, so what the hell! He knew about the box. Maggy, knew all the time it was there and he thought he could get what was in it for himself.'

Maggy looked at Oliver, at the pouched sagging face and the bloodshot eyes and thought. How could I ever have wept for him? How could I have ever cared? Poor devil. Poor pathetic devil.

'Did you, Oliver? Well, you'll have to face disappointment. Because there was damn all in either of them.'

'Either of them?' Oliver came in and sat down on Ida's desk with a little thump, staring at Maggy. 'There was only the one, B 11 it was. I took her there over and over, to B 11.'

'And all the time there was nother one. B 9', Maggy said softly. 'And it was stuffed full of bank notes. Fivers and pounds and ten-shilling notes.'

'Ten-shilling notes,' Ida said, and laughed again, but shortly this time, without any of the abandon she had shown before. 'Bloody ten-shilling notes. Isn't that rich?'

'But there haven't been ten-shilling notes for – ' He stopped and stared at Maggy, his eyes widening. 'Oh, no,' he almost whispered it. 'Oh, no.'

'By George, he's got it!' Maggy sang it, her voice high and shrill. 'By George, he's got it!' She was almost hysterical with it all now, and her head was buzzing and everything she looked at seemed to have a haze of light round it, like a nimbus. 'By George, I think he's got it – '

Theo moved impatiently in his chair. 'All right, Maggy, love. Calm down, will you? I know it's all – but calm down.'

'I'm sorry.' She took a deep breath, and then, deliberately, made her shoulders relax and looked at Oliver. 'Listen, Oliver. She left two boxes. One the lawyer told me about. He said I'd find the money to pay off the debts in it. You knew that.'

'Yes,', Oliver said, still almost whispering. He was staring at her with his eyes wide and somehow desolate and that sobered her more than anything else could, and she leaned forwards and patted his hand. ' – And you thought there might be something in it for you, Oliver?'

He shook his head, dumbly, still not taking his eyes from her face but she sighed softly and said, 'But you did, didn't you? It was you who hung about on the stairs outside my flat, wasn't it, that first time I went to the safe deposit? You wanted the key and you thought – oh, Oliver, but you're stupid, you really are. No one can get into those boxes just by having the key. You have to have a proper authorization! You have to sign. I'm the only one who can sign for either of them. So you wasted your time, didn't you?'

'It was him? The mugger?' Theo said sharply. 'You stinking little – '

'Oh, shut up, Theo. He did no harm. He was too damned inefficient, anyway. Poor devil – '

268

'I just wanted – I'd have given it to you back. I would, honestly. All I wanted was enough to take care of myself, that's all. All those years with Dolly, and not blowing a note all that time, and the music was dead in me and – what else can I do? What am I without something of my own? I had to – '

'I told you you were a fool,' Ida said dispassionately. 'I told you when you tried it you were a bloody fool.'

'It all seemed meant, you know?' Oliver said, and looked earnestly at Maggy. 'Honestly, Maggy, I meant you no harm, but you talked about it and then you got that taxi and I thought – if I can only get the key from her and see what's in there I'll be all right. I meant to ask you again, that was all, and I went to your flat in the train and you weren't home yet and I had to wait on the stairs and then when you came – it just seemed – oh, it just happened, really – '

'Bloody fool,' Ida said again. 'Because even if you'd got into it there was nothing there. Nothing at all.'

'It was in another box,' Maggy said kindly, and reached out and patted his lax damp hand. Poor, poor Oliver. It was amazing that she had ever felt anything for this pathetic creature. 'So you'd have got nothing, even if you had managed to get the key.'

'No one's got anything,' Ida said then, and once more her mouth curved. It was almost as though she was going to make up for the years when she had not laughed or smiled at all in one short hour. 'Not a bloody penny.'

'Is it what I thought?' Oliver said, and Maggy nodded.

'Useless out-of-date money,' she said. 'White fivers – you remember the old white fivers? Some of them, but mostly pound notes and ten-shilling notes. The whole box stuffed full. And not one of them legal tender any more. They've been in there for more than twenty-five years, those notes, with Dolly thinking she was sitting on a fortune and all of it just so much waste paper.'

A little silence fell on the room, and then Oliver took a deep breath and nodded slowly. 'I can see why you laughed, Ida,' he said. 'It's bloody funny, really.' But there was no hint of laughter in his face at all.

'I'll call Friese later this afternoon,' Maggy said after a moment. 'Tell him the place is yours. I'm refusing to employ you, formally, so it reverts to you.'

'Yes,' said Ida. 'You do that.'

'What will you do, Ida?' Theo said. 'The place is more trouble than it's worth, isn't it?'

She shook her head. 'Nothing's worthless when you can work in it. There's bricks and morter and furniture and kitchens and – nothing's worthless. I'll find a way. I've managed before when Dolly was alive, so I'm bloody sure to be able to manage now.'

'Ida – ' Oliver said and then shook his head and got to his feet. 'I'd better go, I think. Got things to do – ' He stumbled to the door, and then Ida said harshly, 'Oh, for Christ's sake, man, stop feeling so bloody sorry for yourself. You can stay if you like. No skin off my nose. I'll find something for you to do, I dare say. Just keep out of my hair, that's all. I want no trouble, you hear me? None of your boy-friends and if there's any hint of drugs here, then out you go – '

He blinked, standing there at the doorway and then slowly nodded. 'I see. Well, that's a generous offer, Ida. Thank you. I'll think about it.' And he went away and Maggy could hear his feet shuffling on the floor of the lobby outside.

Theo coughed, embarrassed, and said, 'I suppose you were right, Maggy. I mean, that the money was useless. That the banks wouldn't have changed it – '

Ida snorted, a thick little sound. 'Use your head, man! Stolen money? Can you just see it! Oh, hello, Bank Manager! I happen to have here a few hundred thousand pounds in out-of-date banknotes. Just change it, will you, there's a good chap! Can you just see it?'

Theo grinned. 'Maybe Andy's little friends'll try that?'

'I hope they do,' Maggy said it with real venom. 'Oh, Christ, I hope they do. They won't know the money's dead, will they? Americans – they won't know. They'll probably march into a bank and – oh, please God, make them do it! It'll be marvellous.'

'Marvellous,' Theo said and stood up. 'Marvellous. But Maggy – it's not just money, is it? That's not the only reason Lancaster was after you.'

She stared at him, puzzled, and then, slowly her face straightened as the realization came hom.

'Oh, my God,' she said, her voice flat. 'Oh, my God.'

There was a little silence and then Theo said carefully, 'Blackmail.'

'What? Blackmail? Who?'

'Lancaster. You could blackmail him. That's what he's afraid of.'

'Are you mad? Do you really think that – '

He shook his head, almost irritably. 'No. Of course not. But there's only one way to convince him that you won't. To make it pointless for him to chase you any more.'

'I'm not sure I – '

Theo reached for the phone, and dialled, and watched her, smiling a little as he waited for an answer. And then said, crisply, 'Is that the *Daily Mail*? Good – get me the News Desk, will you. Joe Gerrard, if possible – yes. I'll hold – '

They finished their sherry, and then Ida, looked at her watch, pointedly and Theo said, 'Maggy – I ought to go to the office, I really should.'

She looked up at him and grinned, a wide relaxed grin. 'Yes, love, I reckon you should. I'll come with you. There's a lot to be done, what with the new album and making up for that concert I blew. Can we get another?'

'After Lincoln Center? No hassle,' he said and held out a hand to her and she took it and stood up.

'I'll see you, Ida, maybe,' she said after a moment, a little awkwardly, and Ida, still sitting behind her desk, didn't look up. 'Yes,' she said perfunctorily, 'I'll see you. Some time. Don't forget to call Friese.'

'I won't,' Maggy said. 'It'll be a pleasure.'

And they went out and across the lobby and out into the street and there was no one waiting there, and no one watching. It was a good feeling.

30

The concert was a sell-out, again, and this time she maintained it all though. The lifting excitement, the sureness, the ripple of the notes, it all worked as perfectly as it was meant to; but the elation that filled her was a different kind, this time. Rich and strong and lasting, and not the exhausting drained feeling it was before. She was a musician and the music came right and she was happy.

There was a girl standing in the wings afterwards, in the middle of all the hubbub, a tall thin girl with long hair flopping round her face, and she was holding a record sleeve close to her chest and watching Maggy with big hungry eyes as she came off stage, her face gleaming with sweat.

'Miss Dundas?' the girl said. 'Please, Miss Dundas, would you sign this for me? I wouldn't bother you, but it's for my mother. She's sick, in the hospital, and she's just crazy about your music, and I want her to have it. If you wouldn't mind, Miss Dundas.'

Maggy looked at her, at the smooth round face and the wide eyes and said, 'Your mother? You want me to sign it for your mother?'

'Yes, please, Miss Dundas,' the girl said and held it out, and put a pen in her hand and Maggy bent her head and signed the sleeve, but it was difficult because her eyes were full of tears and she could hardly see.

She was crying for her own mother, who was dead.